MY BOYFRIEND IS A MONSTER

He Loves Me, He Loves Me Not

#7

OR
DOUBLE DATE
OR
TWO OF A KIND
OR
OPPOSITES ATTRACT
OR
A REAL LOVE-HATE RELATIONSHIP
OR
TWO'S COMPANY, THREE'S A CROWD
OR
YOU CAN'T JUDGE A JOCK BY HIS COVER
OR
HAVEN'T I SEEN YOU SOMEPLACE BEFORE?

ROBIN MAYHALL

Illustrated by KRISTEN CELLA

with additional illustrations by JANE IRWIN, DIRK TIEDE, and JENN MANLEY LEE

GRAPHIC UNIVERSE™ · MINNEAPOLIS · NEW YORK

STORY BY
ROBIN MAYHALL
ILLUSTRATIONS BY
KRISTEN CELLA

WITH ADDITIONAL ILLUSTRATIONS BY
JANE IRWIN, DIRK TIEDE, AND JENN MANLEY LEE
ARTIST'S LAB ASSISTANTS
MO OH AND ALEX VALLEAU

LETTERING BY
ZACK GIALLONGO AND GRACE LU
COVER COLORING BY
JENN MANLEY LEE

Copyright © 2013 by Lerner Publishing Group, Inc.

Graphic Universe™ is a trademark of Lerner Publishing Group, Inc.

Graphic Universe™
A division of Lerner Publishing Group, Inc.
241 First Avenue North
Minneapolis, MN 55401 U.S.A.

Website address: www.lernerbooks.com

Main body text set in CCWildwords. Typeface provided by Comicraft Design.

Library of Congress Cataloging-in-Publication Data

Mayhall, Robin.
    He loves me, he loves me not / by Robin Mayhall ; illustrated by Kristen Cella with additional illustrations by Jane Irwin and Dirk Tiede.
        p.   cm. — (My boyfriend is a monster ; #07)
    Summary: Upon moving to small-town Texas partway into her junior year of high school, Serena sees parallels between the novel her class is studying, Dr. Jekyll and Mr. Hyde, and the two men in her life: boyfriend Lance, the quarterback, and outsider Cam.
    ISBN 978–0–7613–6005–6 (lib. bdg. : alk. paper)
    1. Graphic novels. [1. Graphic novels. 2. High schools—Fiction. 3. Schools—Fiction. 4. Dating (Social customs)—Fiction. 5. Moving, Household—Fiction. 6. Family life—Texas—Fiction. 7. Texas—Fiction. 8. Horror stories.] I. Cella, Kristen, ill. II. Title.
PZ7.7.M39He 2013
741.5′973—dc23   2011044491

Manufactured in the United States of America
1 – PP – 12/31/12

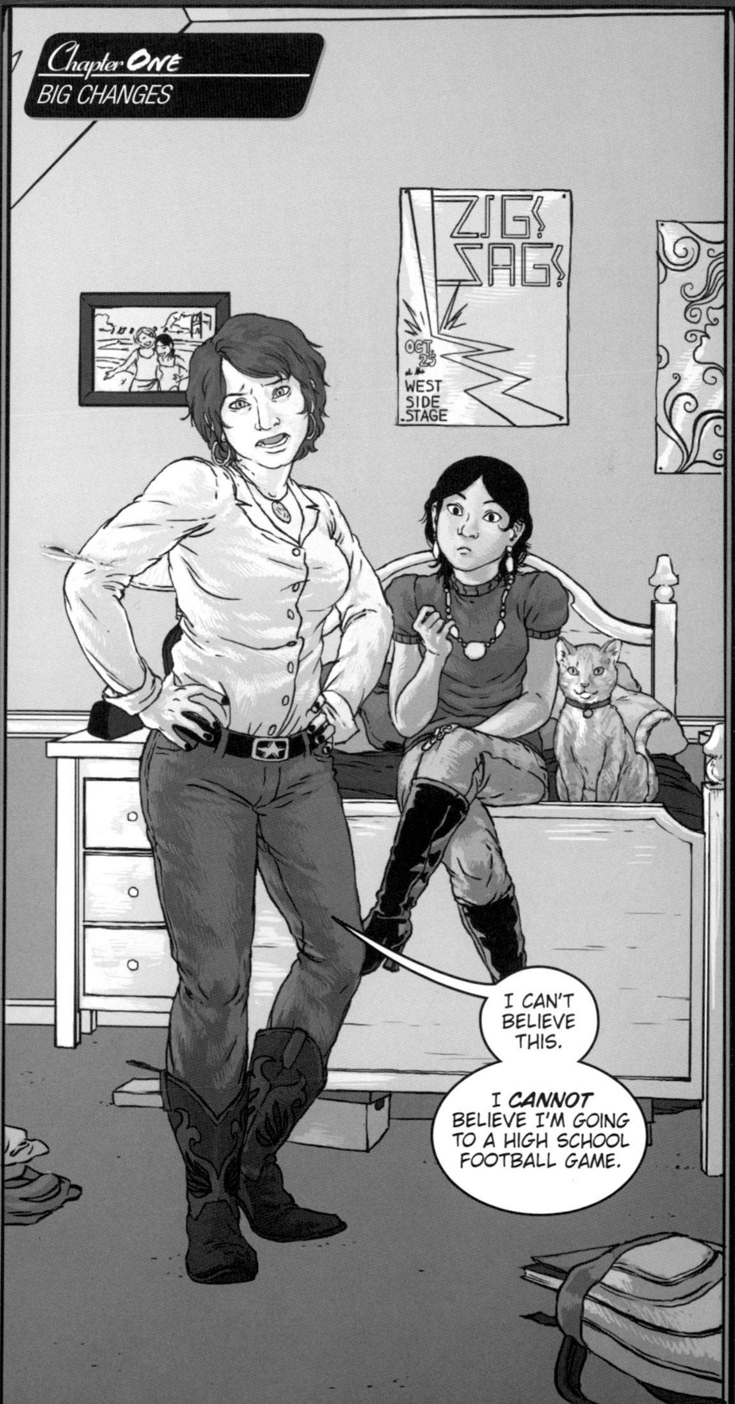
Chapter ONE
BIG CHANGES
ZIG! ZAG!
OCT. 25
WEST SIDE STAGE
I CAN'T BELIEVE THIS.
I **CANNOT** BELIEVE I'M GOING TO A HIGH SCHOOL FOOTBALL GAME.

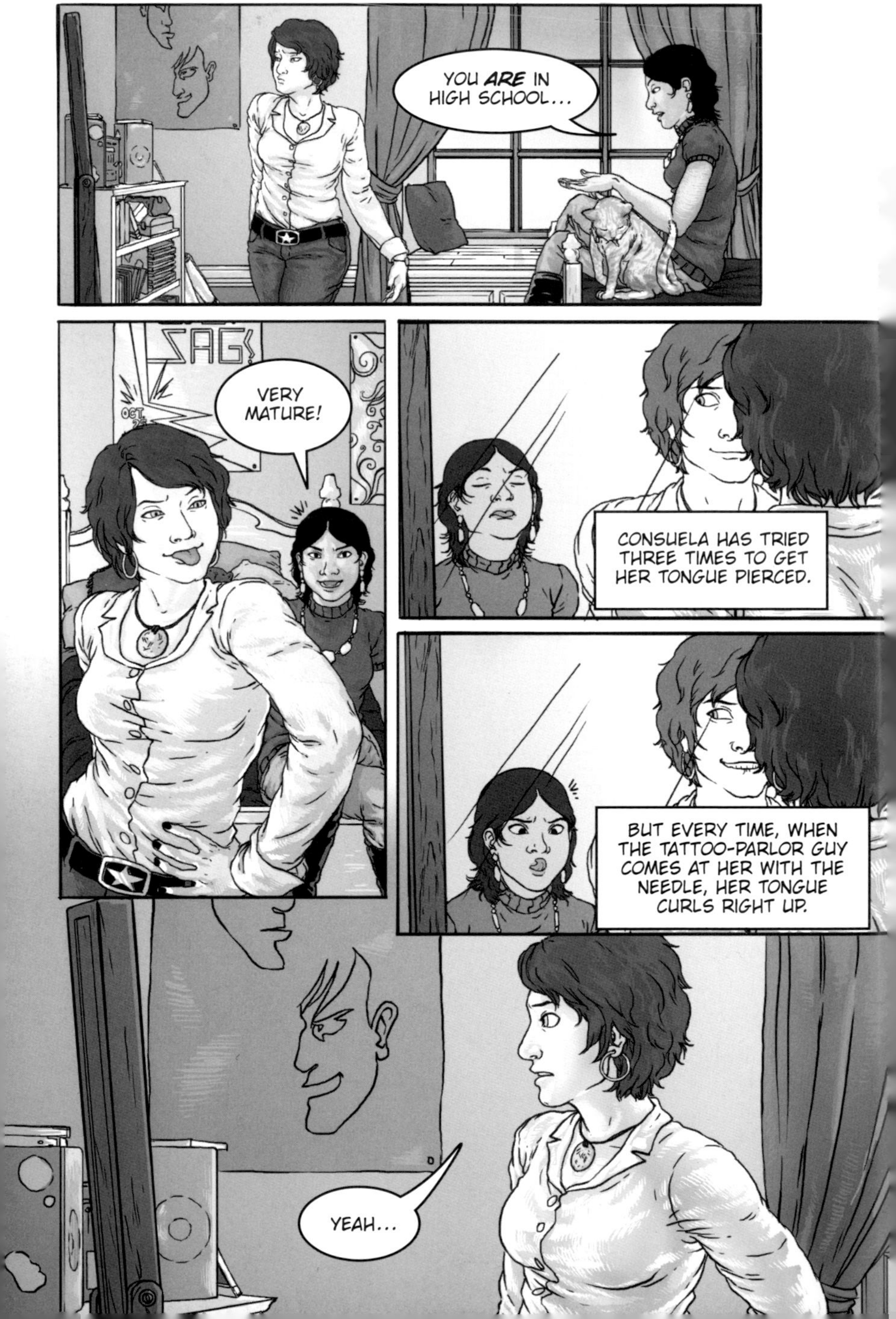
YOU *ARE* IN HIGH SCHOOL...
SAG!
OCT. 25
VERY MATURE!
CONSUELA HAS TRIED THREE TIMES TO GET HER TONGUE PIERCED.
BUT EVERY TIME, WHEN THE TATTOO-PARLOR GUY COMES AT HER WITH THE NEEDLE, HER TONGUE CURLS RIGHT UP.
YEAH...

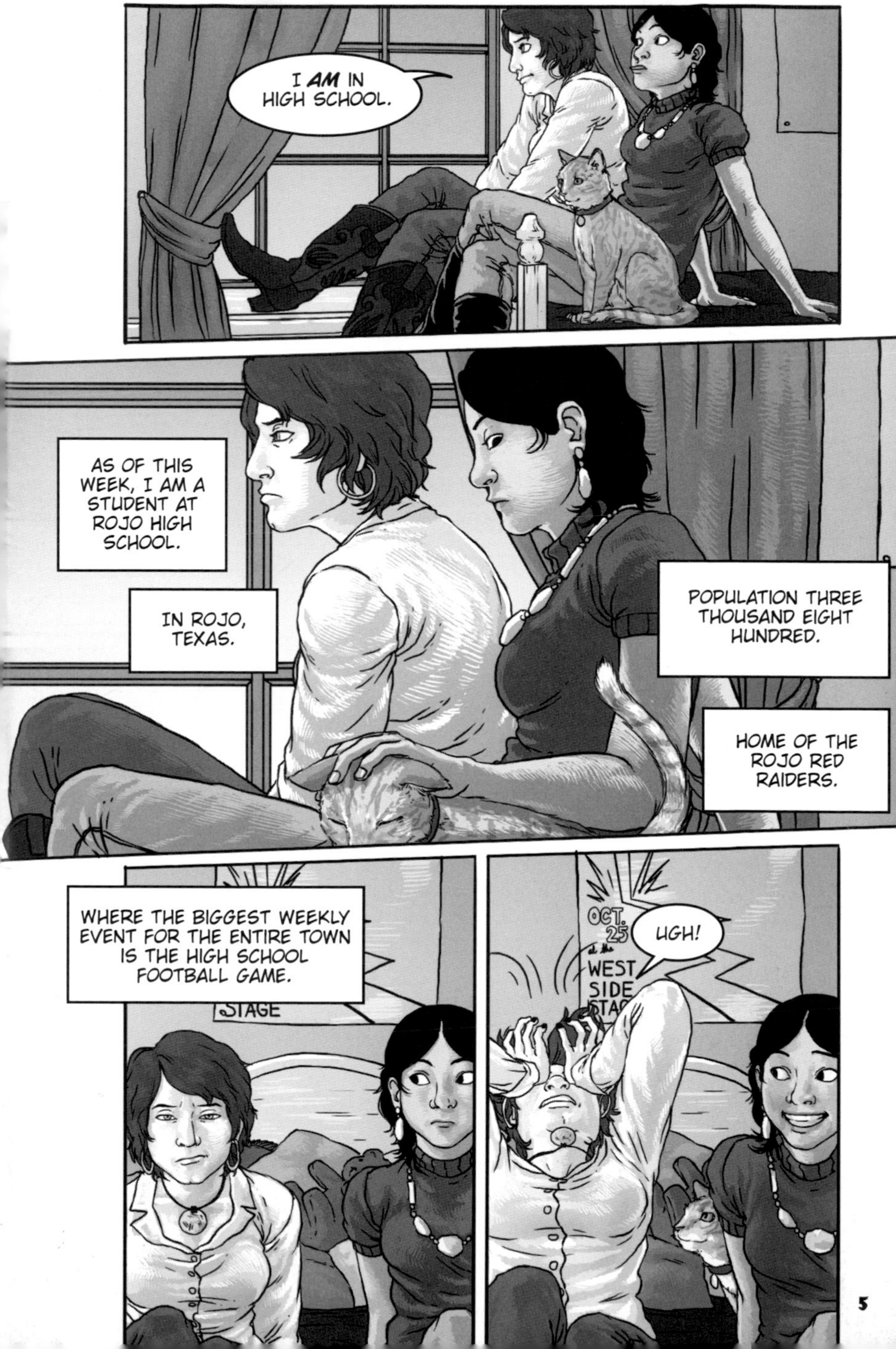
I AM IN HIGH SCHOOL.
AS OF THIS WEEK, I AM A STUDENT AT ROJO HIGH SCHOOL.
IN ROJO, TEXAS.
POPULATION THREE THOUSAND EIGHT HUNDRED.
HOME OF THE ROJO RED RAIDERS.
WHERE THE BIGGEST WEEKLY EVENT FOR THE ENTIRE TOWN IS THE HIGH SCHOOL FOOTBALL GAME.
STAGE
OCT. 25
WEST SIDE
UGH!

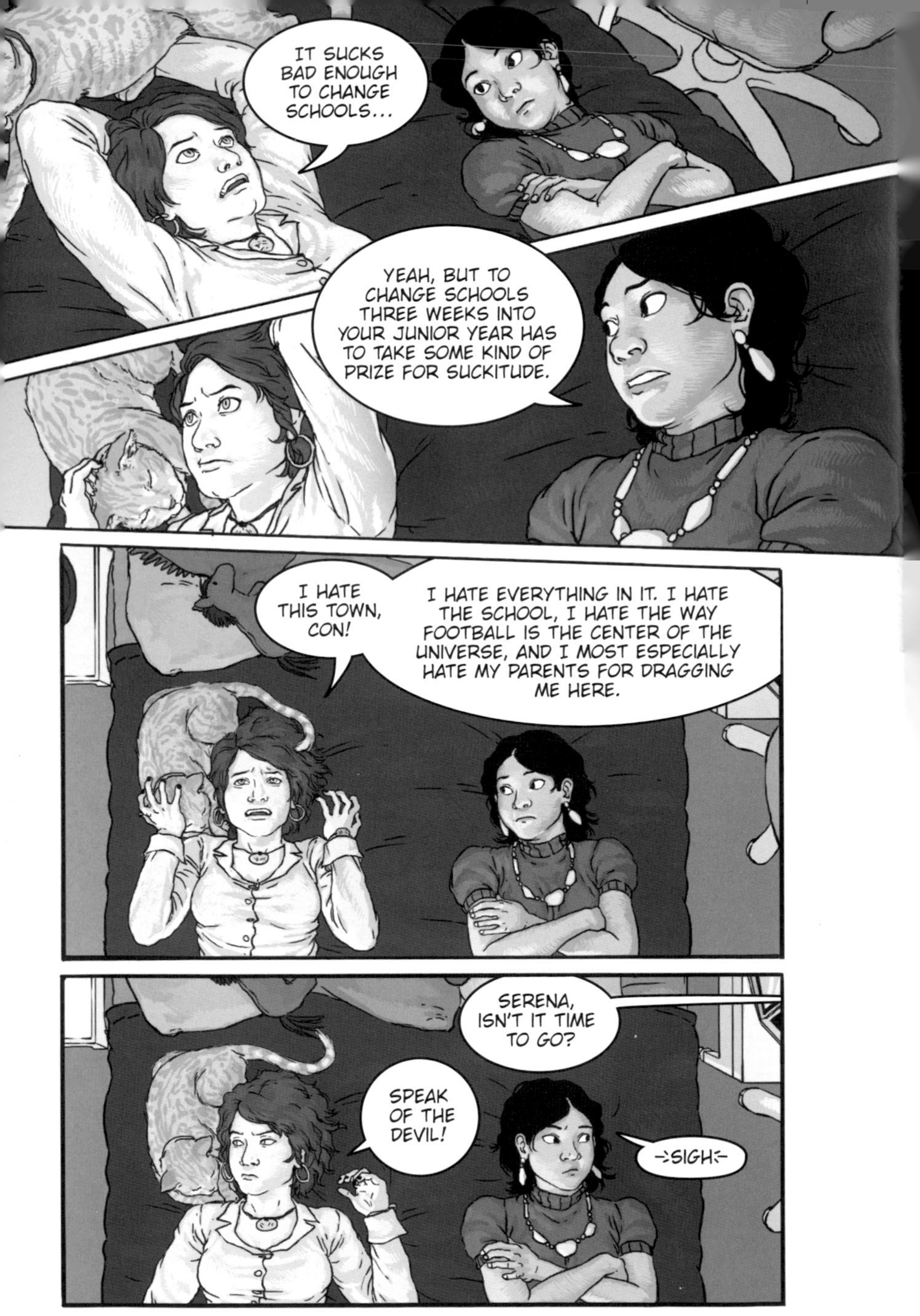
IT SUCKS BAD ENOUGH TO CHANGE SCHOOLS...
YEAH, BUT TO CHANGE SCHOOLS THREE WEEKS INTO YOUR JUNIOR YEAR HAS TO TAKE SOME KIND OF PRIZE FOR SUCKITUDE.
I HATE THIS TOWN, CON!
I HATE EVERYTHING IN IT. I HATE THE SCHOOL, I HATE THE WAY FOOTBALL IS THE CENTER OF THE UNIVERSE, AND I MOST ESPECIALLY HATE MY PARENTS FOR DRAGGING ME HERE.
SERENA, ISN'T IT TIME TO GO?
SPEAK OF THE DEVIL!
SIGH

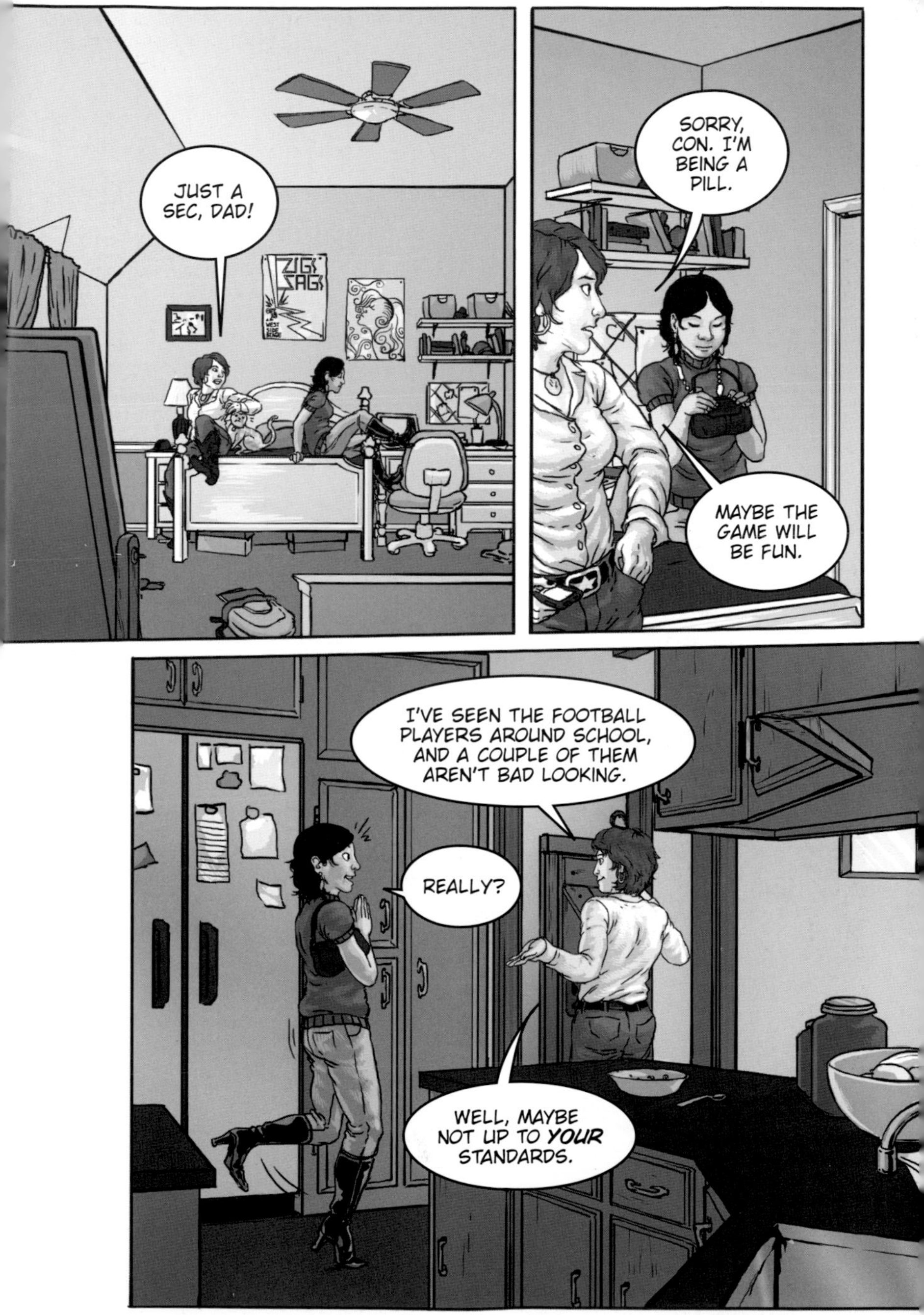
JUST A SEC, DAD!
ZIG SAG
SORRY, CON. I'M BEING A PILL.
MAYBE THE GAME WILL BE FUN.
I'VE SEEN THE FOOTBALL PLAYERS AROUND SCHOOL, AND A COUPLE OF THEM AREN'T BAD LOOKING.
REALLY?
WELL, MAYBE NOT UP TO *YOUR* STANDARDS.

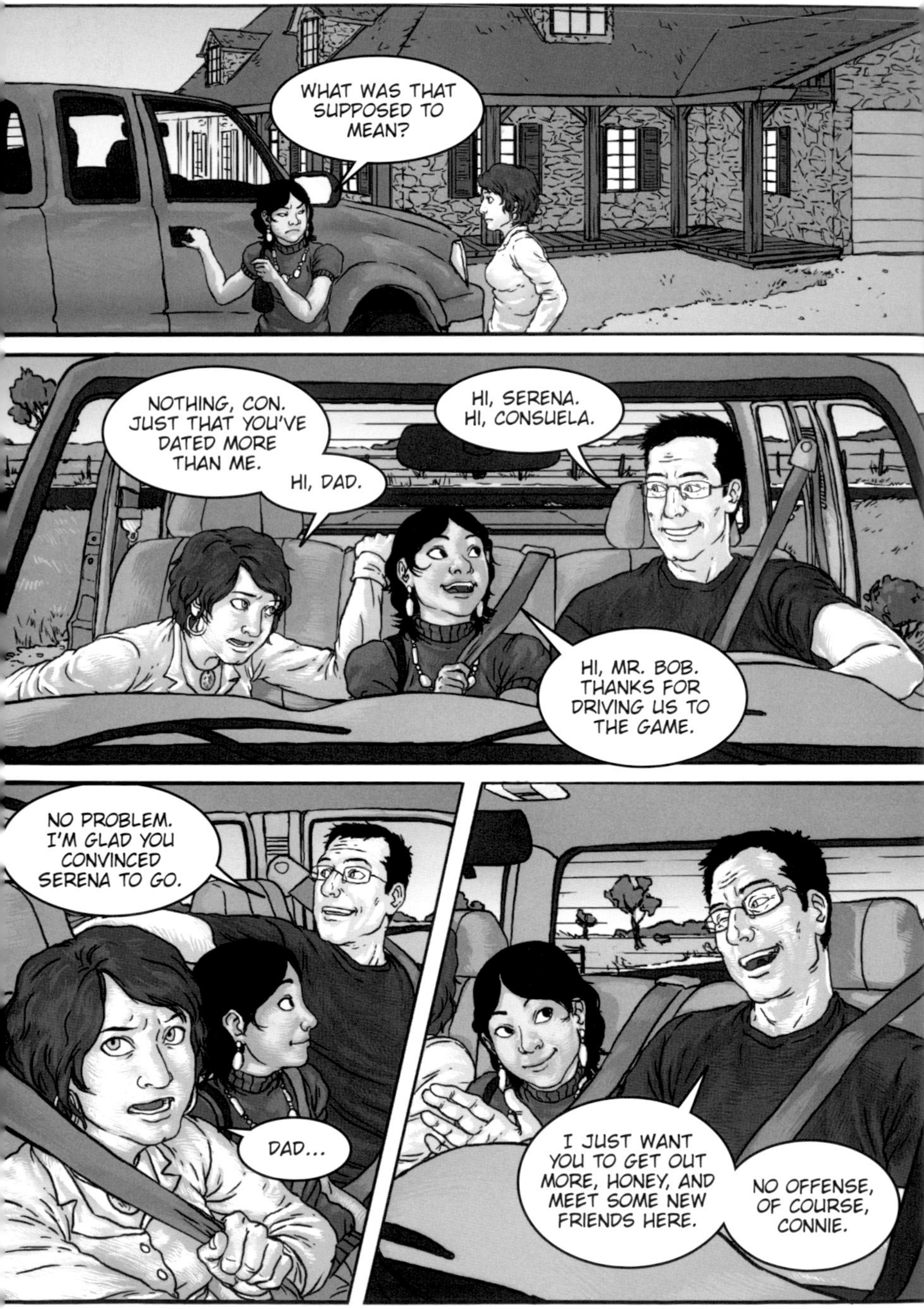
WHAT WAS THAT SUPPOSED TO MEAN?
NOTHING, CON. JUST THAT YOU'VE DATED MORE THAN ME.
HI, DAD.
HI, SERENA. HI, CONSUELA.
HI, MR. BOB. THANKS FOR DRIVING US TO THE GAME.
NO PROBLEM. I'M GLAD YOU CONVINCED SERENA TO GO.
DAD...
I JUST WANT YOU TO GET OUT MORE, HONEY, AND MEET SOME NEW FRIENDS HERE.
NO OFFENSE, OF COURSE, CONNIE.

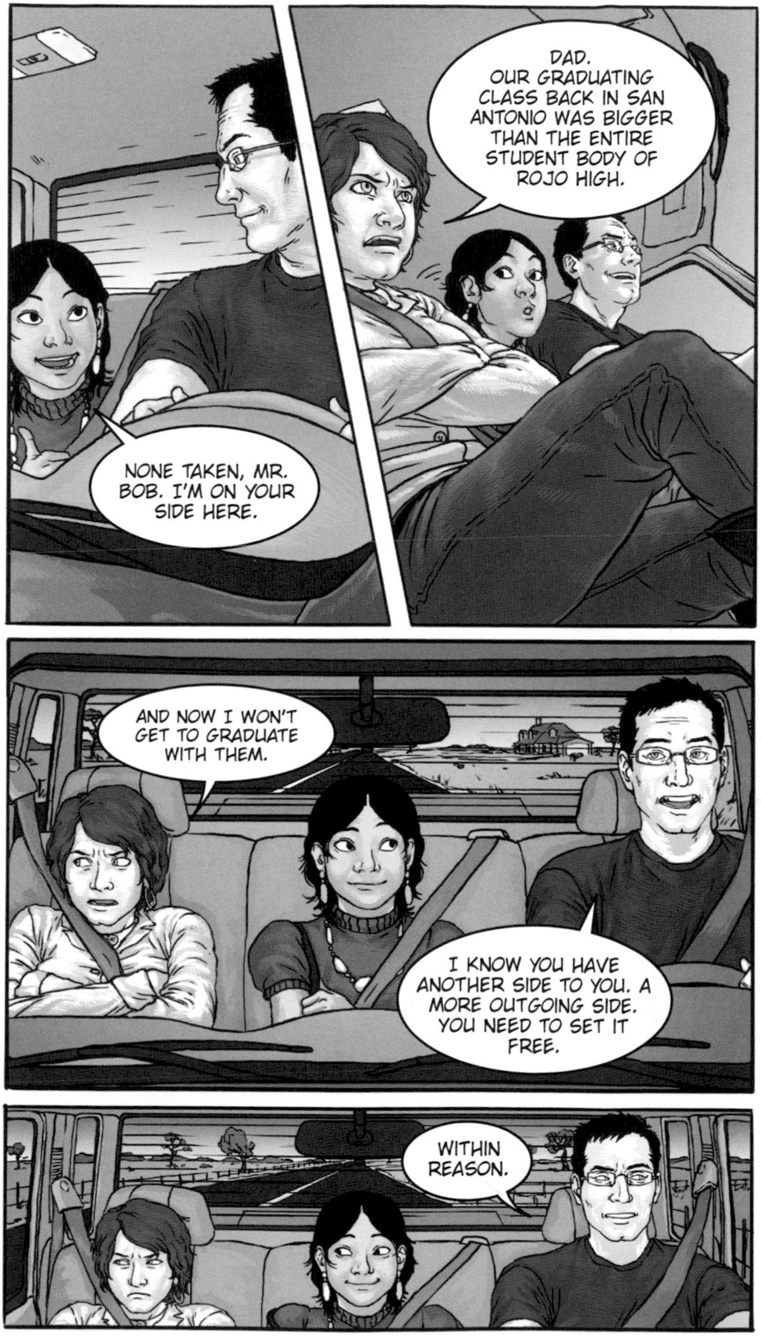
NONE TAKEN, MR. BOB. I'M ON YOUR SIDE HERE.
DAD. OUR GRADUATING CLASS BACK IN SAN ANTONIO WAS BIGGER THAN THE ENTIRE STUDENT BODY OF ROJO HIGH.
AND NOW I WON'T GET TO GRADUATE WITH THEM.
I KNOW YOU HAVE ANOTHER SIDE TO YOU. A MORE OUTGOING SIDE. YOU NEED TO SET IT FREE.
WITHIN REASON.

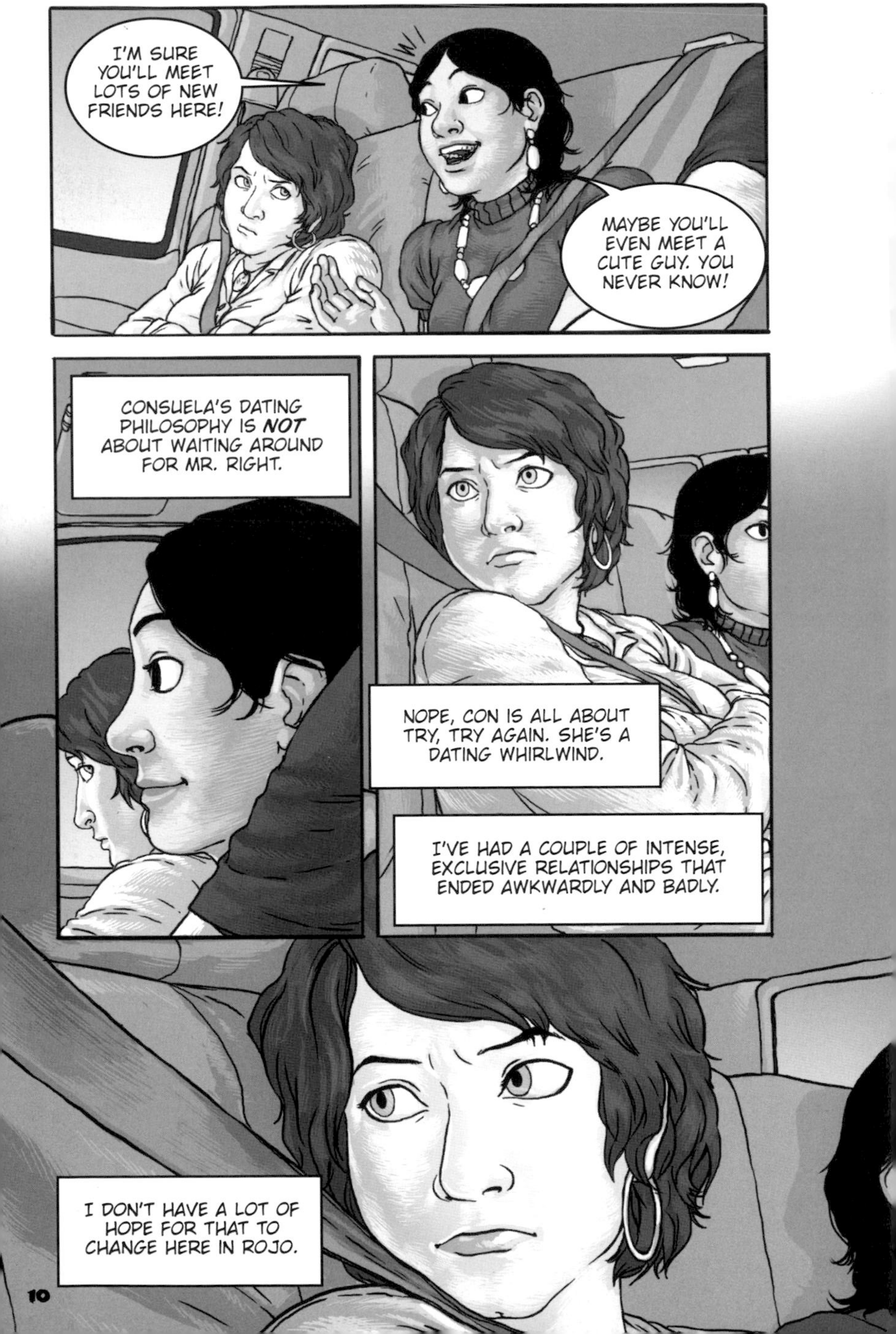
I'M SURE YOU'LL MEET LOTS OF NEW FRIENDS HERE!
MAYBE YOU'LL EVEN MEET A CUTE GUY. YOU NEVER KNOW!
CONSUELA'S DATING PHILOSOPHY IS NOT ABOUT WAITING AROUND FOR MR. RIGHT.
NOPE, CON IS ALL ABOUT TRY, TRY AGAIN. SHE'S A DATING WHIRLWIND.
I'VE HAD A COUPLE OF INTENSE, EXCLUSIVE RELATIONSHIPS THAT ENDED AWKWARDLY AND BADLY.
I DON'T HAVE A LOT OF HOPE FOR THAT TO CHANGE HERE IN ROJO.

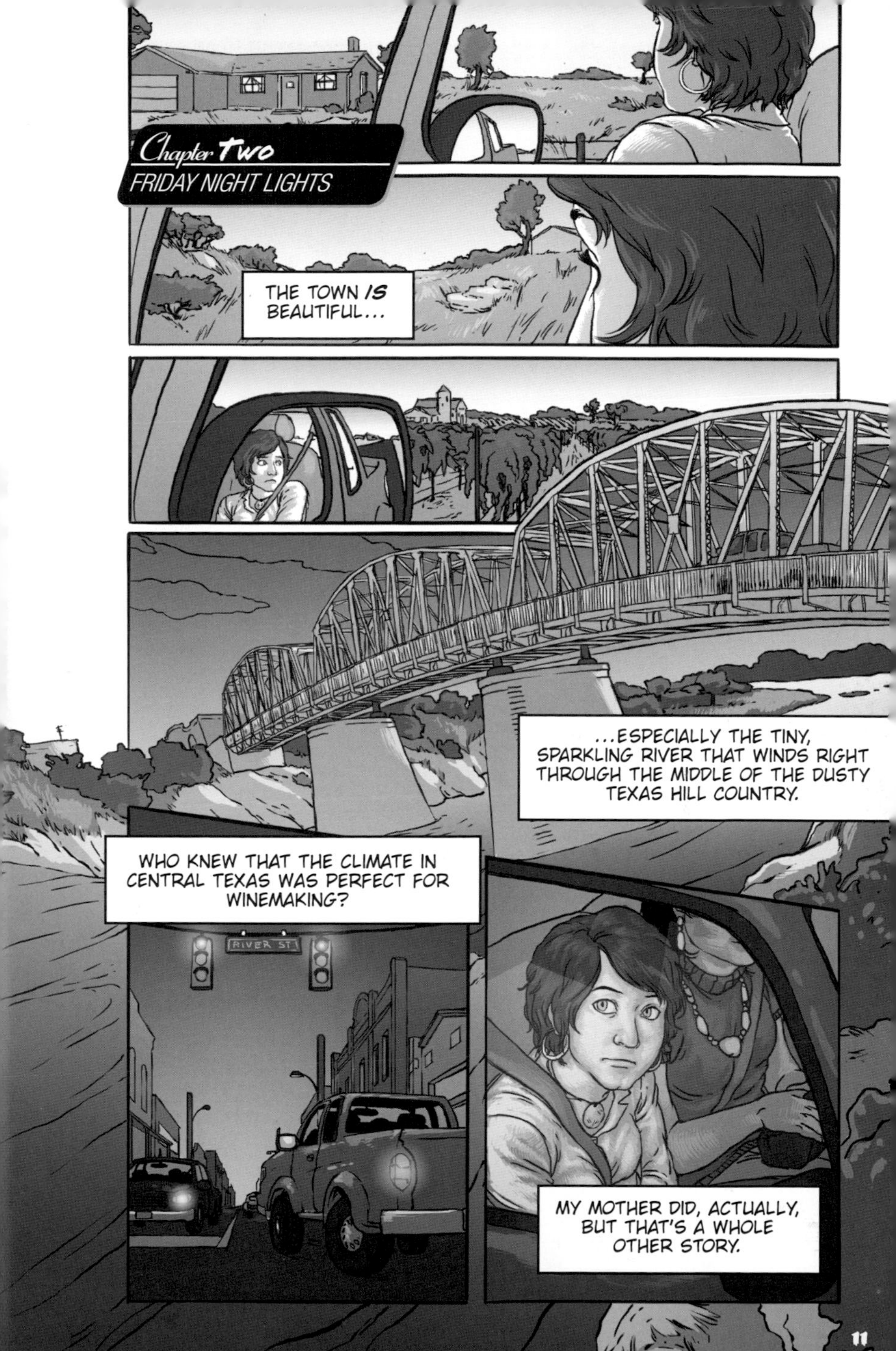
Chapter Two
FRIDAY NIGHT LIGHTS
THE TOWN IS BEAUTIFUL...
...ESPECIALLY THE TINY, SPARKLING RIVER THAT WINDS RIGHT THROUGH THE MIDDLE OF THE DUSTY TEXAS HILL COUNTRY.
WHO KNEW THAT THE CLIMATE IN CENTRAL TEXAS WAS PERFECT FOR WINEMAKING?
RIVER ST
MY MOTHER DID, ACTUALLY, BUT THAT'S A WHOLE OTHER STORY.

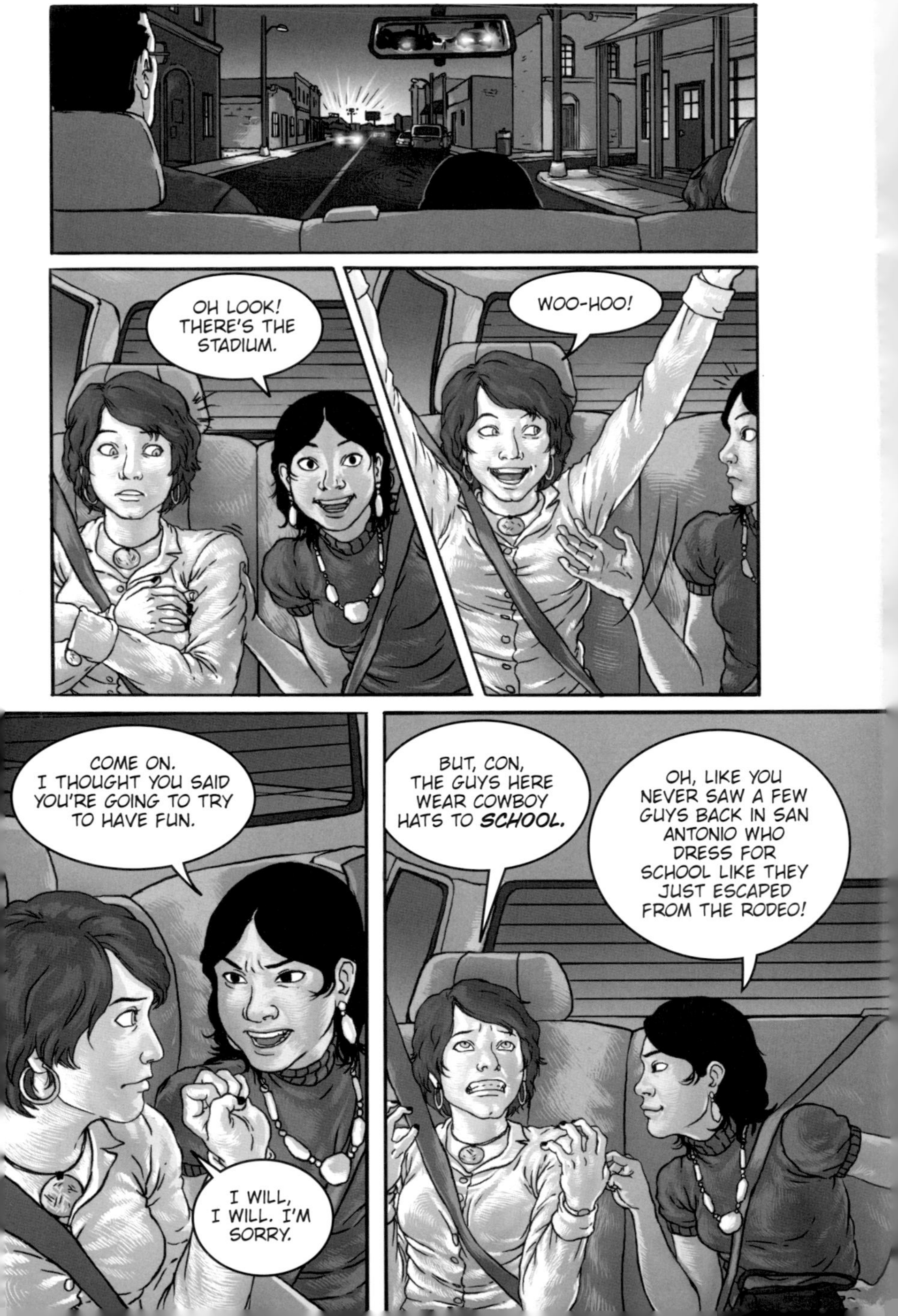
OH LOOK! THERE'S THE STADIUM.
WOO-HOO!
COME ON. I THOUGHT YOU SAID YOU'RE GOING TO TRY TO HAVE FUN.
I WILL, I WILL. I'M SORRY.
BUT, CON, THE GUYS HERE WEAR COWBOY HATS TO SCHOOL.
OH, LIKE YOU NEVER SAW A FEW GUYS BACK IN SAN ANTONIO WHO DRESS FOR SCHOOL LIKE THEY JUST ESCAPED FROM THE RODEO!

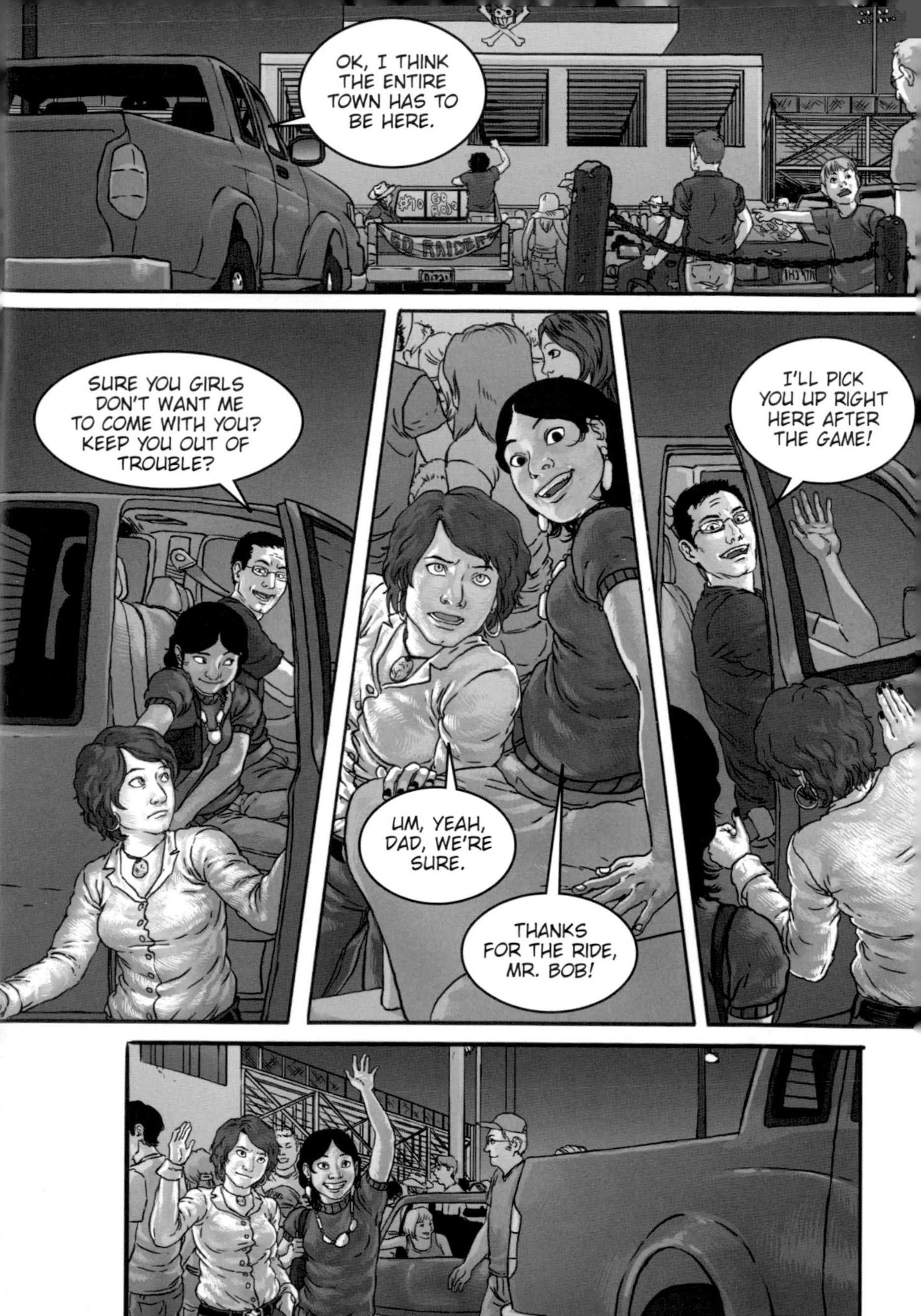
OK, I THINK THE ENTIRE TOWN HAS TO BE HERE.
GO RAIDER
SURE YOU GIRLS DON'T WANT ME TO COME WITH YOU? KEEP YOU OUT OF TROUBLE?
UM, YEAH, DAD, WE'RE SURE.
THANKS FOR THE RIDE, MR. BOB!
I'LL PICK YOU UP RIGHT HERE AFTER THE GAME!

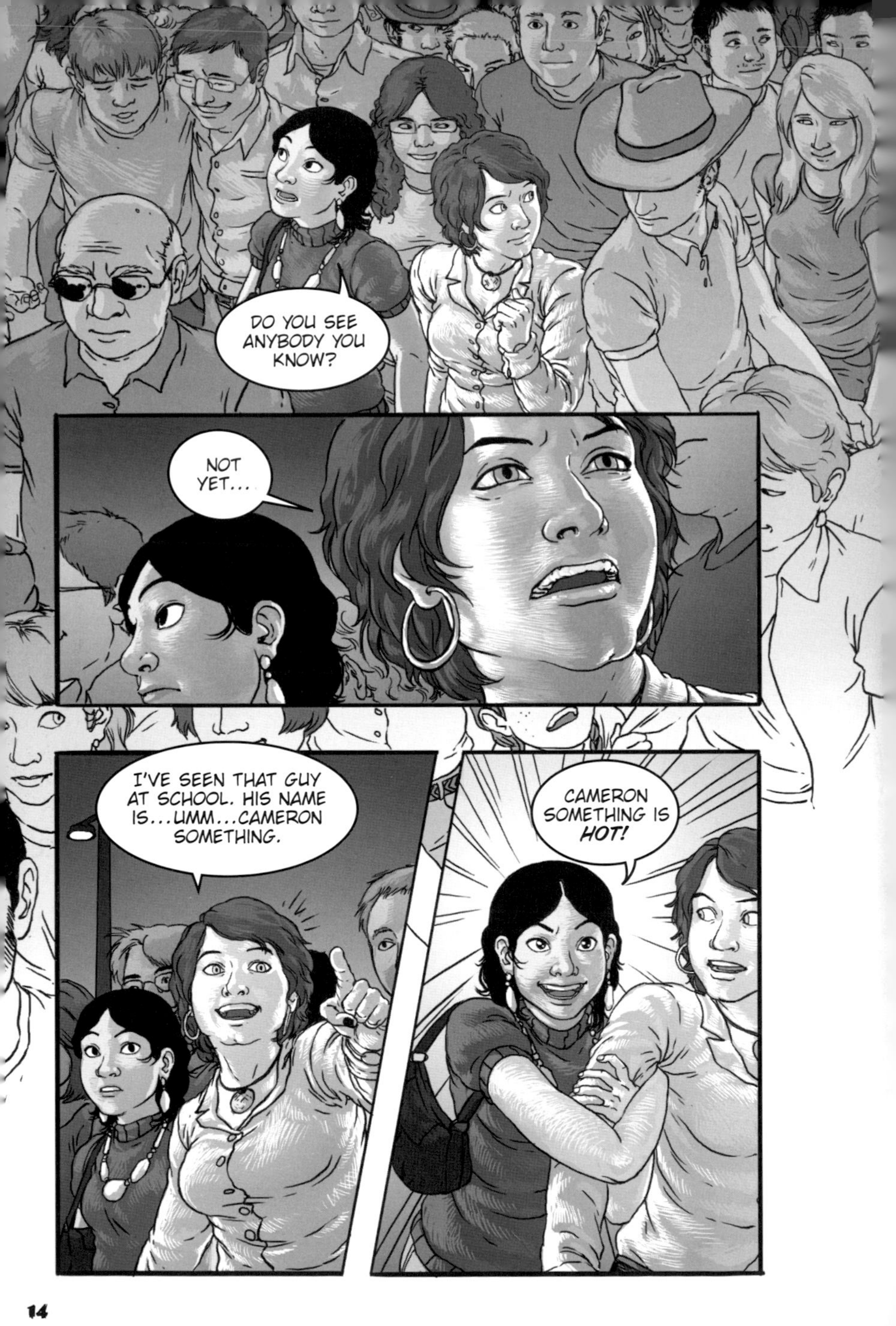
DO YOU SEE ANYBODY YOU KNOW?
NOT YET...
I'VE SEEN THAT GUY AT SCHOOL. HIS NAME IS...UMM...CAMERON SOMETHING.
CAMERON SOMETHING IS *HOT!*

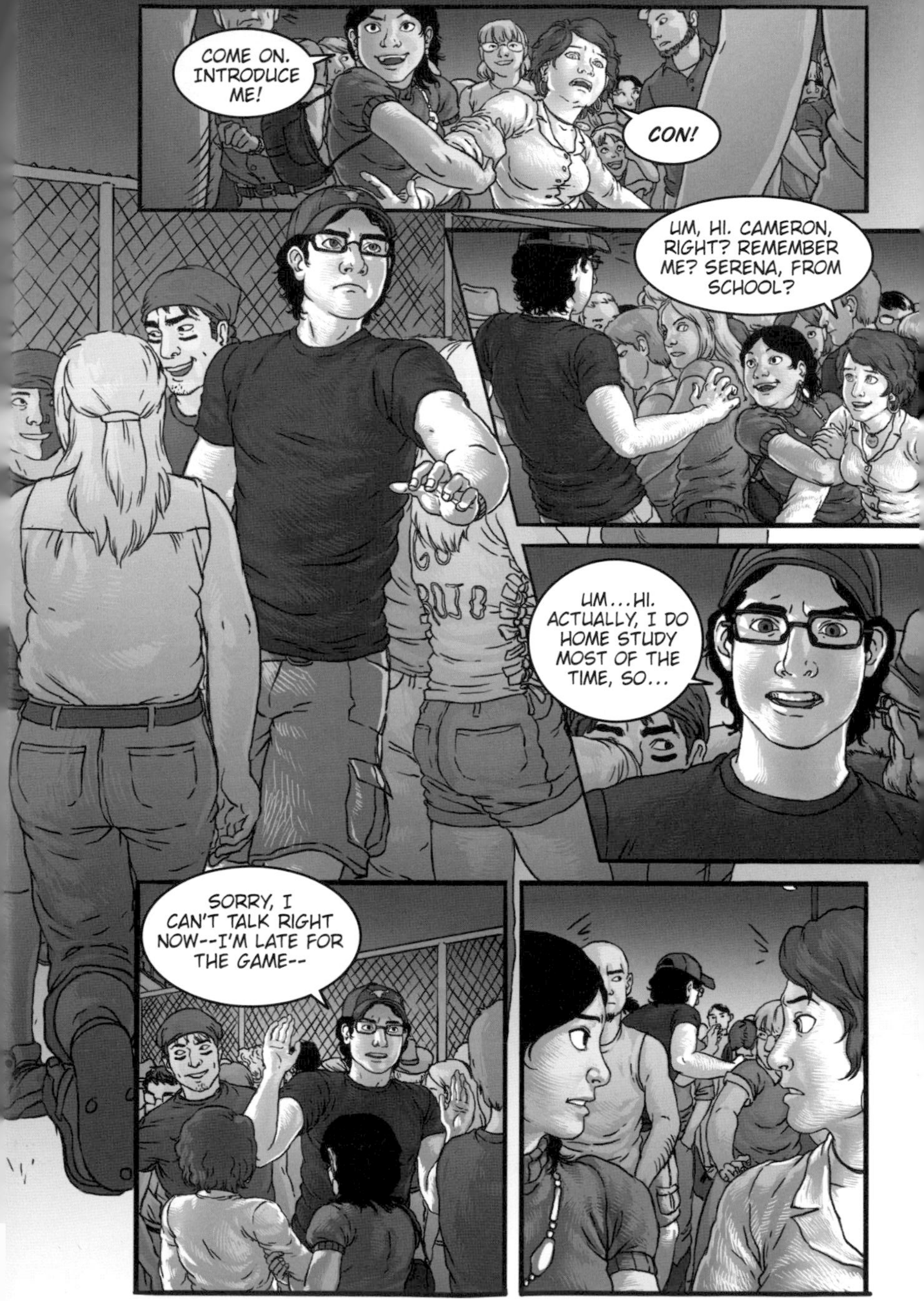
COME ON. INTRODUCE ME!
CON!
UM, HI. CAMERON, RIGHT? REMEMBER ME? SERENA, FROM SCHOOL?
GO ROJO
UM...HI. ACTUALLY, I DO HOME STUDY MOST OF THE TIME, SO...
SORRY, I CAN'T TALK RIGHT NOW--I'M LATE FOR THE GAME--

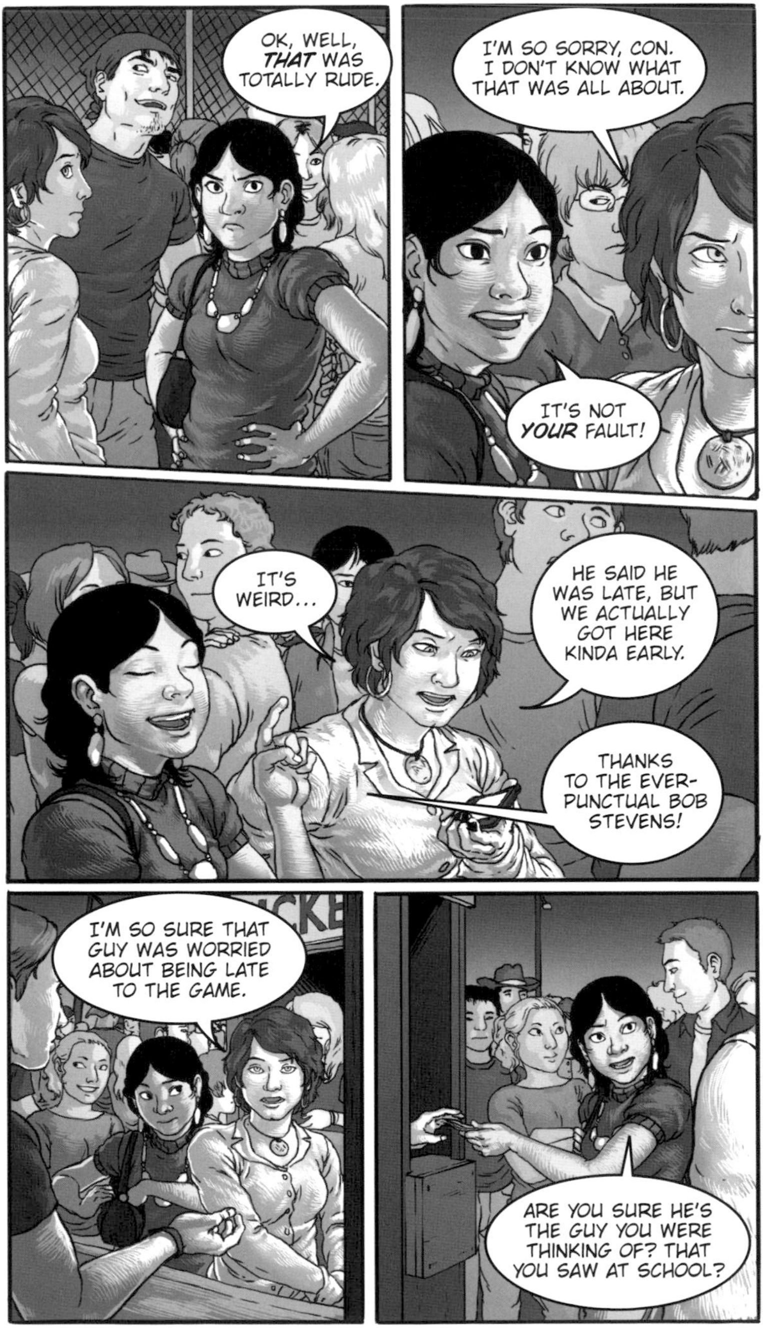
OK, WELL, *THAT* WAS TOTALLY RUDE.
I'M SO SORRY, CON. I DON'T KNOW WHAT THAT WAS ALL ABOUT.
IT'S NOT *YOUR* FAULT!
IT'S WEIRD...
HE SAID HE WAS LATE, BUT WE ACTUALLY GOT HERE KINDA EARLY.
THANKS TO THE EVER-PUNCTUAL BOB STEVENS!
I'M SO SURE THAT GUY WAS WORRIED ABOUT BEING LATE TO THE GAME.
ARE YOU SURE HE'S THE GUY YOU WERE THINKING OF? THAT YOU SAW AT SCHOOL?

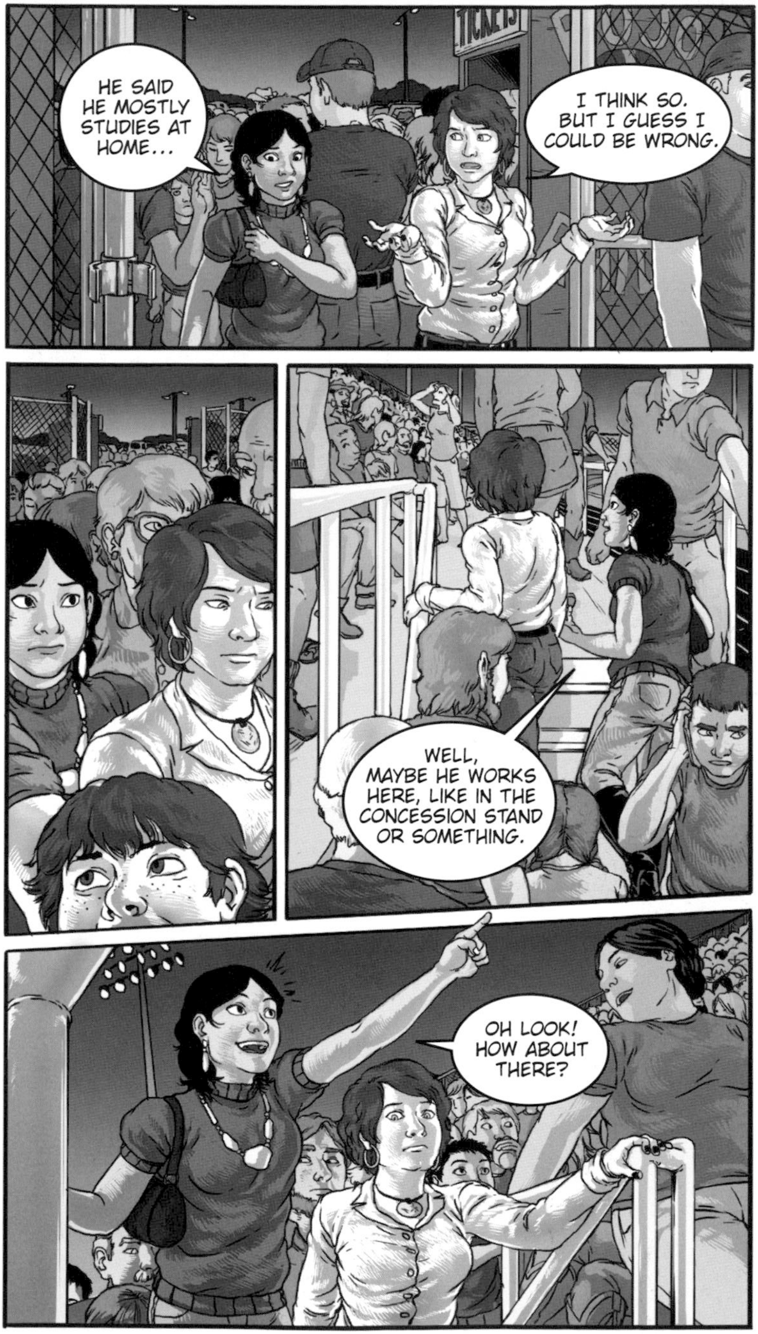
HE SAID HE MOSTLY STUDIES AT HOME...
I THINK SO. BUT I GUESS I COULD BE WRONG.
TICKETS
WELL, MAYBE HE WORKS HERE, LIKE IN THE CONCESSION STAND OR SOMETHING.
OH LOOK! HOW ABOUT THERE?

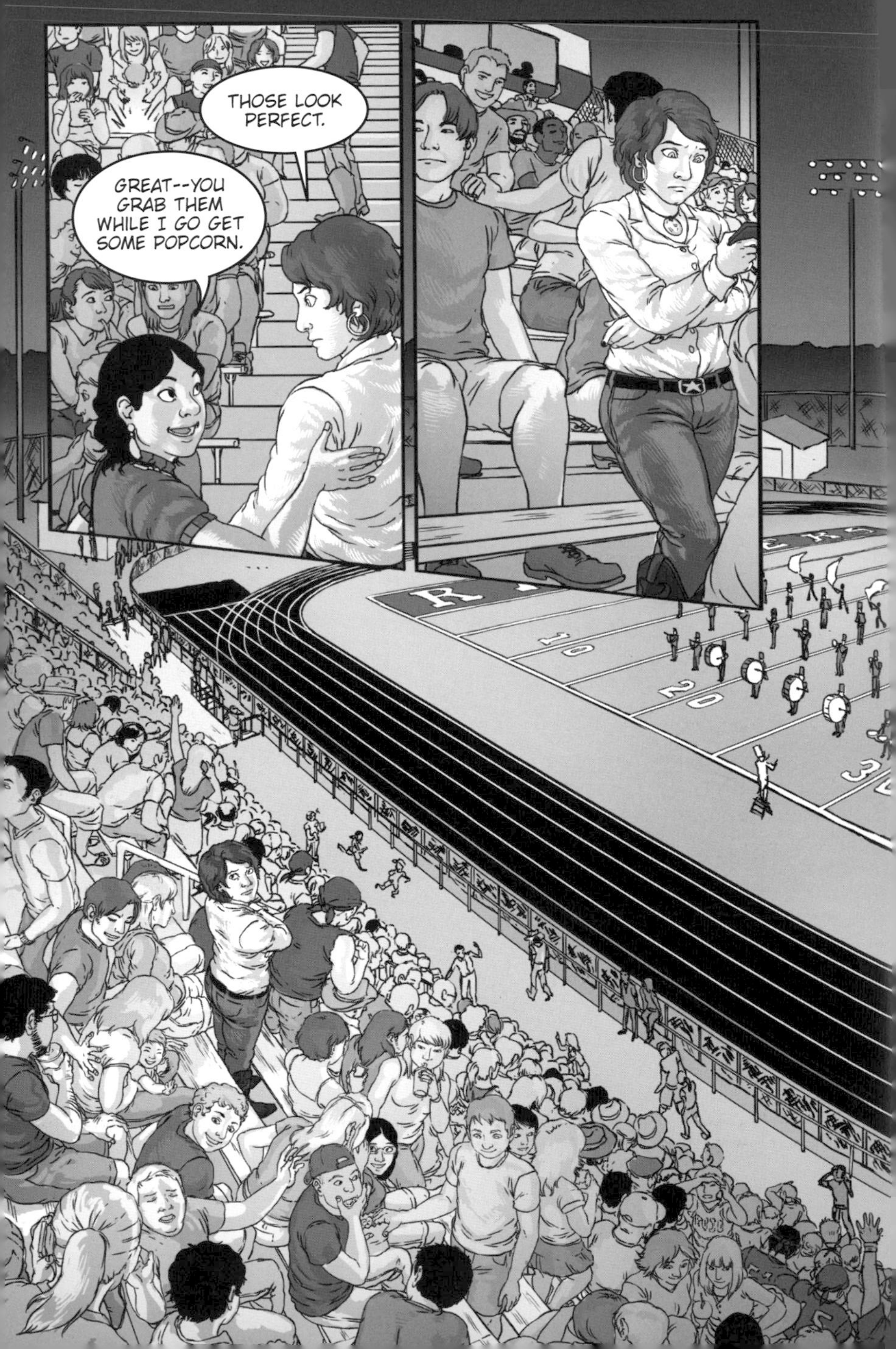
THOSE LOOK PERFECT.
GREAT--YOU GRAB THEM WHILE I GO GET SOME POPCORN.

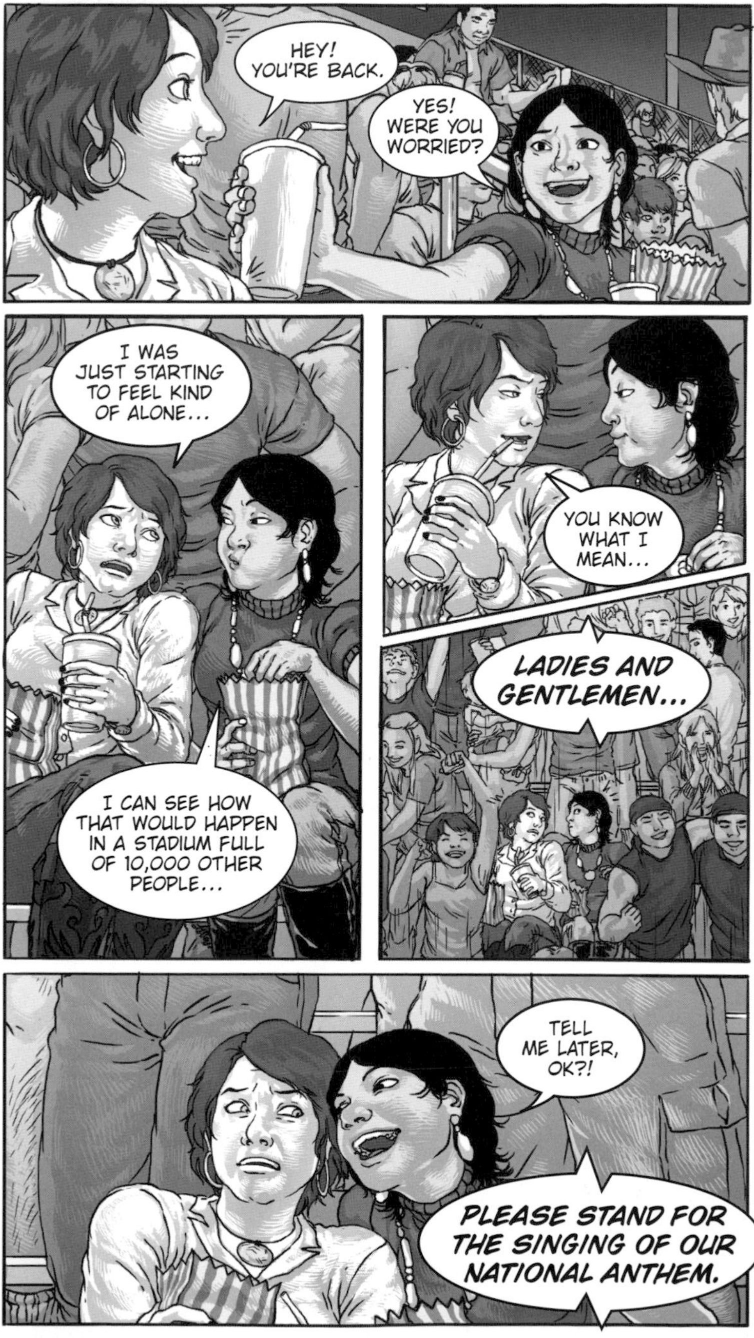
HEY! YOU'RE BACK.
YES! WERE YOU WORRIED?
I WAS JUST STARTING TO FEEL KIND OF ALONE...
I CAN SEE HOW THAT WOULD HAPPEN IN A STADIUM FULL OF 10,000 OTHER PEOPLE...
YOU KNOW WHAT I MEAN...
LADIES AND GENTLEMEN...
TELL ME LATER, OK?!
PLEASE STAND FOR THE SINGING OF OUR NATIONAL ANTHEM.

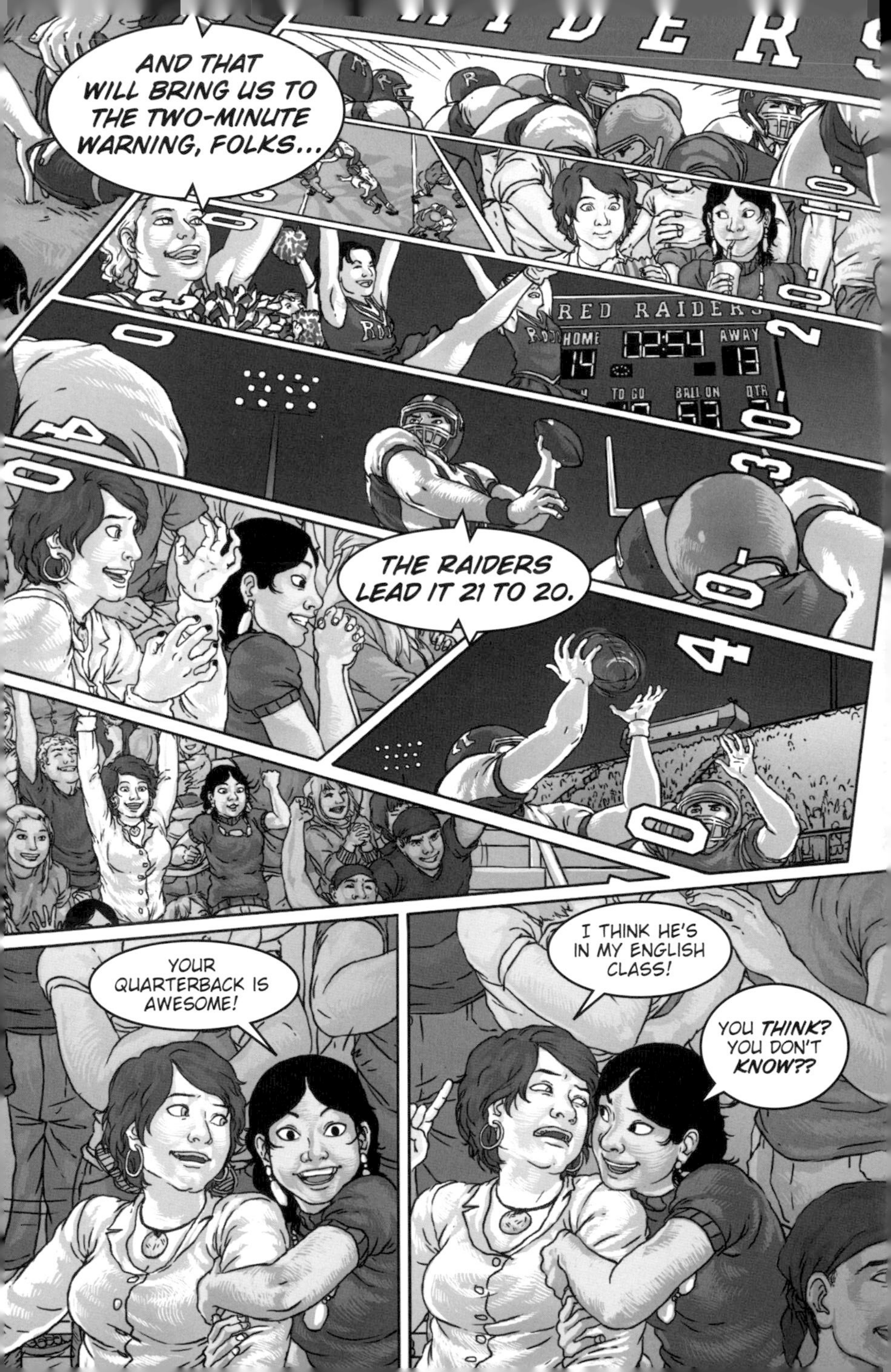
AND THAT WILL BRING US TO THE TWO-MINUTE WARNING, FOLKS...
RED RAIDERS
HOME
AWAY
14
13
TO GO
BALL ON
QTR
THE RAIDERS LEAD IT 21 TO 20.
YOUR QUARTERBACK IS AWESOME!
I THINK HE'S IN MY ENGLISH CLASS!
YOU *THINK*? YOU DON'T *KNOW*??

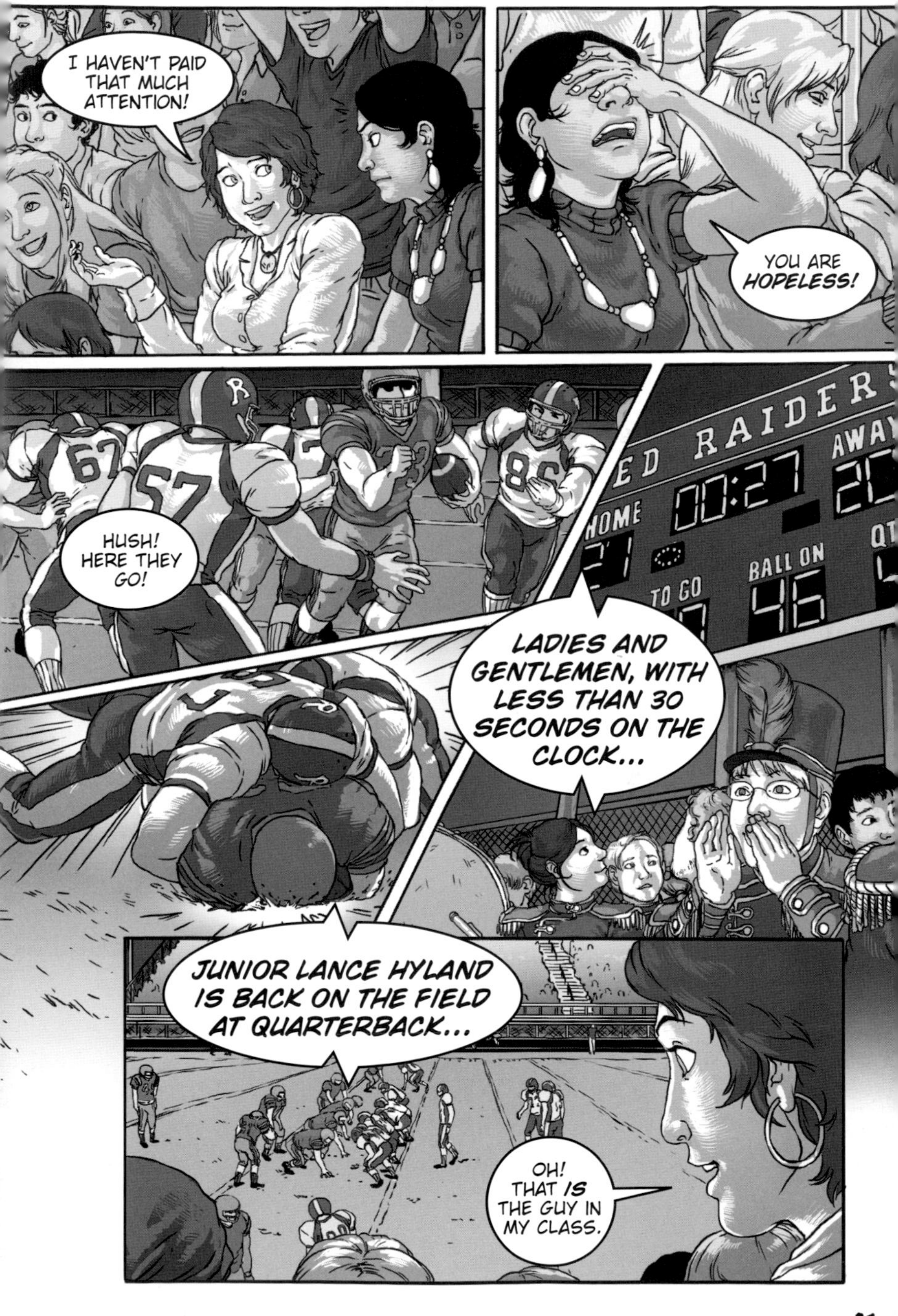
I HAVEN'T PAID THAT MUCH ATTENTION!
YOU ARE HOPELESS!
HUSH! HERE THEY GO!
RED RAIDERS
00:27
AWAY
HOME
BALL ON
46
TO GO
QTR
LADIES AND GENTLEMEN, WITH LESS THAN 30 SECONDS ON THE CLOCK...
JUNIOR LANCE HYLAND IS BACK ON THE FIELD AT QUARTERBACK...
OH! THAT IS THE GUY IN MY CLASS.

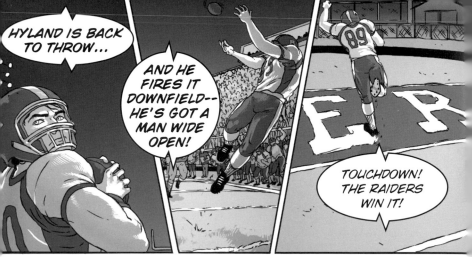

HYLAND IS BACK TO THROW...

AND HE FIRES IT DOWNFIELD-- HE'S GOT A MAN WIDE OPEN!

TOUCHDOWN! THE RAIDERS WIN IT!

DOES HE HAVE A GIRLFRIEND?

I DON'T KNOW! I'VE ONLY BEEN HERE TWO WEEKS!

YOU *HAVE* TO FIND OUT.

HAVE TO.

HAVE TO.

Chapter THREE
MONDAY MORNING QUARTERBACK

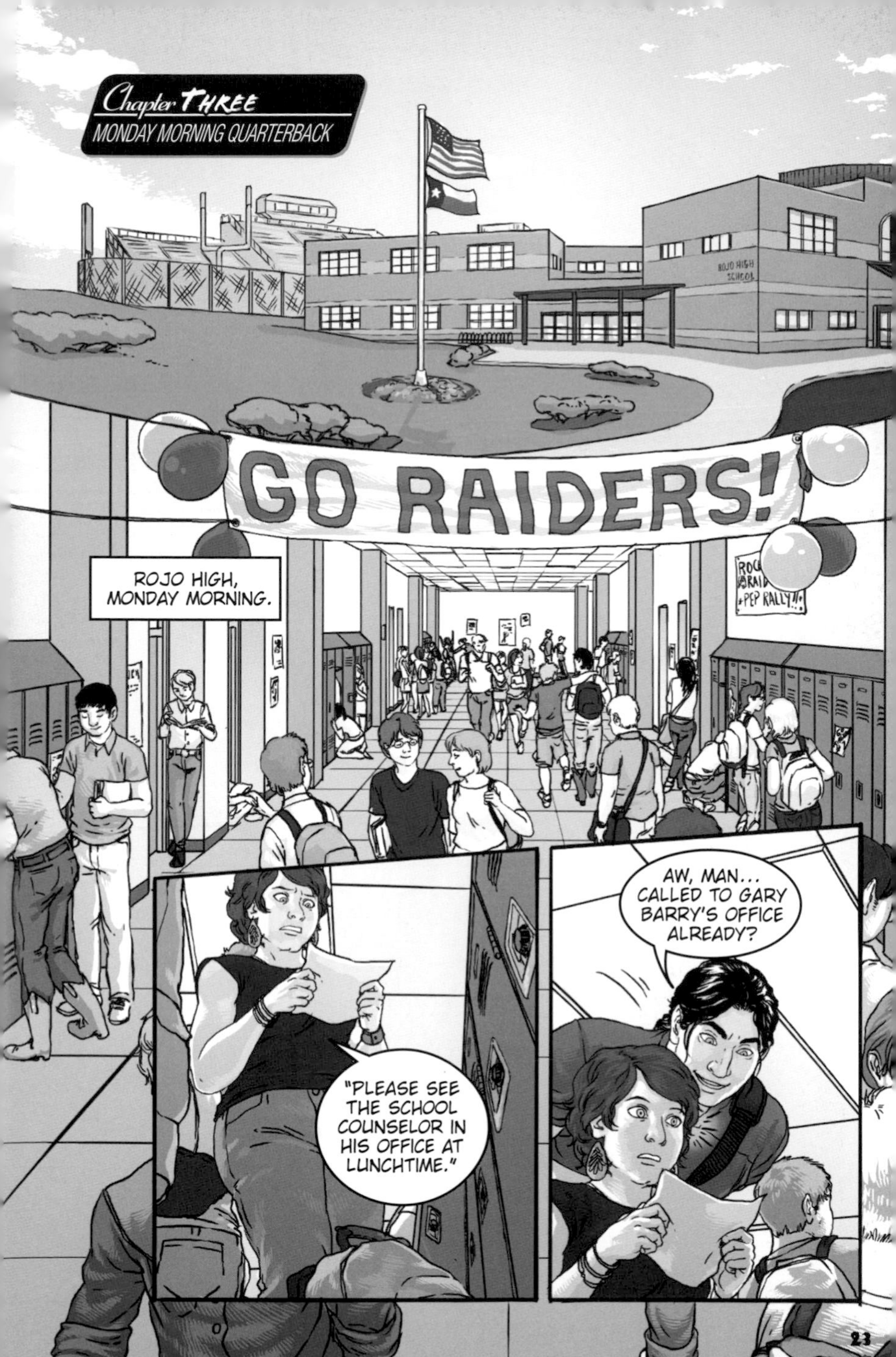
ROJO HIGH SCHOOL
GO RAIDERS!
ROJO HIGH, MONDAY MORNING.
PEP RALLY!!
"PLEASE SEE THE SCHOOL COUNSELOR IN HIS OFFICE AT LUNCHTIME."
AW, MAN... CALLED TO GARY BARRY'S OFFICE ALREADY?

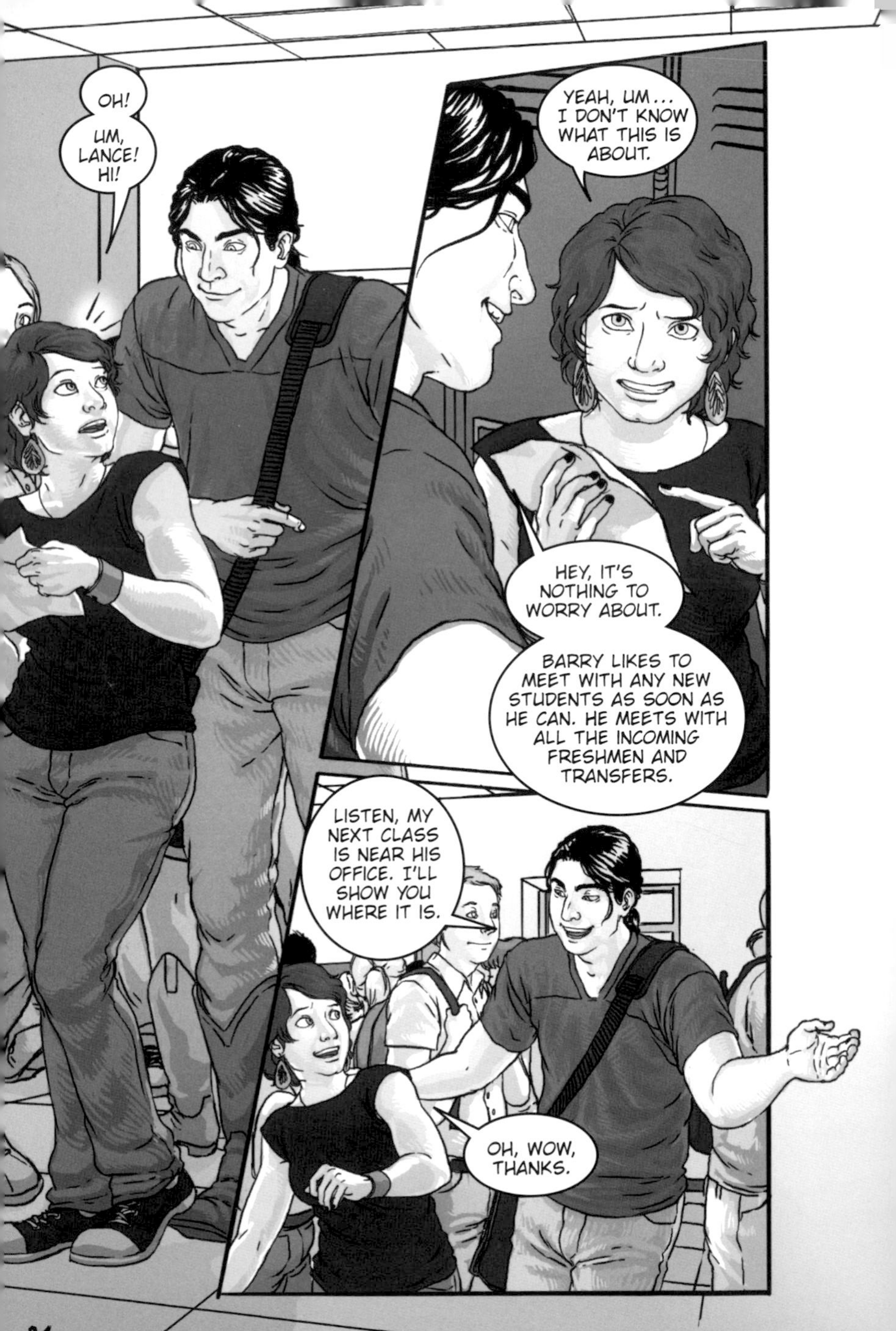
OH!
UM, LANCE! HI!
YEAH, UM... I DON'T KNOW WHAT THIS IS ABOUT.
HEY, IT'S NOTHING TO WORRY ABOUT.
BARRY LIKES TO MEET WITH ANY NEW STUDENTS AS SOON AS HE CAN. HE MEETS WITH ALL THE INCOMING FRESHMEN AND TRANSFERS.
LISTEN, MY NEXT CLASS IS NEAR HIS OFFICE. I'LL SHOW YOU WHERE IT IS.
OH, WOW, THANKS.

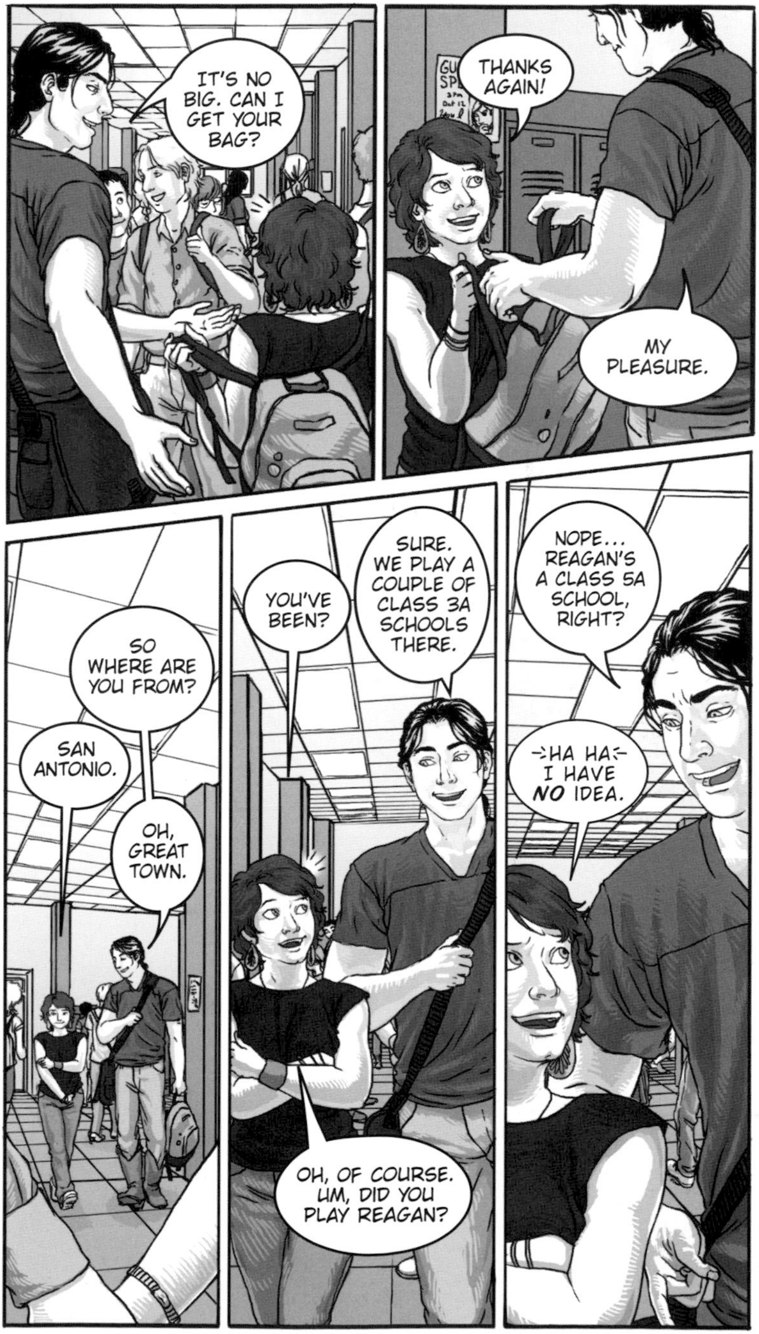
IT'S NO BIG. CAN I GET YOUR BAG?
THANKS AGAIN!
MY PLEASURE.
SO WHERE ARE YOU FROM?
SAN ANTONIO.
OH, GREAT TOWN.
YOU'VE BEEN?
SURE. WE PLAY A COUPLE OF CLASS 3A SCHOOLS THERE.
OH, OF COURSE. UM, DID YOU PLAY REAGAN?
NOPE... REAGAN'S A CLASS 5A SCHOOL, RIGHT?
HA HA I HAVE **NO** IDEA.

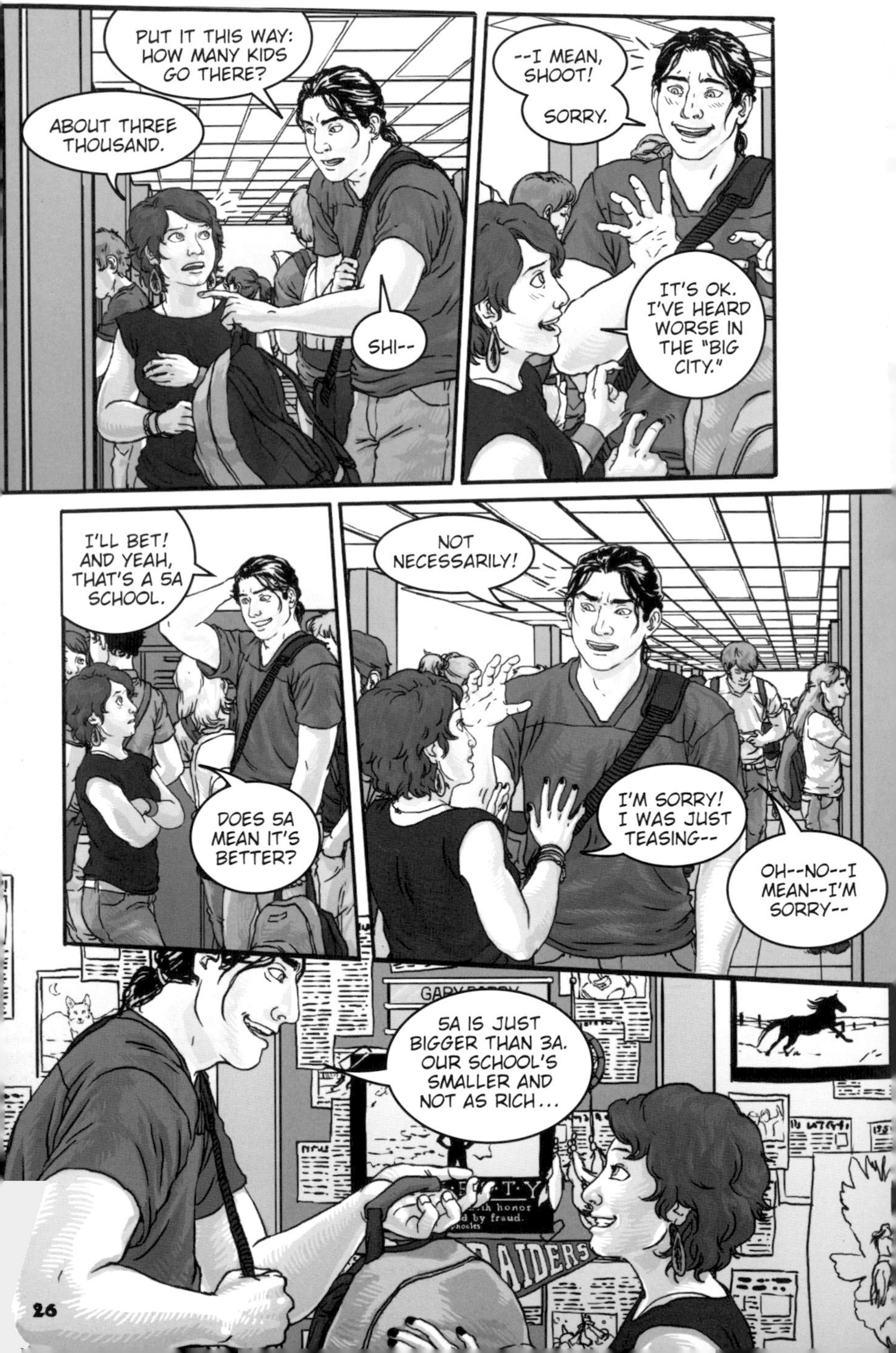
PUT IT THIS WAY: HOW MANY KIDS GO THERE?
ABOUT THREE THOUSAND.
SHI--
--I MEAN, SHOOT!
SORRY.
IT'S OK. I'VE HEARD WORSE IN THE "BIG CITY."
I'LL BET! AND YEAH, THAT'S A 5A SCHOOL.
DOES 5A MEAN IT'S BETTER?
NOT NECESSARILY!
I'M SORRY! I WAS JUST TEASING--
OH--NO--I MEAN--I'M SORRY--
5A IS JUST BIGGER THAN 3A. OUR SCHOOL'S SMALLER AND NOT AS RICH...

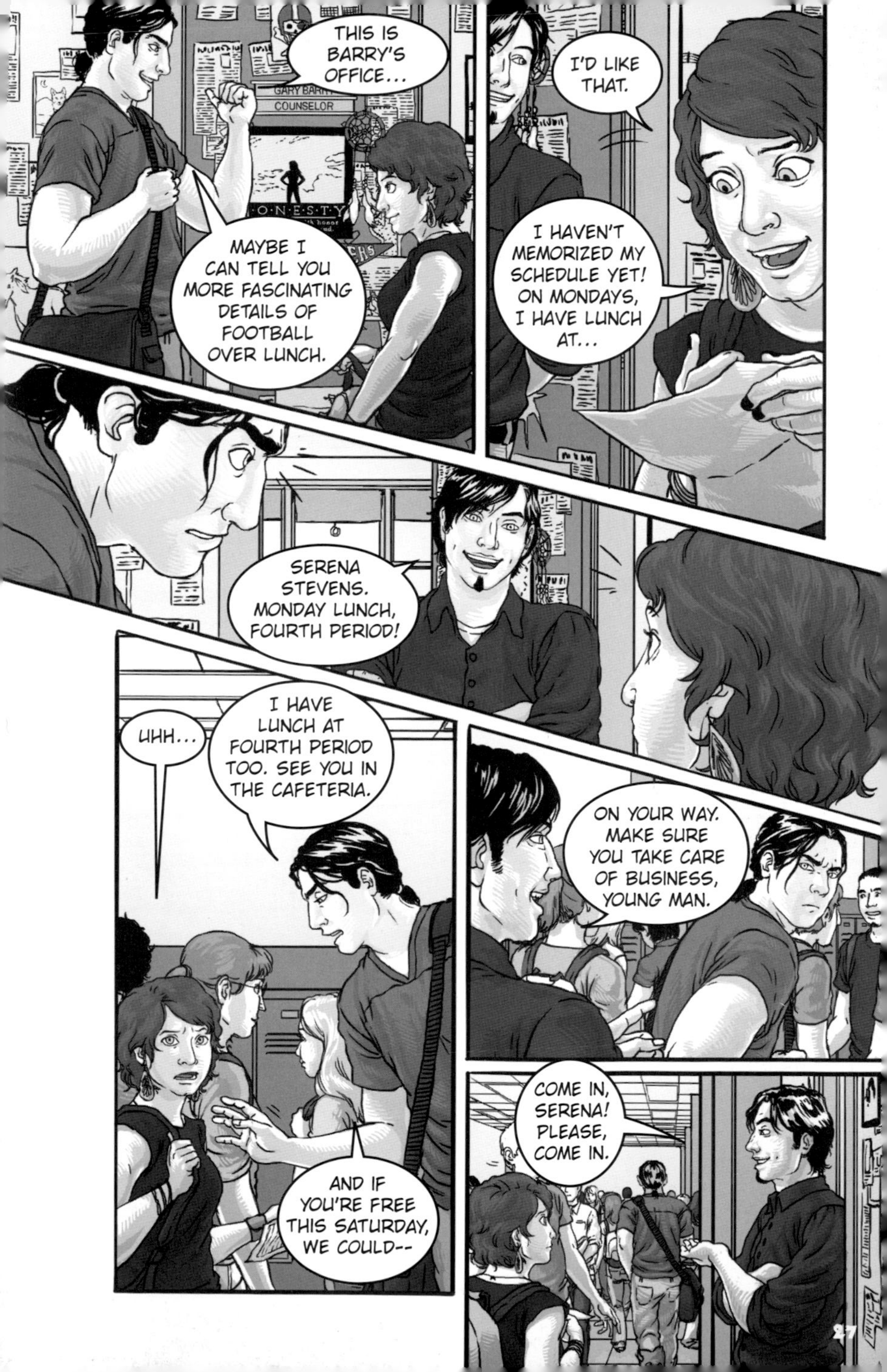

GARY BARRY
COUNSELOR
O·N·E·S·T·Y
THIS IS BARRY'S OFFICE...
MAYBE I CAN TELL YOU MORE FASCINATING DETAILS OF FOOTBALL OVER LUNCH.
I'D LIKE THAT.
I HAVEN'T MEMORIZED MY SCHEDULE YET! ON MONDAYS, I HAVE LUNCH AT...
SERENA STEVENS. MONDAY LUNCH, FOURTH PERIOD!
UHH...
I HAVE LUNCH AT FOURTH PERIOD TOO. SEE YOU IN THE CAFETERIA.
AND IF YOU'RE FREE THIS SATURDAY, WE COULD--
ON YOUR WAY. MAKE SURE YOU TAKE CARE OF BUSINESS, YOUNG MAN.
COME IN, SERENA! PLEASE, COME IN.

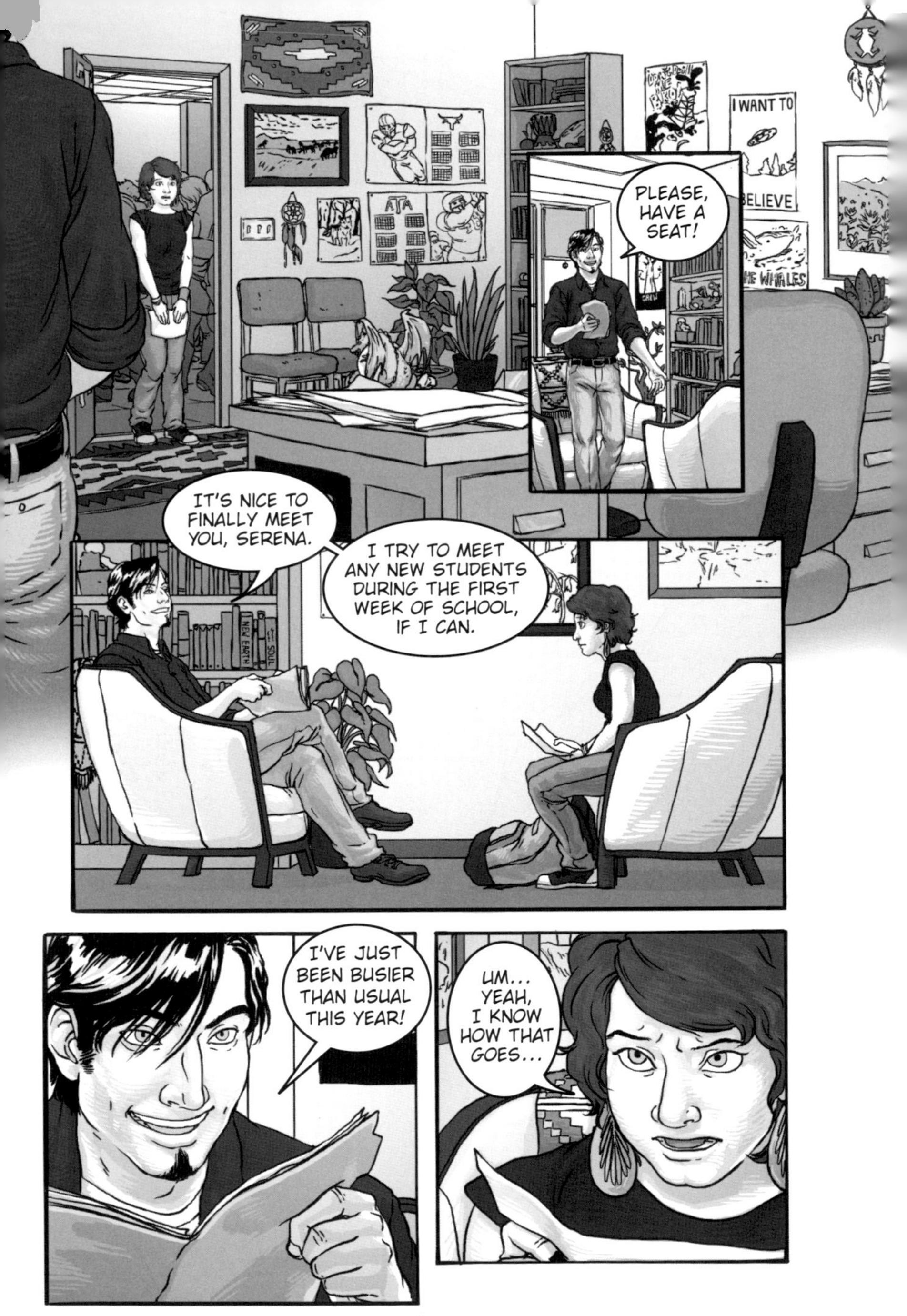

I WANT TO
BELIEVE
THE WHALES
PLEASE, HAVE A SEAT!
IT'S NICE TO FINALLY MEET YOU, SERENA.
I TRY TO MEET ANY NEW STUDENTS DURING THE FIRST WEEK OF SCHOOL, IF I CAN.
NEW EARTH
SOUL
I'VE JUST BEEN BUSIER THAN USUAL THIS YEAR!
UM... YEAH, I KNOW HOW THAT GOES...

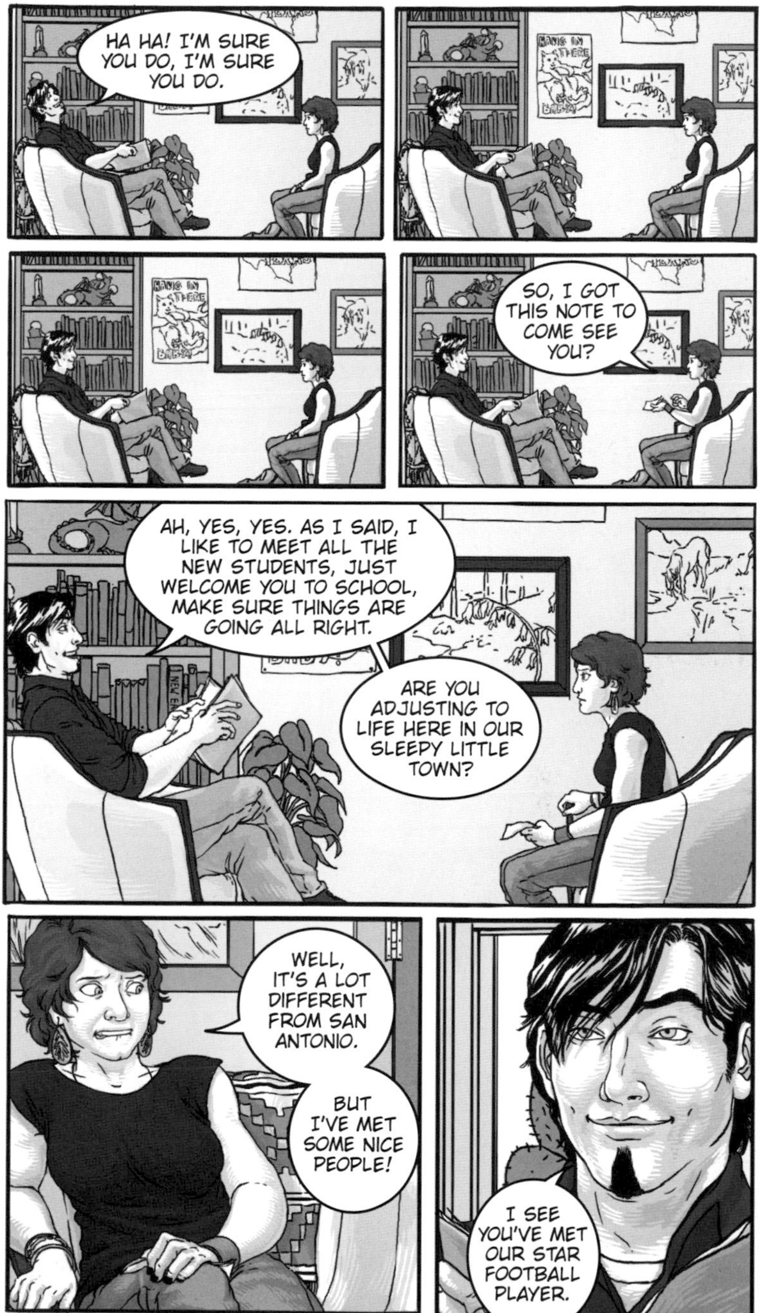
HA HA! I'M SURE YOU DO, I'M SURE YOU DO.
SO, I GOT THIS NOTE TO COME SEE YOU?
AH, YES, YES. AS I SAID, I LIKE TO MEET ALL THE NEW STUDENTS, JUST WELCOME YOU TO SCHOOL, MAKE SURE THINGS ARE GOING ALL RIGHT.
ARE YOU ADJUSTING TO LIFE HERE IN OUR SLEEPY LITTLE TOWN?
WELL, IT'S A LOT DIFFERENT FROM SAN ANTONIO.
BUT I'VE MET SOME NICE PEOPLE!
I SEE YOU'VE MET OUR STAR FOOTBALL PLAYER.

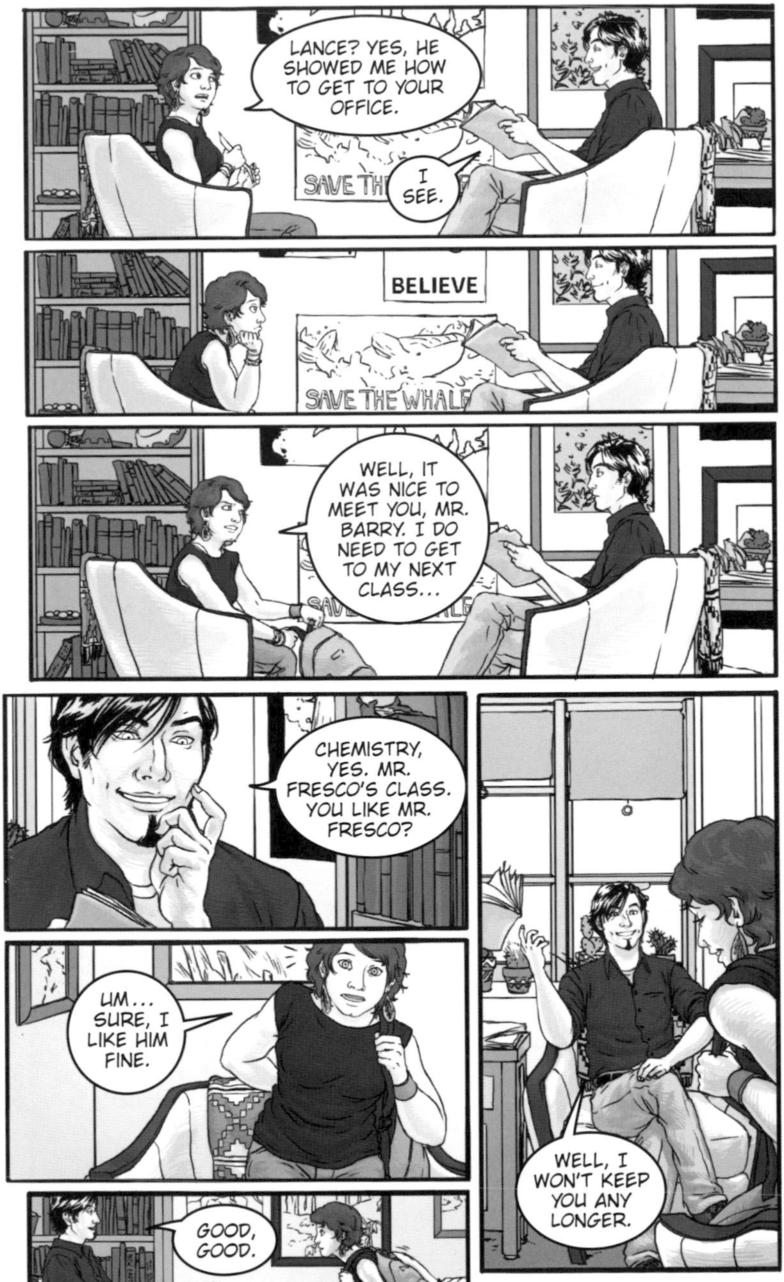
LANCE? YES, HE SHOWED ME HOW TO GET TO YOUR OFFICE.
I SEE.
BELIEVE
SAVE THE WHALE
WELL, IT WAS NICE TO MEET YOU, MR. BARRY. I DO NEED TO GET TO MY NEXT CLASS...
CHEMISTRY, YES. MR. FRESCO'S CLASS. YOU LIKE MR. FRESCO?
UM... SURE, I LIKE HIM FINE.
GOOD, GOOD.
WELL, I WON'T KEEP YOU ANY LONGER.

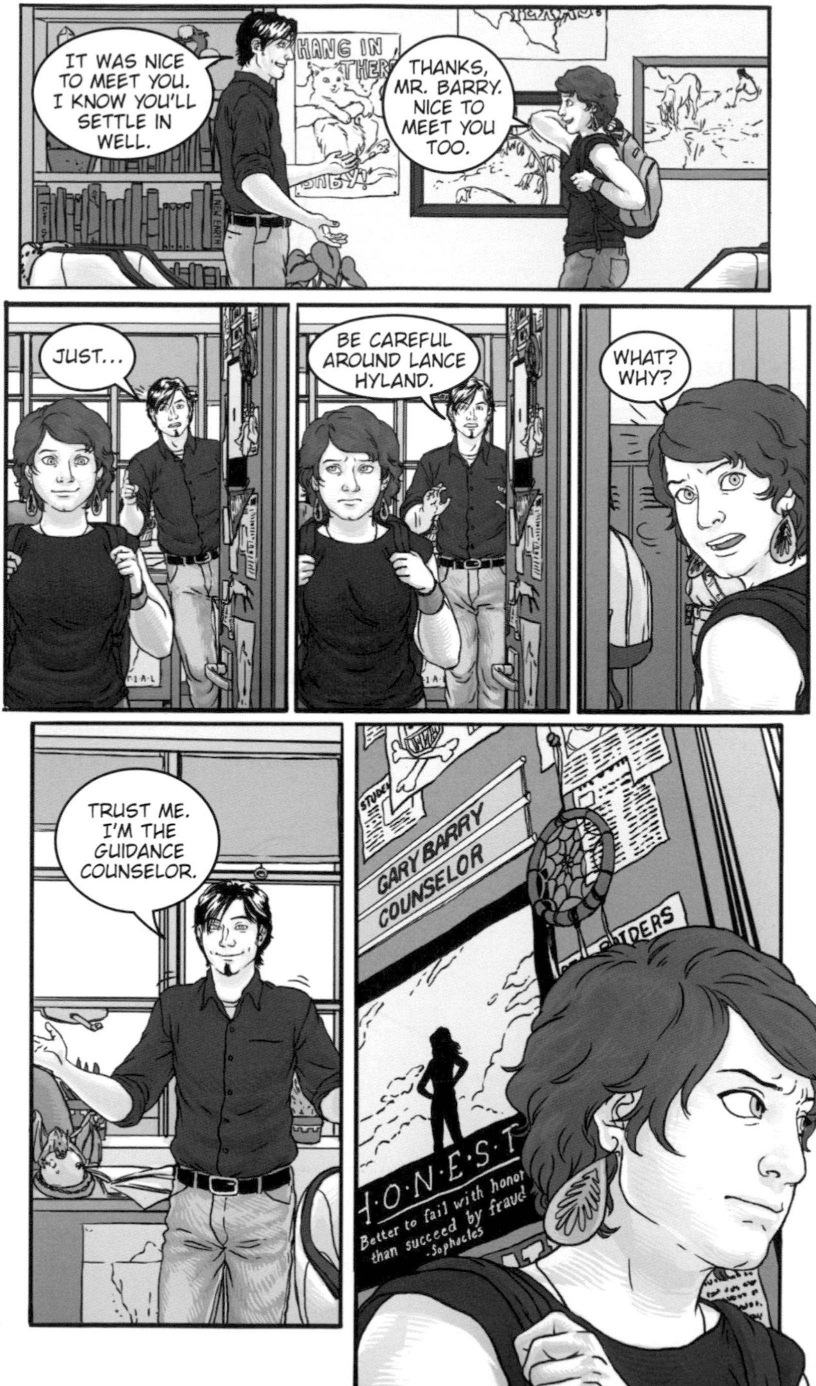
IT WAS NICE TO MEET YOU. I KNOW YOU'LL SETTLE IN WELL.
THANKS, MR. BARRY. NICE TO MEET YOU TOO.
JUST...
BE CAREFUL AROUND LANCE HYLAND.
WHAT? WHY?
TRUST ME. I'M THE GUIDANCE COUNSELOR.
GARY BARRY
COUNSELOR
H·O·N·E·S·T
Better to fail with honor than succeed by fraud
-Sophocles

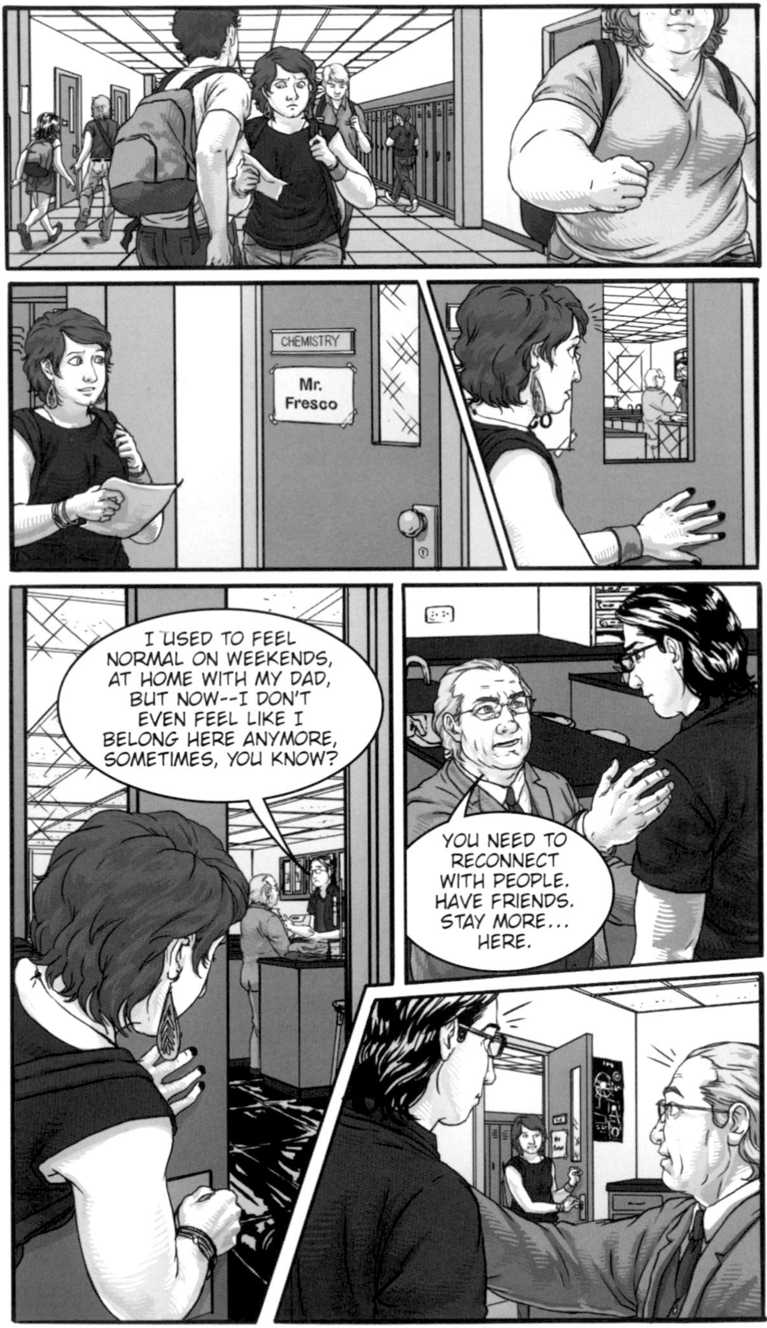
CHEMISTRY
Mr. Fresco
I USED TO FEEL NORMAL ON WEEKENDS, AT HOME WITH MY DAD, BUT NOW--I DON'T EVEN FEEL LIKE I BELONG HERE ANYMORE, SOMETIMES, YOU KNOW?
YOU NEED TO RECONNECT WITH PEOPLE. HAVE FRIENDS. STAY MORE... HERE.

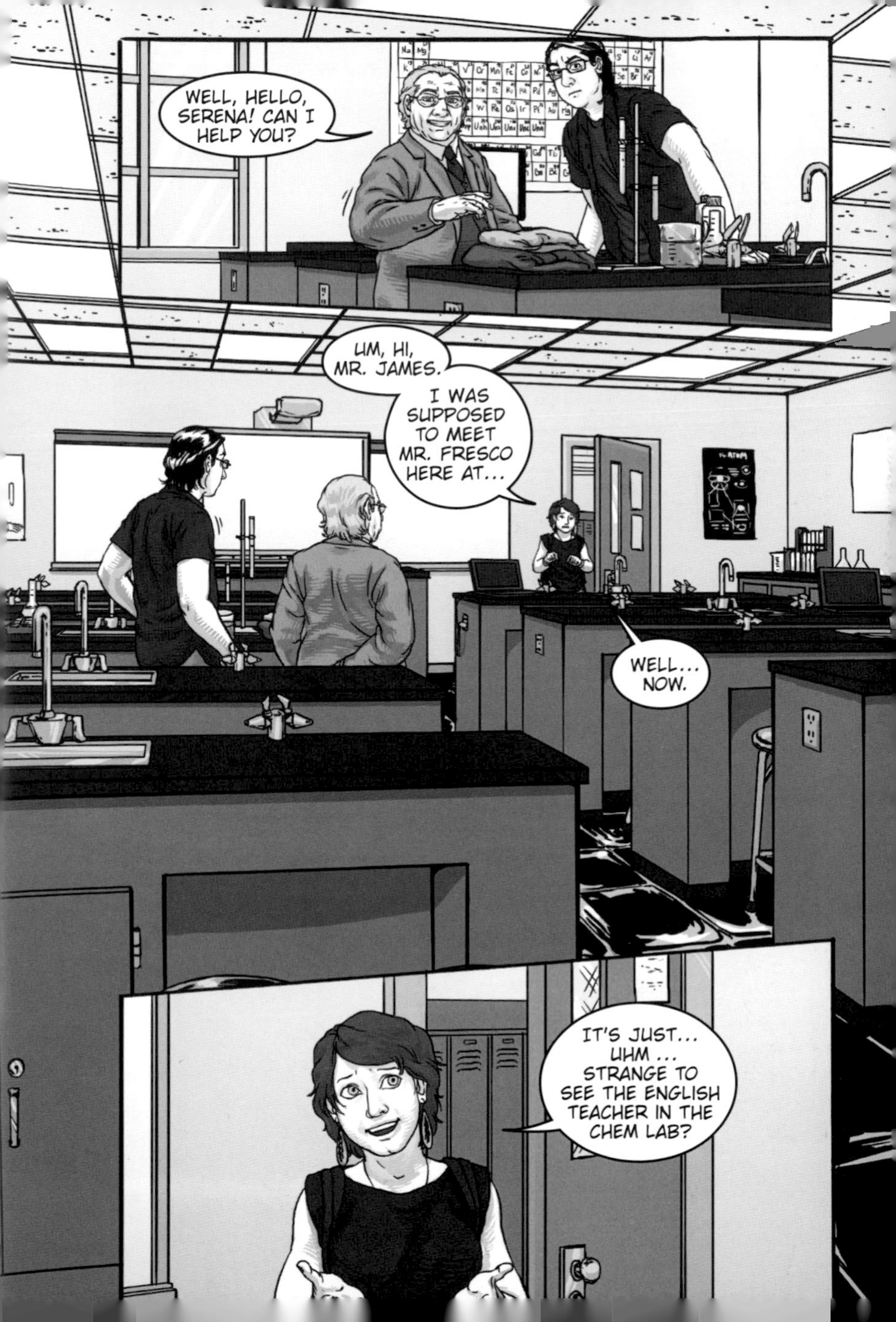
WELL, HELLO, SERENA! CAN I HELP YOU?
UM, HI, MR. JAMES.
I WAS SUPPOSED TO MEET MR. FRESCO HERE AT...
WELL... NOW.
IT'S JUST... UHM ... STRANGE TO SEE THE ENGLISH TEACHER IN THE CHEM LAB?

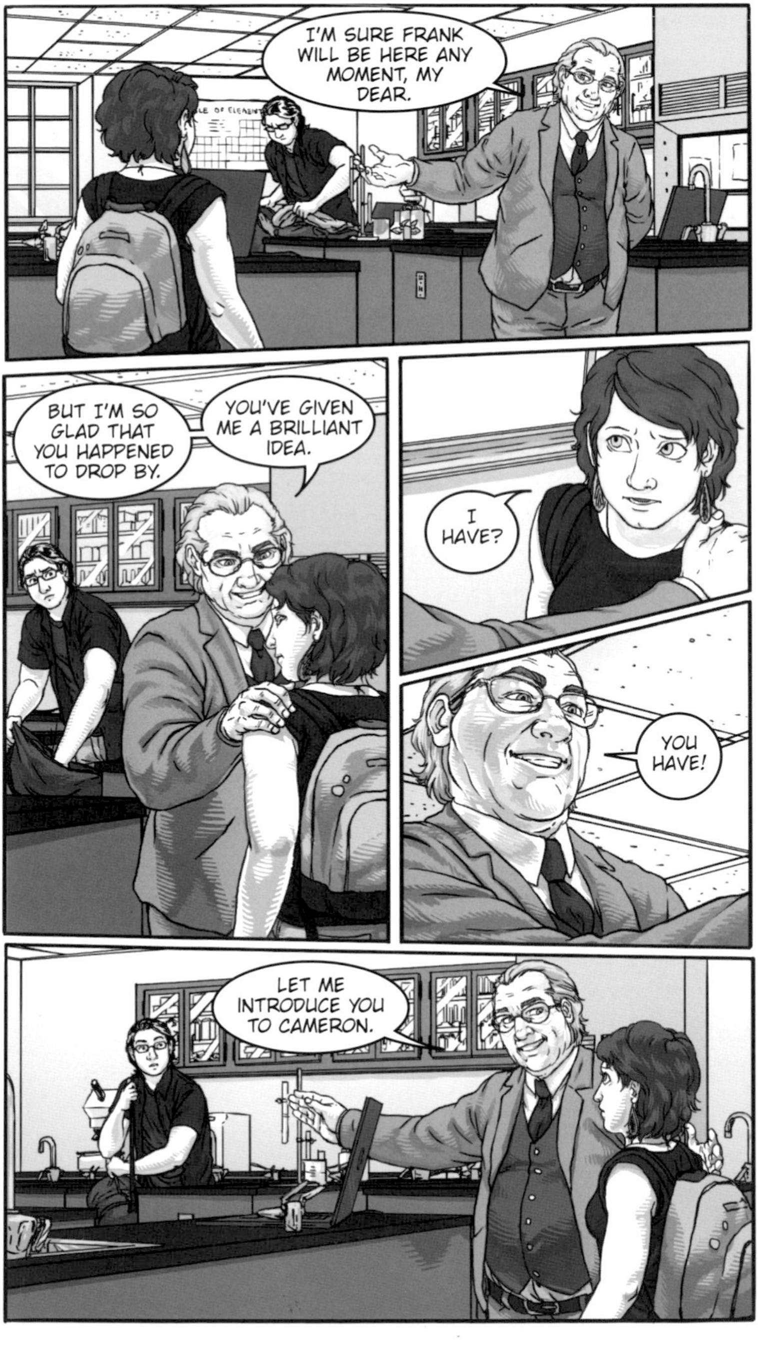
I'M SURE FRANK WILL BE HERE ANY MOMENT, MY DEAR.
BUT I'M SO GLAD THAT YOU HAPPENED TO DROP BY.
YOU'VE GIVEN ME A BRILLIANT IDEA.
I HAVE?
YOU HAVE!
LET ME INTRODUCE YOU TO CAMERON.

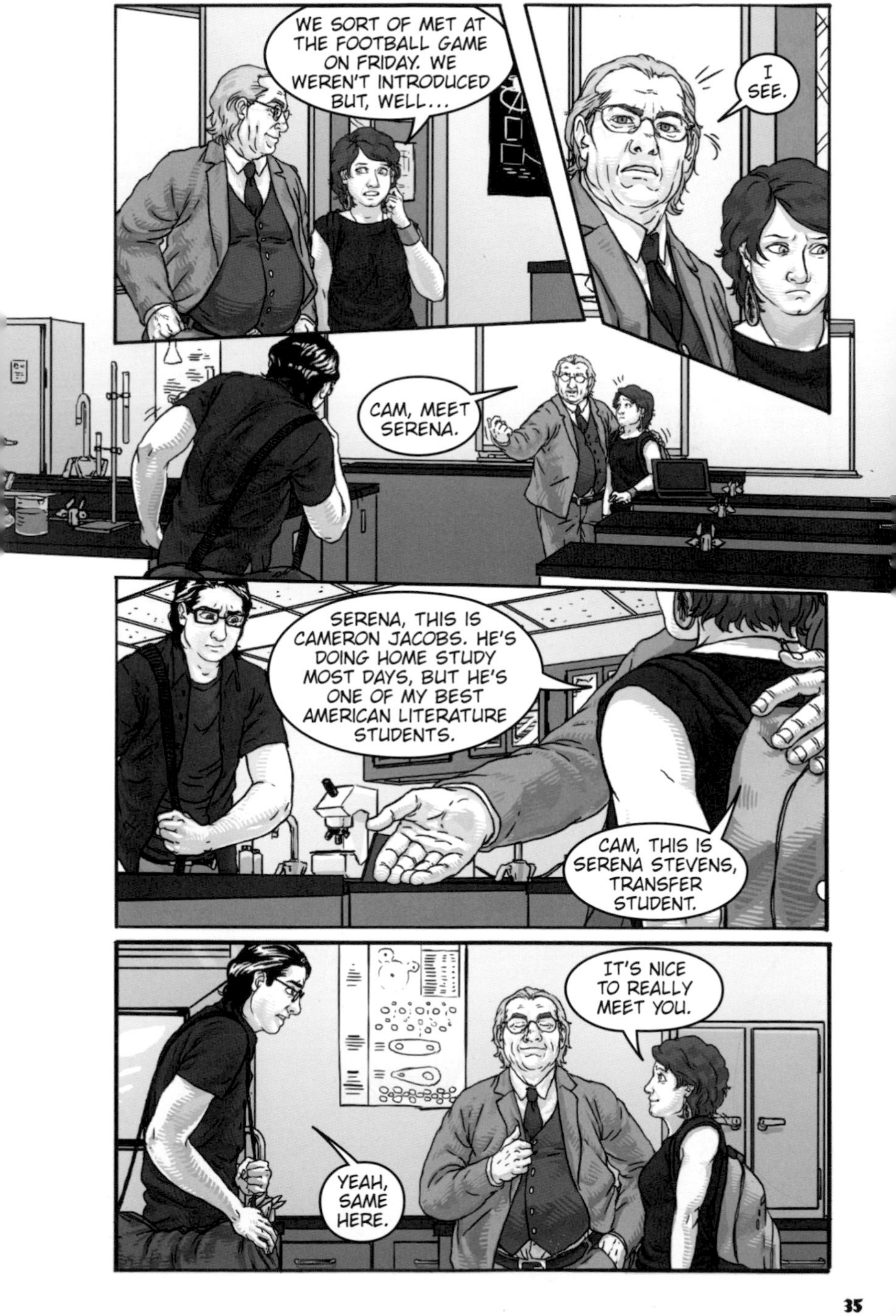
WE SORT OF MET AT THE FOOTBALL GAME ON FRIDAY. WE WEREN'T INTRODUCED BUT, WELL...
I SEE.
CAM, MEET SERENA.
SERENA, THIS IS CAMERON JACOBS. HE'S DOING HOME STUDY MOST DAYS, BUT HE'S ONE OF MY BEST AMERICAN LITERATURE STUDENTS.
CAM, THIS IS SERENA STEVENS, TRANSFER STUDENT.
IT'S NICE TO REALLY MEET YOU.
YEAH, SAME HERE.

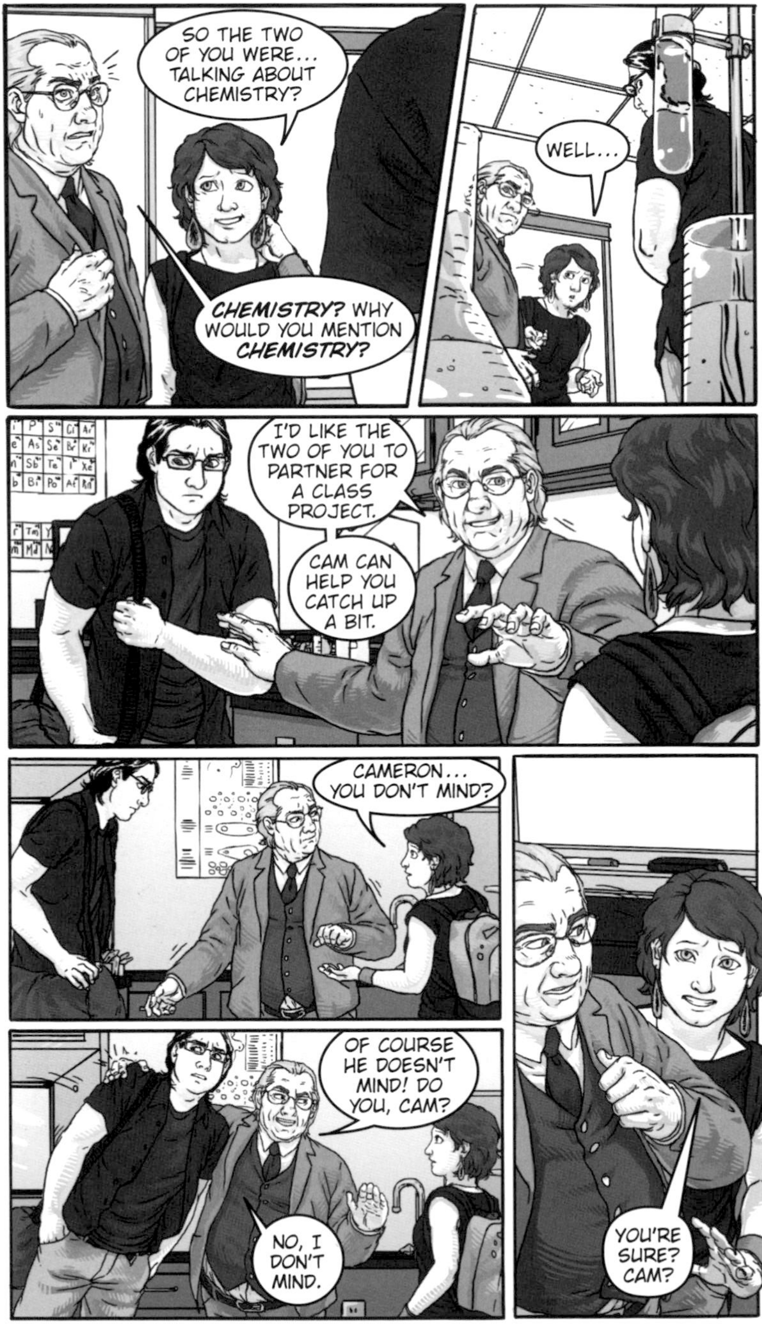
SO THE TWO OF YOU WERE... TALKING ABOUT CHEMISTRY?
CHEMISTRY? WHY WOULD YOU MENTION CHEMISTRY?
WELL...
I'D LIKE THE TWO OF YOU TO PARTNER FOR A CLASS PROJECT.
CAM CAN HELP YOU CATCH UP A BIT.
CAMERON... YOU DON'T MIND?
OF COURSE HE DOESN'T MIND! DO YOU, CAM?
NO, I DON'T MIND.
YOU'RE SURE? CAM?

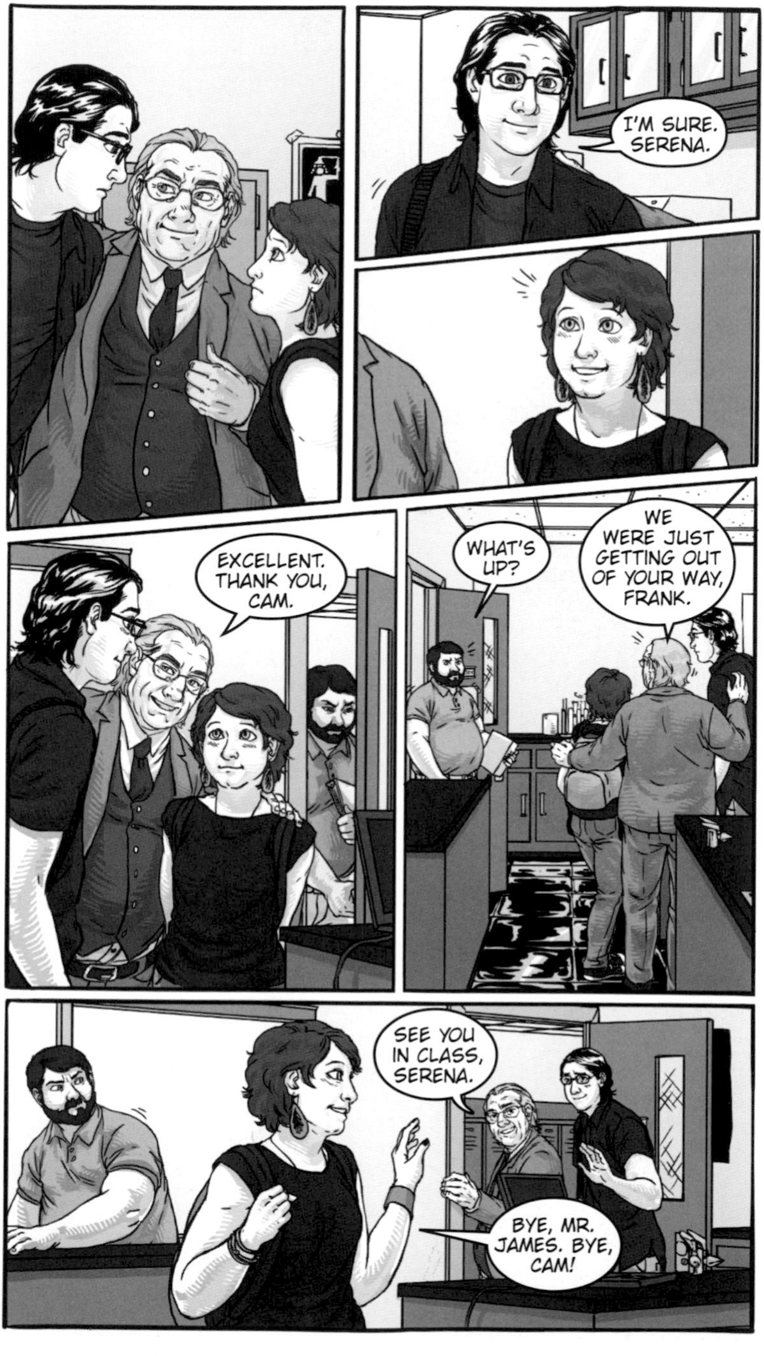
I'M SURE. SERENA.
EXCELLENT. THANK YOU, CAM.
WHAT'S UP?
WE WERE JUST GETTING OUT OF YOUR WAY, FRANK.
SEE YOU IN CLASS, SERENA.
BYE, MR. JAMES. BYE, CAM!

Chapter Four
MEET THE PARENTS

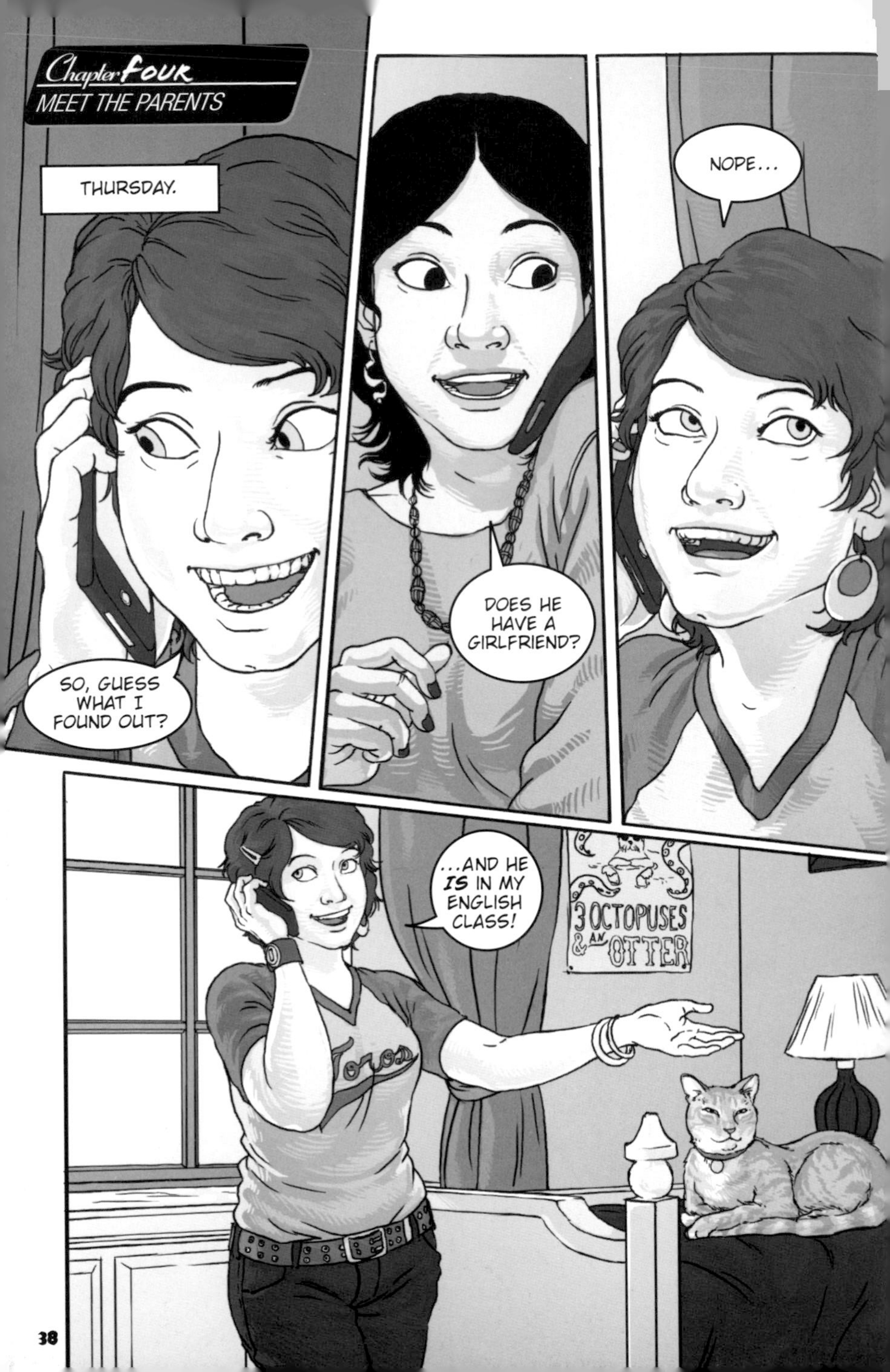
THURSDAY.
SO, GUESS WHAT I FOUND OUT?
DOES HE HAVE A GIRLFRIEND?
NOPE...
...AND HE IS IN MY ENGLISH CLASS!
3 OCTOPUSES & AN OTTER
Toros

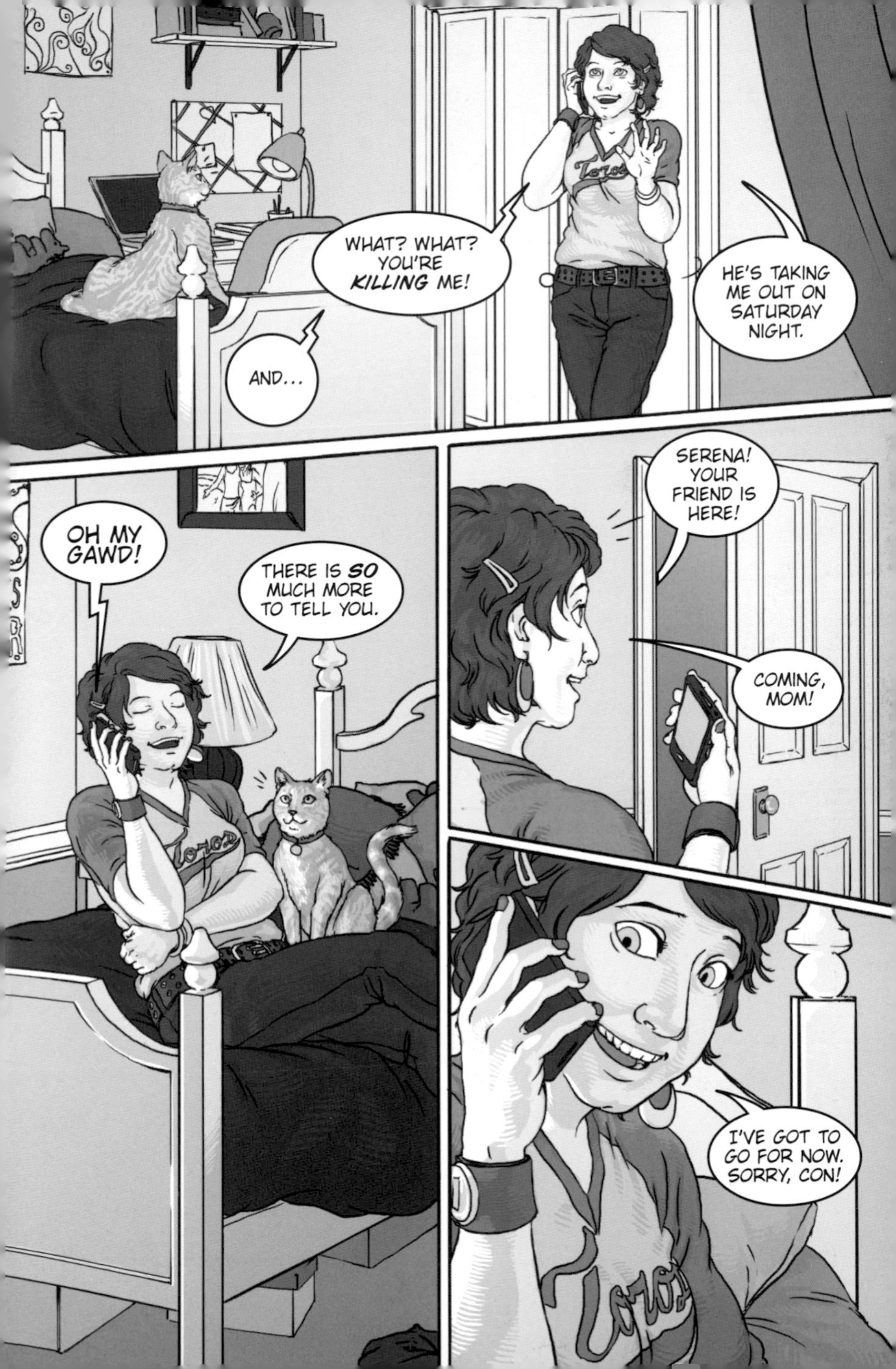
AND...
WHAT? WHAT? YOU'RE *KILLING* ME!
HE'S TAKING ME OUT ON SATURDAY NIGHT.
OH MY GAWD!
THERE IS *SO* MUCH MORE TO TELL YOU.
SERENA! YOUR FRIEND IS HERE!
COMING, MOM!
I'VE GOT TO GO FOR NOW. SORRY, CON!

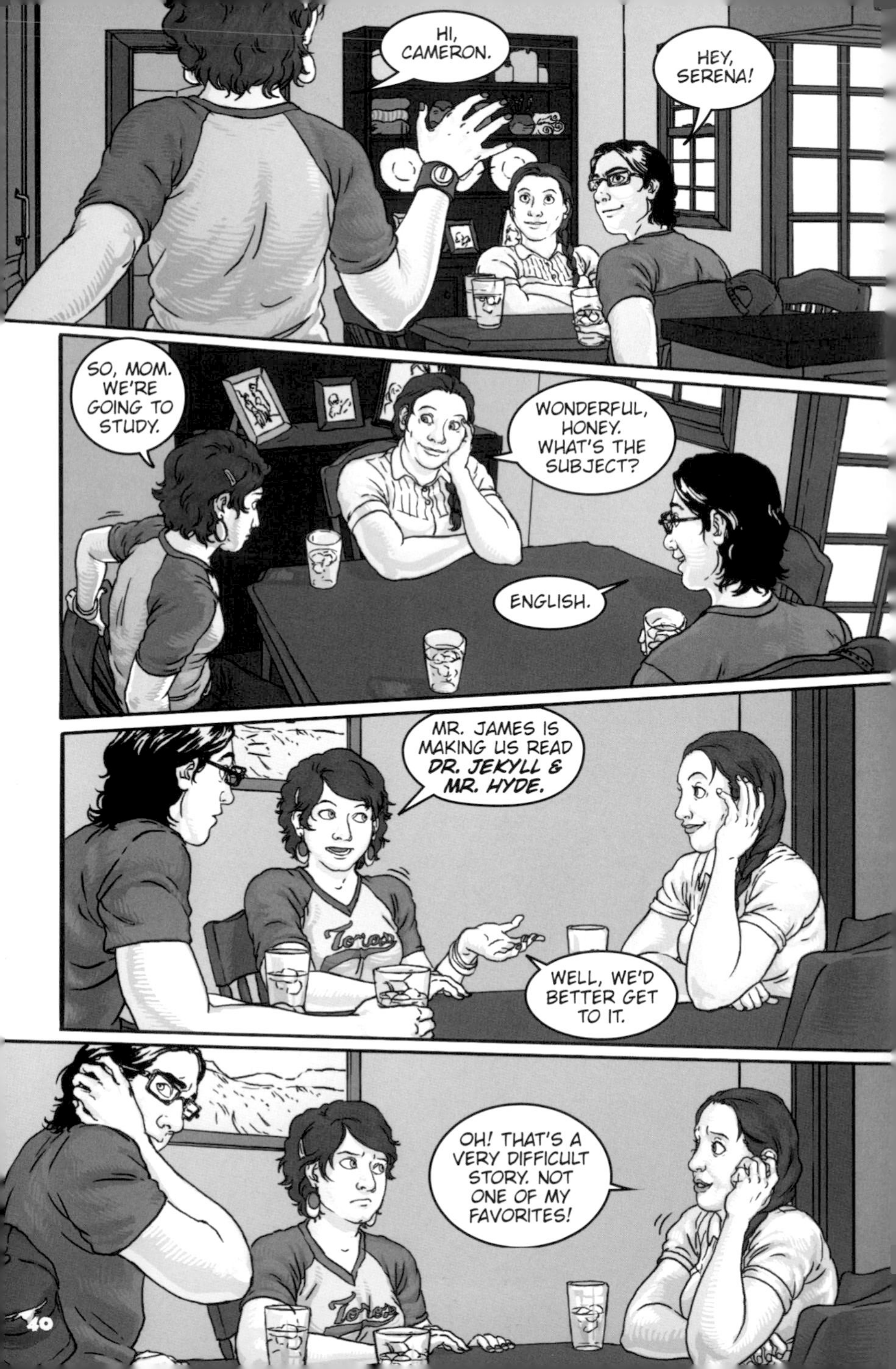
HI, CAMERON.
HEY, SERENA!
SO, MOM. WE'RE GOING TO STUDY.
WONDERFUL, HONEY. WHAT'S THE SUBJECT?
ENGLISH.
MR. JAMES IS MAKING US READ ***DR. JEKYLL & MR. HYDE.***
WELL, WE'D BETTER GET TO IT.
OH! THAT'S A VERY DIFFICULT STORY. NOT ONE OF MY FAVORITES!

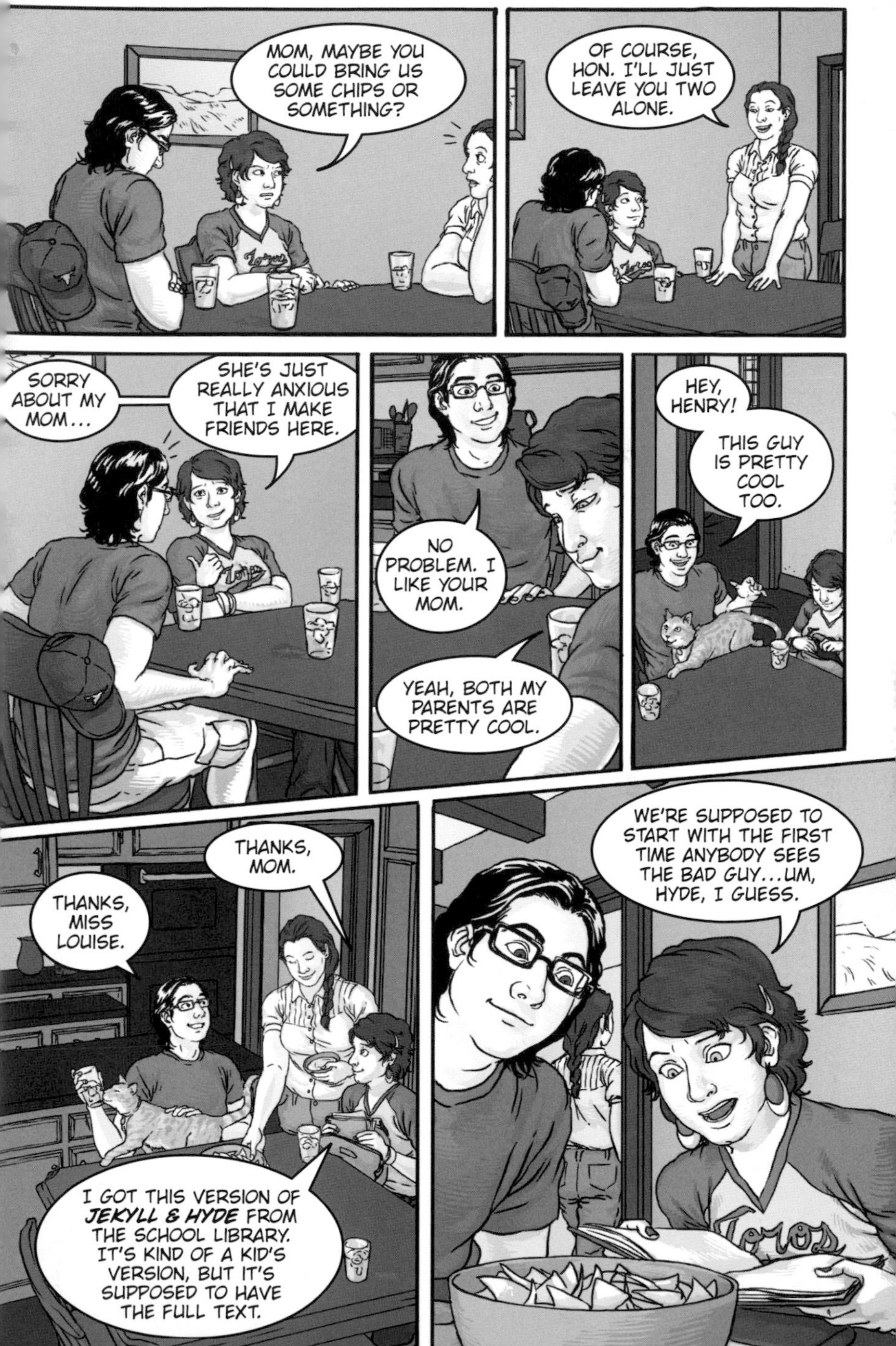
MOM, MAYBE YOU COULD BRING US SOME CHIPS OR SOMETHING?
OF COURSE, HON. I'LL JUST LEAVE YOU TWO ALONE.
SORRY ABOUT MY MOM...
SHE'S JUST REALLY ANXIOUS THAT I MAKE FRIENDS HERE.
NO PROBLEM. I LIKE YOUR MOM.
YEAH, BOTH MY PARENTS ARE PRETTY COOL.
HEY, HENRY!
THIS GUY IS PRETTY COOL TOO.
THANKS, MISS LOUISE.
THANKS, MOM.
I GOT THIS VERSION OF ***JEKYLL & HYDE*** FROM THE SCHOOL LIBRARY. IT'S KIND OF A KID'S VERSION, BUT IT'S SUPPOSED TO HAVE THE FULL TEXT.
WE'RE SUPPOSED TO START WITH THE FIRST TIME ANYBODY SEES THE BAD GUY...UM, HYDE, I GUESS.

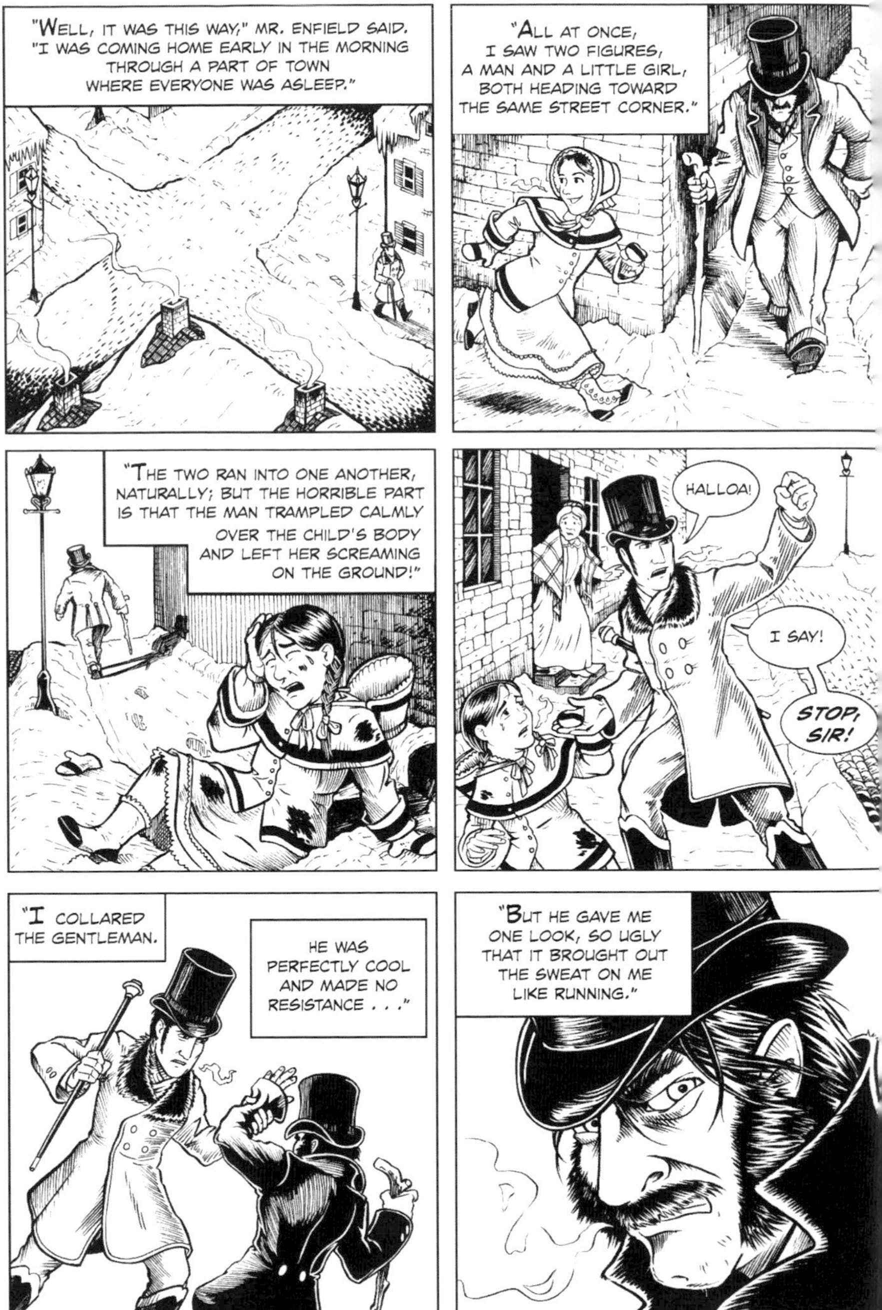
"WELL, IT WAS THIS WAY," MR. ENFIELD SAID. "I WAS COMING HOME EARLY IN THE MORNING THROUGH A PART OF TOWN WHERE EVERYONE WAS ASLEEP."
"ALL AT ONCE, I SAW TWO FIGURES, A MAN AND A LITTLE GIRL, BOTH HEADING TOWARD THE SAME STREET CORNER."
"THE TWO RAN INTO ONE ANOTHER, NATURALLY; BUT THE HORRIBLE PART IS THAT THE MAN TRAMPLED CALMLY OVER THE CHILD'S BODY AND LEFT HER SCREAMING ON THE GROUND!"
HALLOA!
I SAY!
STOP, SIR!
"I COLLARED THE GENTLEMAN.
HE WAS PERFECTLY COOL AND MADE NO RESISTANCE . . ."
"BUT HE GAVE ME ONE LOOK, SO UGLY THAT IT BROUGHT OUT THE SWEAT ON ME LIKE RUNNING."

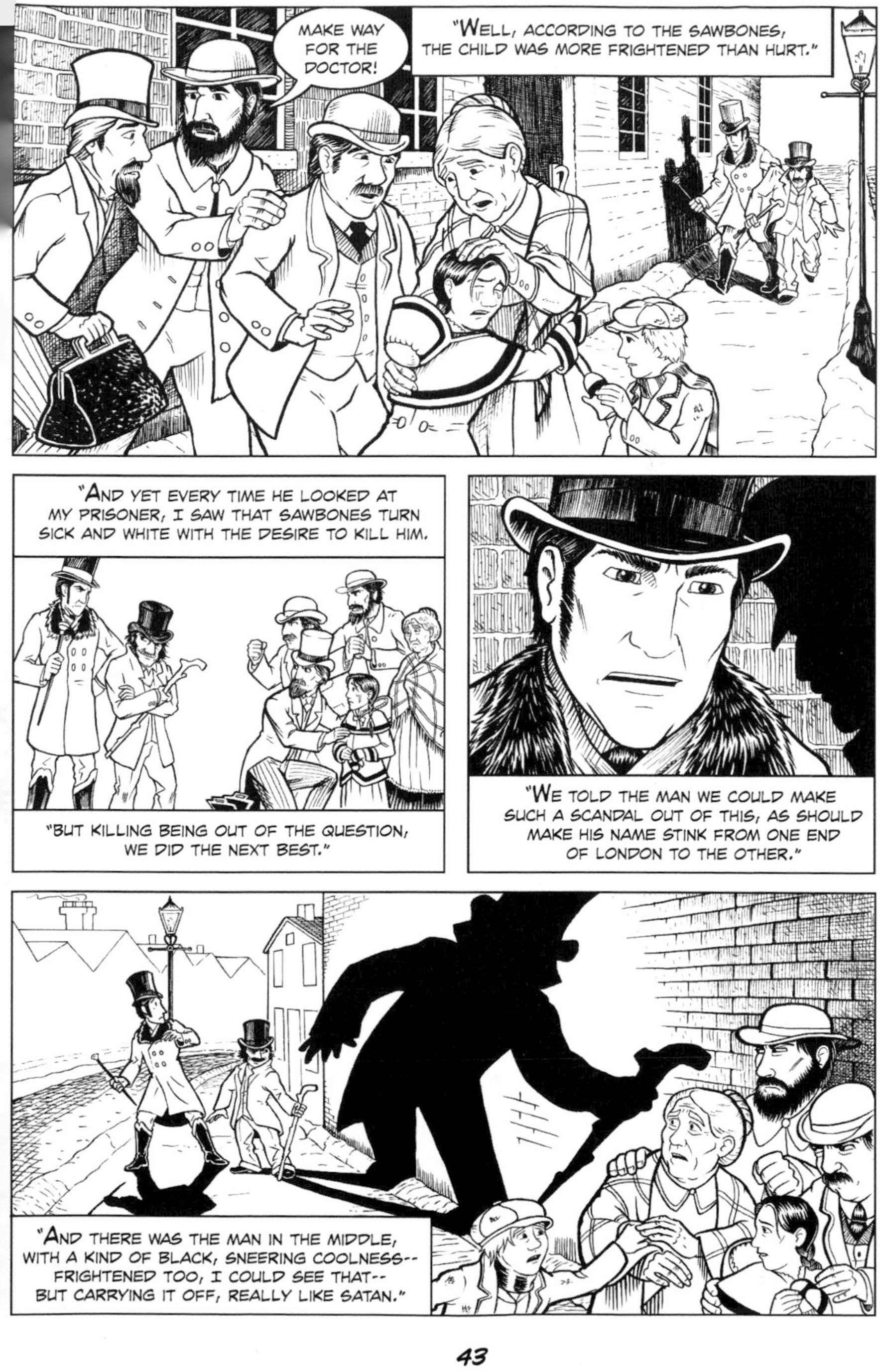
MAKE WAY FOR THE DOCTOR!
"WELL, ACCORDING TO THE SAWBONES, THE CHILD WAS MORE FRIGHTENED THAN HURT."
"AND YET EVERY TIME HE LOOKED AT MY PRISONER, I SAW THAT SAWBONES TURN SICK AND WHITE WITH THE DESIRE TO KILL HIM.
"BUT KILLING BEING OUT OF THE QUESTION, WE DID THE NEXT BEST."
"WE TOLD THE MAN WE COULD MAKE SUCH A SCANDAL OUT OF THIS, AS SHOULD MAKE HIS NAME STINK FROM ONE END OF LONDON TO THE OTHER."
"AND THERE WAS THE MAN IN THE MIDDLE, WITH A KIND OF BLACK, SNEERING COOLNESS-- FRIGHTENED TOO, I COULD SEE THAT-- BUT CARRYING IT OFF, REALLY LIKE SATAN."

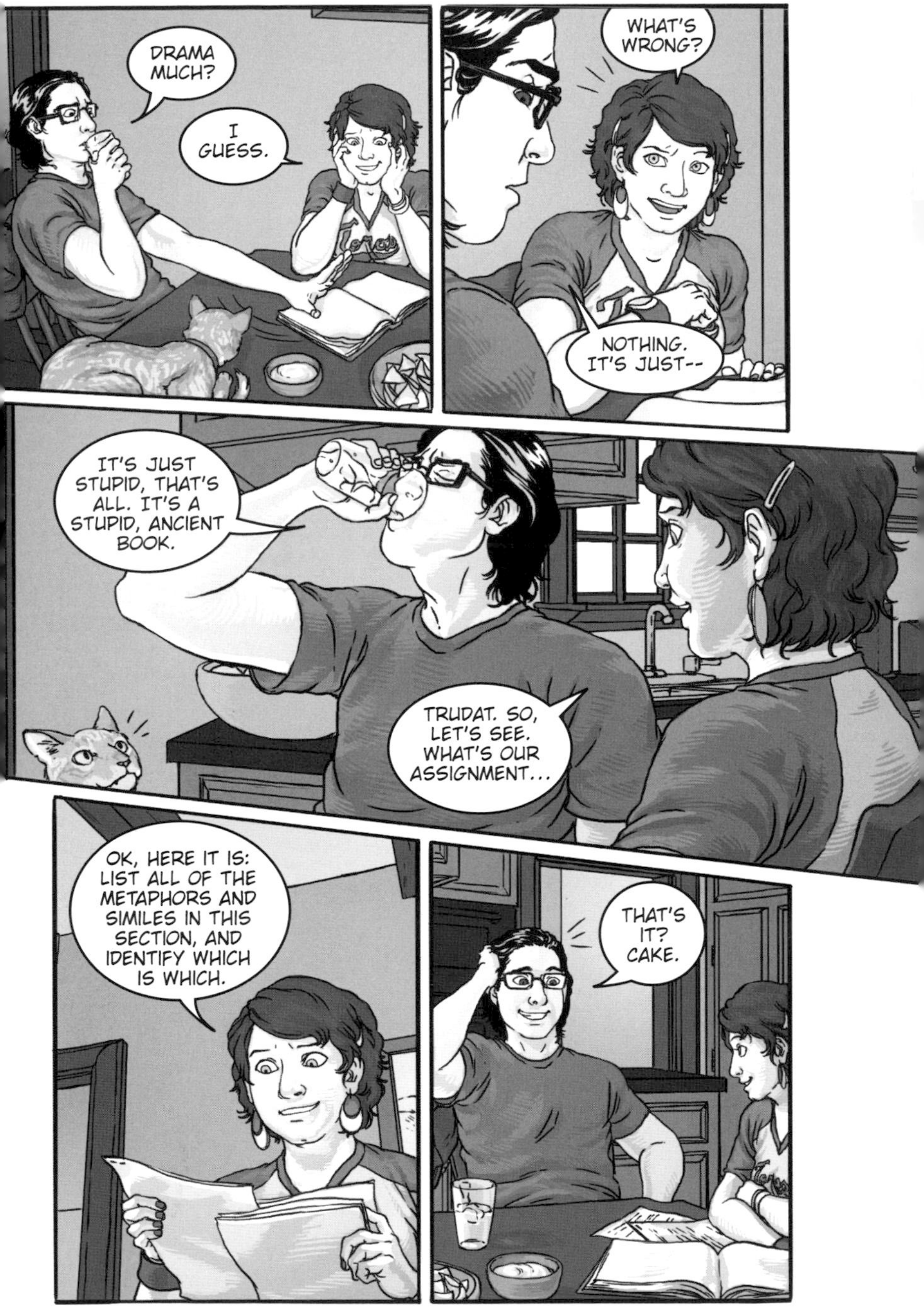
DRAMA MUCH?
I GUESS.
WHAT'S WRONG?
NOTHING. IT'S JUST--
IT'S JUST STUPID, THAT'S ALL. IT'S A STUPID, ANCIENT BOOK.
TRUDAT. SO, LET'S SEE. WHAT'S OUR ASSIGNMENT...
OK, HERE IT IS: LIST ALL OF THE METAPHORS AND SIMILES IN THIS SECTION, AND IDENTIFY WHICH IS WHICH.
THAT'S IT? CAKE.

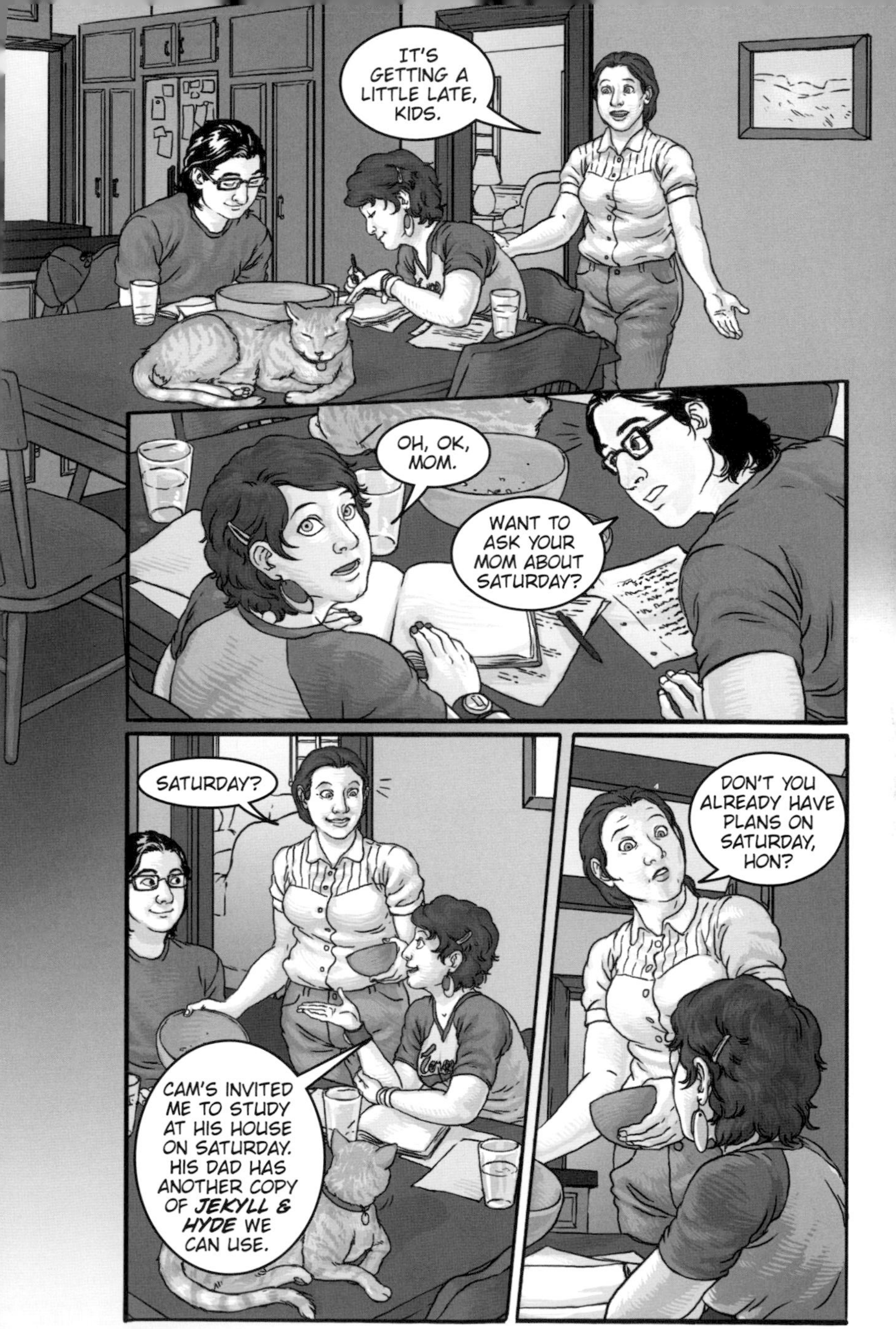
IT'S GETTING A LITTLE LATE, KIDS.
OH, OK, MOM.
WANT TO ASK YOUR MOM ABOUT SATURDAY?
SATURDAY?
CAM'S INVITED ME TO STUDY AT HIS HOUSE ON SATURDAY. HIS DAD HAS ANOTHER COPY OF ***JEKYLL & HYDE*** WE CAN USE.
DON'T YOU ALREADY HAVE PLANS ON SATURDAY, HON?

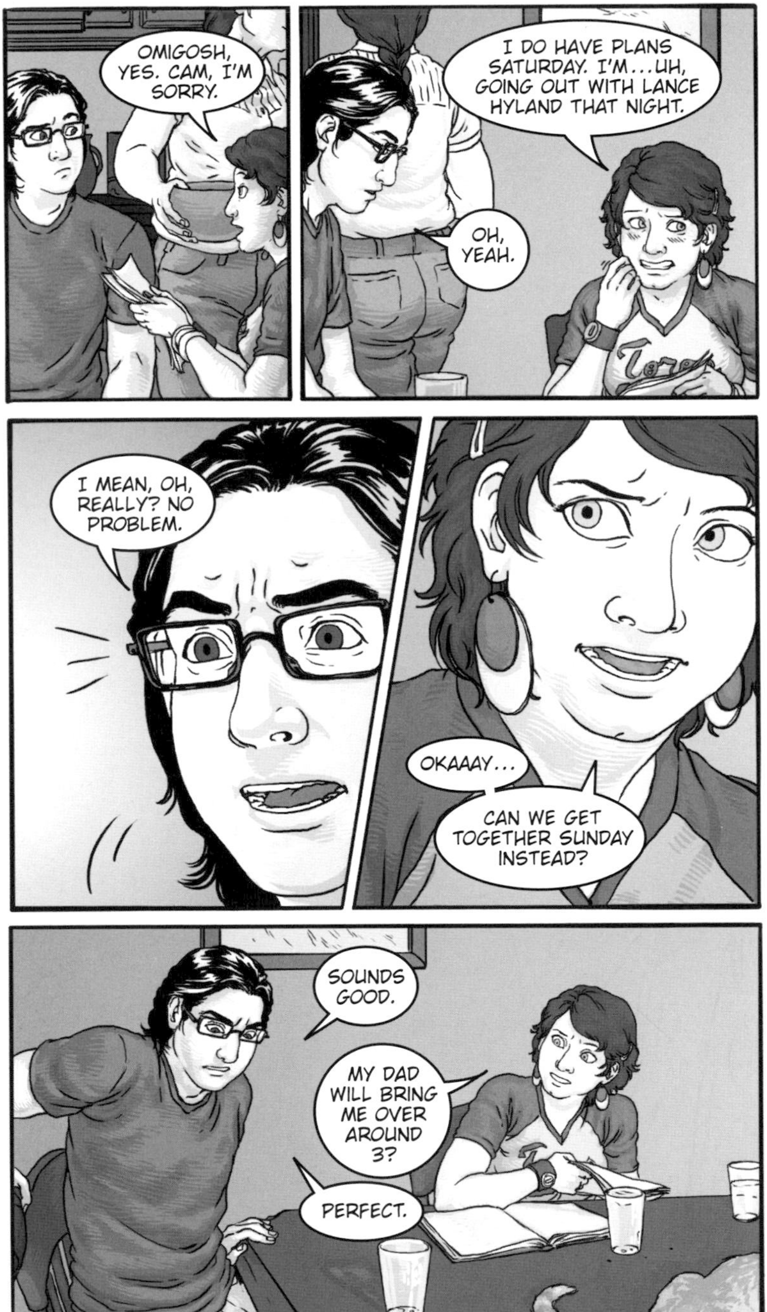
OMIGOSH, YES. CAM, I'M SORRY.
I DO HAVE PLANS SATURDAY. I'M...UH, GOING OUT WITH LANCE HYLAND THAT NIGHT.
OH, YEAH.
I MEAN, OH, REALLY? NO PROBLEM.
OKAAAY...
CAN WE GET TOGETHER SUNDAY INSTEAD?
SOUNDS GOOD.
MY DAD WILL BRING ME OVER AROUND 3?
PERFECT.

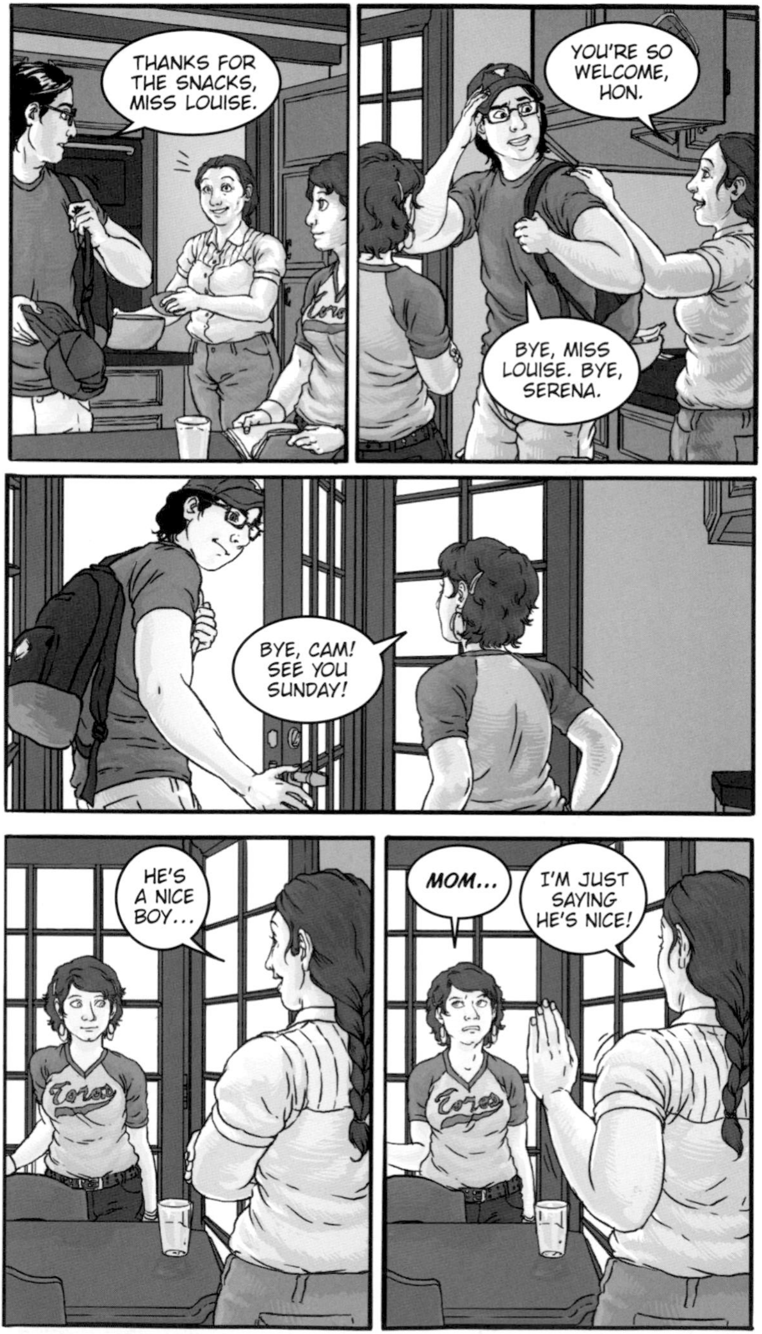
THANKS FOR THE SNACKS, MISS LOUISE.
YOU'RE SO WELCOME, HON.
BYE, MISS LOUISE. BYE, SERENA.
BYE, CAM! SEE YOU SUNDAY!
HE'S A NICE BOY...
MOM...
I'M JUST SAYING HE'S NICE!

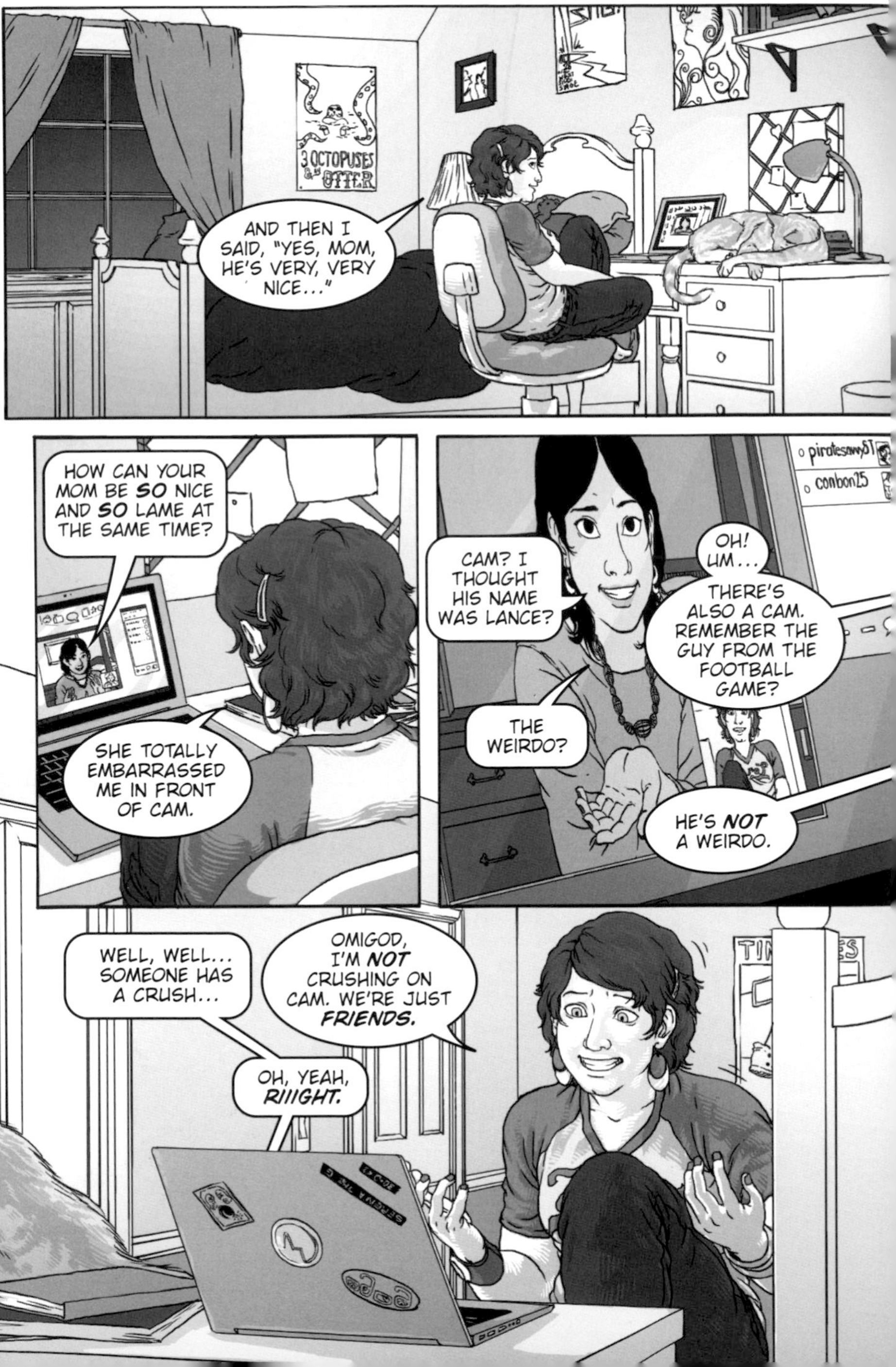
3 OCTOPUSES & an OTTER
AND THEN I SAID, "YES, MOM, HE'S VERY, VERY NICE..."
HOW CAN YOUR MOM BE **SO** NICE AND **SO** LAME AT THE SAME TIME?
SHE TOTALLY EMBARRASSED ME IN FRONT OF CAM.
piratesavvy87
conbon25
CAM? I THOUGHT HIS NAME WAS LANCE?
OH! UM...
THERE'S ALSO A CAM. REMEMBER THE GUY FROM THE FOOTBALL GAME?
THE WEIRDO?
HE'S ***NOT*** A WEIRDO.
WELL, WELL... SOMEONE HAS A CRUSH...
OMIGOD, I'M ***NOT*** CRUSHING ON CAM. WE'RE JUST ***FRIENDS.***
OH, YEAH, ***RIIIGHT.***

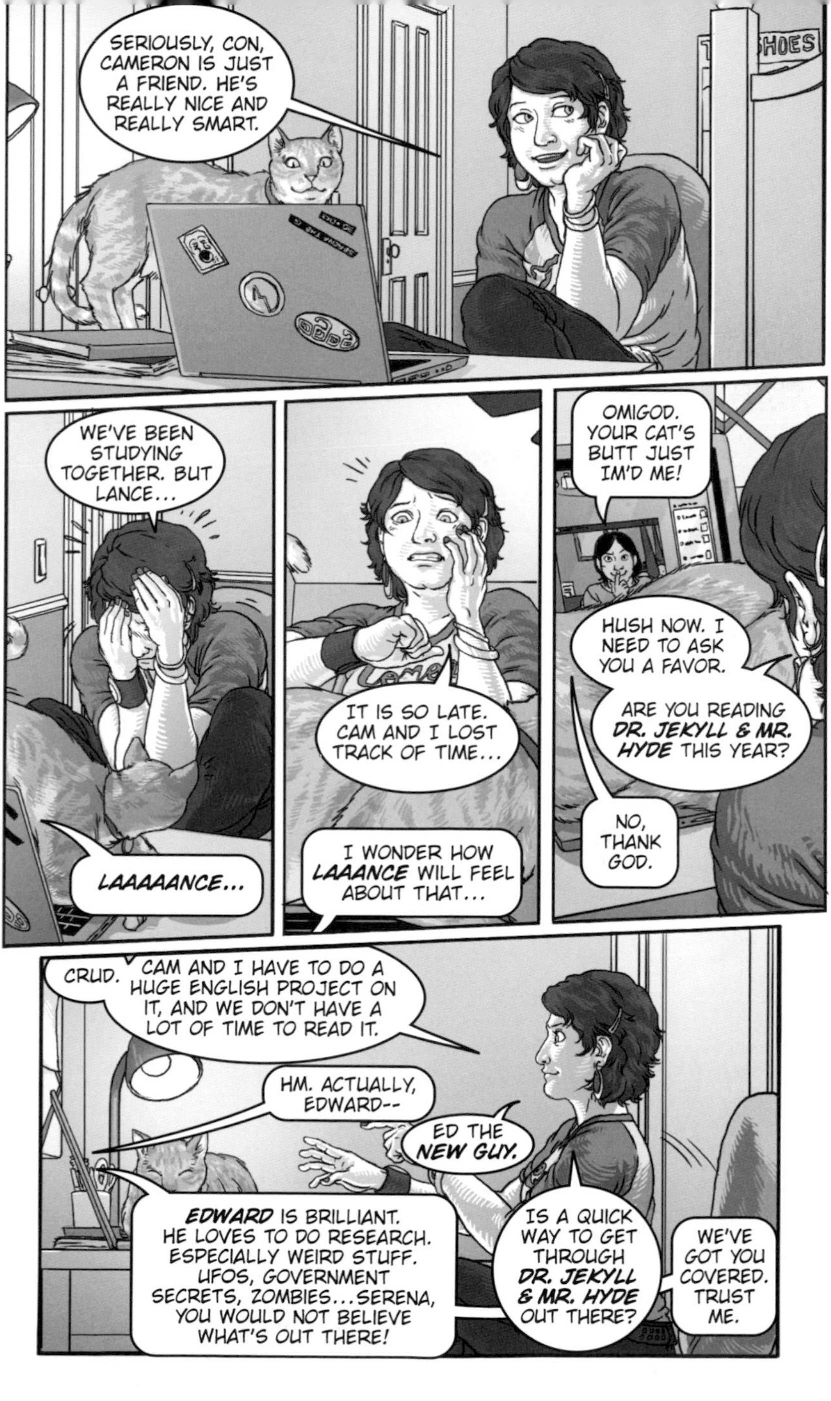

SHOES
SERIOUSLY, CON, CAMERON IS JUST A FRIEND. HE'S REALLY NICE AND REALLY SMART.
WE'VE BEEN STUDYING TOGETHER. BUT LANCE...
LAAAAANCE...
IT IS SO LATE. CAM AND I LOST TRACK OF TIME...
I WONDER HOW LAAANCE WILL FEEL ABOUT THAT...
OMIGOD. YOUR CAT'S BUTT JUST IM'D ME!
HUSH NOW. I NEED TO ASK YOU A FAVOR.
ARE YOU READING DR. JEKYLL & MR. HYDE THIS YEAR?
NO, THANK GOD.
CRUD.
CAM AND I HAVE TO DO A HUGE ENGLISH PROJECT ON IT, AND WE DON'T HAVE A LOT OF TIME TO READ IT.
HM. ACTUALLY, EDWARD--
ED THE NEW GUY.
EDWARD IS BRILLIANT. HE LOVES TO DO RESEARCH. ESPECIALLY WEIRD STUFF. UFOS, GOVERNMENT SECRETS, ZOMBIES...SERENA, YOU WOULD NOT BELIEVE WHAT'S OUT THERE!
IS A QUICK WAY TO GET THROUGH DR. JEKYLL & MR. HYDE OUT THERE?
WE'VE GOT YOU COVERED. TRUST ME.

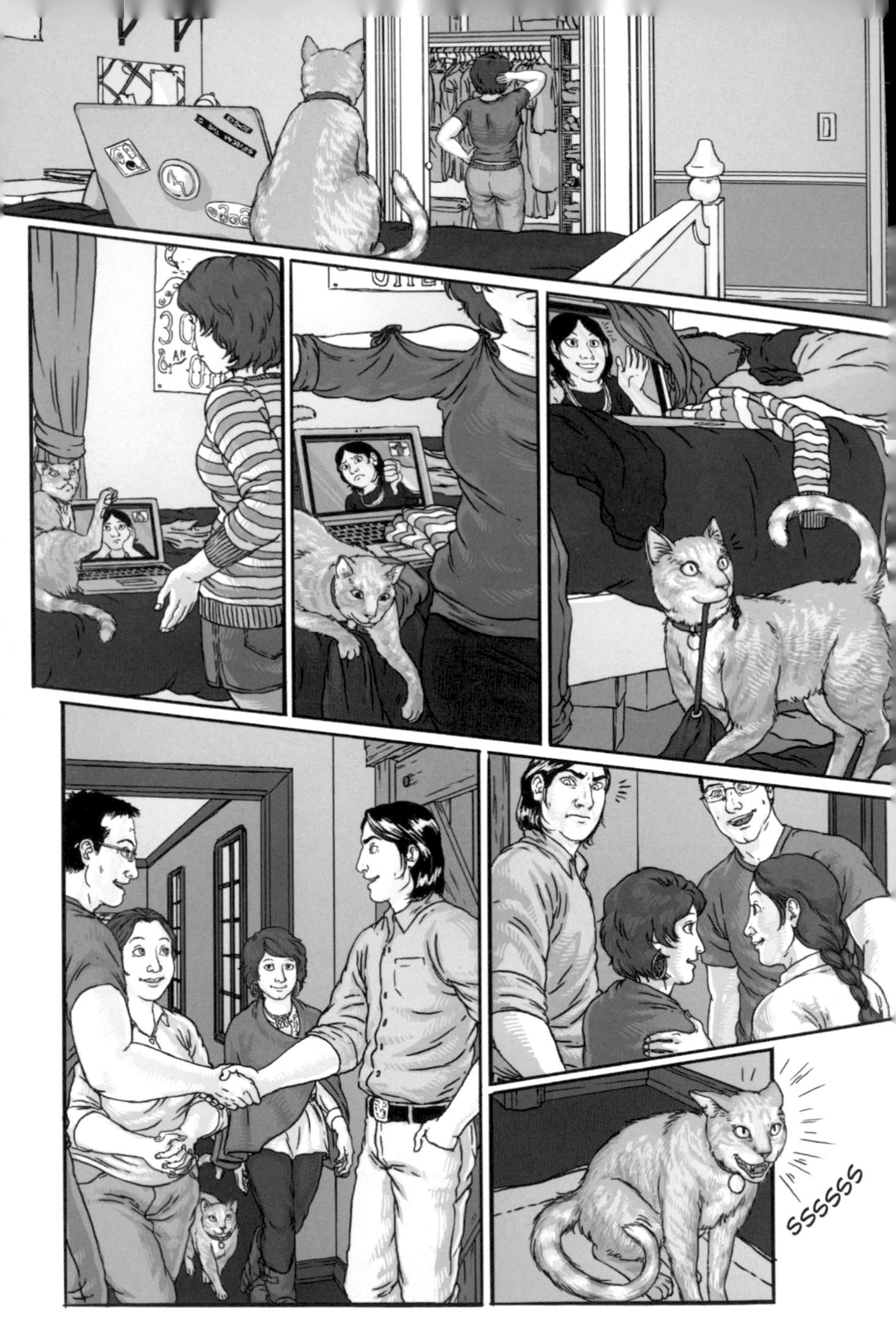
SSSSSS

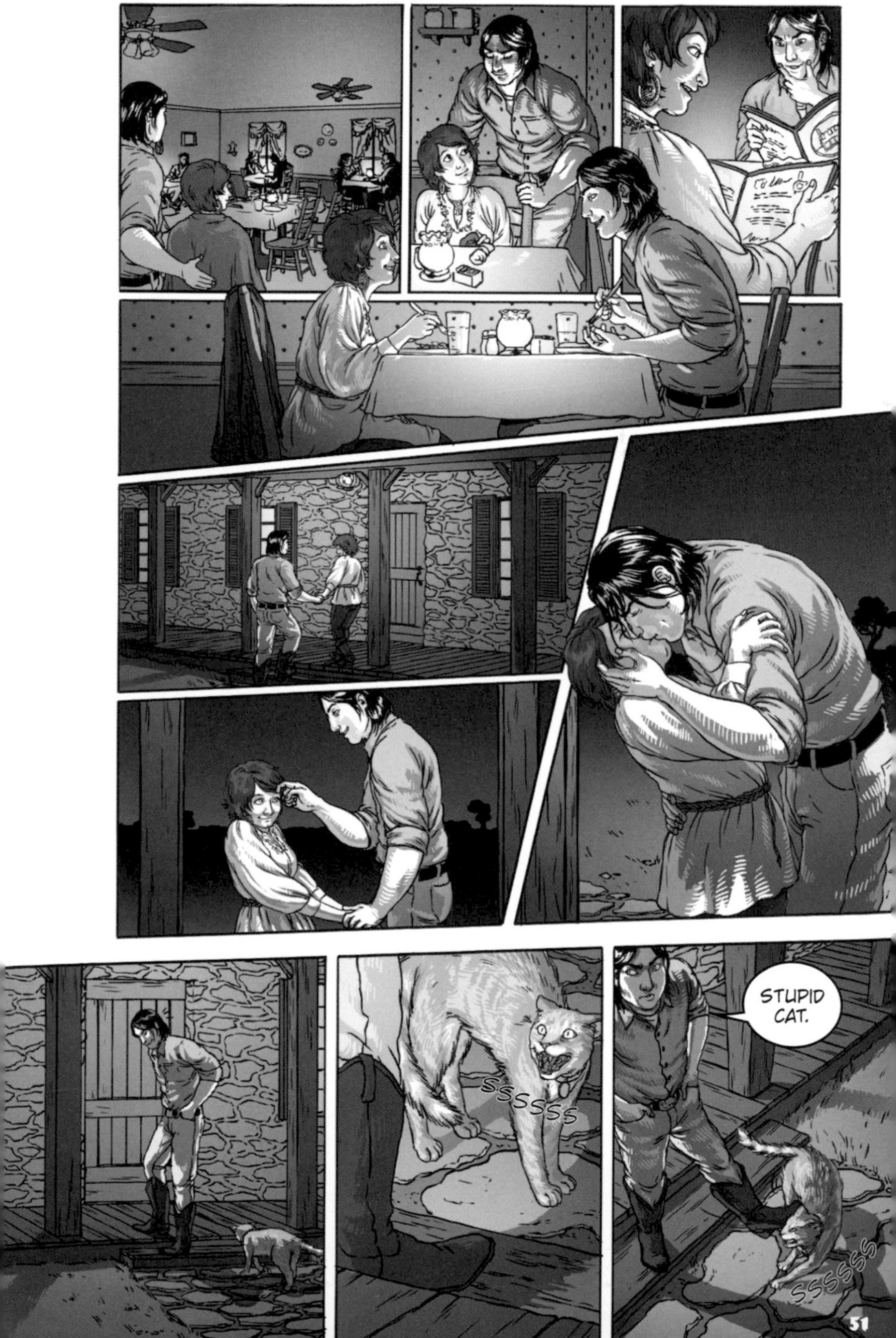
SSSSSS
STUPID CAT.
SSSSSS

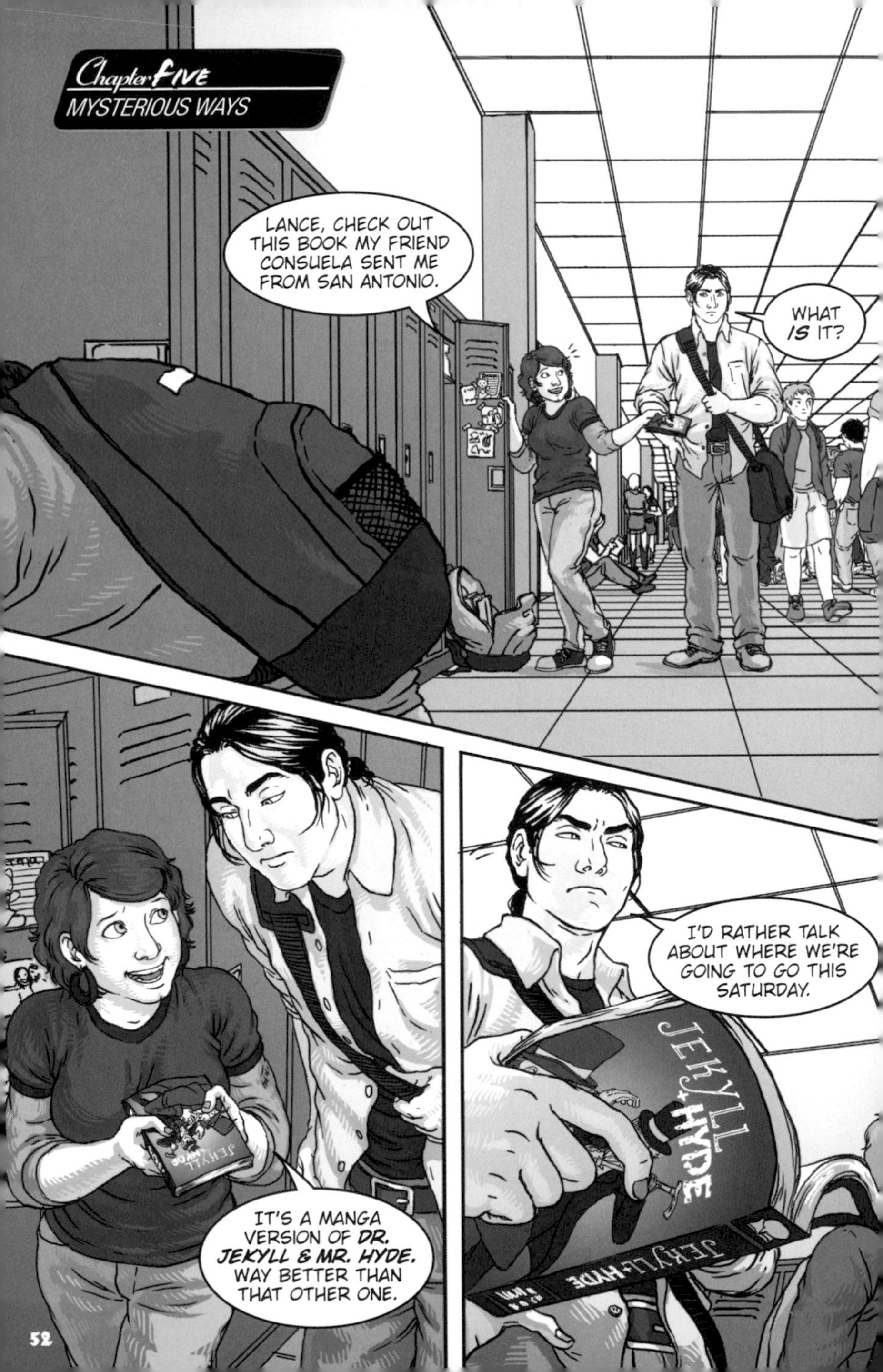
Chapter FIVE
MYSTERIOUS WAYS
LANCE, CHECK OUT THIS BOOK MY FRIEND CONSUELA SENT ME FROM SAN ANTONIO.
WHAT IS IT?
IT'S A MANGA VERSION OF DR. JEKYLL & MR. HYDE. WAY BETTER THAN THAT OTHER ONE.
I'D RATHER TALK ABOUT WHERE WE'RE GOING TO GO THIS SATURDAY.
JEKYLL + HYDE
JEKYLL+HYDE

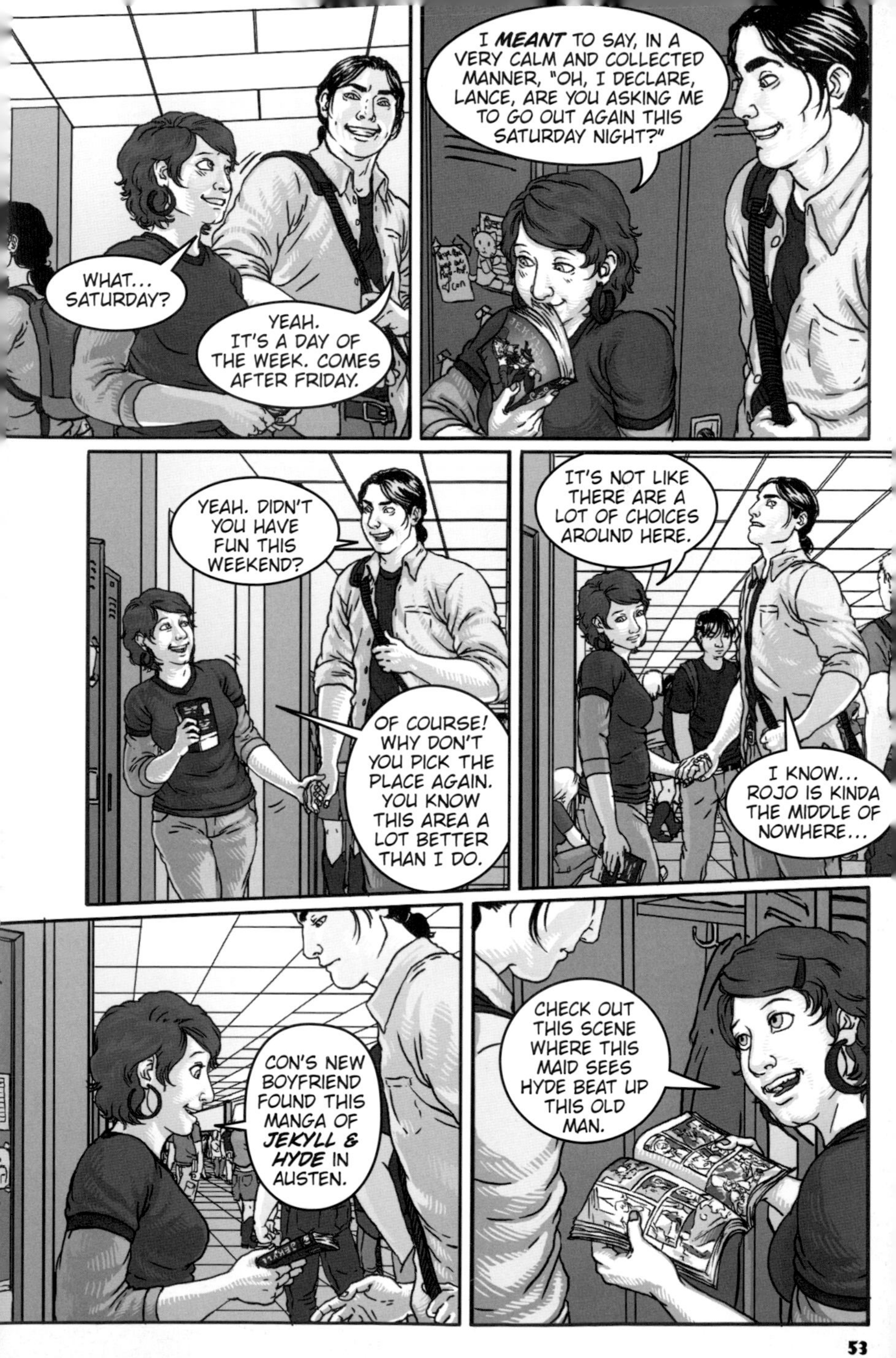
WHAT... SATURDAY?
YEAH. IT'S A DAY OF THE WEEK. COMES AFTER FRIDAY.
I *MEANT* TO SAY, IN A VERY CALM AND COLLECTED MANNER, "OH, I DECLARE, LANCE, ARE YOU ASKING ME TO GO OUT AGAIN THIS SATURDAY NIGHT?"
YEAH. DIDN'T YOU HAVE FUN THIS WEEKEND?
OF COURSE! WHY DON'T YOU PICK THE PLACE AGAIN. YOU KNOW THIS AREA A LOT BETTER THAN I DO.
IT'S NOT LIKE THERE ARE A LOT OF CHOICES AROUND HERE.
I KNOW... ROJO IS KINDA THE MIDDLE OF NOWHERE...
CON'S NEW BOYFRIEND FOUND THIS MANGA OF *JEKYLL & HYDE* IN AUSTEN.
CHECK OUT THIS SCENE WHERE THIS MAID SEES HYDE BEAT UP THIS OLD MAN.

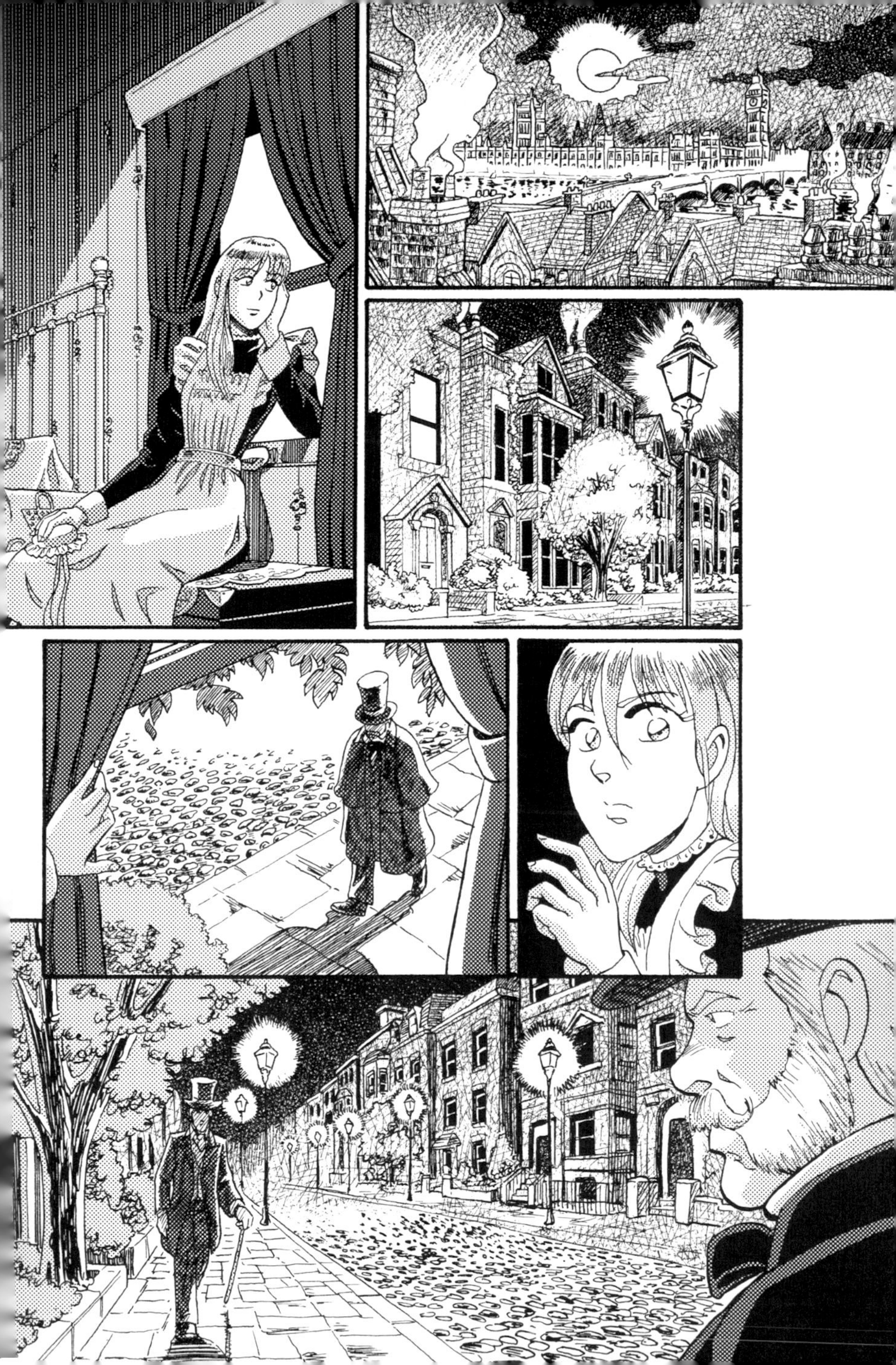

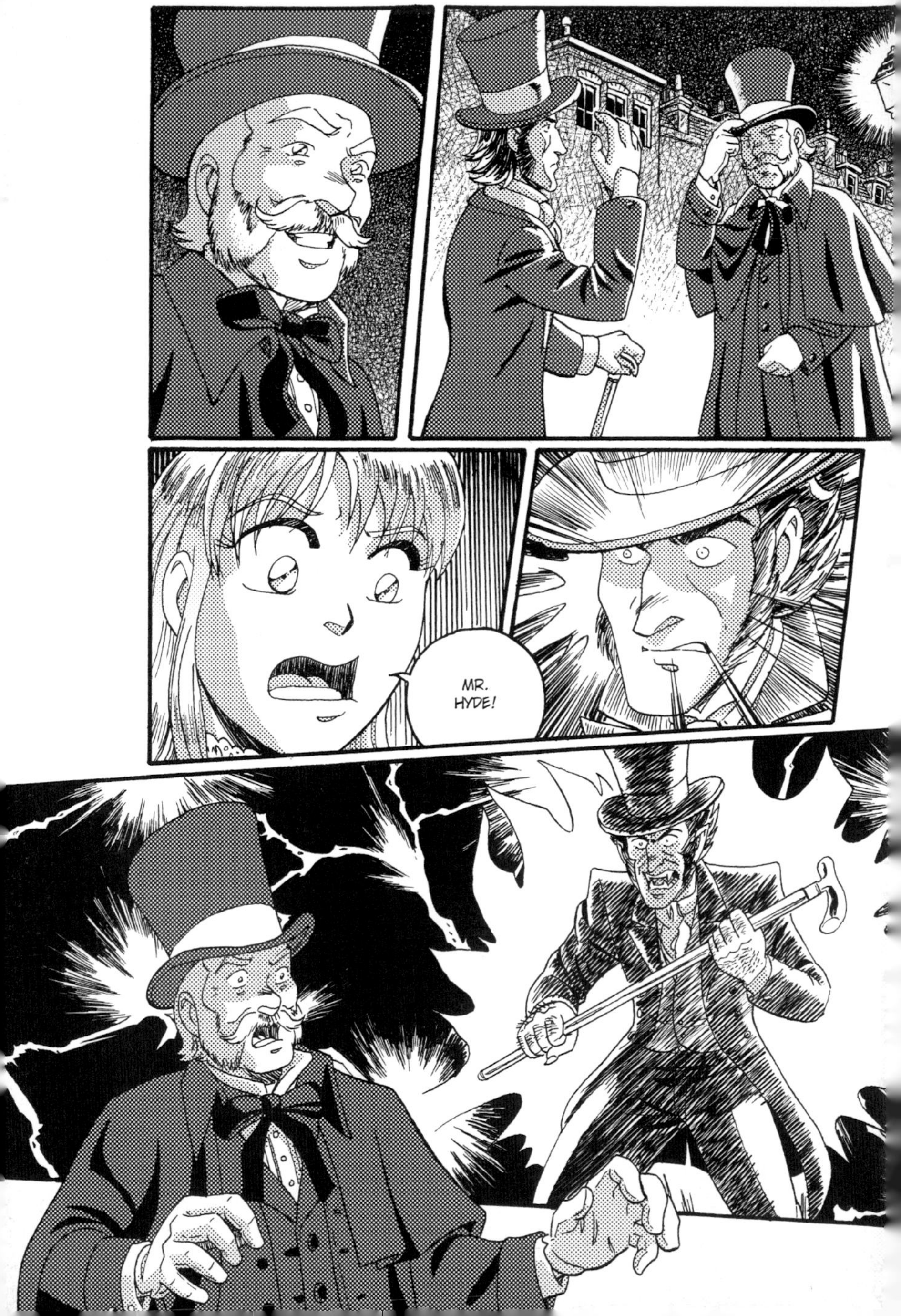
MR. HYDE!

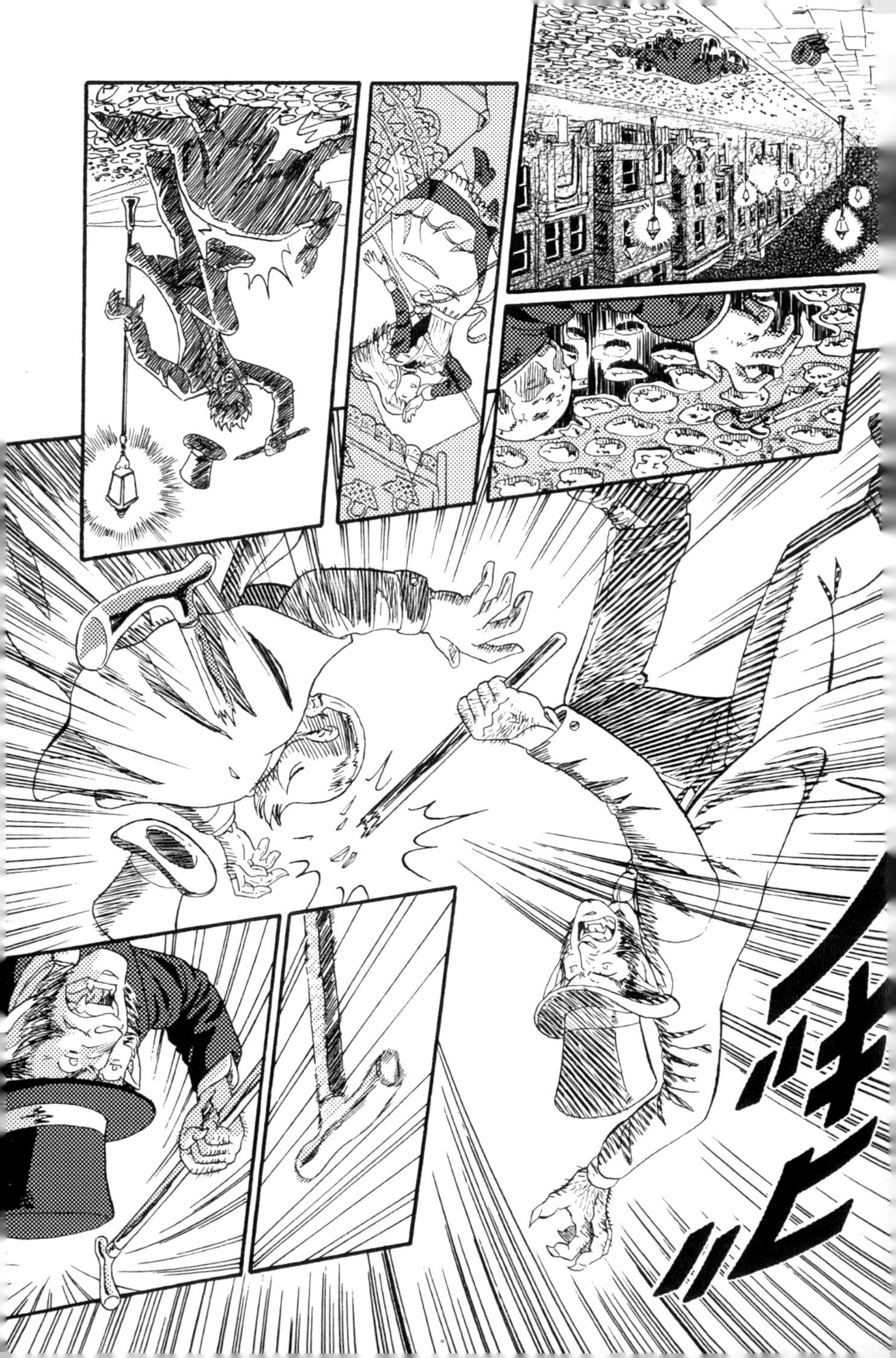
キン

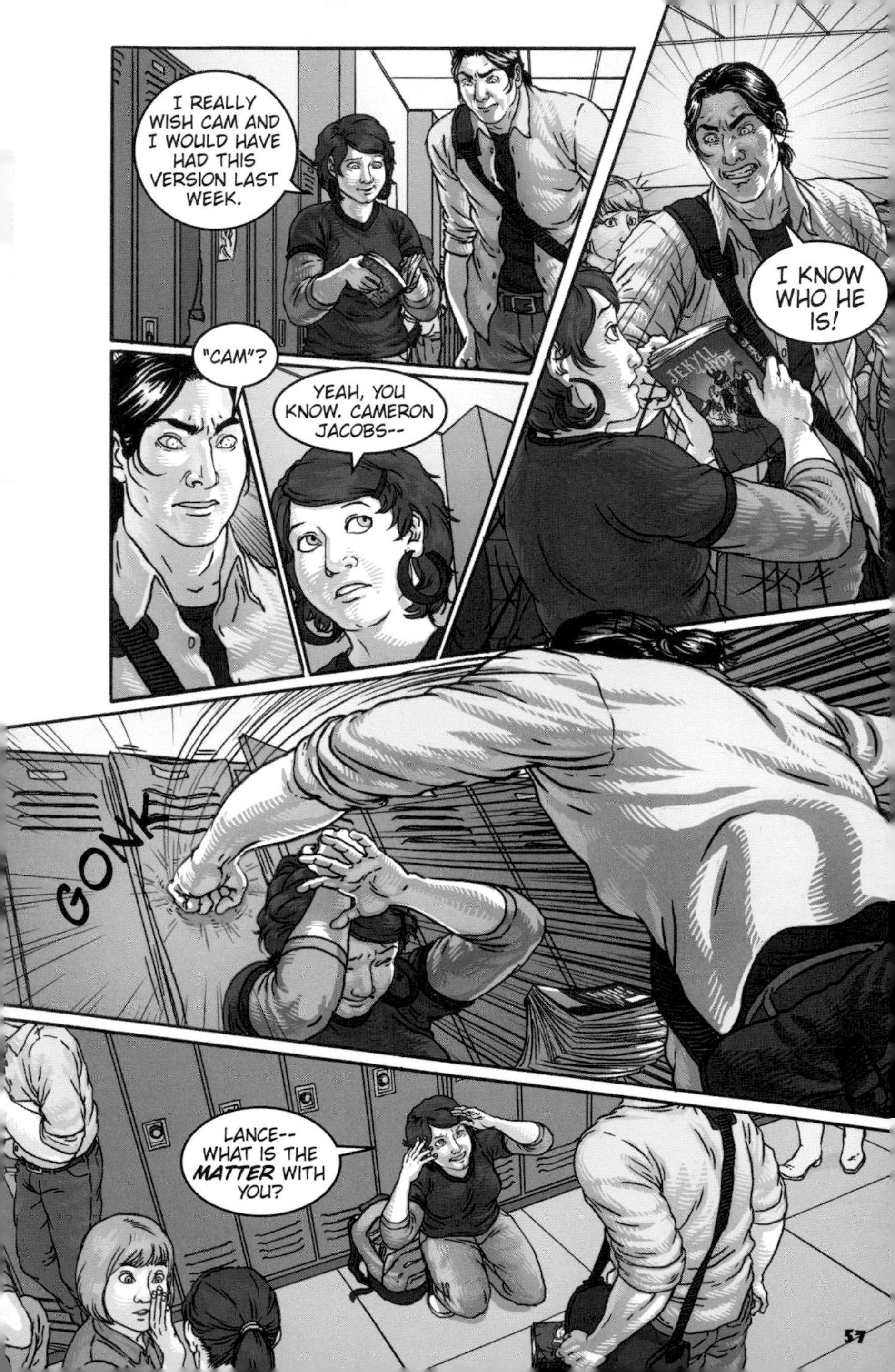

I REALLY WISH CAM AND I WOULD HAVE HAD THIS VERSION LAST WEEK.
"CAM"?
YEAH, YOU KNOW. CAMERON JACOBS--
I KNOW WHO HE IS!
JEKYLL HYDE
GONK
LANCE-- WHAT IS THE ***MATTER*** WITH YOU?

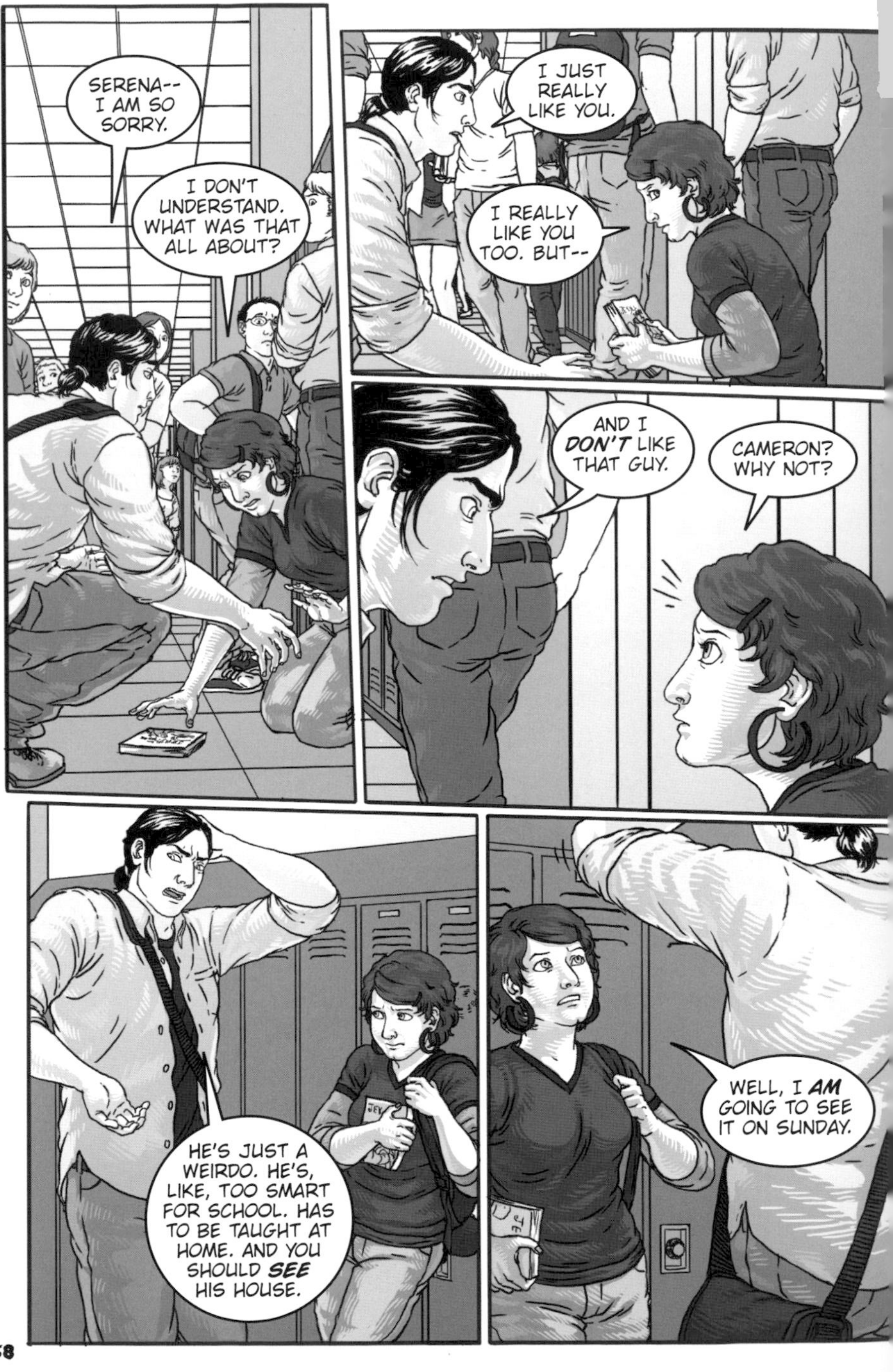
SERENA-- I AM SO SORRY.
I DON'T UNDERSTAND. WHAT WAS THAT ALL ABOUT?
I JUST REALLY LIKE YOU.
I REALLY LIKE YOU TOO. BUT--
AND I DON'T LIKE THAT GUY.
CAMERON? WHY NOT?
HE'S JUST A WEIRDO. HE'S, LIKE, TOO SMART FOR SCHOOL. HAS TO BE TAUGHT AT HOME. AND YOU SHOULD SEE HIS HOUSE.
WELL, I AM GOING TO SEE IT ON SUNDAY.

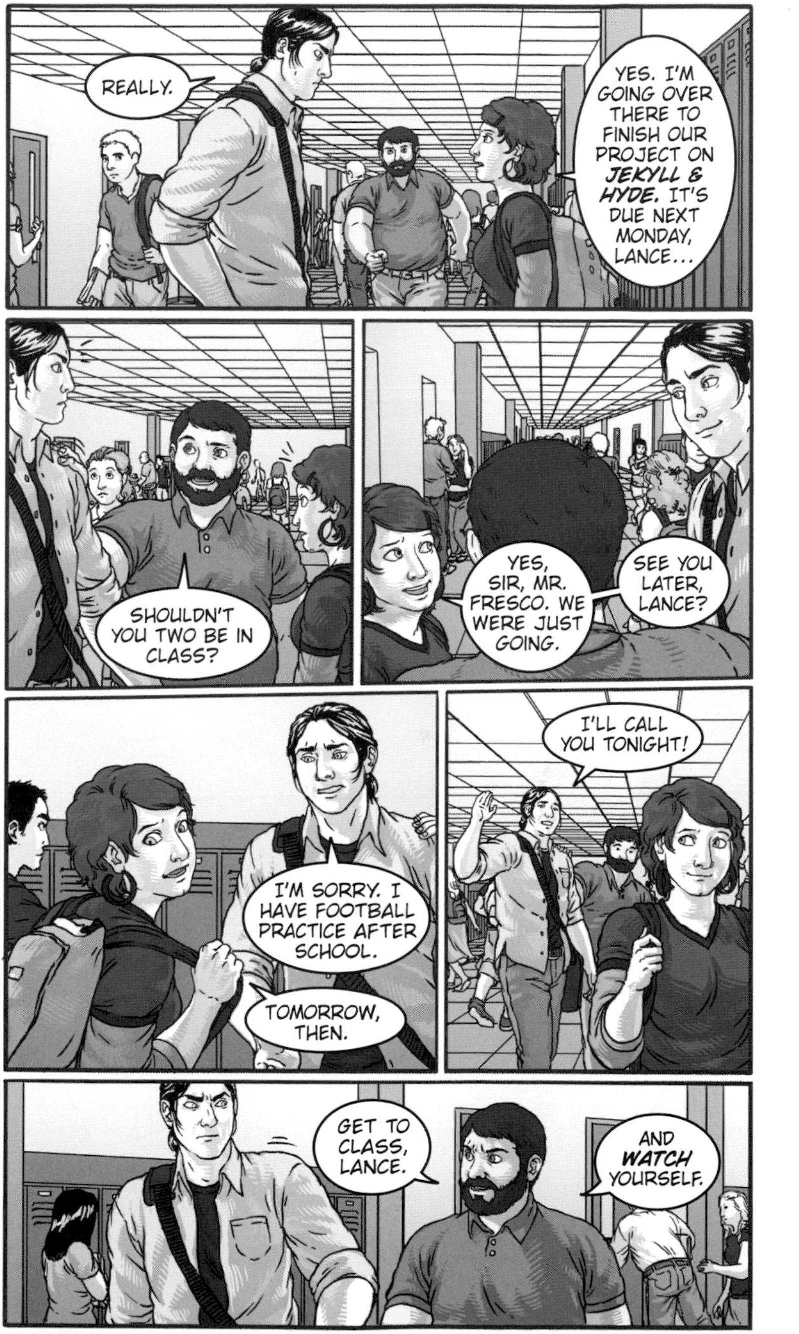
REALLY.
YES. I'M GOING OVER THERE TO FINISH OUR PROJECT ON *JEKYLL & HYDE.* IT'S DUE NEXT MONDAY, LANCE...
SHOULDN'T YOU TWO BE IN CLASS?
YES, SIR, MR. FRESCO. WE WERE JUST GOING.
SEE YOU LATER, LANCE?
I'M SORRY. I HAVE FOOTBALL PRACTICE AFTER SCHOOL.
TOMORROW, THEN.
I'LL CALL YOU TONIGHT!
GET TO CLASS, LANCE.
AND *WATCH* YOURSELF.

Chapter SIX
OMG, It's FRIDAY

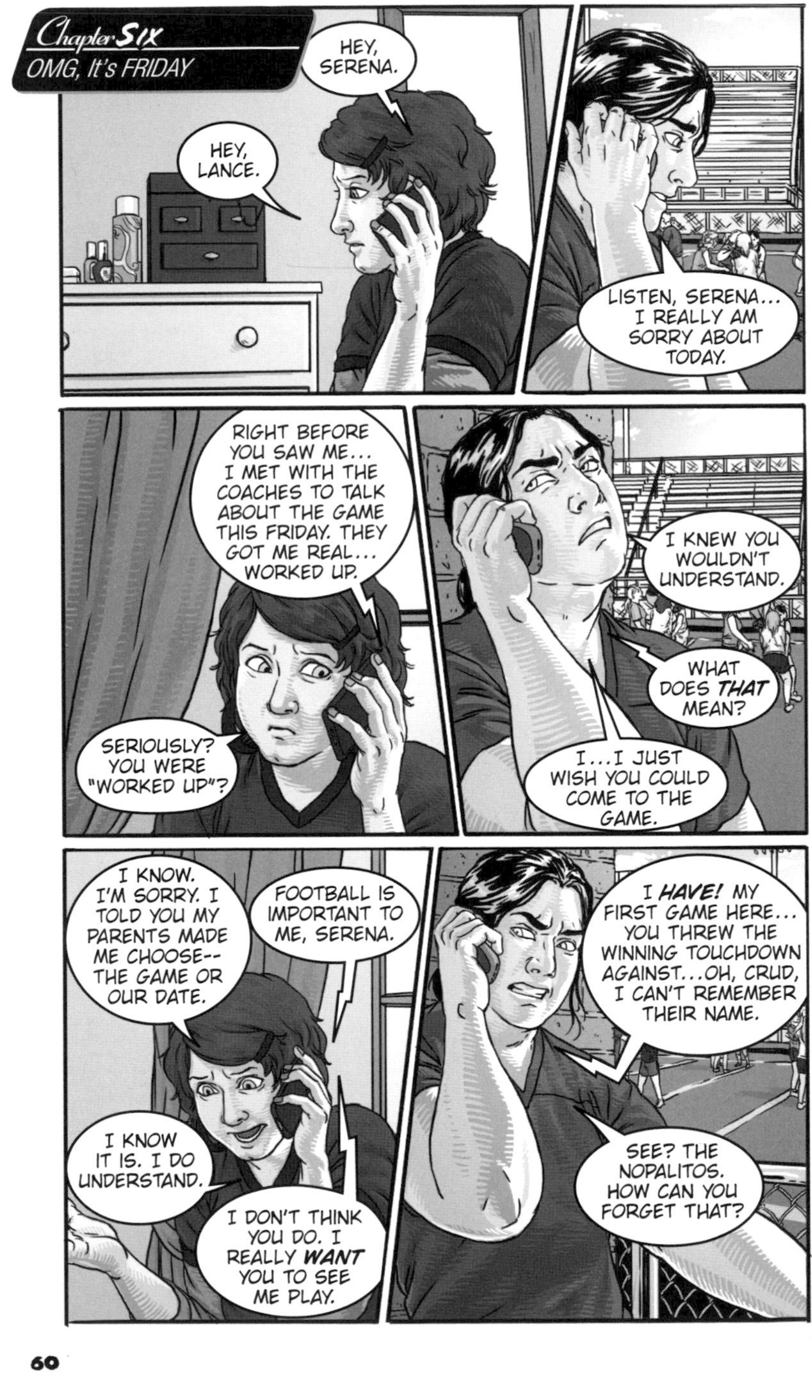

HEY, SERENA.
HEY, LANCE.
LISTEN, SERENA... I REALLY AM SORRY ABOUT TODAY.
RIGHT BEFORE YOU SAW ME... I MET WITH THE COACHES TO TALK ABOUT THE GAME THIS FRIDAY. THEY GOT ME REAL... WORKED UP.
SERIOUSLY? YOU WERE "WORKED UP"?
I KNEW YOU WOULDN'T UNDERSTAND.
WHAT DOES *THAT* MEAN?
I...I JUST WISH YOU COULD COME TO THE GAME.
I KNOW. I'M SORRY. I TOLD YOU MY PARENTS MADE ME CHOOSE-- THE GAME OR OUR DATE.
FOOTBALL IS IMPORTANT TO ME, SERENA.
I KNOW IT IS. I DO UNDERSTAND.
I DON'T THINK YOU DO. I REALLY *WANT* YOU TO SEE ME PLAY.
I *HAVE!* MY FIRST GAME HERE... YOU THREW THE WINNING TOUCHDOWN AGAINST...OH, CRUD, I CAN'T REMEMBER THEIR NAME.
SEE? THE NOPALITOS. HOW CAN YOU FORGET THAT?

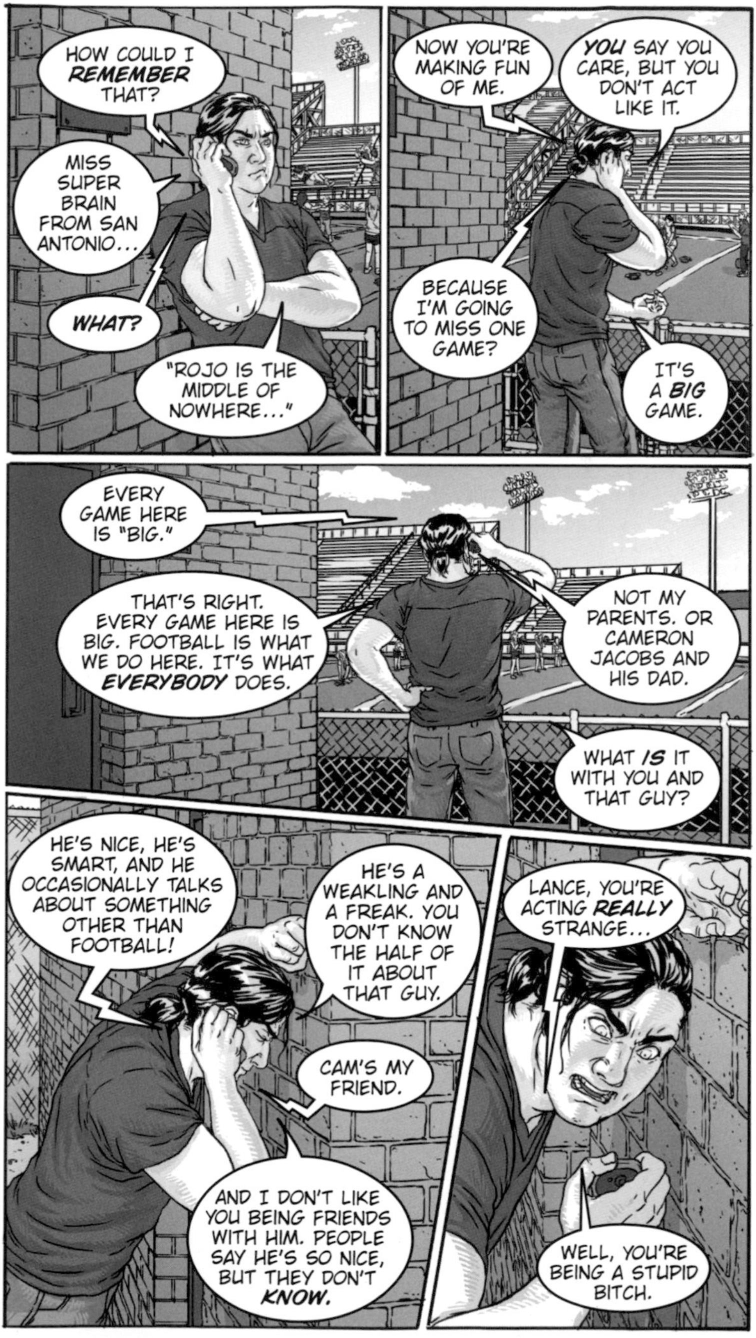
HOW COULD I REMEMBER THAT?
MISS SUPER BRAIN FROM SAN ANTONIO...
WHAT?
"ROJO IS THE MIDDLE OF NOWHERE..."
NOW YOU'RE MAKING FUN OF ME.
YOU SAY YOU CARE, BUT YOU DON'T ACT LIKE IT.
BECAUSE I'M GOING TO MISS ONE GAME?
IT'S A BIG GAME.
EVERY GAME HERE IS "BIG."
THAT'S RIGHT. EVERY GAME HERE IS BIG. FOOTBALL IS WHAT WE DO HERE. IT'S WHAT EVERYBODY DOES.
NOT MY PARENTS. OR CAMERON JACOBS AND HIS DAD.
WHAT IS IT WITH YOU AND THAT GUY?
HE'S NICE, HE'S SMART, AND HE OCCASIONALLY TALKS ABOUT SOMETHING OTHER THAN FOOTBALL!
HE'S A WEAKLING AND A FREAK. YOU DON'T KNOW THE HALF OF IT ABOUT THAT GUY.
CAM'S MY FRIEND.
AND I DON'T LIKE YOU BEING FRIENDS WITH HIM. PEOPLE SAY HE'S SO NICE, BUT THEY DON'T KNOW.
LANCE, YOU'RE ACTING REALLY STRANGE...
WELL, YOU'RE BEING A STUPID BITCH.

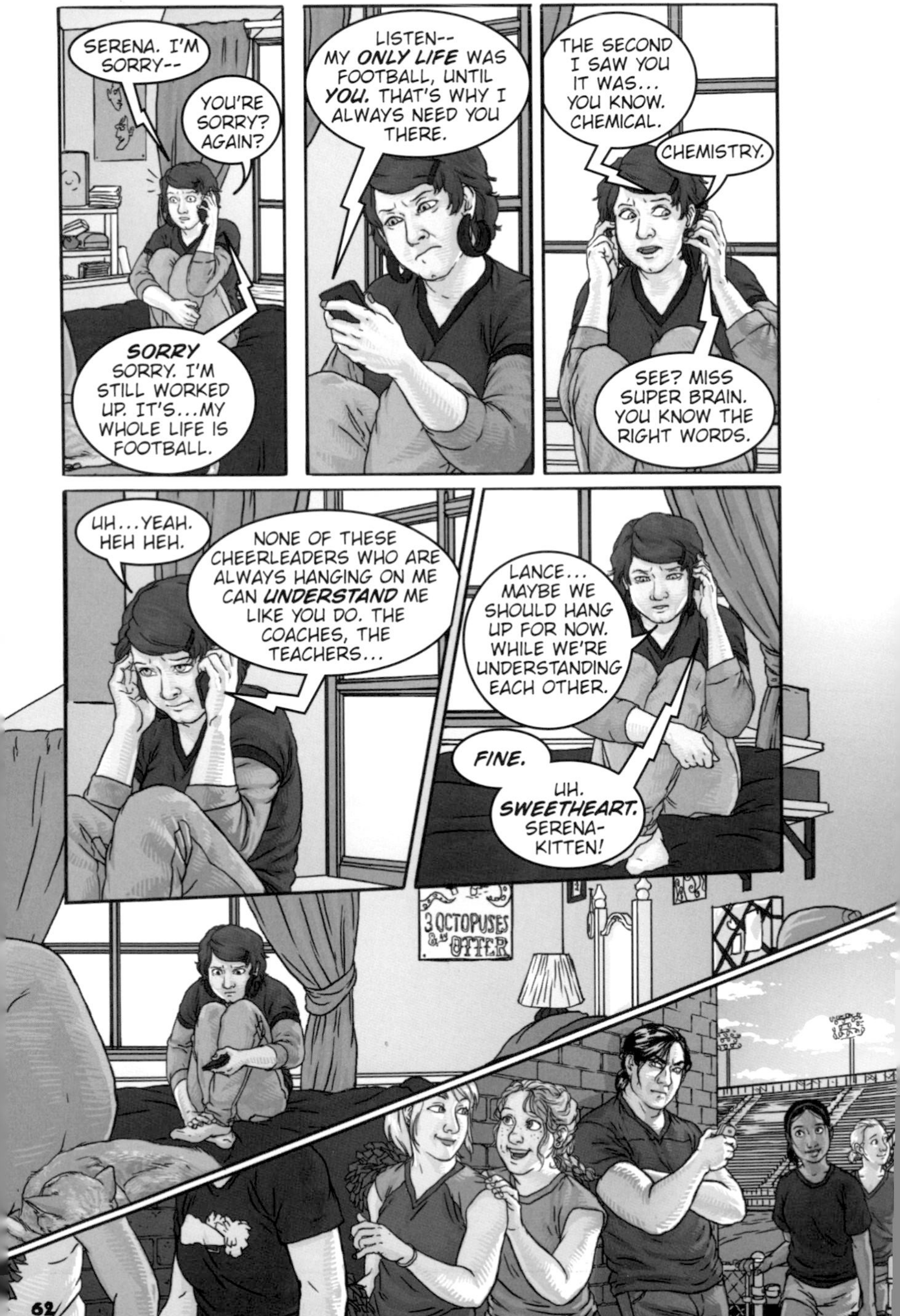

SERENA. I'M SORRY--
YOU'RE SORRY? AGAIN?
SORRY SORRY. I'M STILL WORKED UP. IT'S...MY WHOLE LIFE IS FOOTBALL.
LISTEN-- MY ONLY LIFE WAS FOOTBALL, UNTIL YOU. THAT'S WHY I ALWAYS NEED YOU THERE.
THE SECOND I SAW YOU IT WAS... YOU KNOW. CHEMICAL.
CHEMISTRY.
SEE? MISS SUPER BRAIN. YOU KNOW THE RIGHT WORDS.
UH...YEAH. HEH HEH.
NONE OF THESE CHEERLEADERS WHO ARE ALWAYS HANGING ON ME CAN UNDERSTAND ME LIKE YOU DO. THE COACHES, THE TEACHERS...
LANCE... MAYBE WE SHOULD HANG UP FOR NOW. WHILE WE'RE UNDERSTANDING EACH OTHER.
FINE.
UH. SWEETHEART. SERENA-KITTEN!
3 OCTOPUSES & 1 OTTER

"BITCH..."

C'MON, CON... BE THERE.

DARN IT!

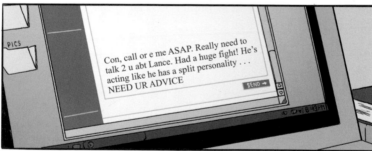

PICS

Con, call or e me ASAP. Really need to talk 2 u abt Lance. Had a huge fight! He's acting like he has a split personality . . .
NEED UR ADVICE

SEND →

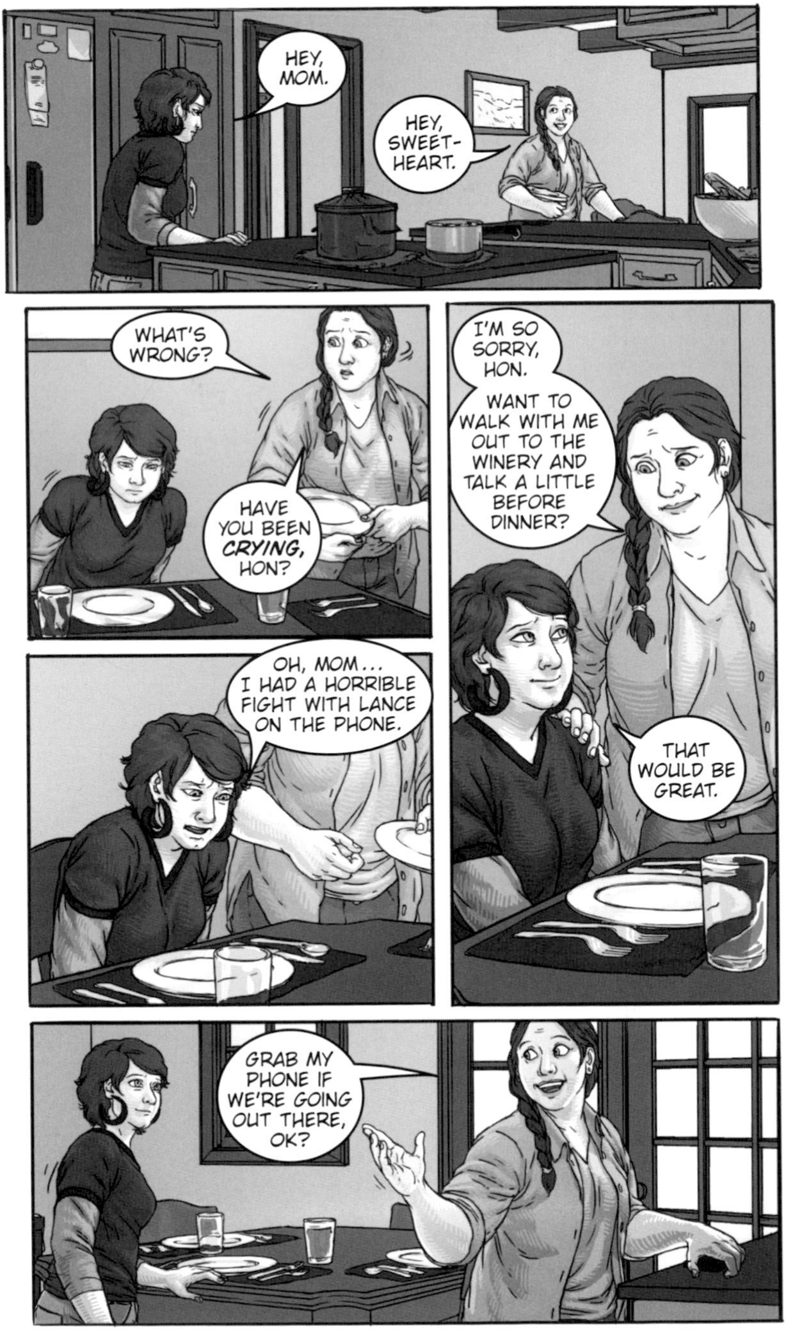
HEY, MOM.
HEY, SWEET-HEART.
WHAT'S WRONG?
HAVE YOU BEEN *CRYING,* HON?
I'M SO SORRY, HON.
WANT TO WALK WITH ME OUT TO THE WINERY AND TALK A LITTLE BEFORE DINNER?
OH, MOM... I HAD A HORRIBLE FIGHT WITH LANCE ON THE PHONE.
THAT WOULD BE GREAT.
GRAB MY PHONE IF WE'RE GOING OUT THERE, OK?

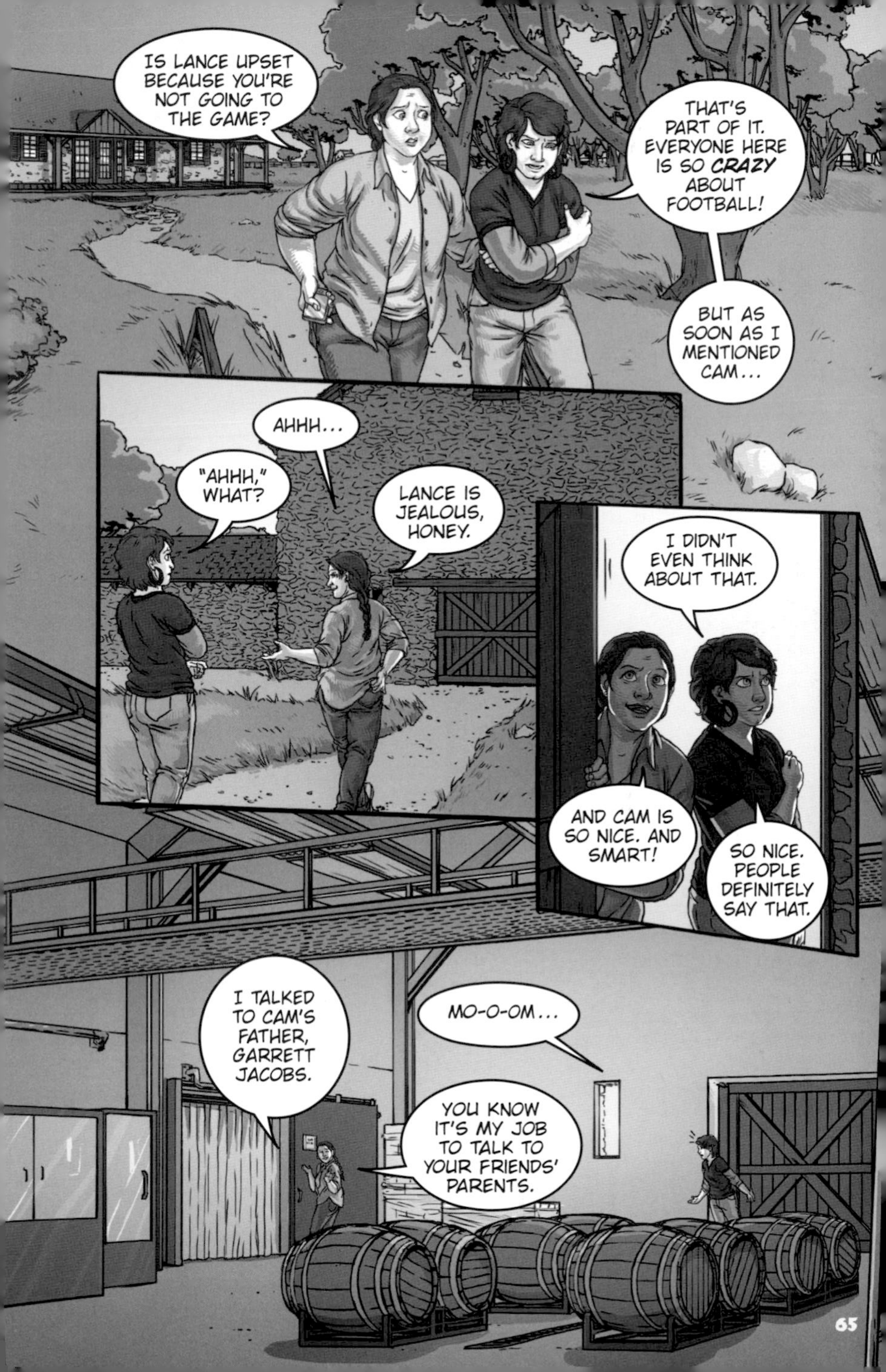
IS LANCE UPSET BECAUSE YOU'RE NOT GOING TO THE GAME?
THAT'S PART OF IT. EVERYONE HERE IS SO *CRAZY* ABOUT FOOTBALL!
BUT AS SOON AS I MENTIONED CAM...
AHHH...
"AHHH," WHAT?
LANCE IS JEALOUS, HONEY.
I DIDN'T EVEN THINK ABOUT THAT.
AND CAM IS SO NICE. AND SMART!
SO NICE. PEOPLE DEFINITELY SAY THAT.
I TALKED TO CAM'S FATHER, GARRETT JACOBS.
MO-O-OM...
YOU KNOW IT'S MY JOB TO TALK TO YOUR FRIENDS' PARENTS.

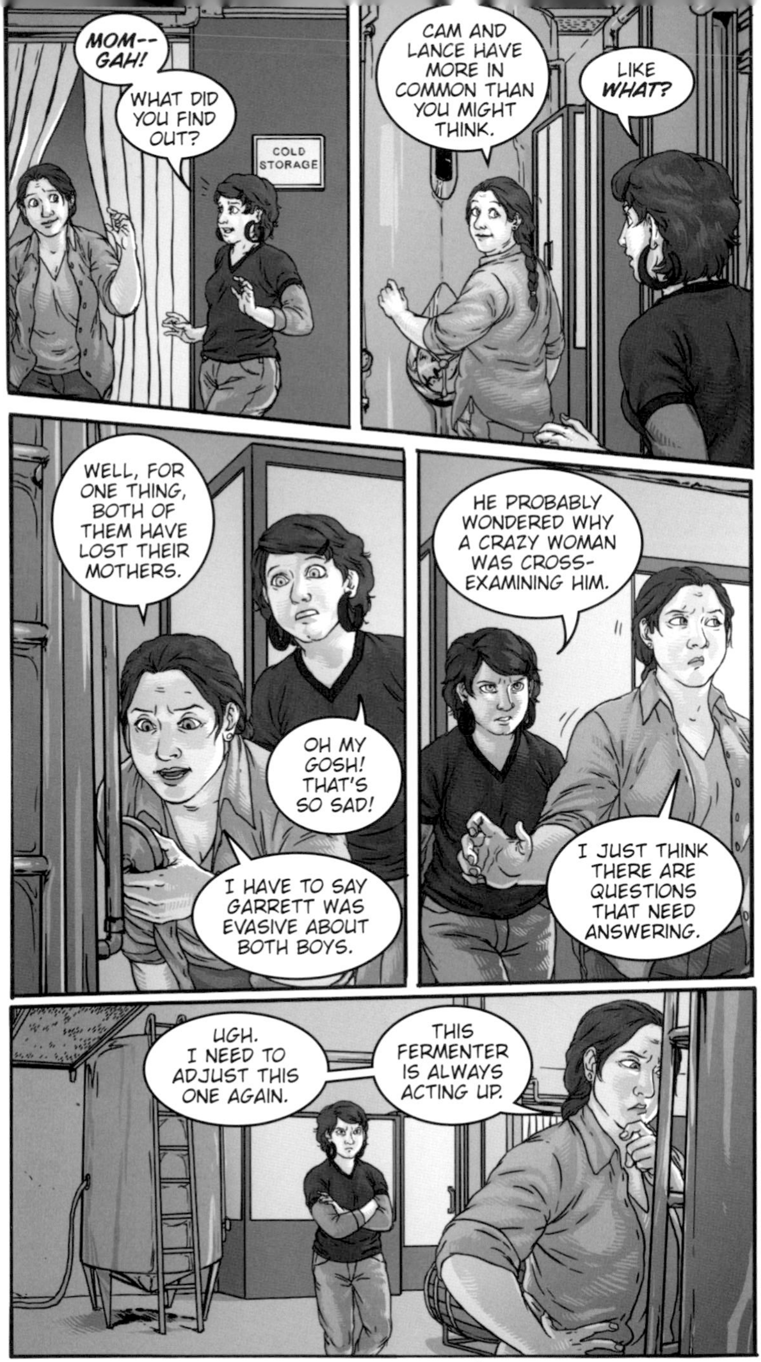
MOM-- GAH!
WHAT DID YOU FIND OUT?
COLD STORAGE
CAM AND LANCE HAVE MORE IN COMMON THAN YOU MIGHT THINK.
LIKE *WHAT?*
WELL, FOR ONE THING, BOTH OF THEM HAVE LOST THEIR MOTHERS.
OH MY GOSH! THAT'S SO SAD!
I HAVE TO SAY GARRETT WAS EVASIVE ABOUT BOTH BOYS.
HE PROBABLY WONDERED WHY A CRAZY WOMAN WAS CROSS-EXAMINING HIM.
I JUST THINK THERE ARE QUESTIONS THAT NEED ANSWERING.
UGH. I NEED TO ADJUST THIS ONE AGAIN.
THIS FERMENTER IS ALWAYS ACTING UP.

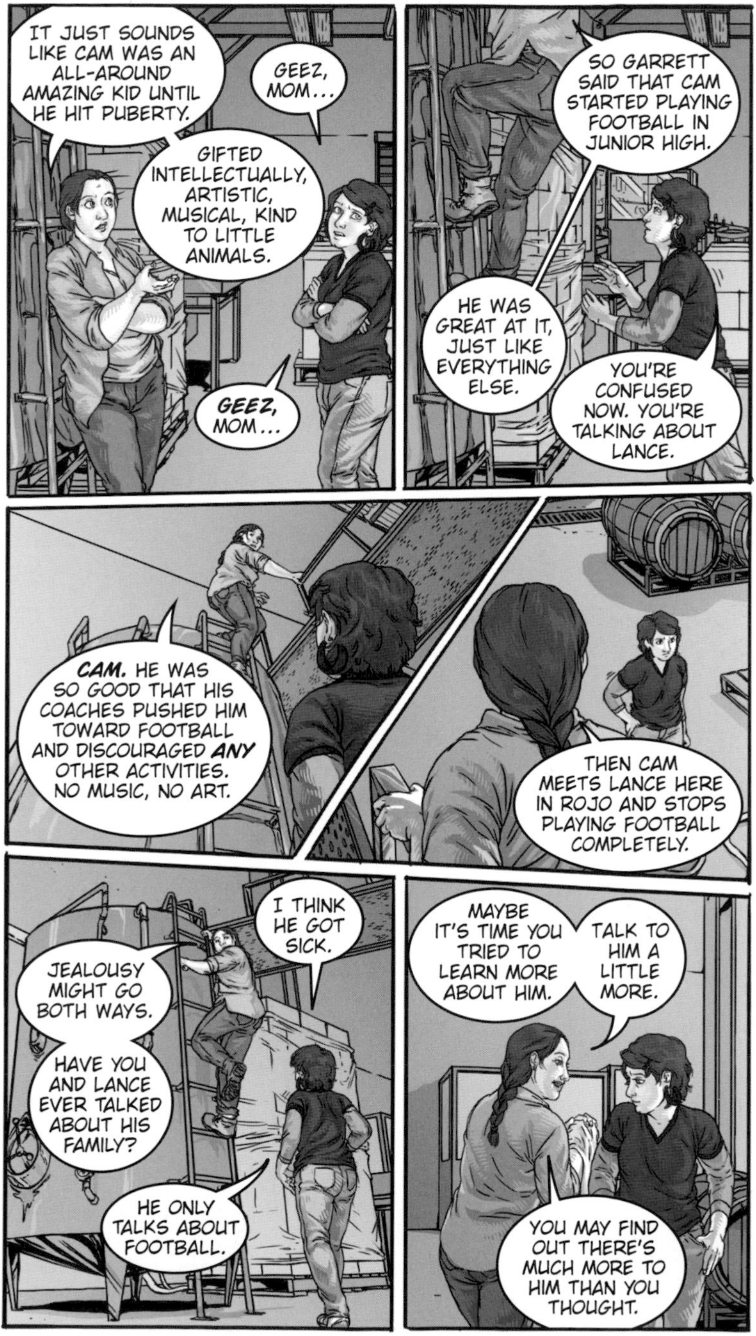
IT JUST SOUNDS LIKE CAM WAS AN ALL-AROUND AMAZING KID UNTIL HE HIT PUBERTY.
GEEZ, MOM...
GIFTED INTELLECTUALLY, ARTISTIC, MUSICAL, KIND TO LITTLE ANIMALS.
GEEZ, MOM...
SO GARRETT SAID THAT CAM STARTED PLAYING FOOTBALL IN JUNIOR HIGH.
HE WAS GREAT AT IT, JUST LIKE EVERYTHING ELSE.
YOU'RE CONFUSED NOW. YOU'RE TALKING ABOUT LANCE.
CAM. HE WAS SO GOOD THAT HIS COACHES PUSHED HIM TOWARD FOOTBALL AND DISCOURAGED ANY OTHER ACTIVITIES. NO MUSIC, NO ART.
THEN CAM MEETS LANCE HERE IN ROJO AND STOPS PLAYING FOOTBALL COMPLETELY.
I THINK HE GOT SICK.
JEALOUSY MIGHT GO BOTH WAYS.
HAVE YOU AND LANCE EVER TALKED ABOUT HIS FAMILY?
HE ONLY TALKS ABOUT FOOTBALL.
MAYBE IT'S TIME YOU TRIED TO LEARN MORE ABOUT HIM.
TALK TO HIM A LITTLE MORE.
YOU MAY FIND OUT THERE'S MUCH MORE TO HIM THAN YOU THOUGHT.

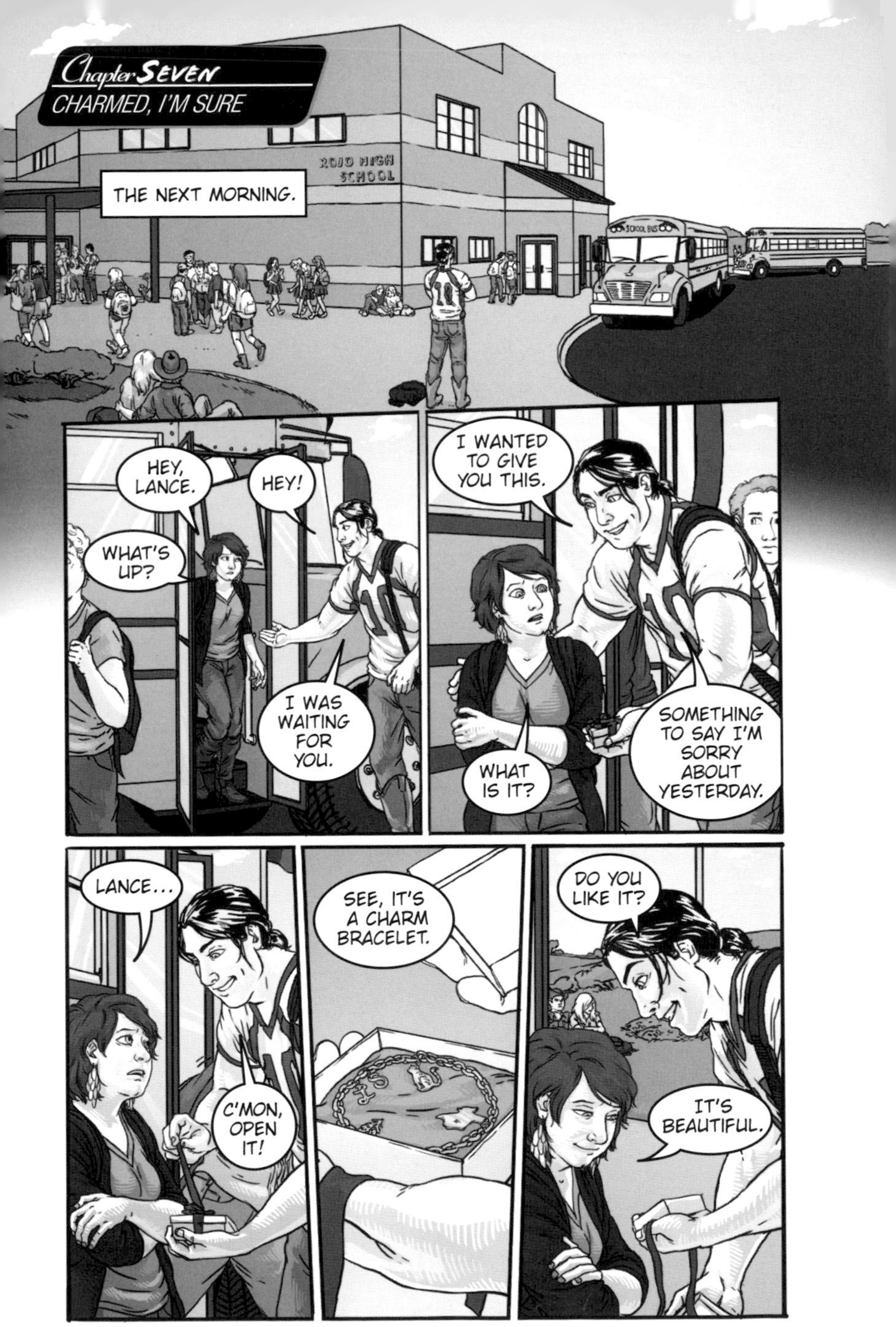
Chapter SEVEN
CHARMED, I'M SURE
ROJO HIGH SCHOOL
THE NEXT MORNING.
SCHOOL BUS
HEY, LANCE.
HEY!
WHAT'S UP?
I WAS WAITING FOR YOU.
I WANTED TO GIVE YOU THIS.
WHAT IS IT?
SOMETHING TO SAY I'M SORRY ABOUT YESTERDAY.
LANCE...
C'MON, OPEN IT!
SEE, IT'S A CHARM BRACELET.
DO YOU LIKE IT?
IT'S BEAUTIFUL.

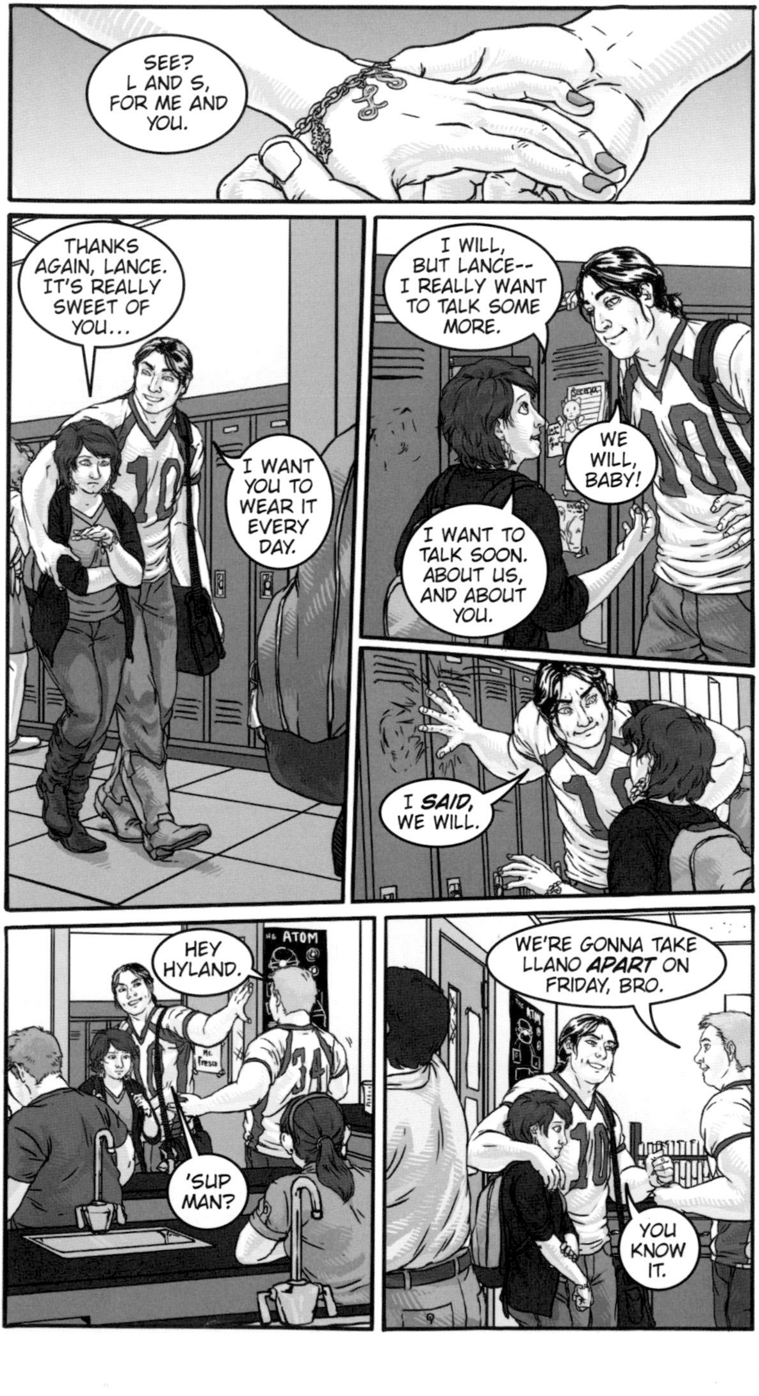
SEE? L AND S, FOR ME AND YOU.
THANKS AGAIN, LANCE. IT'S REALLY SWEET OF YOU...
I WANT YOU TO WEAR IT EVERY DAY.
I WILL, BUT LANCE-- I REALLY WANT TO TALK SOME MORE.
WE WILL, BABY!
I WANT TO TALK SOON. ABOUT US, AND ABOUT YOU.
I *SAID,* WE WILL.
HEY HYLAND.
'SUP MAN?
WE'RE GONNA TAKE LLANO *APART* ON FRIDAY, BRO.
YOU KNOW IT.

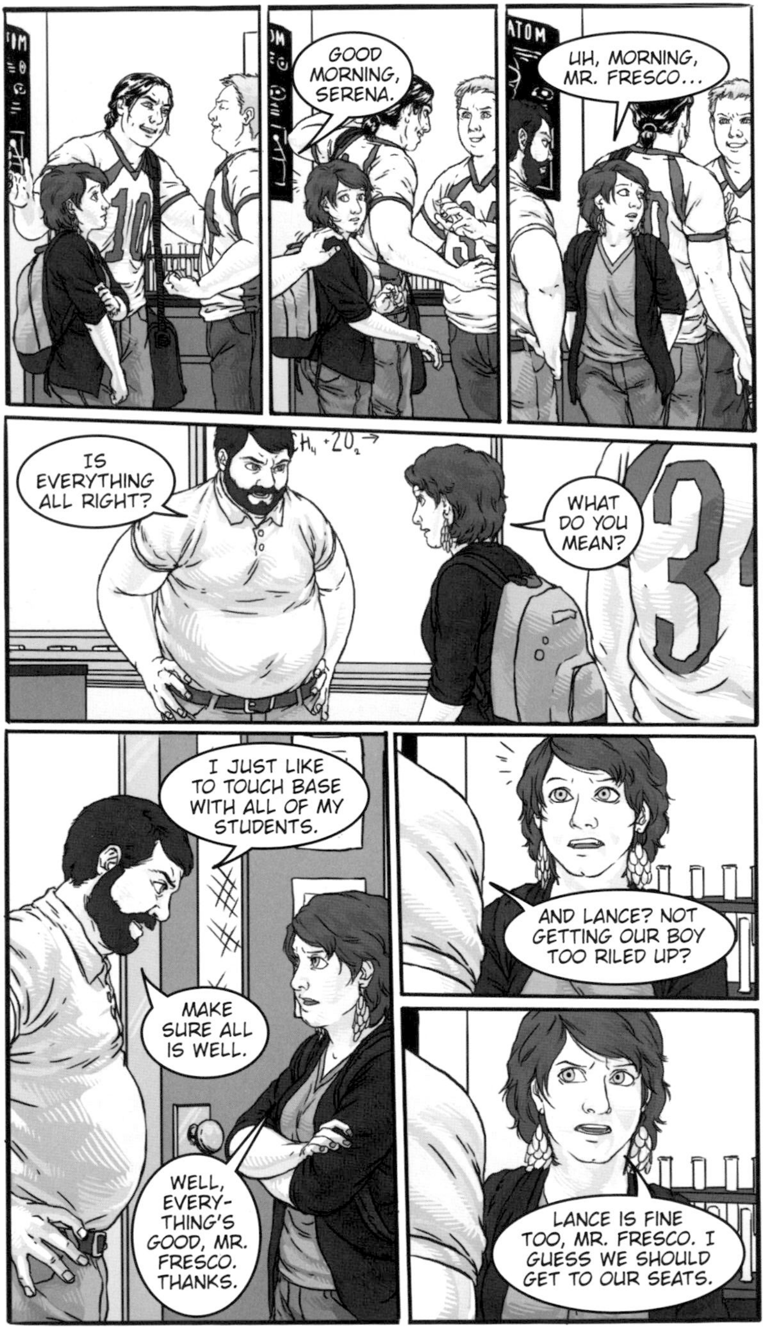
GOOD MORNING, SERENA.
UH, MORNING, MR. FRESCO...
IS EVERYTHING ALL RIGHT?
WHAT DO YOU MEAN?
I JUST LIKE TO TOUCH BASE WITH ALL OF MY STUDENTS.
MAKE SURE ALL IS WELL.
WELL, EVERY-THING'S GOOD, MR. FRESCO. THANKS.
AND LANCE? NOT GETTING OUR BOY TOO RILED UP?
LANCE IS FINE TOO, MR. FRESCO. I GUESS WE SHOULD GET TO OUR SEATS.

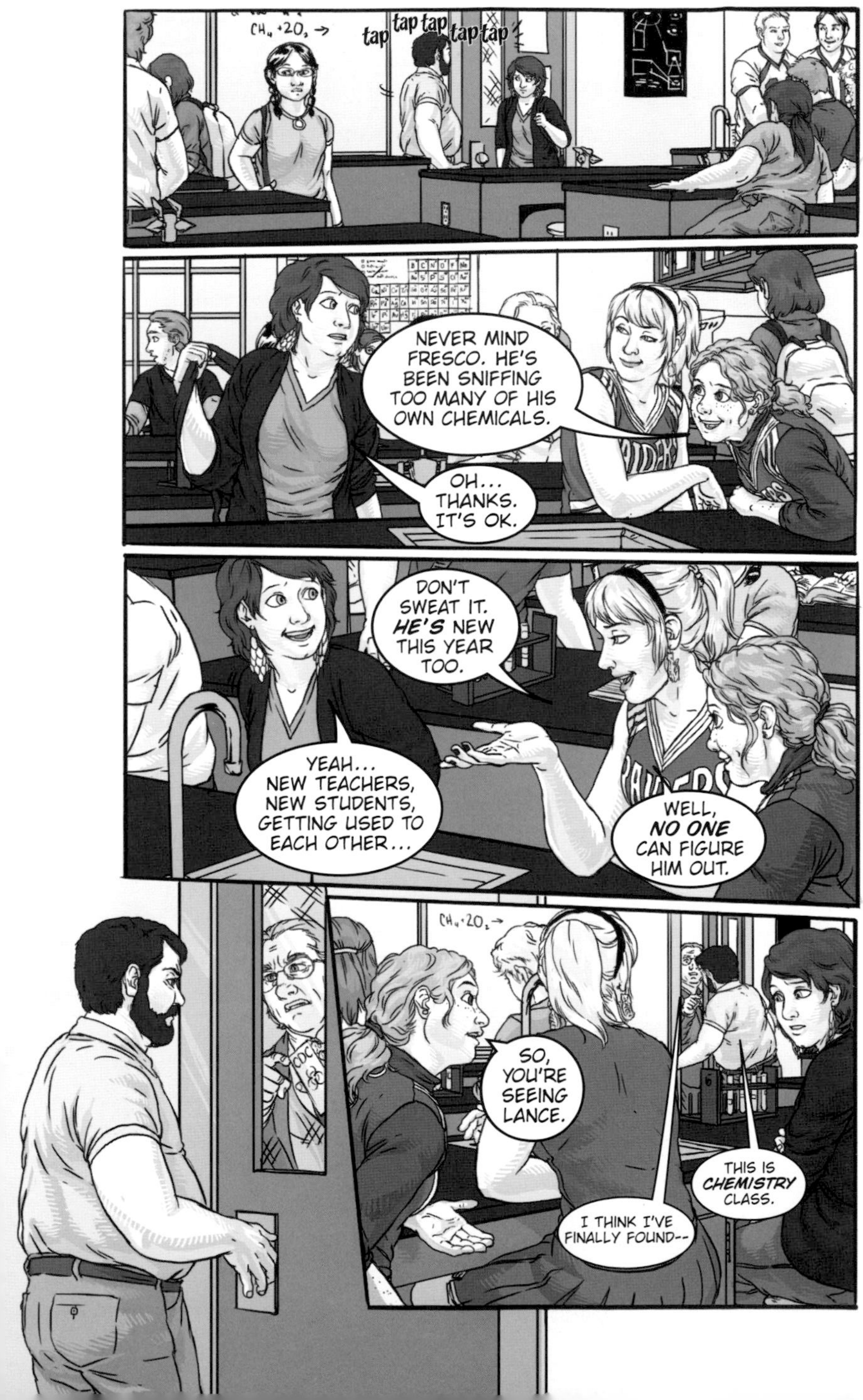
tap tap tap tap tap
NEVER MIND FRESCO. HE'S BEEN SNIFFING TOO MANY OF HIS OWN CHEMICALS.
OH... THANKS. IT'S OK.
DON'T SWEAT IT. HE'S NEW THIS YEAR TOO.
YEAH... NEW TEACHERS, NEW STUDENTS, GETTING USED TO EACH OTHER...
WELL, NO ONE CAN FIGURE HIM OUT.
SO, YOU'RE SEEING LANCE.
THIS IS CHEMISTRY CLASS.
I THINK I'VE FINALLY FOUND--

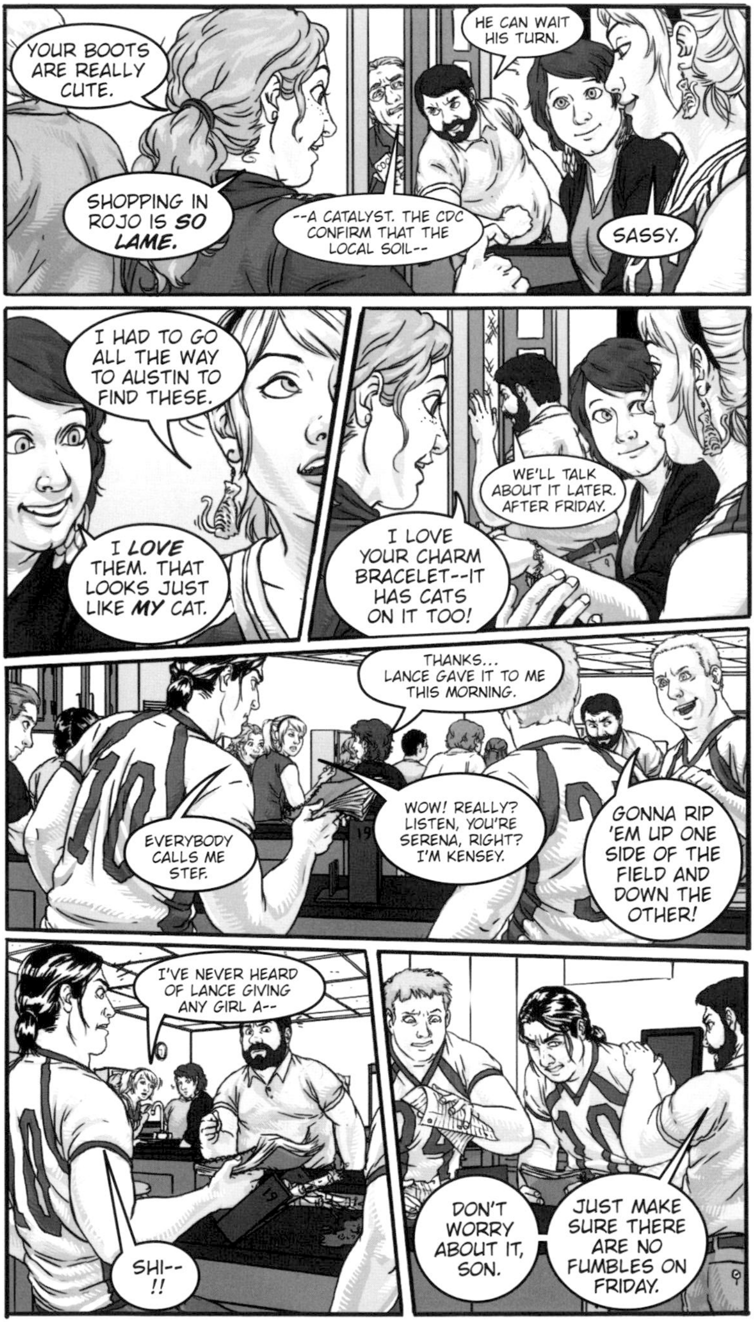
YOUR BOOTS ARE REALLY CUTE.
HE CAN WAIT HIS TURN.
SHOPPING IN ROJO IS SO LAME.
--A CATALYST. THE CDC CONFIRM THAT THE LOCAL SOIL--
SASSY.
I HAD TO GO ALL THE WAY TO AUSTIN TO FIND THESE.
I LOVE THEM. THAT LOOKS JUST LIKE MY CAT.
WE'LL TALK ABOUT IT LATER. AFTER FRIDAY.
I LOVE YOUR CHARM BRACELET--IT HAS CATS ON IT TOO!
THANKS... LANCE GAVE IT TO ME THIS MORNING.
EVERYBODY CALLS ME STEF.
WOW! REALLY? LISTEN, YOU'RE SERENA, RIGHT? I'M KENSEY.
GONNA RIP 'EM UP ONE SIDE OF THE FIELD AND DOWN THE OTHER!
I'VE NEVER HEARD OF LANCE GIVING ANY GIRL A--
SHI-- !!
DON'T WORRY ABOUT IT, SON.
JUST MAKE SURE THERE ARE NO FUMBLES ON FRIDAY.

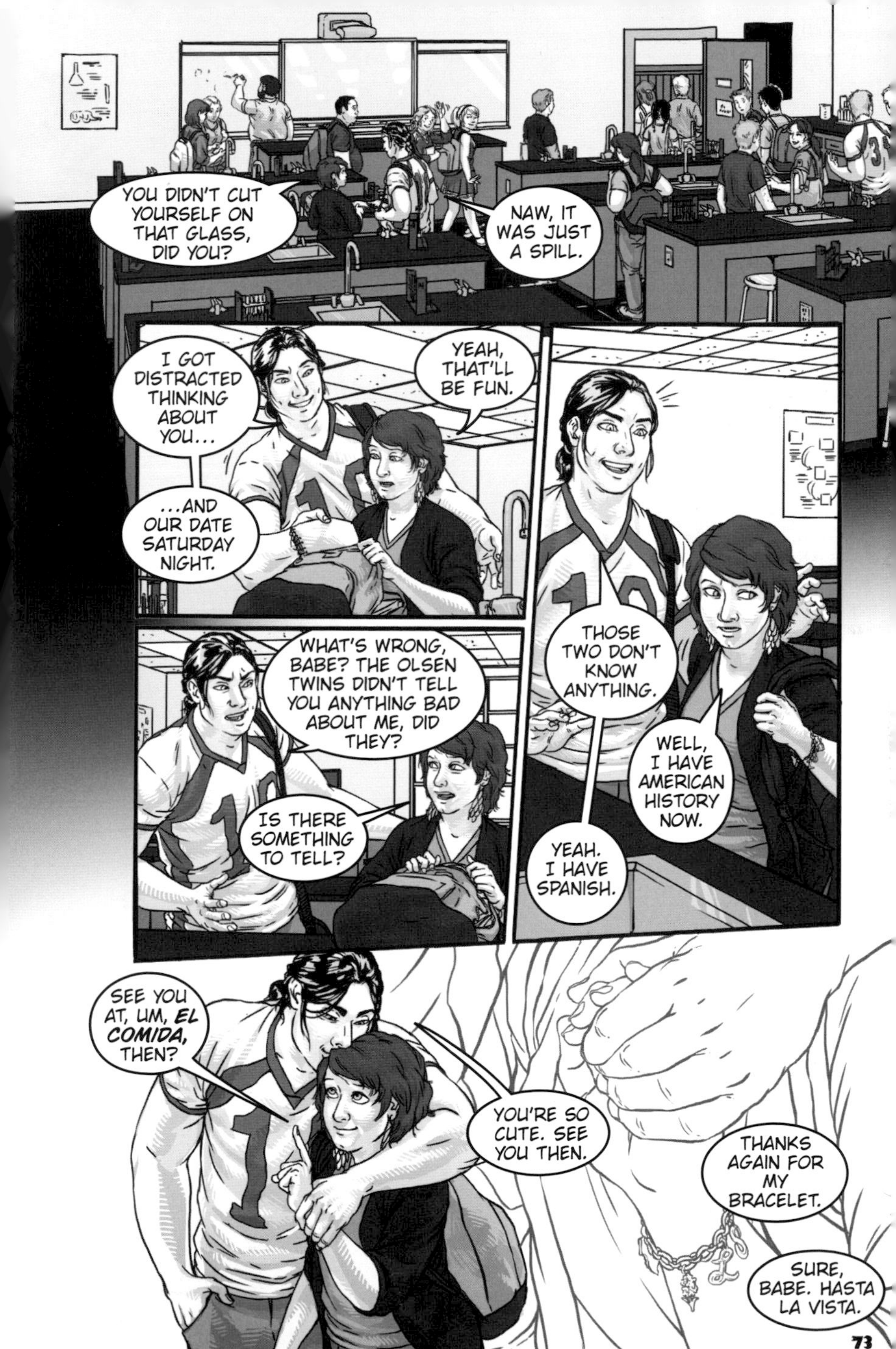
YOU DIDN'T CUT YOURSELF ON THAT GLASS, DID YOU?
NAW, IT WAS JUST A SPILL.
I GOT DISTRACTED THINKING ABOUT YOU...
YEAH, THAT'LL BE FUN.
...AND OUR DATE SATURDAY NIGHT.
THOSE TWO DON'T KNOW ANYTHING.
WHAT'S WRONG, BABE? THE OLSEN TWINS DIDN'T TELL YOU ANYTHING BAD ABOUT ME, DID THEY?
IS THERE SOMETHING TO TELL?
WELL, I HAVE AMERICAN HISTORY NOW.
YEAH. I HAVE SPANISH.
SEE YOU AT, UM, ***EL COMIDA,*** THEN?
YOU'RE SO CUTE. SEE YOU THEN.
THANKS AGAIN FOR MY BRACELET.
SURE, BABE. HASTA LA VISTA.

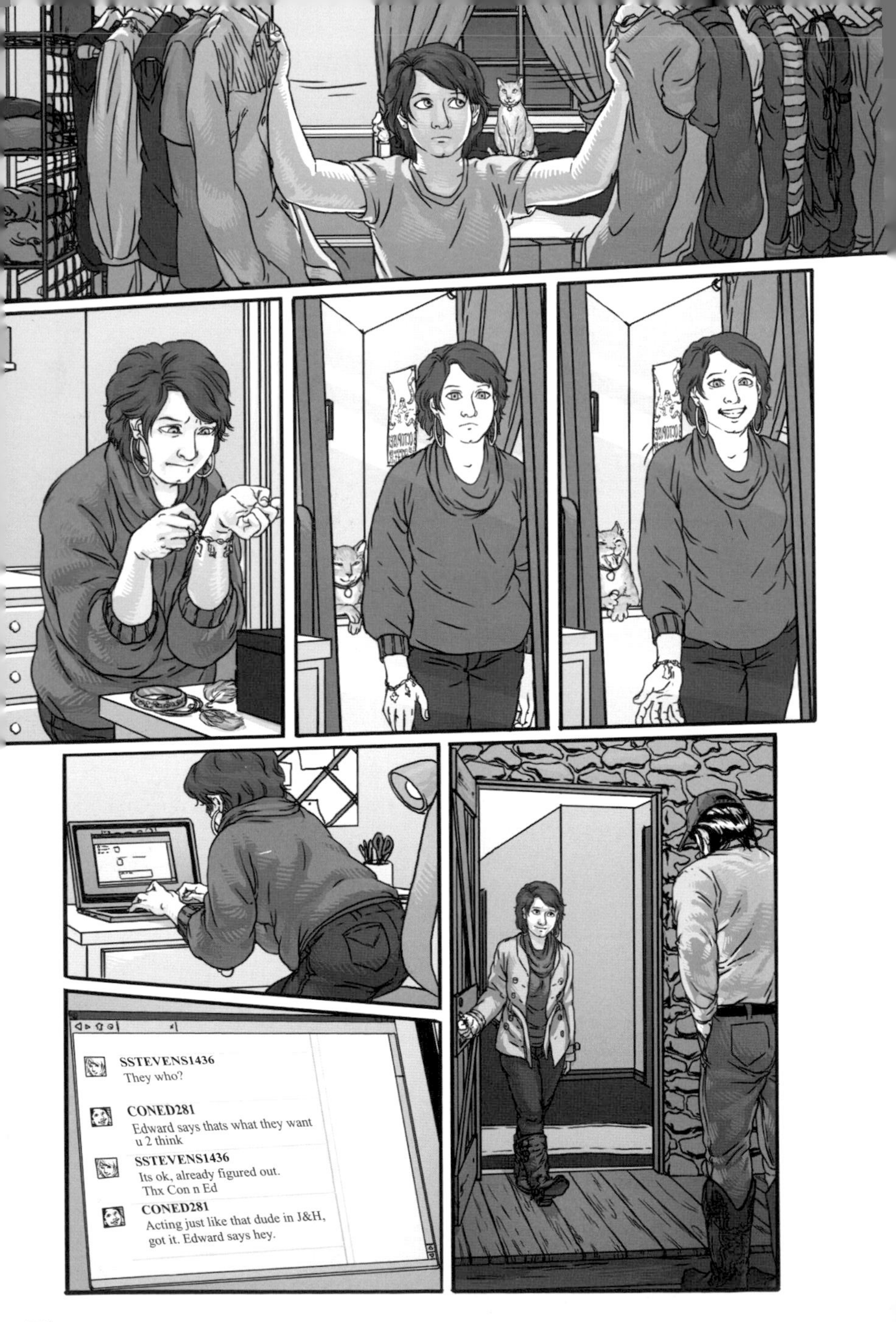

SSTEVENS1436
They who?
CONED281
Edward says thats what they want u 2 think
SSTEVENS1436
Its ok, already figured out. Thx Con n Ed
CONED281
Acting just like that dude in J&H, got it. Edward says hey.

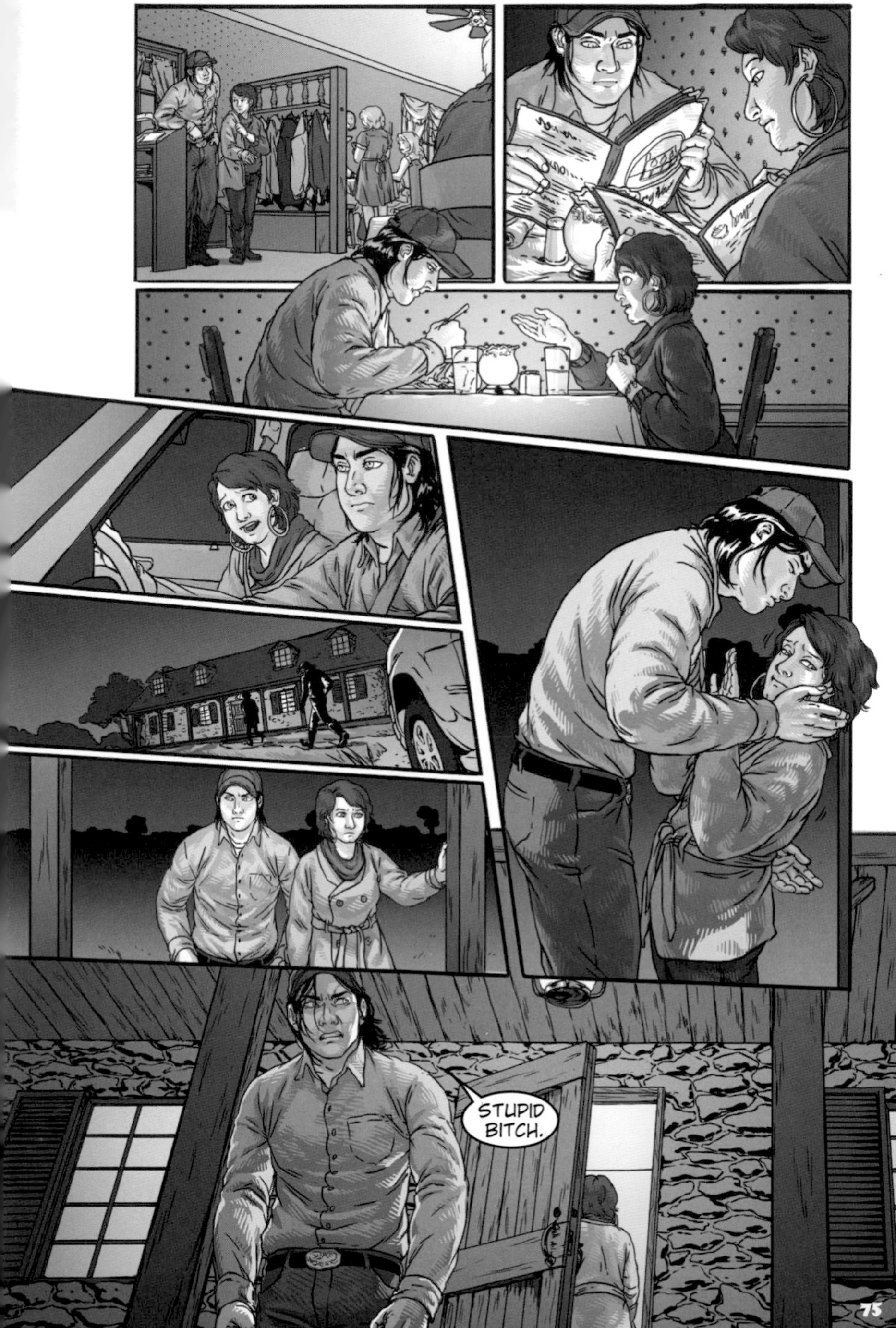
STUPID BITCH.

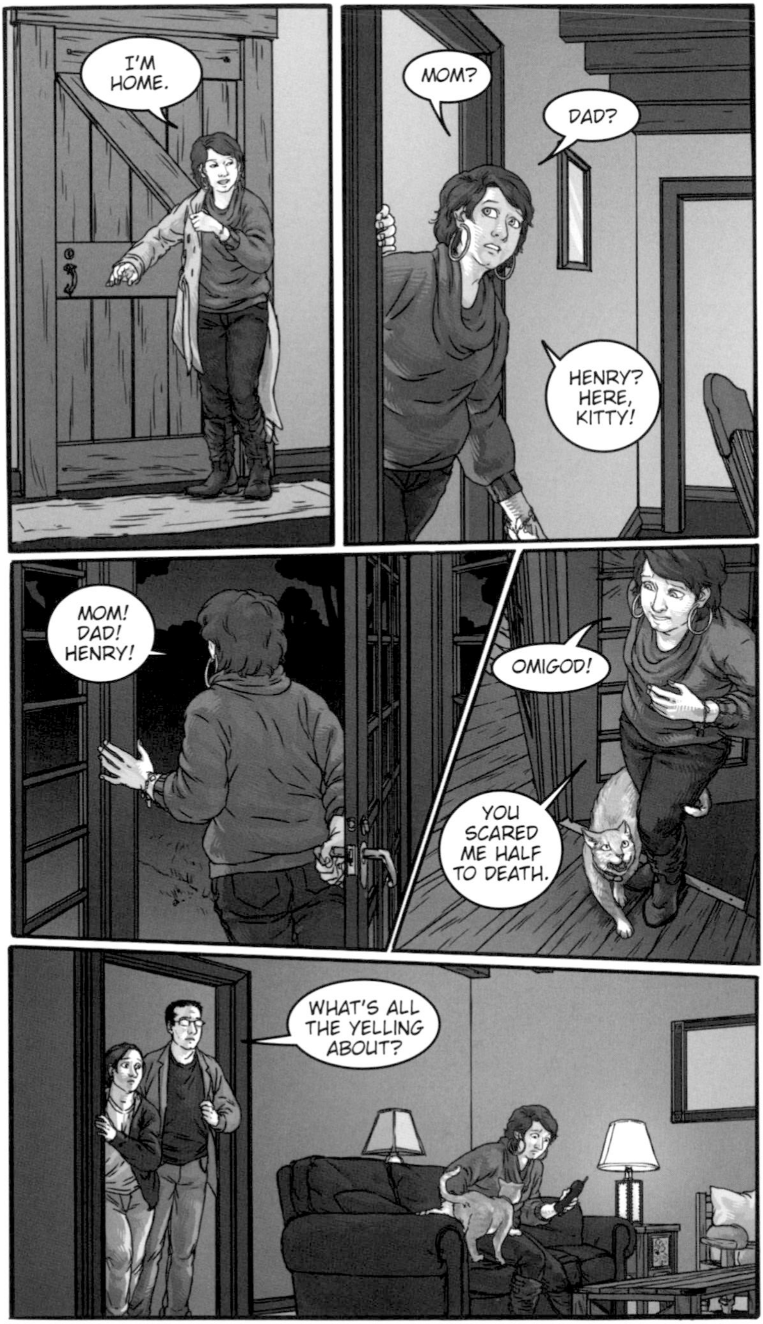
I'M HOME.
MOM?
DAD?
HENRY? HERE, KITTY!
MOM! DAD! HENRY!
OMIGOD!
YOU SCARED ME HALF TO DEATH.
WHAT'S ALL THE YELLING ABOUT?

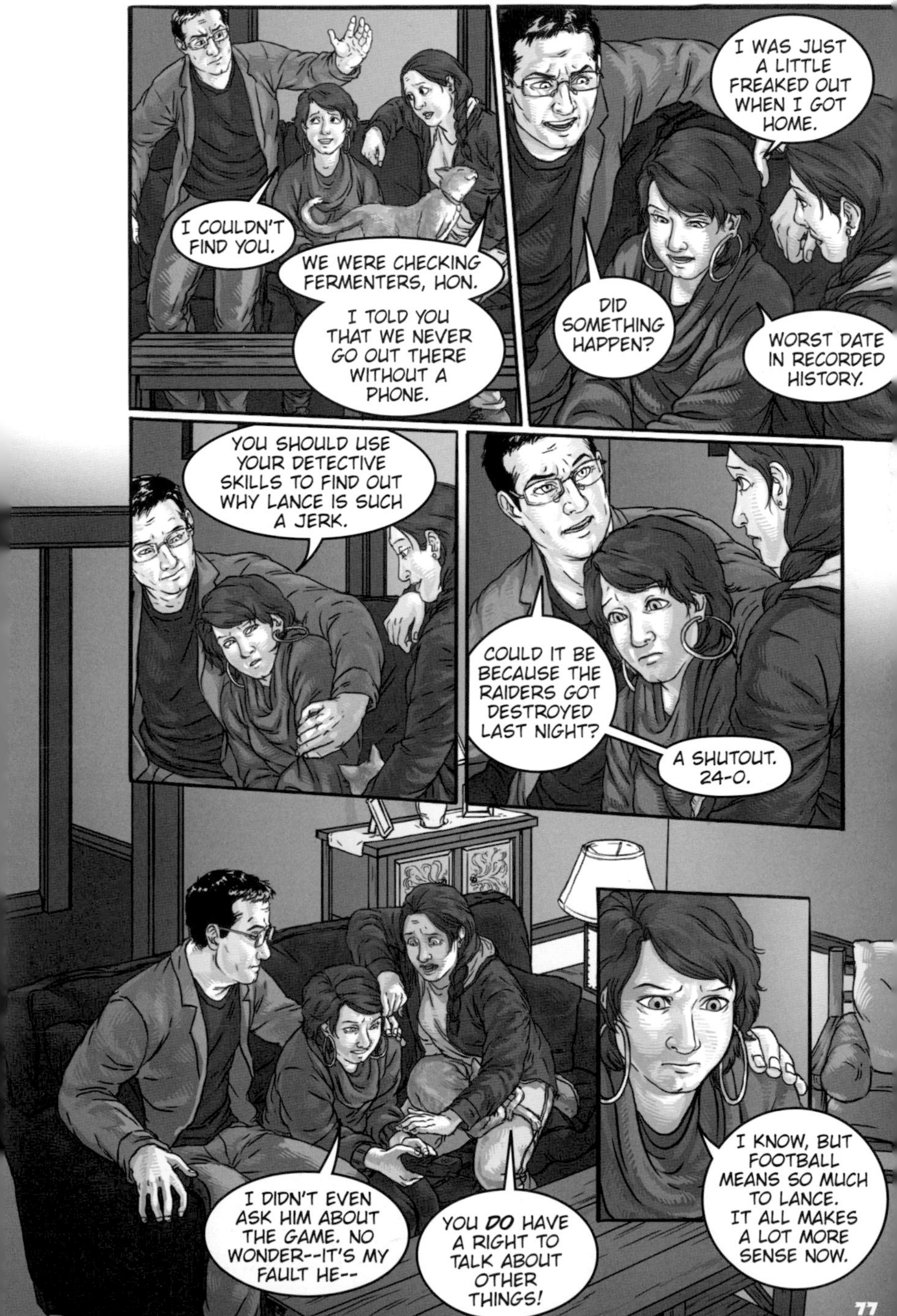

I COULDN'T FIND YOU.
WE WERE CHECKING FERMENTERS, HON.
I TOLD YOU THAT WE NEVER GO OUT THERE WITHOUT A PHONE.
I WAS JUST A LITTLE FREAKED OUT WHEN I GOT HOME.
DID SOMETHING HAPPEN?
WORST DATE IN RECORDED HISTORY.
YOU SHOULD USE YOUR DETECTIVE SKILLS TO FIND OUT WHY LANCE IS SUCH A JERK.
COULD IT BE BECAUSE THE RAIDERS GOT DESTROYED LAST NIGHT?
A SHUTOUT. 24-0.
I DIDN'T EVEN ASK HIM ABOUT THE GAME. NO WONDER--IT'S MY FAULT HE--
YOU *DO* HAVE A RIGHT TO TALK ABOUT OTHER THINGS!
I KNOW, BUT FOOTBALL MEANS SO MUCH TO LANCE. IT ALL MAKES A LOT MORE SENSE NOW.

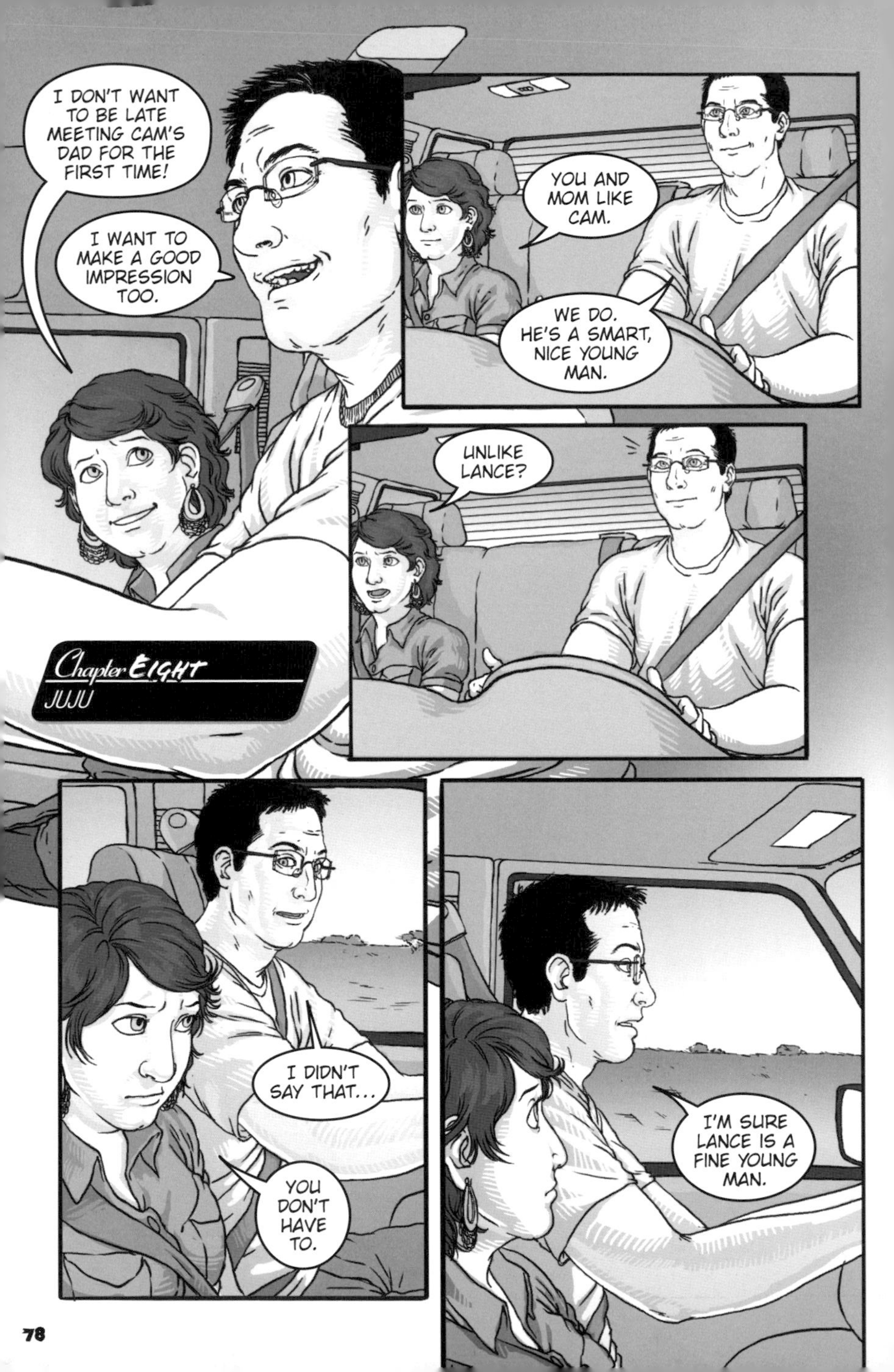
I DON'T WANT TO BE LATE MEETING CAM'S DAD FOR THE FIRST TIME!
I WANT TO MAKE A GOOD IMPRESSION TOO.
Chapter EIGHT
JUJU
YOU AND MOM LIKE CAM.
WE DO. HE'S A SMART, NICE YOUNG MAN.
UNLIKE LANCE?
I DIDN'T SAY THAT...
YOU DON'T HAVE TO.
I'M SURE LANCE IS A FINE YOUNG MAN.

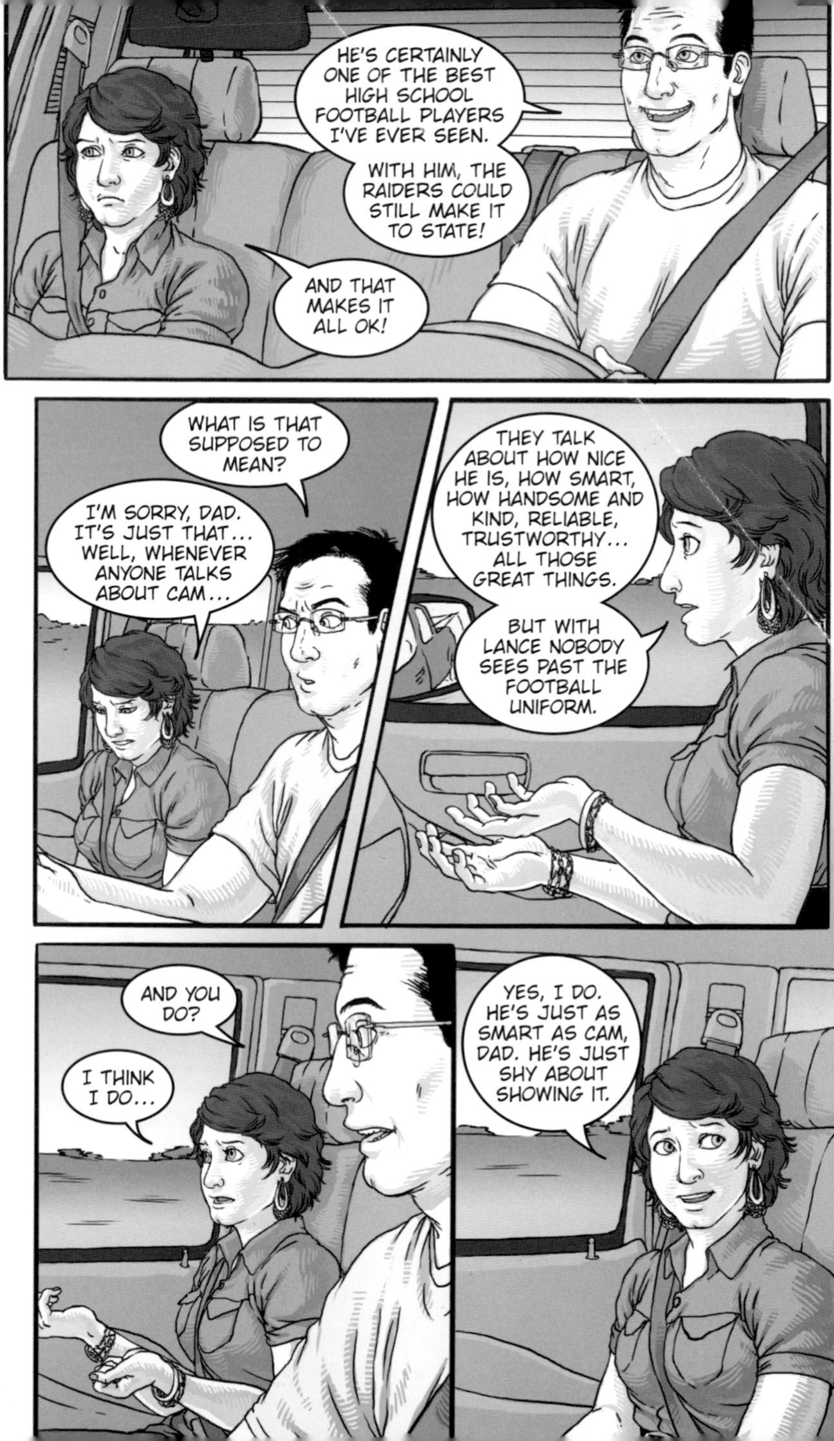
HE'S CERTAINLY ONE OF THE BEST HIGH SCHOOL FOOTBALL PLAYERS I'VE EVER SEEN.
WITH HIM, THE RAIDERS COULD STILL MAKE IT TO STATE!
AND THAT MAKES IT ALL OK!
WHAT IS THAT SUPPOSED TO MEAN?
I'M SORRY, DAD. IT'S JUST THAT... WELL, WHENEVER ANYONE TALKS ABOUT CAM...
THEY TALK ABOUT HOW NICE HE IS, HOW SMART, HOW HANDSOME AND KIND, RELIABLE, TRUSTWORTHY... ALL THOSE GREAT THINGS.
BUT WITH LANCE NOBODY SEES PAST THE FOOTBALL UNIFORM.
AND YOU DO?
I THINK I DO...
YES, I DO. HE'S JUST AS SMART AS CAM, DAD. HE'S JUST SHY ABOUT SHOWING IT.

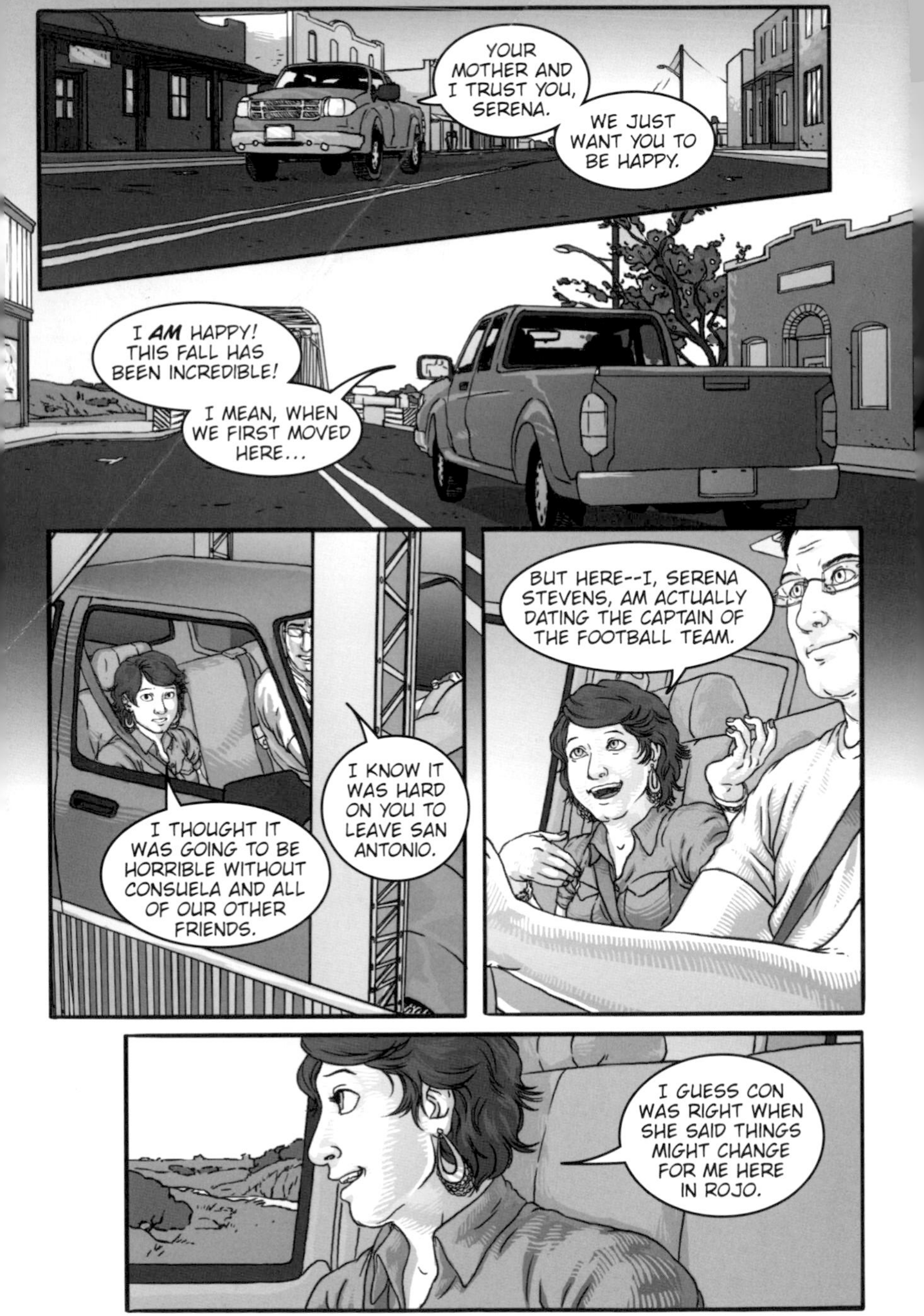
YOUR MOTHER AND I TRUST YOU, SERENA.
WE JUST WANT YOU TO BE HAPPY.
I **AM** HAPPY! THIS FALL HAS BEEN INCREDIBLE!
I MEAN, WHEN WE FIRST MOVED HERE...
I THOUGHT IT WAS GOING TO BE HORRIBLE WITHOUT CONSUELA AND ALL OF OUR OTHER FRIENDS.
I KNOW IT WAS HARD ON YOU TO LEAVE SAN ANTONIO.
BUT HERE--I, SERENA STEVENS, AM ACTUALLY DATING THE CAPTAIN OF THE FOOTBALL TEAM.
I GUESS CON WAS RIGHT WHEN SHE SAID THINGS MIGHT CHANGE FOR ME HERE IN ROJO.

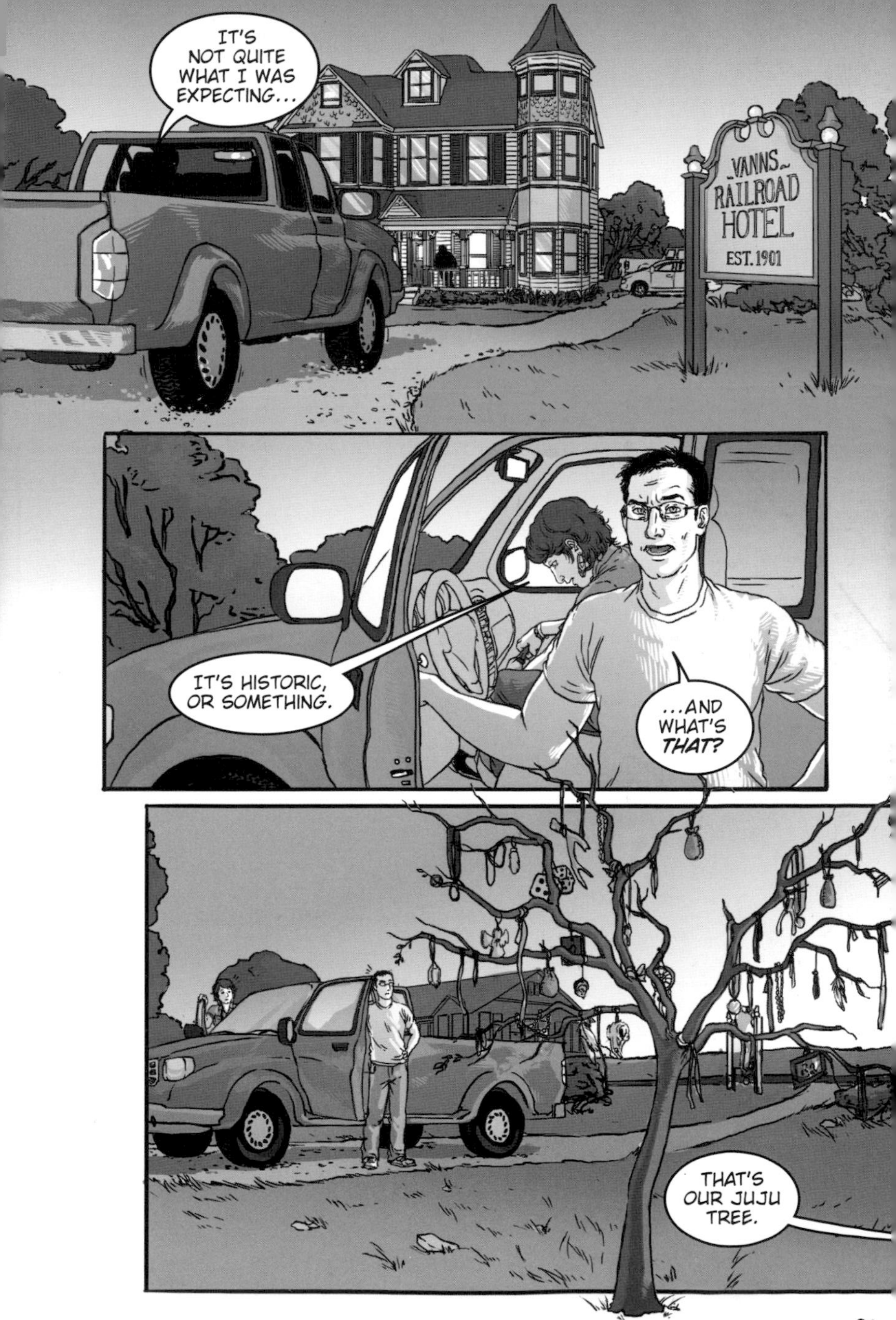
IT'S NOT QUITE WHAT I WAS EXPECTING...
VANNS RAILROAD HOTEL
EST. 1901
IT'S HISTORIC, OR SOMETHING.
...AND WHAT'S *THAT?*
THAT'S OUR JUJU TREE.

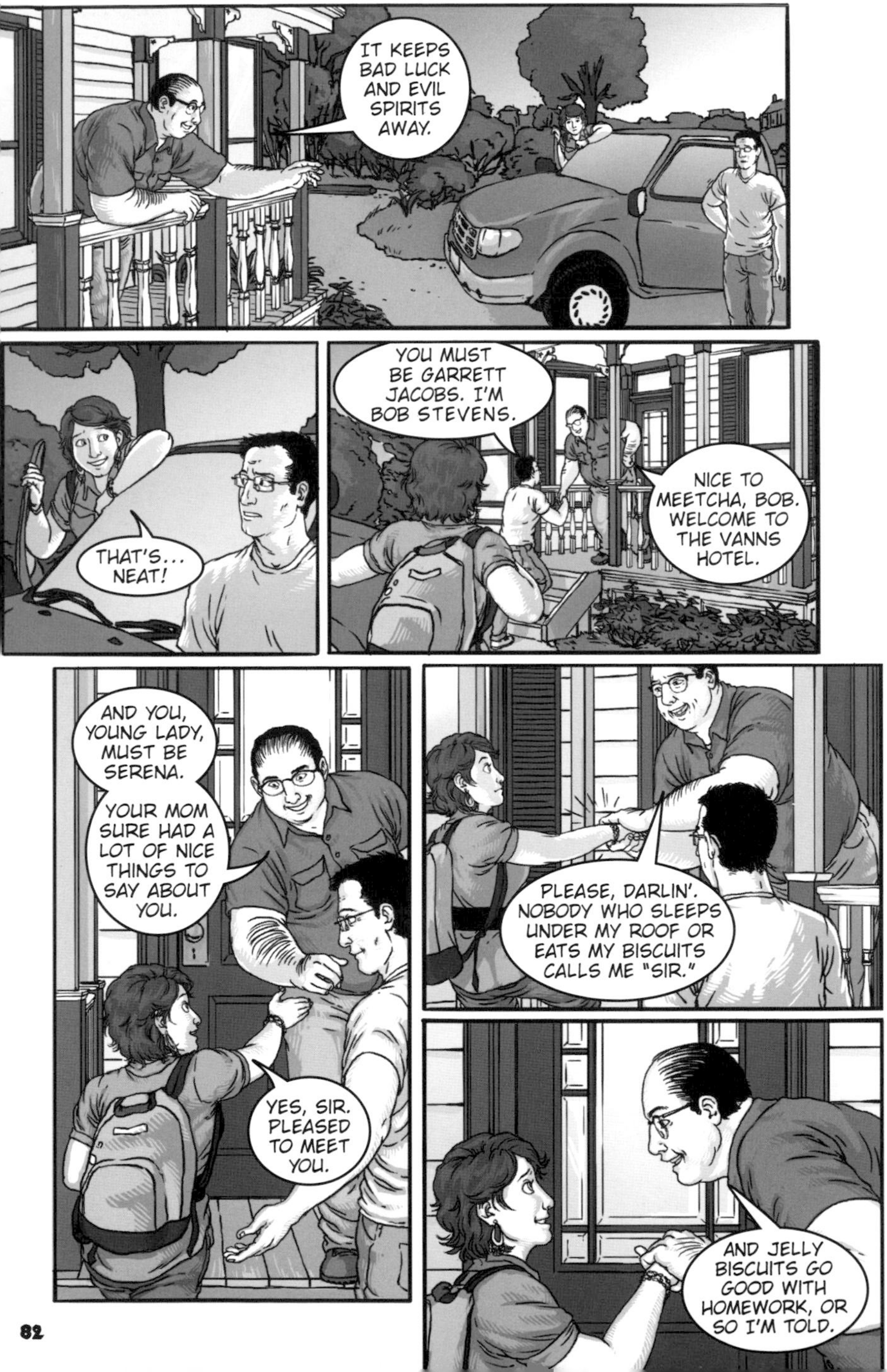
IT KEEPS BAD LUCK AND EVIL SPIRITS AWAY.
THAT'S... NEAT!
YOU MUST BE GARRETT JACOBS. I'M BOB STEVENS.
NICE TO MEETCHA, BOB. WELCOME TO THE VANNS HOTEL.
AND YOU, YOUNG LADY, MUST BE SERENA.
YOUR MOM SURE HAD A LOT OF NICE THINGS TO SAY ABOUT YOU.
YES, SIR. PLEASED TO MEET YOU.
PLEASE, DARLIN'. NOBODY WHO SLEEPS UNDER MY ROOF OR EATS MY BISCUITS CALLS ME "SIR."
AND JELLY BISCUITS GO GOOD WITH HOMEWORK, OR SO I'M TOLD.

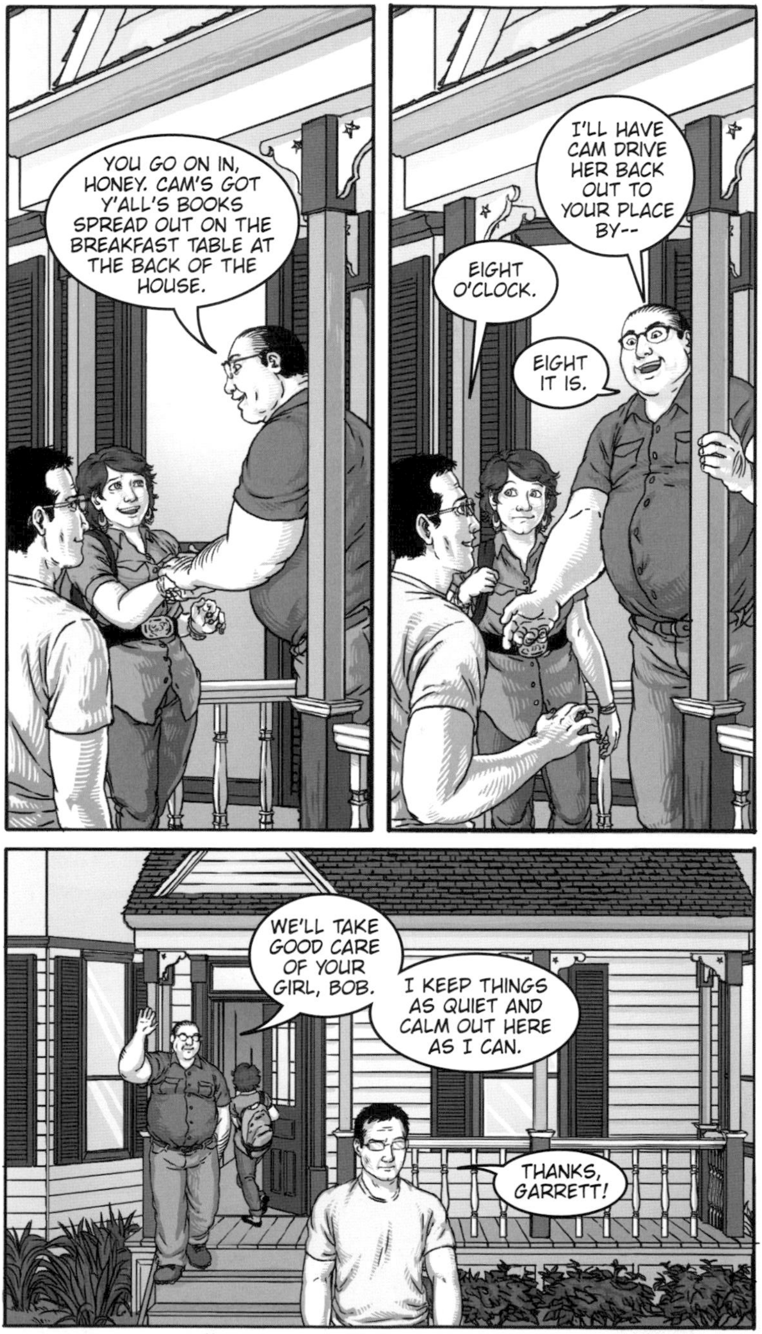
YOU GO ON IN, HONEY. CAM'S GOT Y'ALL'S BOOKS SPREAD OUT ON THE BREAKFAST TABLE AT THE BACK OF THE HOUSE.
I'LL HAVE CAM DRIVE HER BACK OUT TO YOUR PLACE BY--
EIGHT O'CLOCK.
EIGHT IT IS.
WE'LL TAKE GOOD CARE OF YOUR GIRL, BOB.
I KEEP THINGS AS QUIET AND CALM OUT HERE AS I CAN.
THANKS, GARRETT!

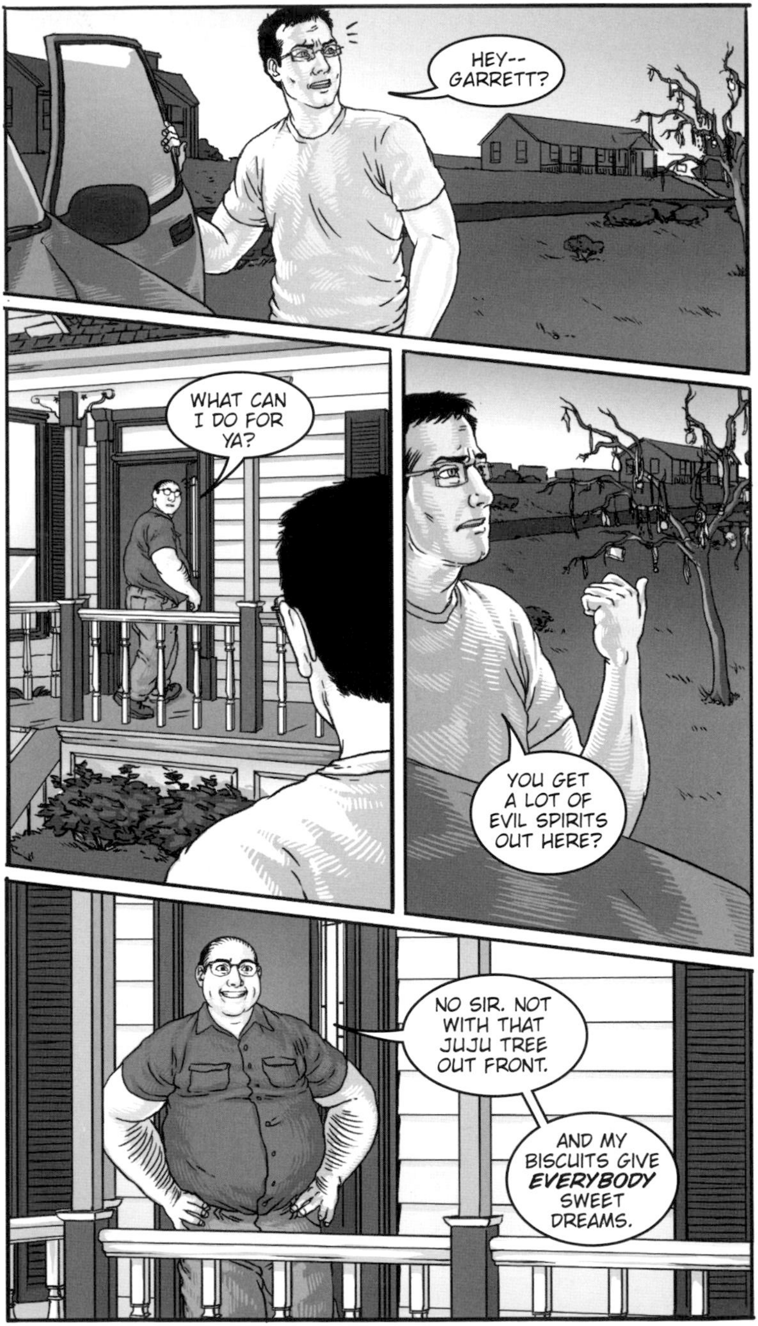
HEY--
GARRETT?
WHAT CAN I DO FOR YA?
YOU GET A LOT OF EVIL SPIRITS OUT HERE?
NO SIR. NOT WITH THAT JUJU TREE OUT FRONT.
AND MY BISCUITS GIVE *EVERYBODY* SWEET DREAMS.

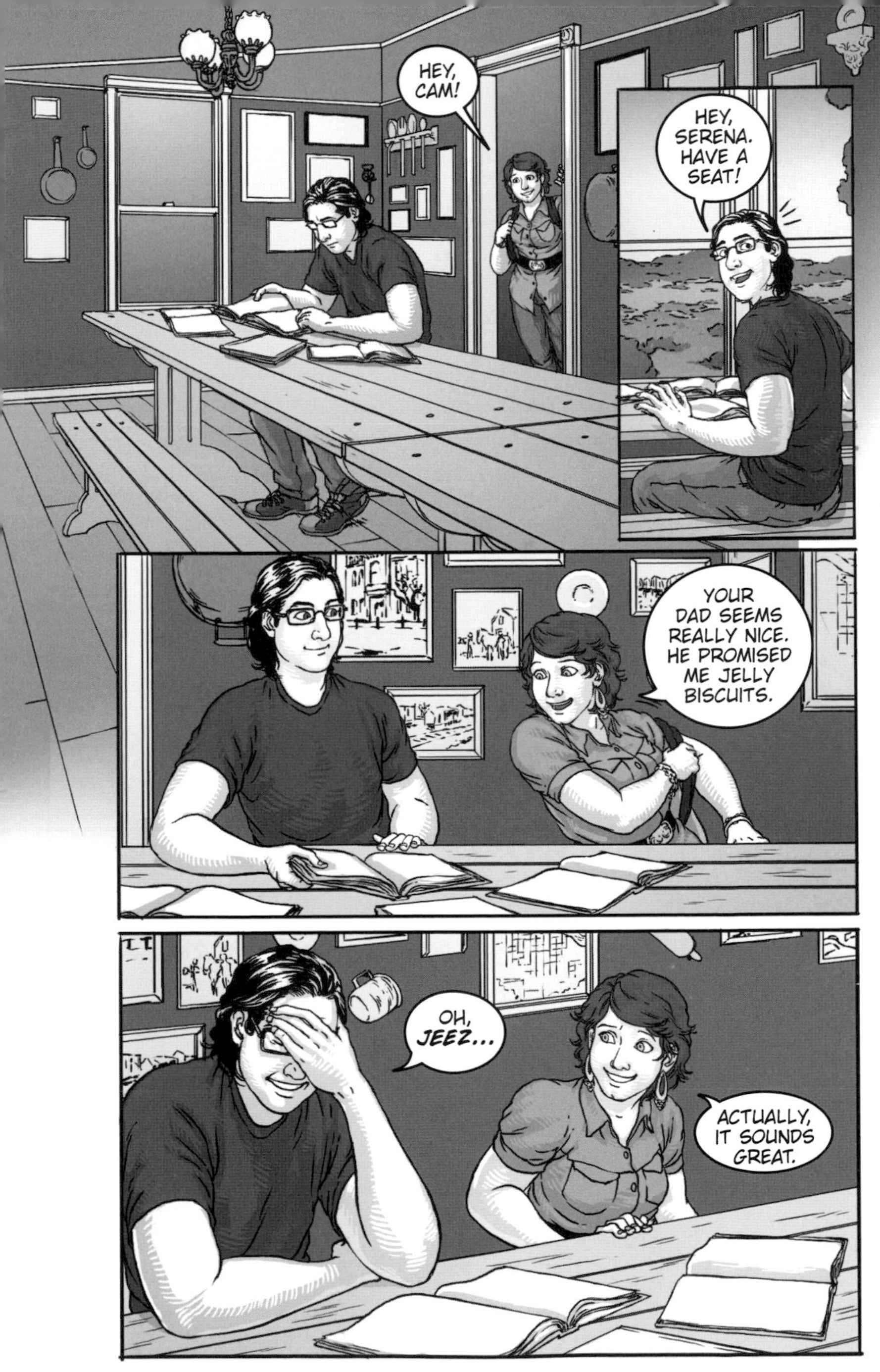
HEY, CAM!
HEY, SERENA. HAVE A SEAT!
YOUR DAD SEEMS REALLY NICE. HE PROMISED ME JELLY BISCUITS.
OH, JEEZ...
ACTUALLY, IT SOUNDS GREAT.

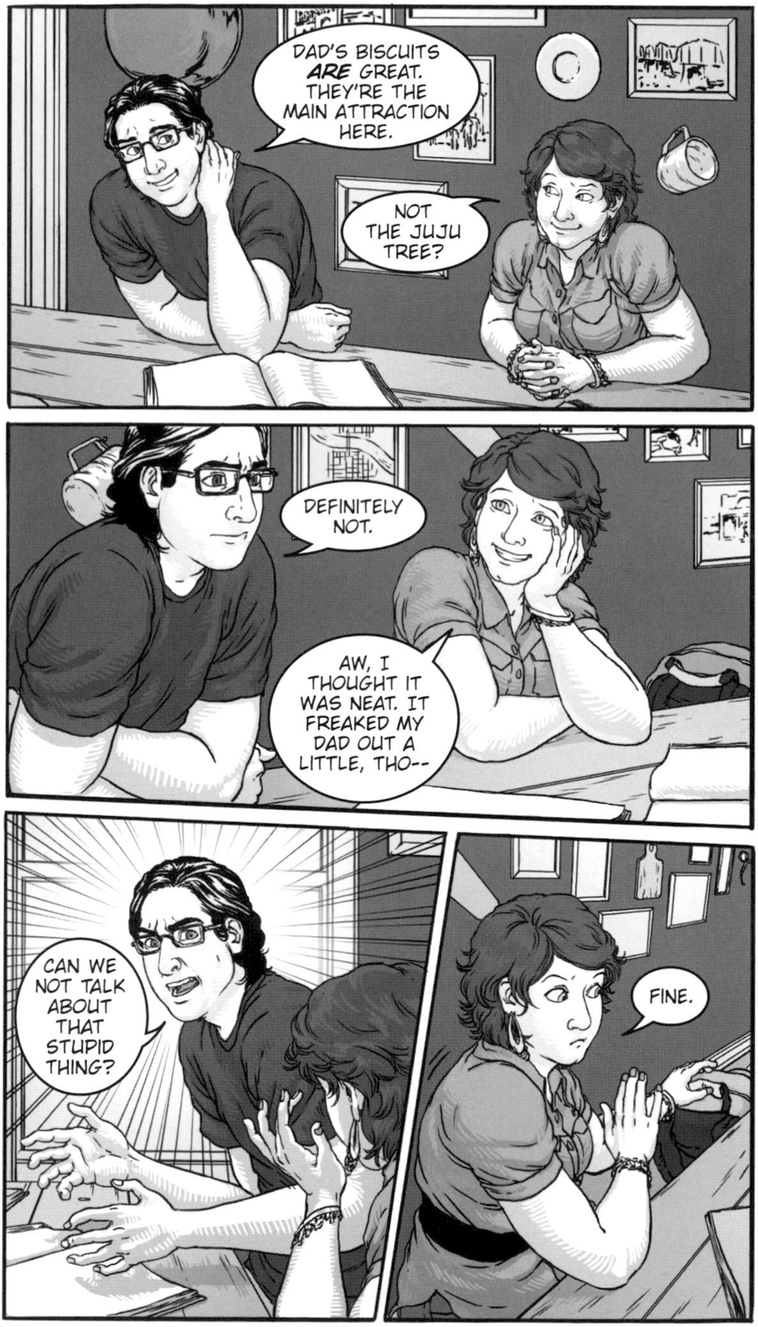
DAD'S BISCUITS *ARE* GREAT. THEY'RE THE MAIN ATTRACTION HERE.
NOT THE JUJU TREE?
DEFINITELY NOT.
AW, I THOUGHT IT WAS NEAT. IT FREAKED MY DAD OUT A LITTLE, THO--
CAN WE NOT TALK ABOUT THAT STUPID THING?
FINE.

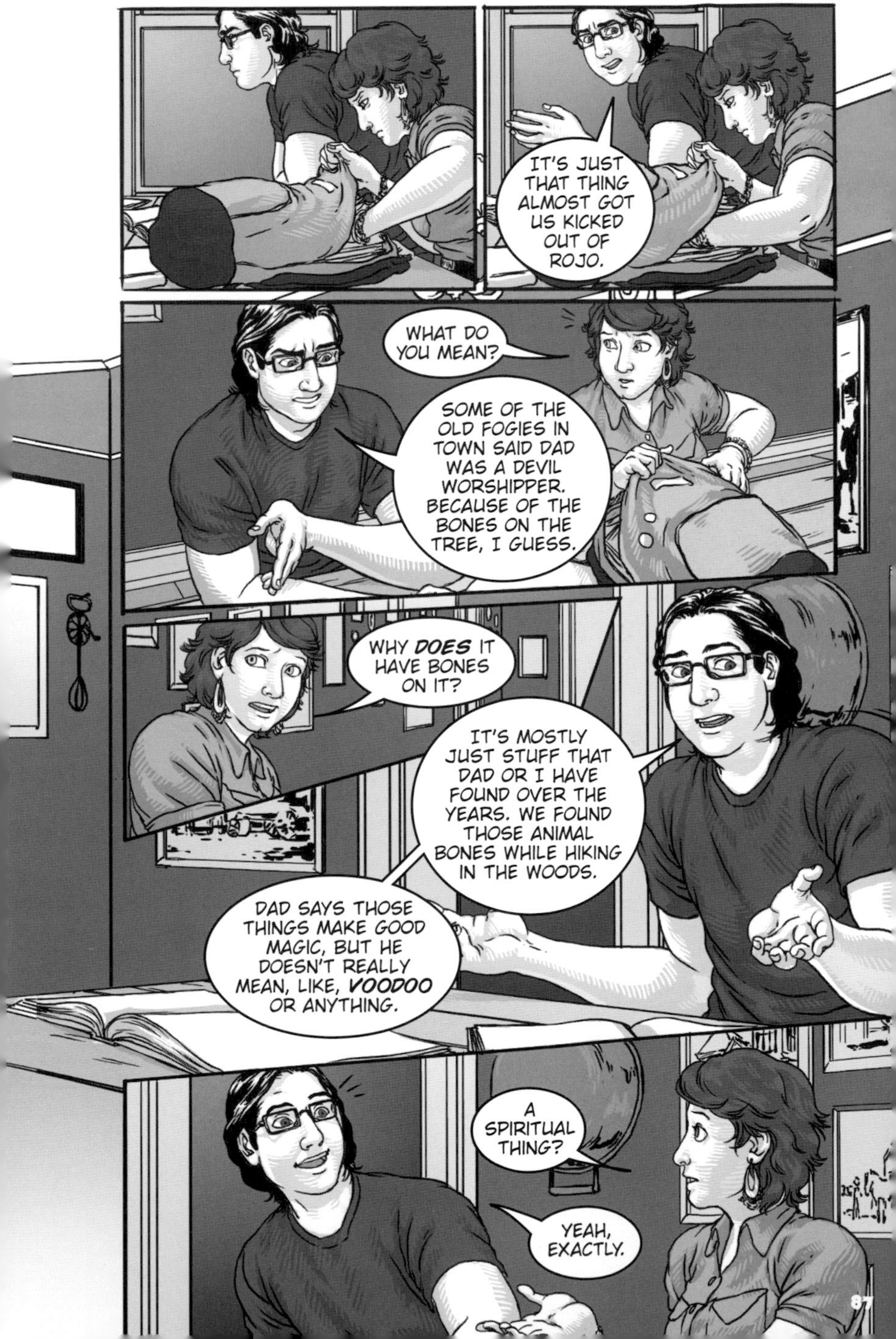
IT'S JUST THAT THING ALMOST GOT US KICKED OUT OF ROJO.
WHAT DO YOU MEAN?
SOME OF THE OLD FOGIES IN TOWN SAID DAD WAS A DEVIL WORSHIPPER. BECAUSE OF THE BONES ON THE TREE, I GUESS.
WHY *DOES* IT HAVE BONES ON IT?
IT'S MOSTLY JUST STUFF THAT DAD OR I HAVE FOUND OVER THE YEARS. WE FOUND THOSE ANIMAL BONES WHILE HIKING IN THE WOODS.
DAD SAYS THOSE THINGS MAKE GOOD MAGIC, BUT HE DOESN'T REALLY MEAN, LIKE, *VOODOO* OR ANYTHING.
A SPIRITUAL THING?
YEAH, EXACTLY.

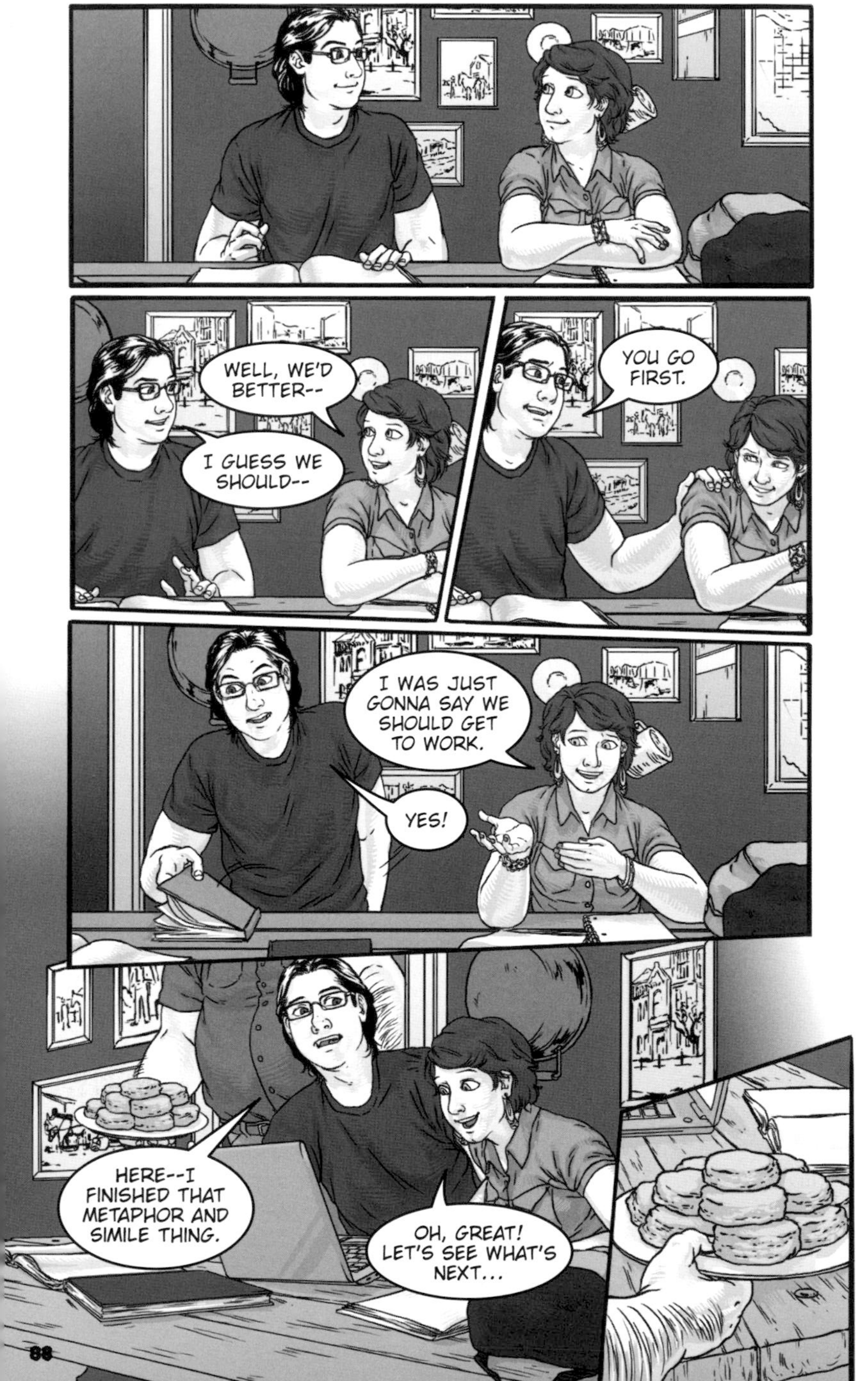
WELL, WE'D BETTER--
I GUESS WE SHOULD--
YOU GO FIRST.
I WAS JUST GONNA SAY WE SHOULD GET TO WORK.
YES!
HERE--I FINISHED THAT METAPHOR AND SIMILE THING.
OH, GREAT! LET'S SEE WHAT'S NEXT...

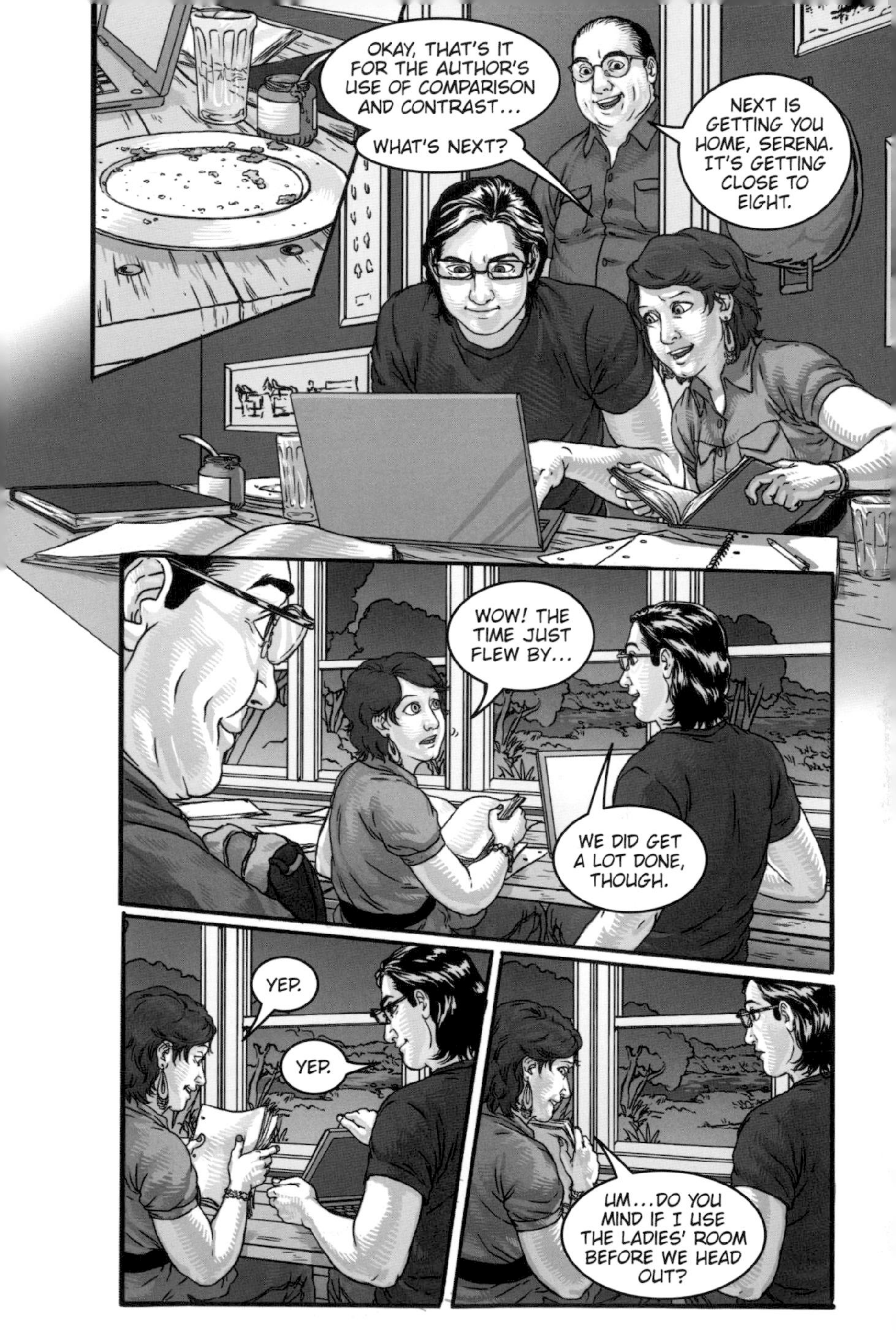

OKAY, THAT'S IT FOR THE AUTHOR'S USE OF COMPARISON AND CONTRAST...
WHAT'S NEXT?
NEXT IS GETTING YOU HOME, SERENA. IT'S GETTING CLOSE TO EIGHT.
WOW! THE TIME JUST FLEW BY...
WE DID GET A LOT DONE, THOUGH.
YEP.
YEP.
UM...DO YOU MIND IF I USE THE LADIES' ROOM BEFORE WE HEAD OUT?

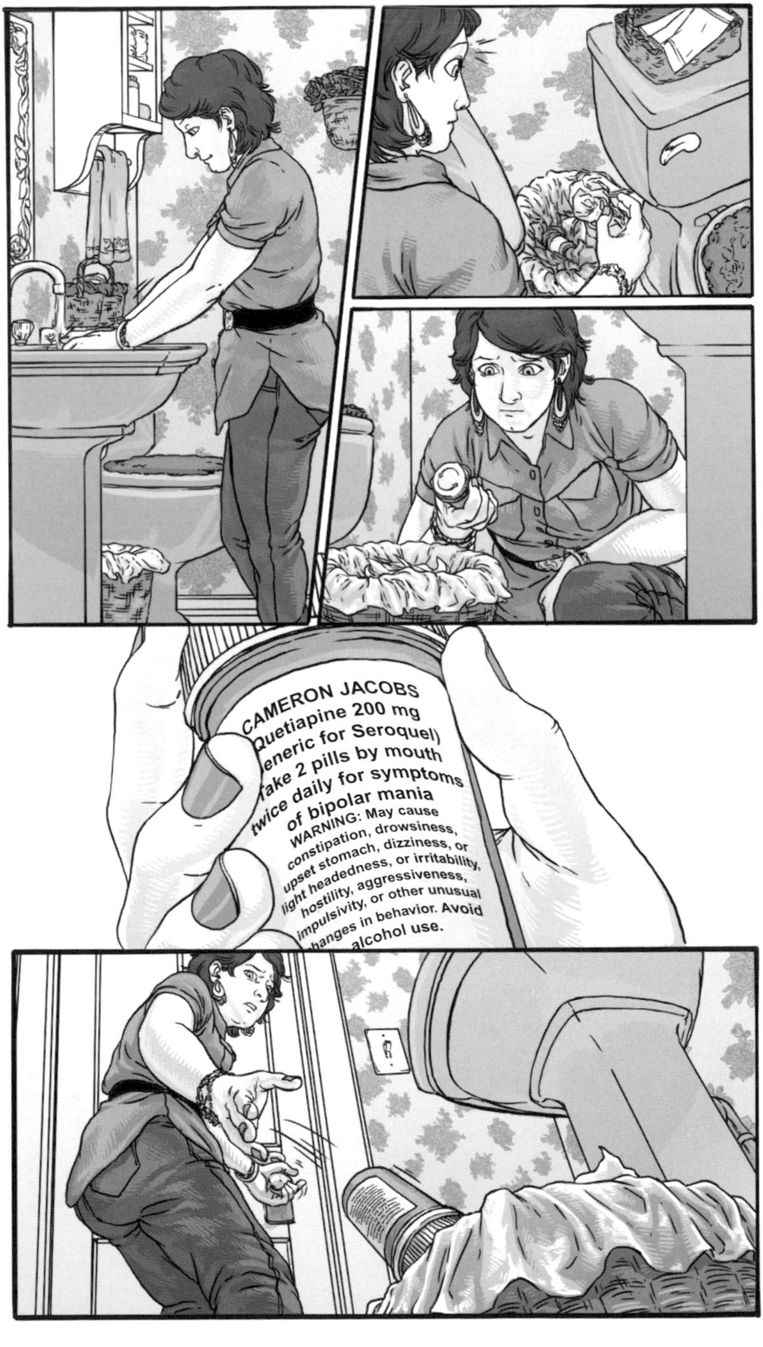
CAMERON JACOBS
Quetiapine 200 mg
eneric for Seroquel)
Take 2 pills by mouth
twice daily for symptoms
of bipolar mania
WARNING: May cause
constipation, drowsiness,
upset stomach, dizziness, or
light headedness, or irritability,
hostility, aggressiveness,
impulsivity, or other unusual
hanges in behavior. Avoid
alcohol use.

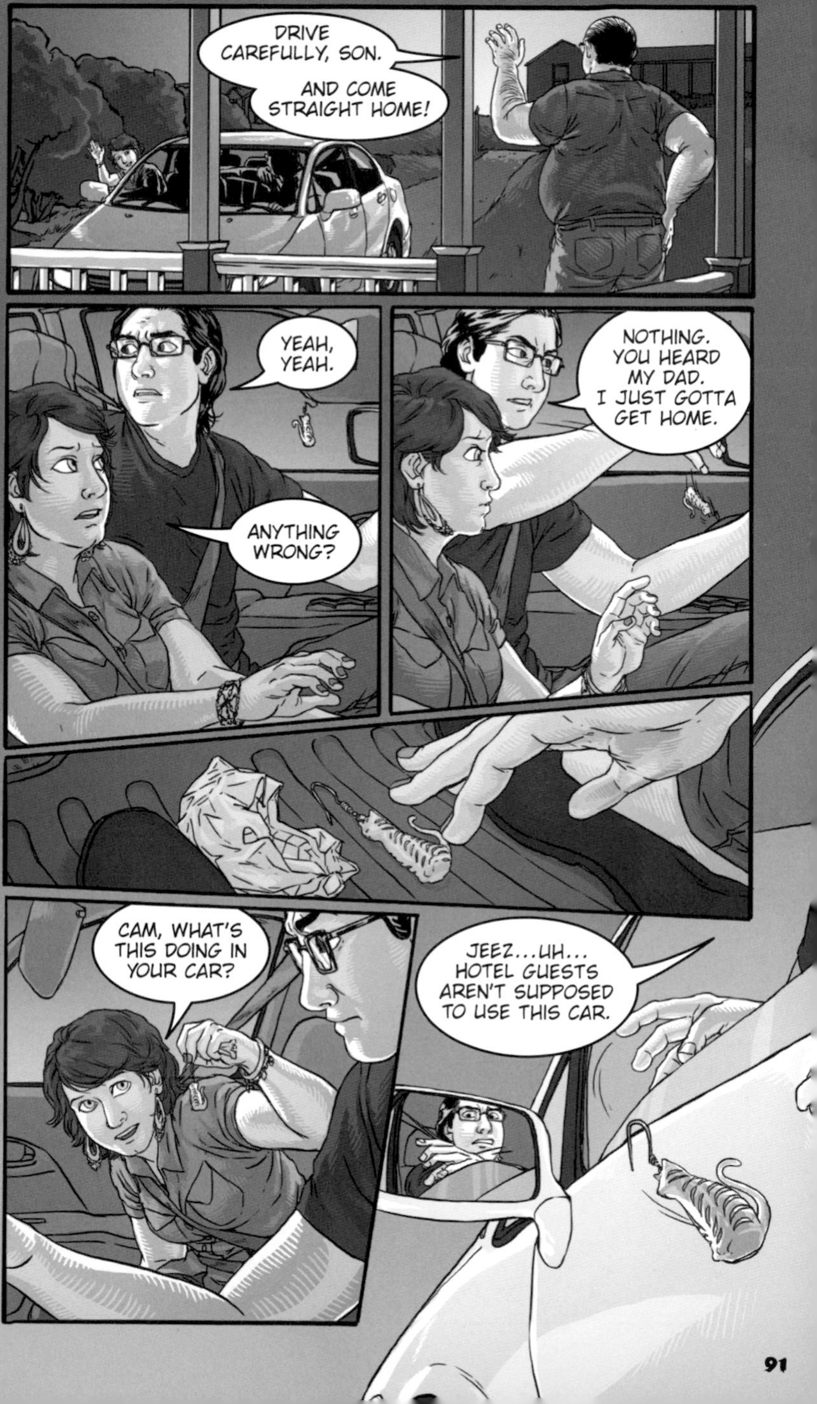
DRIVE CAREFULLY, SON.
AND COME STRAIGHT HOME!
YEAH, YEAH.
ANYTHING WRONG?
NOTHING. YOU HEARD MY DAD. I JUST GOTTA GET HOME.
CAM, WHAT'S THIS DOING IN YOUR CAR?
JEEZ...UH... HOTEL GUESTS AREN'T SUPPOSED TO USE THIS CAR.

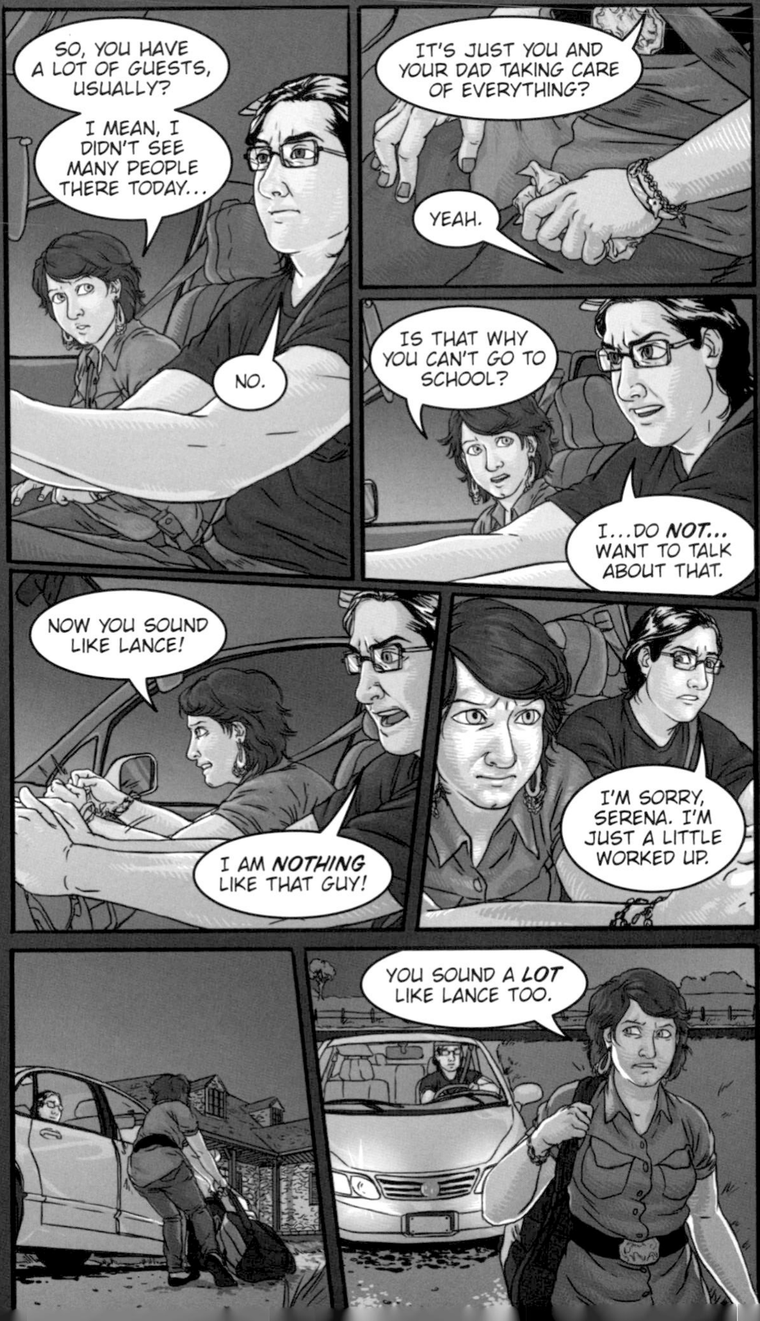
SO, YOU HAVE A LOT OF GUESTS, USUALLY?
I MEAN, I DIDN'T SEE MANY PEOPLE THERE TODAY...
NO.
IT'S JUST YOU AND YOUR DAD TAKING CARE OF EVERYTHING?
YEAH.
IS THAT WHY YOU CAN'T GO TO SCHOOL?
I...DO **NOT...** WANT TO TALK ABOUT THAT.
NOW YOU SOUND LIKE LANCE!
I AM **NOTHING** LIKE THAT GUY!
I'M SORRY, SERENA. I'M JUST A LITTLE WORKED UP.
YOU SOUND A **LOT** LIKE LANCE TOO.

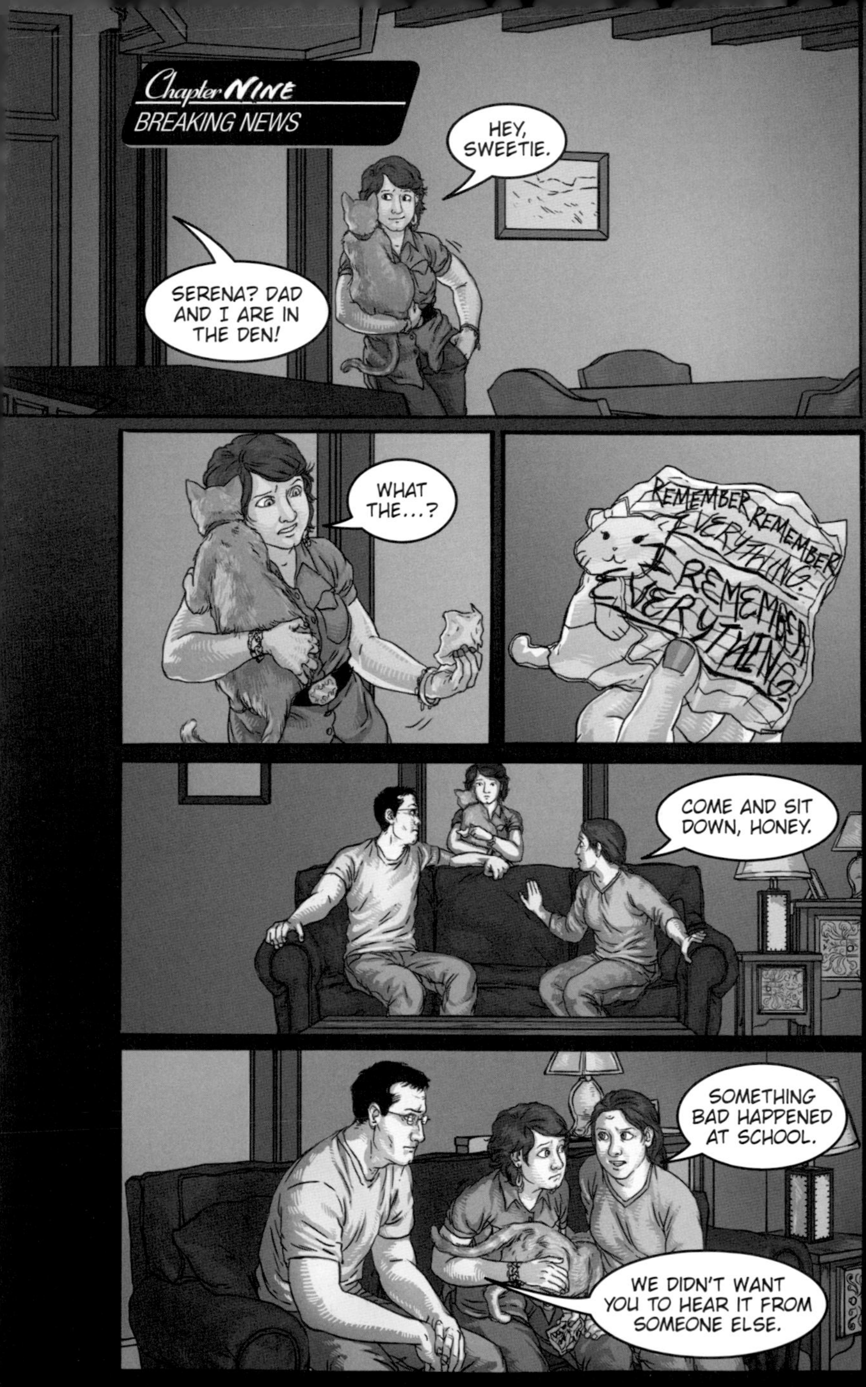
Chapter NINE
BREAKING NEWS
HEY, SWEETIE.
SERENA? DAD AND I ARE IN THE DEN!
WHAT THE...?
REMEMBER REMEMBER EVERYTHING. I REMEMBER EVERYTHING.
COME AND SIT DOWN, HONEY.
SOMETHING BAD HAPPENED AT SCHOOL.
WE DIDN'T WANT YOU TO HEAR IT FROM SOMEONE ELSE.

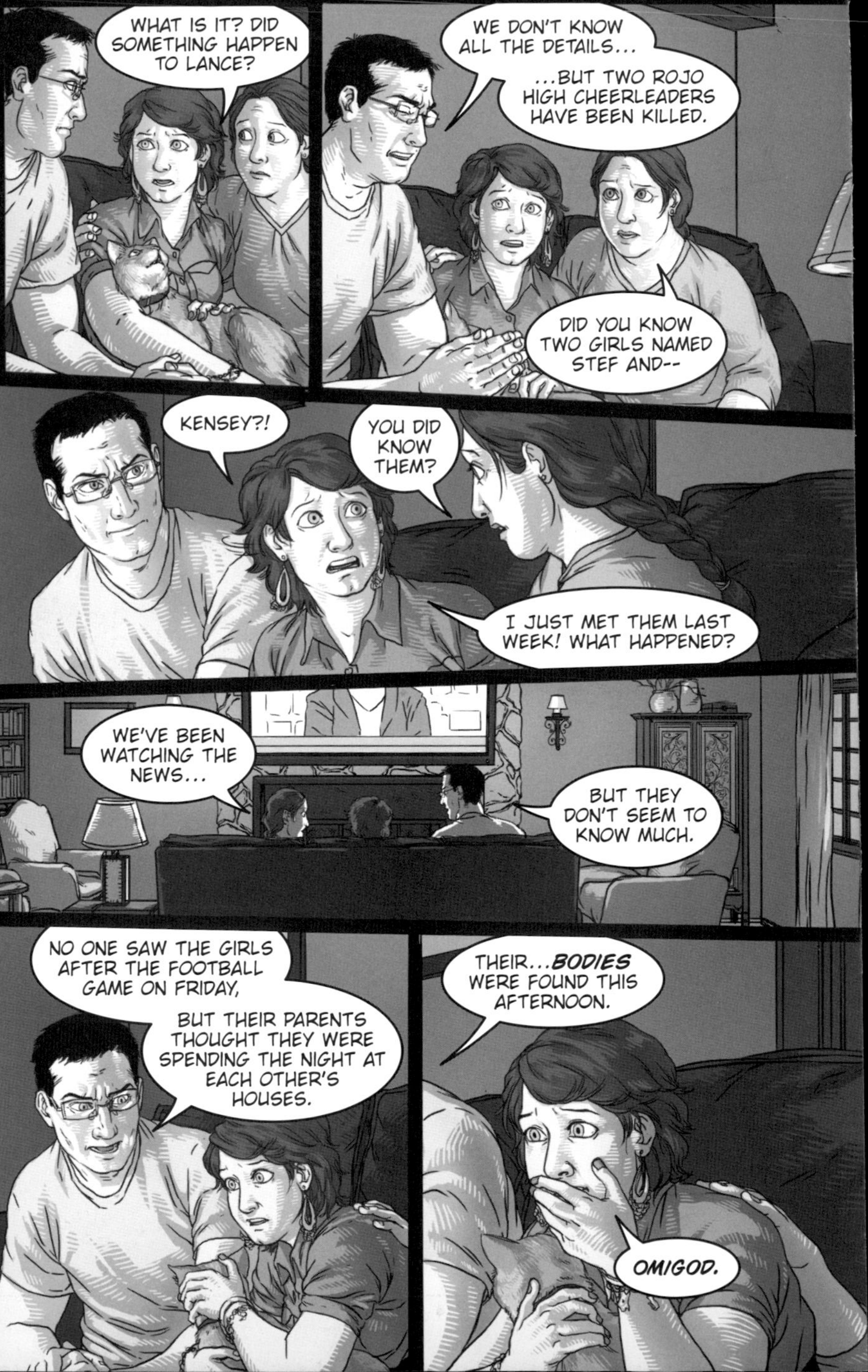
WHAT IS IT? DID SOMETHING HAPPEN TO LANCE?
WE DON'T KNOW ALL THE DETAILS...
...BUT TWO ROJO HIGH CHEERLEADERS HAVE BEEN KILLED.
DID YOU KNOW TWO GIRLS NAMED STEF AND--
KENSEY?!
YOU DID KNOW THEM?
I JUST MET THEM LAST WEEK! WHAT HAPPENED?
WE'VE BEEN WATCHING THE NEWS...
BUT THEY DON'T SEEM TO KNOW MUCH.
NO ONE SAW THE GIRLS AFTER THE FOOTBALL GAME ON FRIDAY,
BUT THEIR PARENTS THOUGHT THEY WERE SPENDING THE NIGHT AT EACH OTHER'S HOUSES.
THEIR...BODIES WERE FOUND THIS AFTERNOON.
OMIGOD.

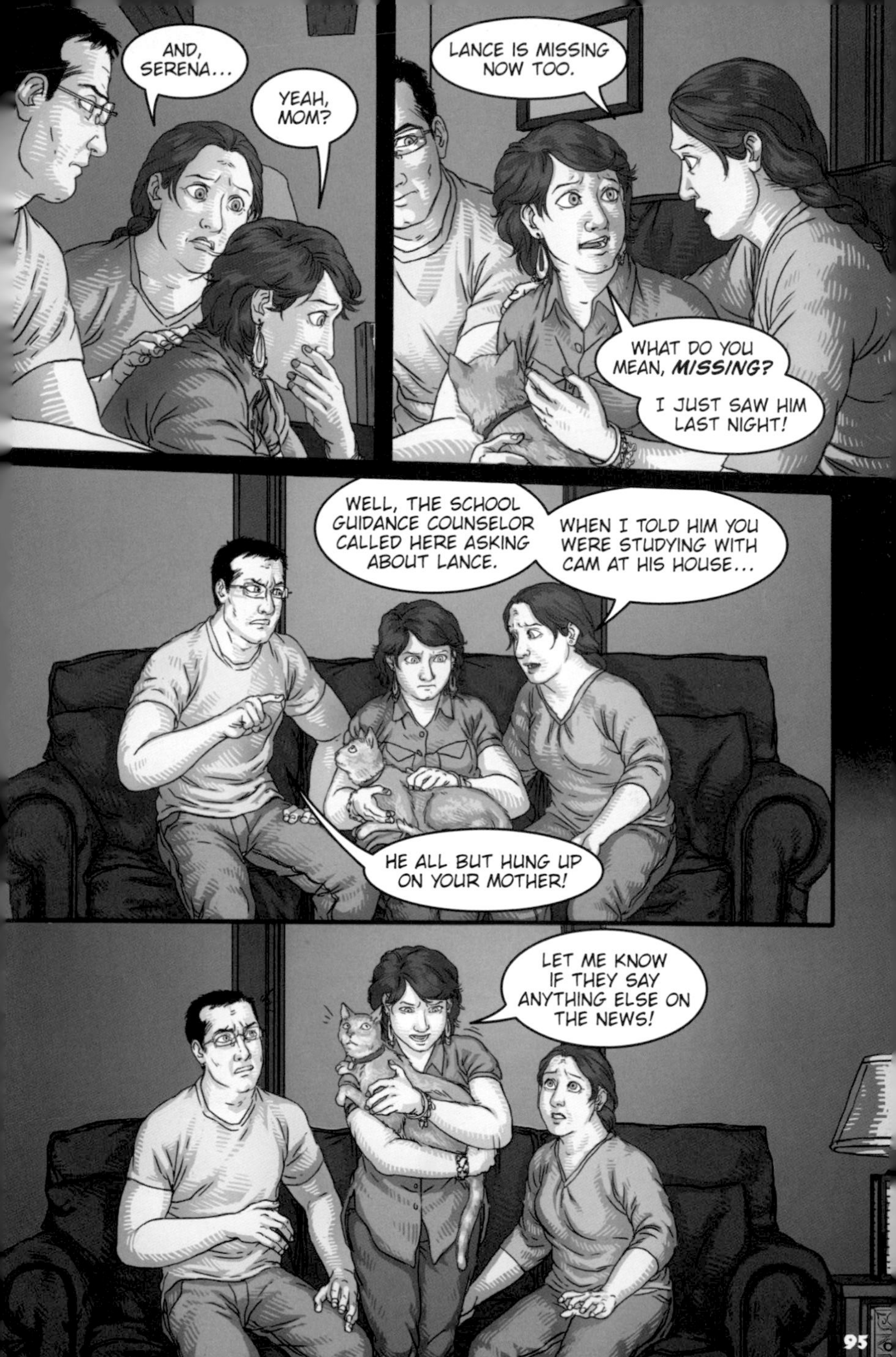
AND, SERENA...
YEAH, MOM?
LANCE IS MISSING NOW TOO.
WHAT DO YOU MEAN, ***MISSING?***
I JUST SAW HIM LAST NIGHT!
WELL, THE SCHOOL GUIDANCE COUNSELOR CALLED HERE ASKING ABOUT LANCE.
WHEN I TOLD HIM YOU WERE STUDYING WITH CAM AT HIS HOUSE...
HE ALL BUT HUNG UP ON YOUR MOTHER!
LET ME KNOW IF THEY SAY ANYTHING ELSE ON THE NEWS!

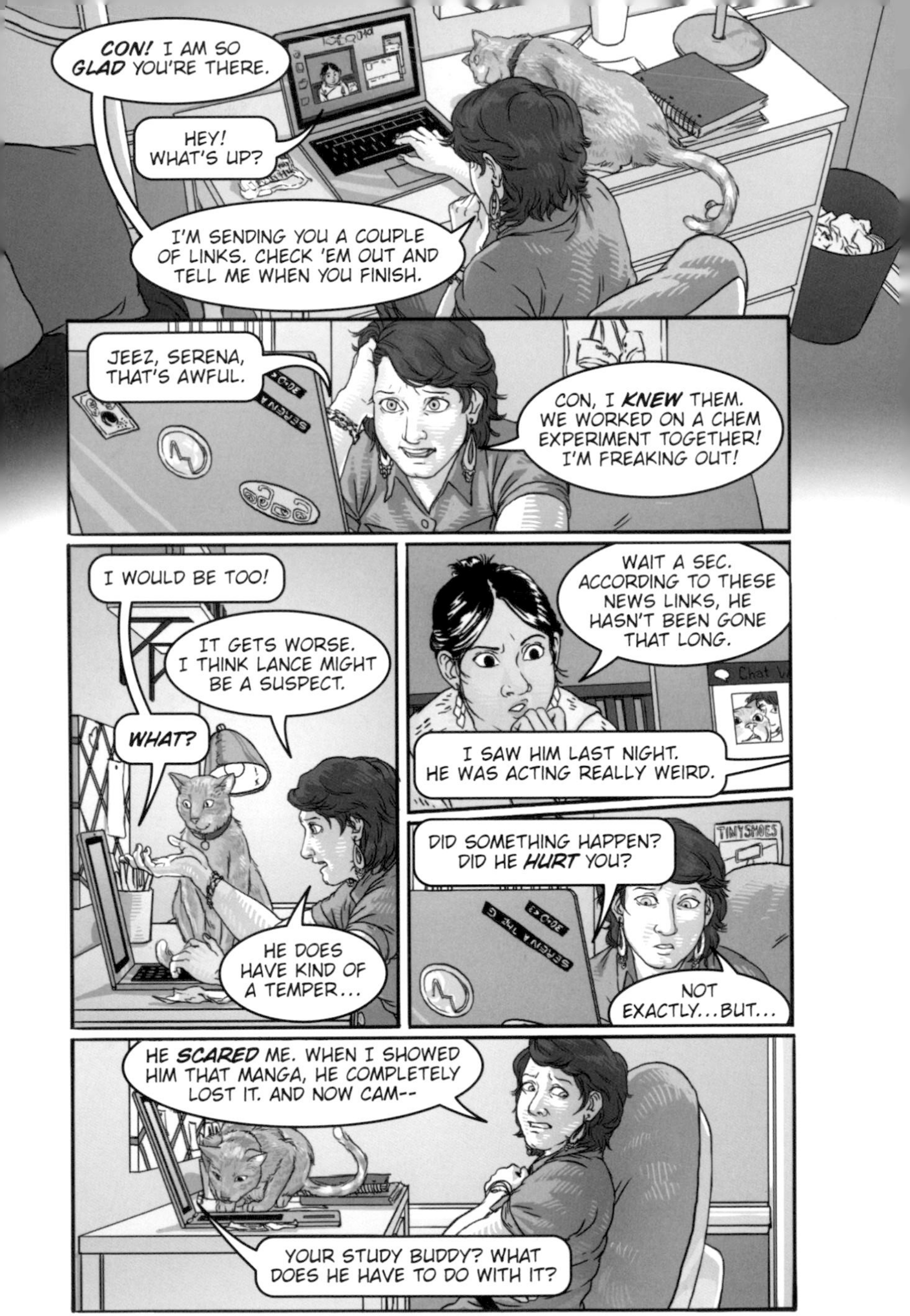
CON! I AM SO GLAD YOU'RE THERE.
HEY! WHAT'S UP?
I'M SENDING YOU A COUPLE OF LINKS. CHECK 'EM OUT AND TELL ME WHEN YOU FINISH.
JEEZ, SERENA, THAT'S AWFUL.
CON, I KNEW THEM. WE WORKED ON A CHEM EXPERIMENT TOGETHER! I'M FREAKING OUT!
I WOULD BE TOO!
IT GETS WORSE. I THINK LANCE MIGHT BE A SUSPECT.
WHAT?
HE DOES HAVE KIND OF A TEMPER...
WAIT A SEC. ACCORDING TO THESE NEWS LINKS, HE HASN'T BEEN GONE THAT LONG.
I SAW HIM LAST NIGHT. HE WAS ACTING REALLY WEIRD.
DID SOMETHING HAPPEN? DID HE HURT YOU?
NOT EXACTLY...BUT...
HE SCARED ME. WHEN I SHOWED HIM THAT MANGA, HE COMPLETELY LOST IT. AND NOW CAM--
YOUR STUDY BUDDY? WHAT DOES HE HAVE TO DO WITH IT?

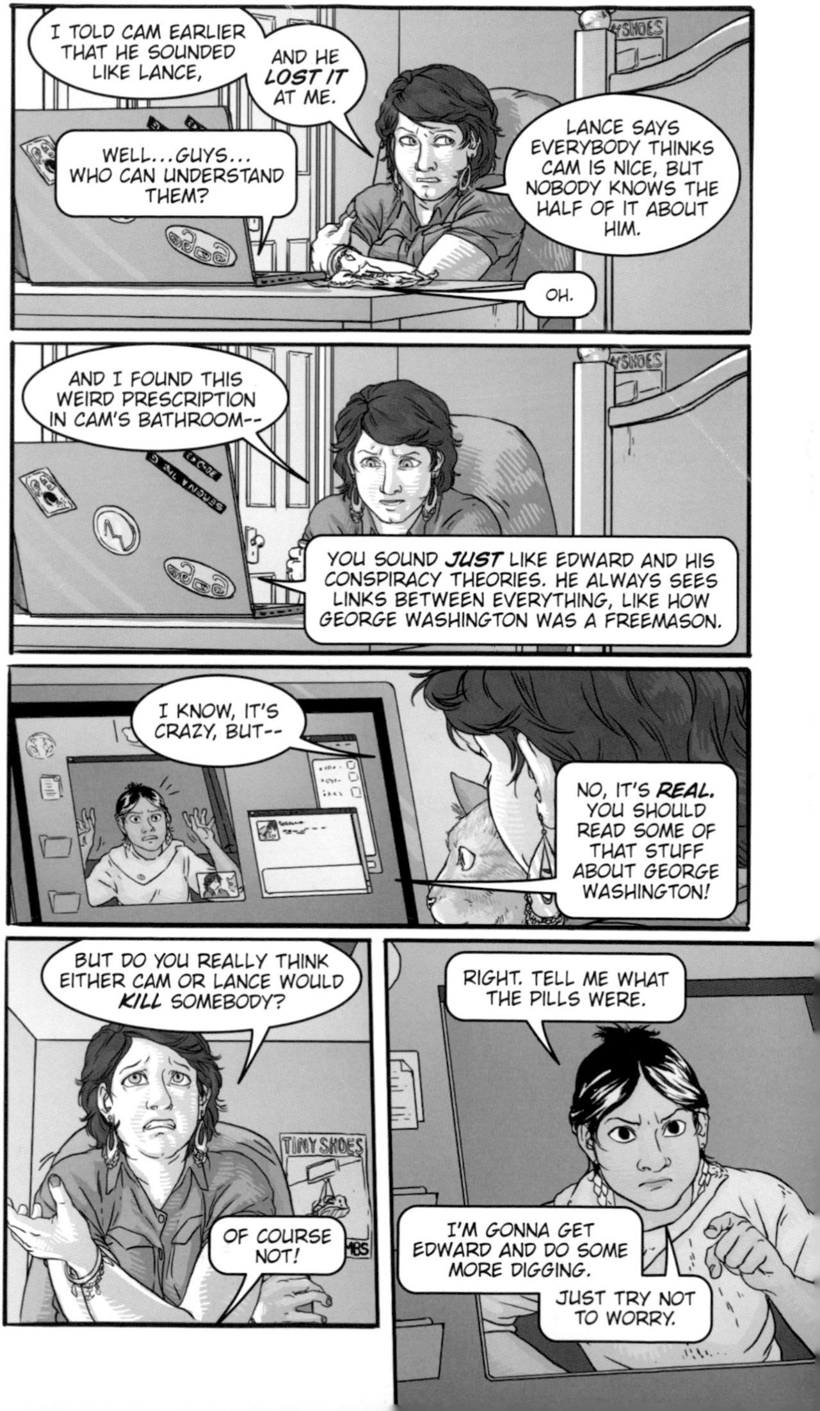
I TOLD CAM EARLIER THAT HE SOUNDED LIKE LANCE,
AND HE *LOST IT* AT ME.
WELL...GUYS... WHO CAN UNDERSTAND THEM?
LANCE SAYS EVERYBODY THINKS CAM IS NICE, BUT NOBODY KNOWS THE HALF OF IT ABOUT HIM.
OH.
AND I FOUND THIS WEIRD PRESCRIPTION IN CAM'S BATHROOM--
YOU SOUND *JUST* LIKE EDWARD AND HIS CONSPIRACY THEORIES. HE ALWAYS SEES LINKS BETWEEN EVERYTHING, LIKE HOW GEORGE WASHINGTON WAS A FREEMASON.
I KNOW, IT'S CRAZY, BUT--
NO, IT'S *REAL.* YOU SHOULD READ SOME OF THAT STUFF ABOUT GEORGE WASHINGTON!
BUT DO YOU REALLY THINK EITHER CAM OR LANCE WOULD *KILL* SOMEBODY?
OF COURSE NOT!
TINY SHOES
RIGHT. TELL ME WHAT THE PILLS WERE.
I'M GONNA GET EDWARD AND DO SOME MORE DIGGING.
JUST TRY NOT TO WORRY.

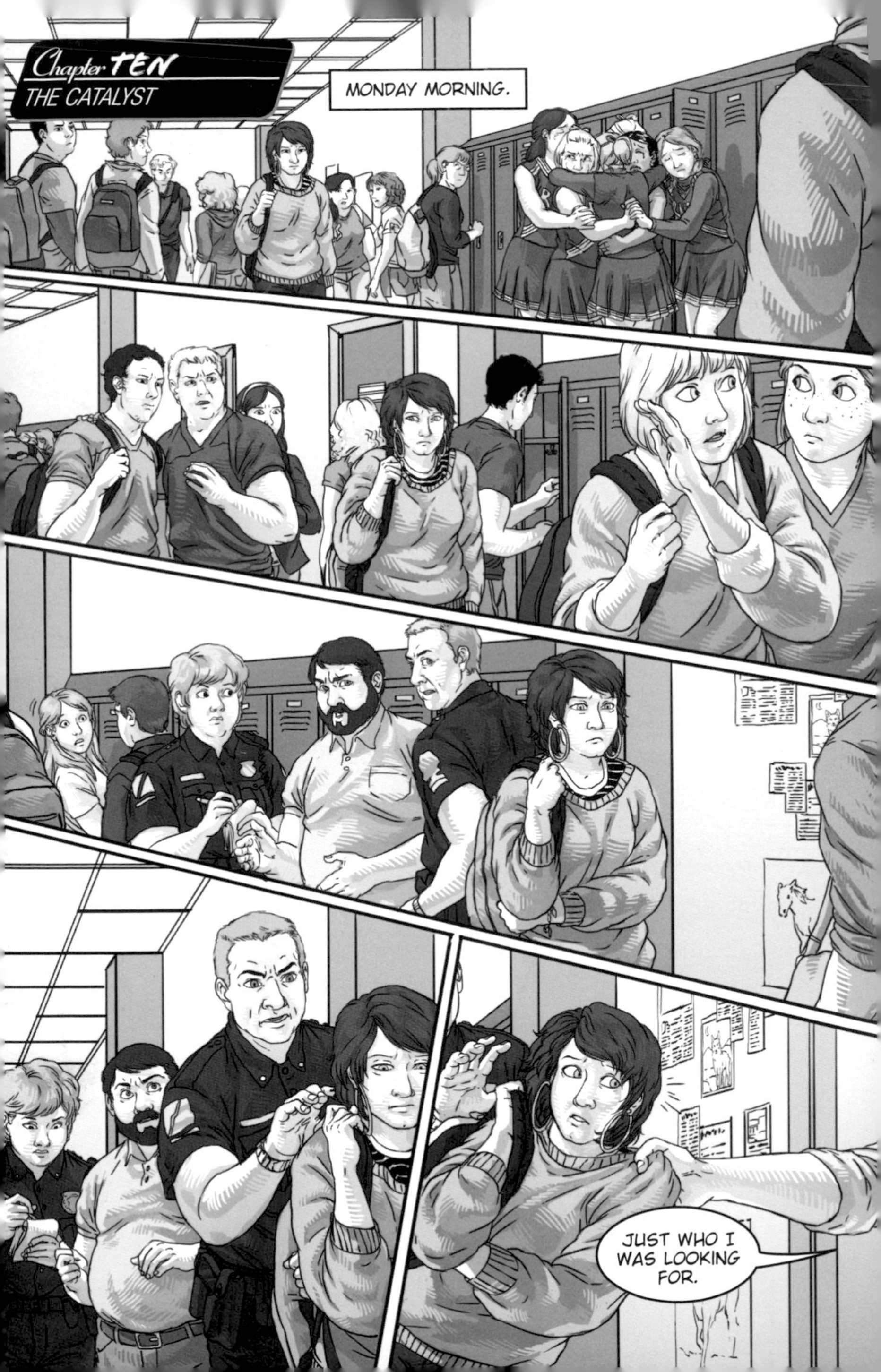
Chapter TEN
THE CATALYST
MONDAY MORNING.
JUST WHO I WAS LOOKING FOR.

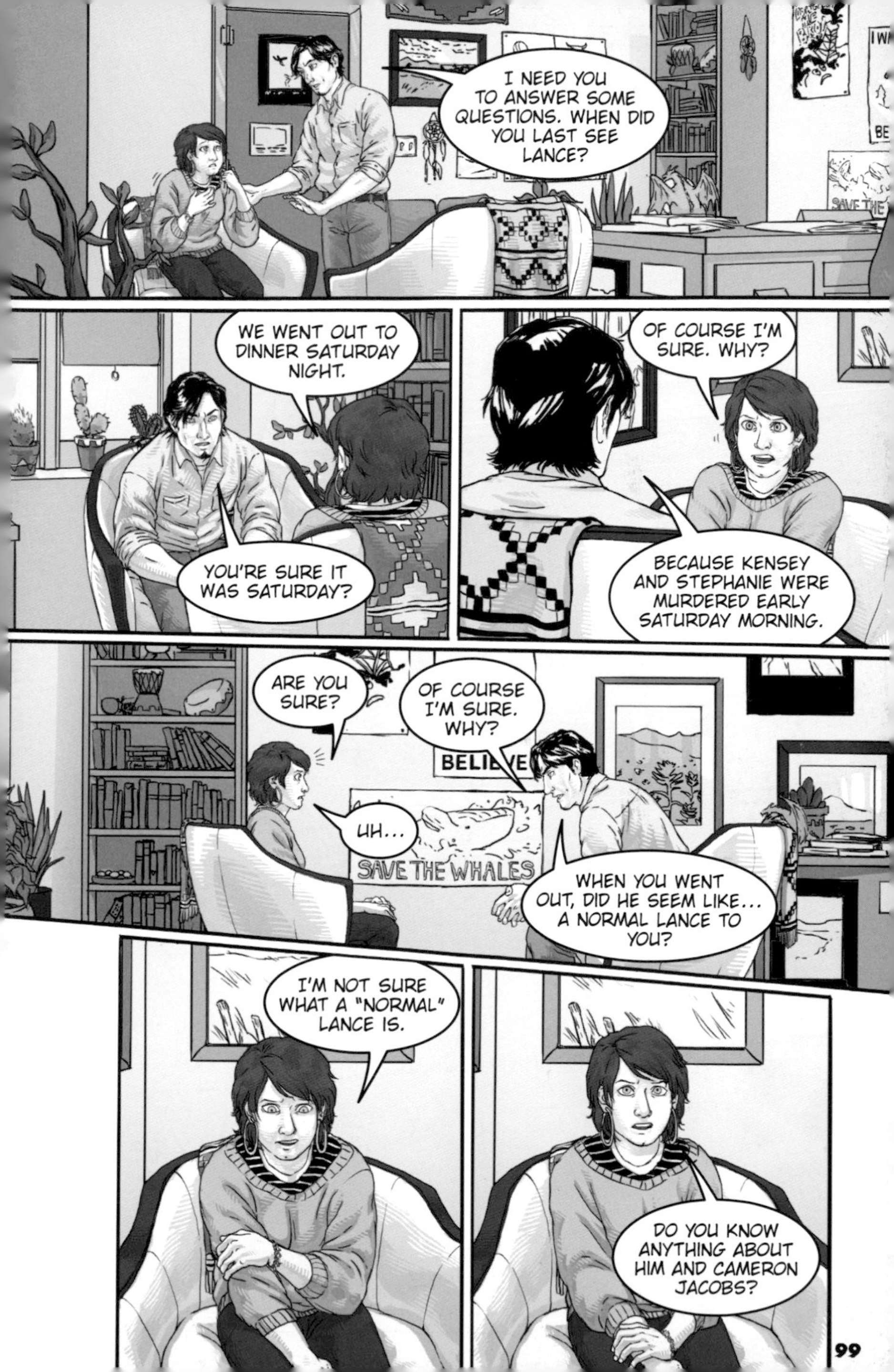
I NEED YOU TO ANSWER SOME QUESTIONS. WHEN DID YOU LAST SEE LANCE?
WE WENT OUT TO DINNER SATURDAY NIGHT.
YOU'RE SURE IT WAS SATURDAY?
OF COURSE I'M SURE. WHY?
BECAUSE KENSEY AND STEPHANIE WERE MURDERED EARLY SATURDAY MORNING.
ARE YOU SURE?
OF COURSE I'M SURE. WHY?
UH...
SAVE THE WHALES
WHEN YOU WENT OUT, DID HE SEEM LIKE... A NORMAL LANCE TO YOU?
I'M NOT SURE WHAT A "NORMAL" LANCE IS.
DO YOU KNOW ANYTHING ABOUT HIM AND CAMERON JACOBS?

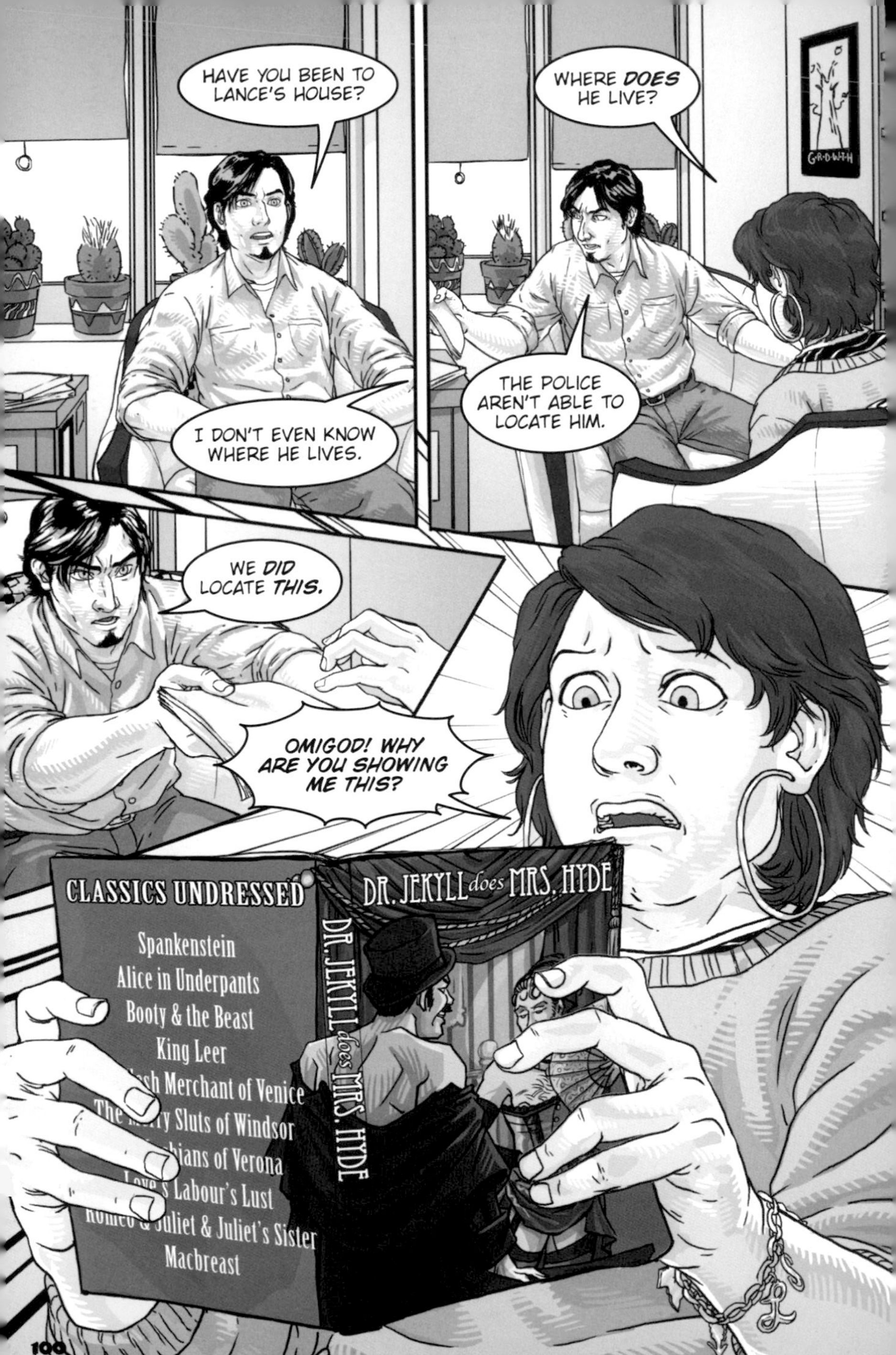
HAVE YOU BEEN TO LANCE'S HOUSE?
I DON'T EVEN KNOW WHERE HE LIVES.
WHERE DOES HE LIVE?
THE POLICE AREN'T ABLE TO LOCATE HIM.
WE DID LOCATE THIS.
OMIGOD! WHY ARE YOU SHOWING ME THIS?
CLASSICS UNDRESSED
Spankenstein
Alice in Underpants
Booty & the Beast
King Leer
Merchant of Venice
Sluts of Windsor
of Verona
Labour's Lust
Juliet & Juliet's Sister
Macbreast
DR. JEKYLL does MRS. HYDE
DR. JEKYLL does MRS. HYDE

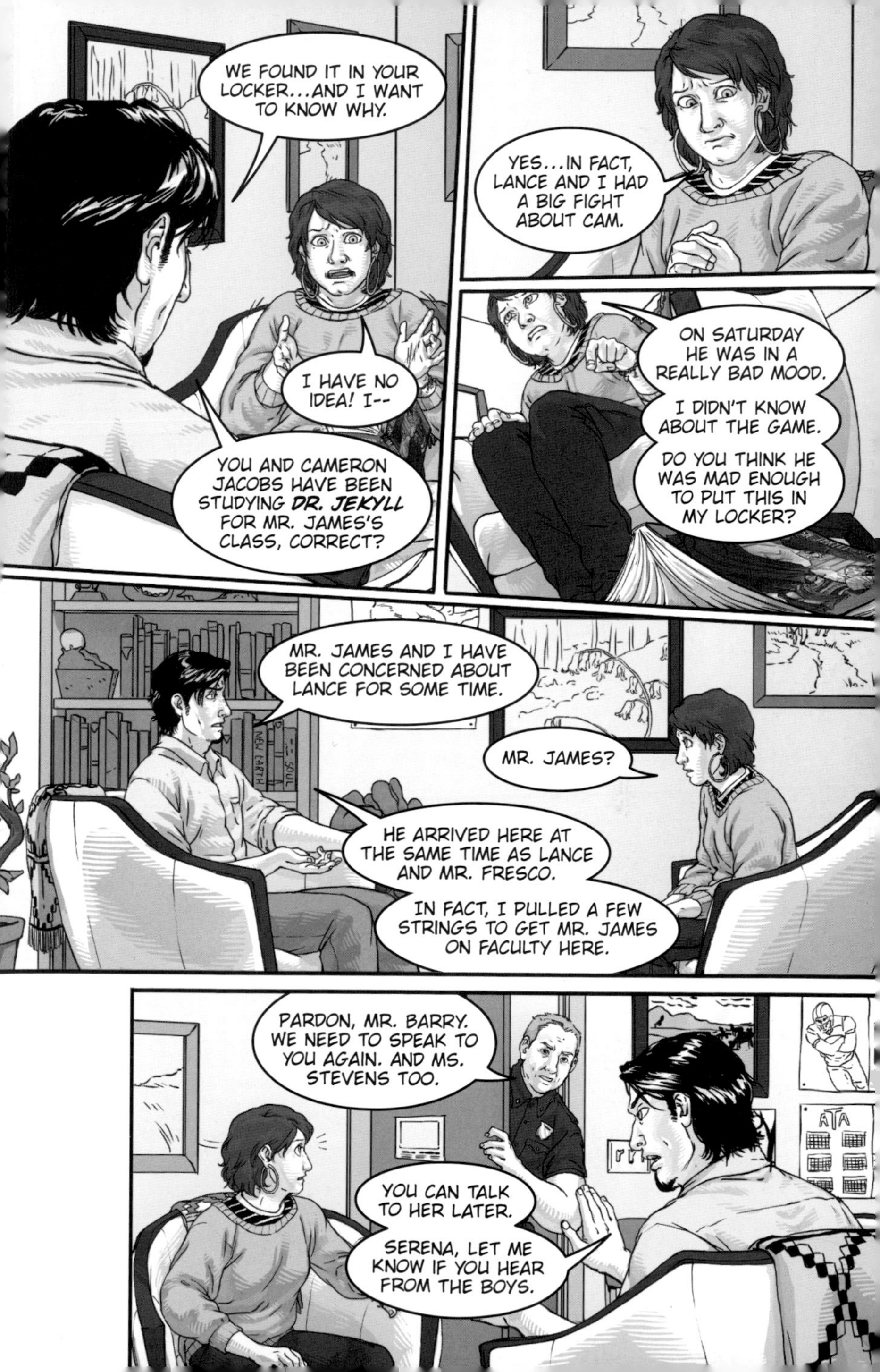
WE FOUND IT IN YOUR LOCKER...AND I WANT TO KNOW WHY.
I HAVE NO IDEA! I--
YOU AND CAMERON JACOBS HAVE BEEN STUDYING *DR. JEKYLL* FOR MR. JAMES'S CLASS, CORRECT?
YES...IN FACT, LANCE AND I HAD A BIG FIGHT ABOUT CAM.
ON SATURDAY HE WAS IN A REALLY BAD MOOD.
I DIDN'T KNOW ABOUT THE GAME.
DO YOU THINK HE WAS MAD ENOUGH TO PUT THIS IN MY LOCKER?
MR. JAMES AND I HAVE BEEN CONCERNED ABOUT LANCE FOR SOME TIME.
MR. JAMES?
HE ARRIVED HERE AT THE SAME TIME AS LANCE AND MR. FRESCO.
IN FACT, I PULLED A FEW STRINGS TO GET MR. JAMES ON FACULTY HERE.
PARDON, MR. BARRY. WE NEED TO SPEAK TO YOU AGAIN. AND MS. STEVENS TOO.
YOU CAN TALK TO HER LATER.
SERENA, LET ME KNOW IF YOU HEAR FROM THE BOYS.

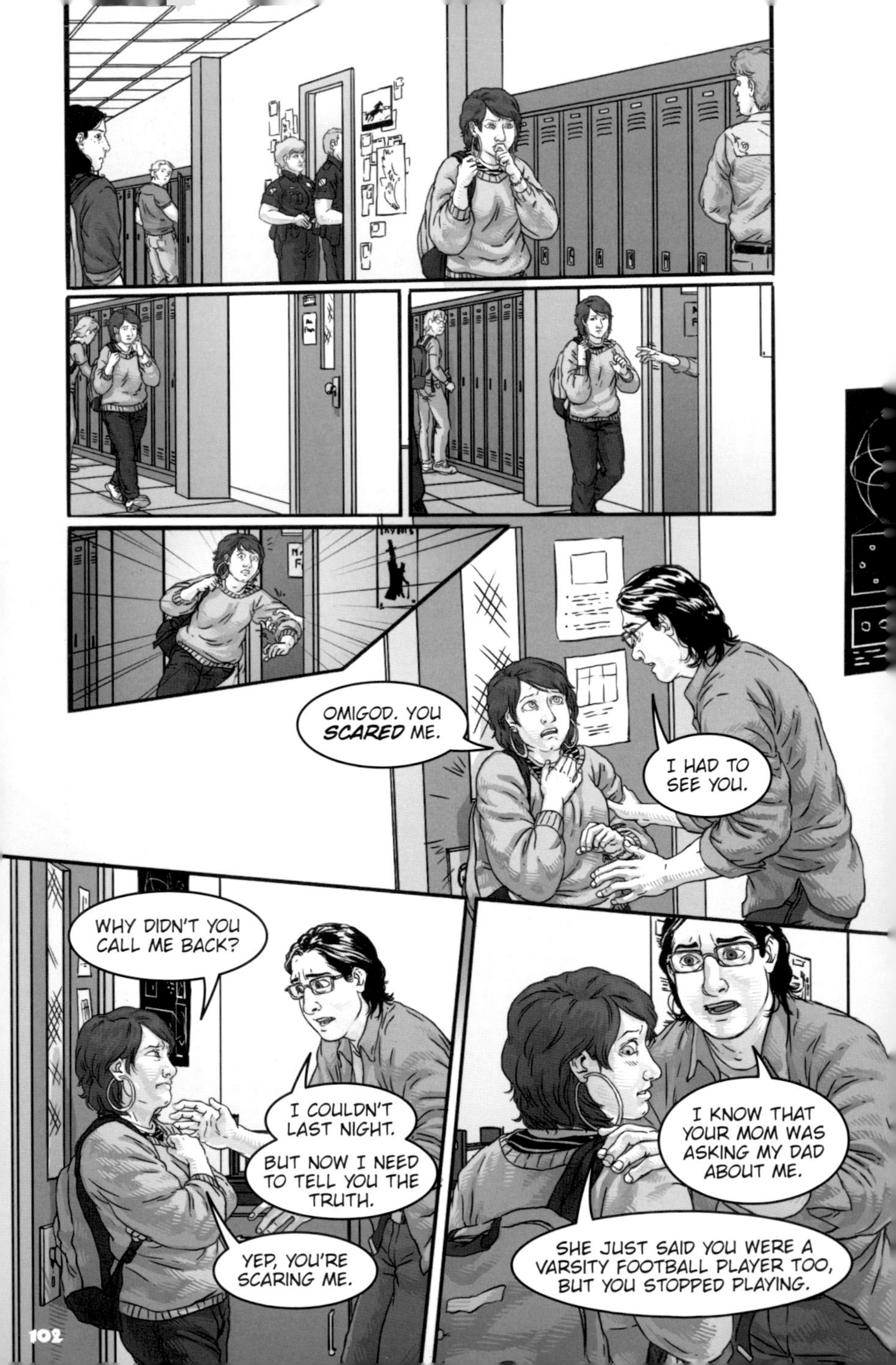

OMIGOD. YOU SCARED ME.
I HAD TO SEE YOU.
WHY DIDN'T YOU CALL ME BACK?
I COULDN'T LAST NIGHT.
BUT NOW I NEED TO TELL YOU THE TRUTH.
YEP, YOU'RE SCARING ME.
I KNOW THAT YOUR MOM WAS ASKING MY DAD ABOUT ME.
SHE JUST SAID YOU WERE A VARSITY FOOTBALL PLAYER TOO, BUT YOU STOPPED PLAYING.

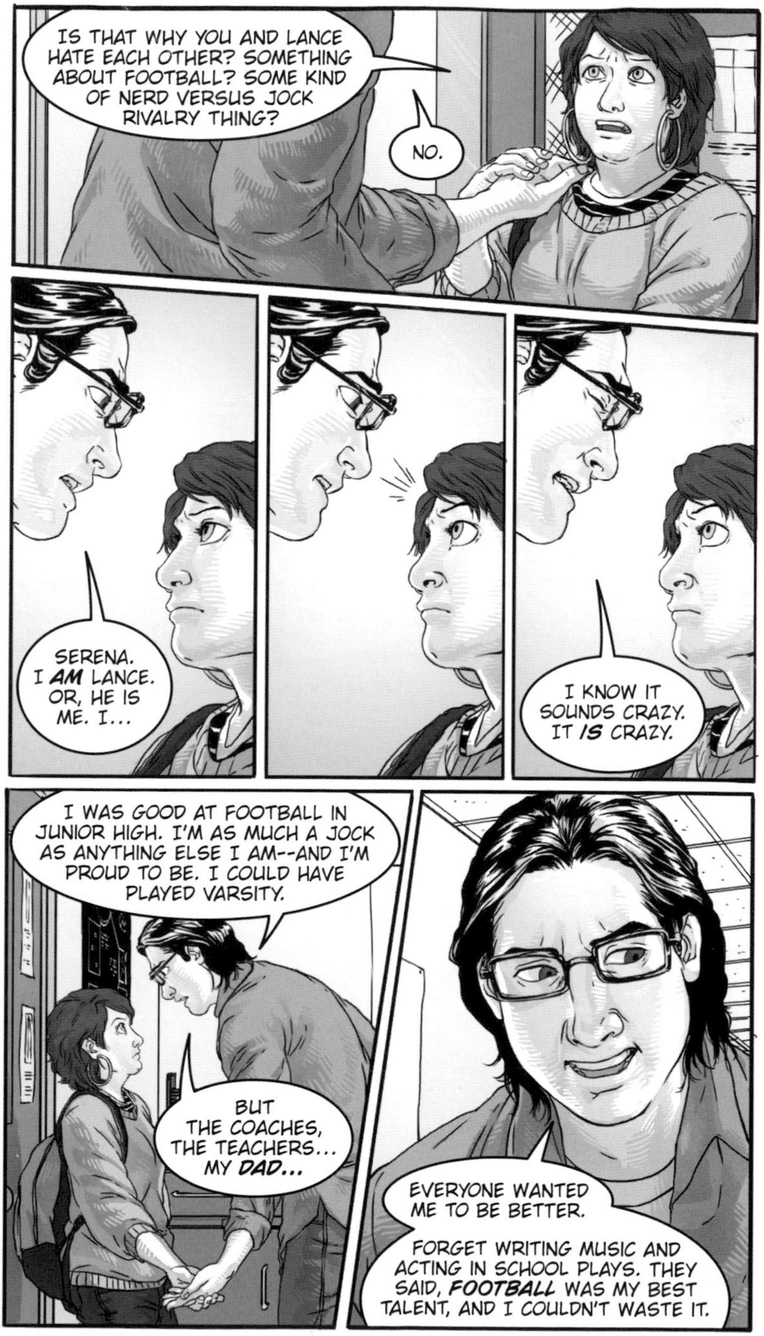
IS THAT WHY YOU AND LANCE HATE EACH OTHER? SOMETHING ABOUT FOOTBALL? SOME KIND OF NERD VERSUS JOCK RIVALRY THING?
NO.
SERENA. I **AM** LANCE. OR, HE IS ME. I...
I KNOW IT SOUNDS CRAZY. IT **IS** CRAZY.
I WAS GOOD AT FOOTBALL IN JUNIOR HIGH. I'M AS MUCH A JOCK AS ANYTHING ELSE I AM--AND I'M PROUD TO BE. I COULD HAVE PLAYED VARSITY.
BUT THE COACHES, THE TEACHERS... MY **DAD...**
EVERYONE WANTED ME TO BE BETTER.
FORGET WRITING MUSIC AND ACTING IN SCHOOL PLAYS. THEY SAID, **FOOTBALL** WAS MY BEST TALENT, AND I COULDN'T WASTE IT.

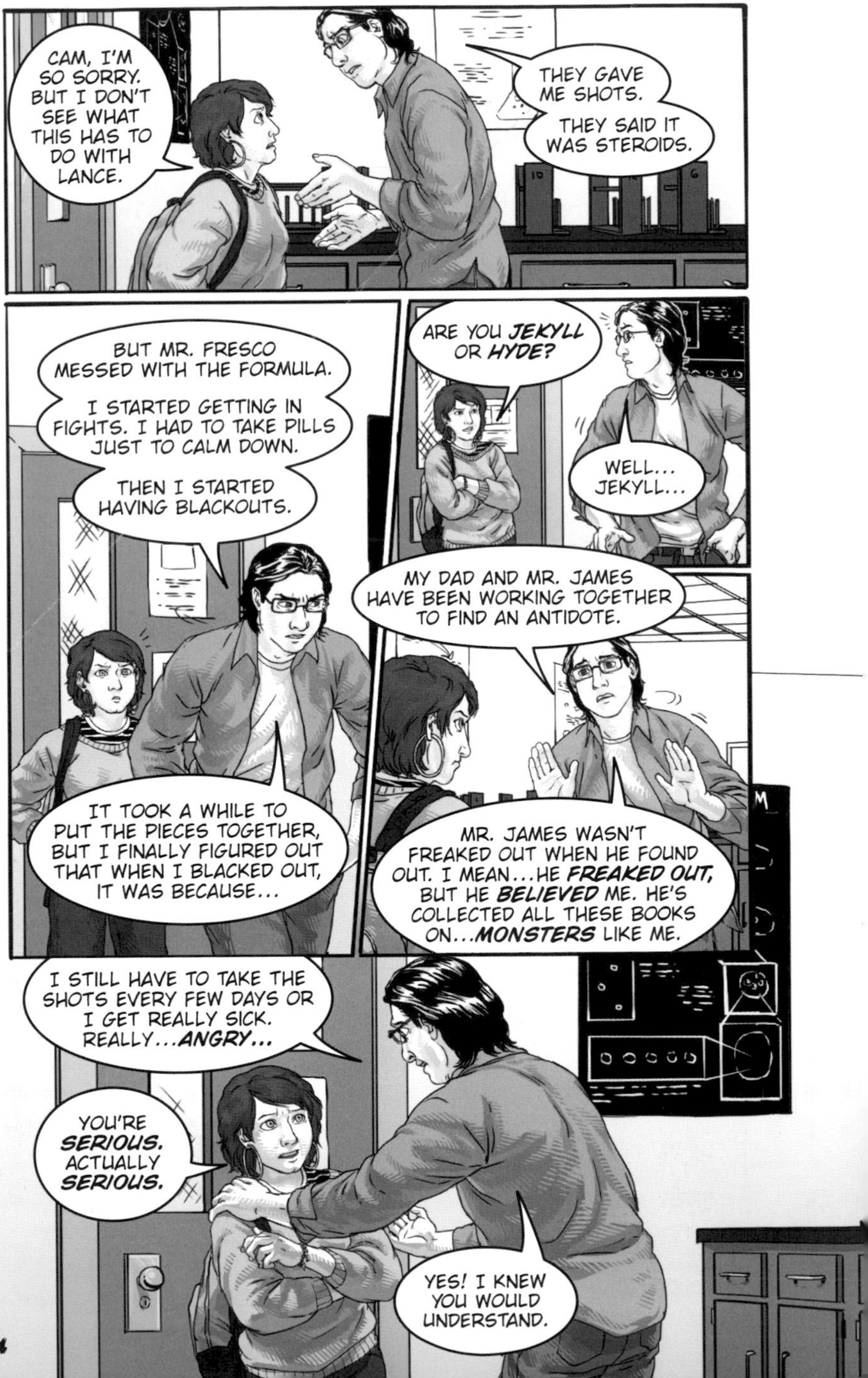
CAM, I'M SO SORRY. BUT I DON'T SEE WHAT THIS HAS TO DO WITH LANCE.
THEY GAVE ME SHOTS.
THEY SAID IT WAS STEROIDS.
BUT MR. FRESCO MESSED WITH THE FORMULA.
I STARTED GETTING IN FIGHTS. I HAD TO TAKE PILLS JUST TO CALM DOWN.
THEN I STARTED HAVING BLACKOUTS.
IT TOOK A WHILE TO PUT THE PIECES TOGETHER, BUT I FINALLY FIGURED OUT THAT WHEN I BLACKED OUT, IT WAS BECAUSE...
ARE YOU *JEKYLL* OR *HYDE?*
WELL... JEKYLL...
MY DAD AND MR. JAMES HAVE BEEN WORKING TOGETHER TO FIND AN ANTIDOTE.
MR. JAMES WASN'T FREAKED OUT WHEN HE FOUND OUT. I MEAN...HE *FREAKED OUT,* BUT HE *BELIEVED* ME. HE'S COLLECTED ALL THESE BOOKS ON...*MONSTERS* LIKE ME.
I STILL HAVE TO TAKE THE SHOTS EVERY FEW DAYS OR I GET REALLY SICK. REALLY...*ANGRY...*
YOU'RE *SERIOUS.* ACTUALLY *SERIOUS.*
YES! I KNEW YOU WOULD UNDERSTAND.

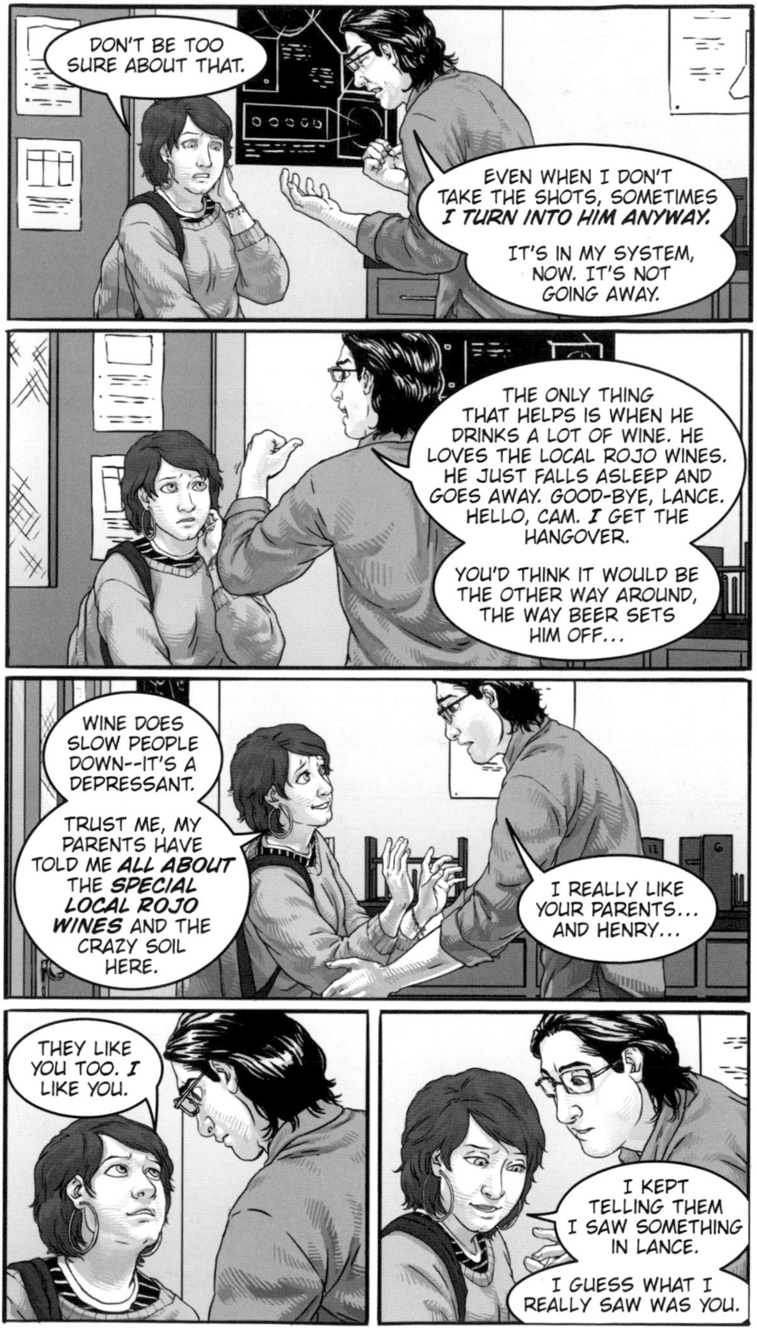
DON'T BE TOO SURE ABOUT THAT.
EVEN WHEN I DON'T TAKE THE SHOTS, SOMETIMES *I TURN INTO HIM ANYWAY.*
IT'S IN MY SYSTEM, NOW. IT'S NOT GOING AWAY.
THE ONLY THING THAT HELPS IS WHEN HE DRINKS A LOT OF WINE. HE LOVES THE LOCAL ROJO WINES. HE JUST FALLS ASLEEP AND GOES AWAY. GOOD-BYE, LANCE. HELLO, CAM. *I* GET THE HANGOVER.
YOU'D THINK IT WOULD BE THE OTHER WAY AROUND, THE WAY BEER SETS HIM OFF...
WINE DOES SLOW PEOPLE DOWN--IT'S A DEPRESSANT.
TRUST ME, MY PARENTS HAVE TOLD ME *ALL ABOUT* THE *SPECIAL LOCAL ROJO WINES* AND THE CRAZY SOIL HERE.
I REALLY LIKE YOUR PARENTS... AND HENRY...
THEY LIKE YOU TOO. *I* LIKE YOU.
I KEPT TELLING THEM I SAW SOMETHING IN LANCE.
I GUESS WHAT I REALLY SAW WAS YOU.

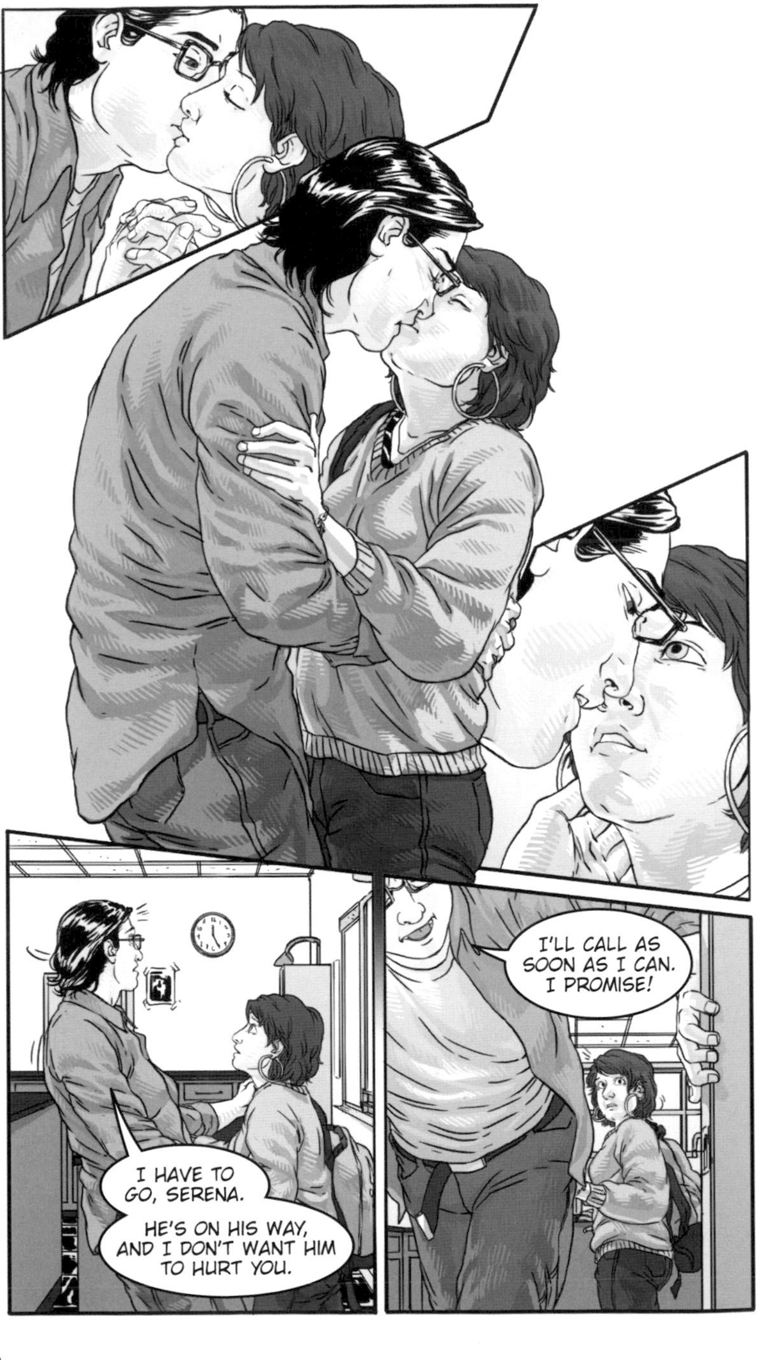
I HAVE TO GO, SERENA.
HE'S ON HIS WAY, AND I DON'T WANT HIM TO HURT YOU.
I'LL CALL AS SOON AS I CAN. I PROMISE!

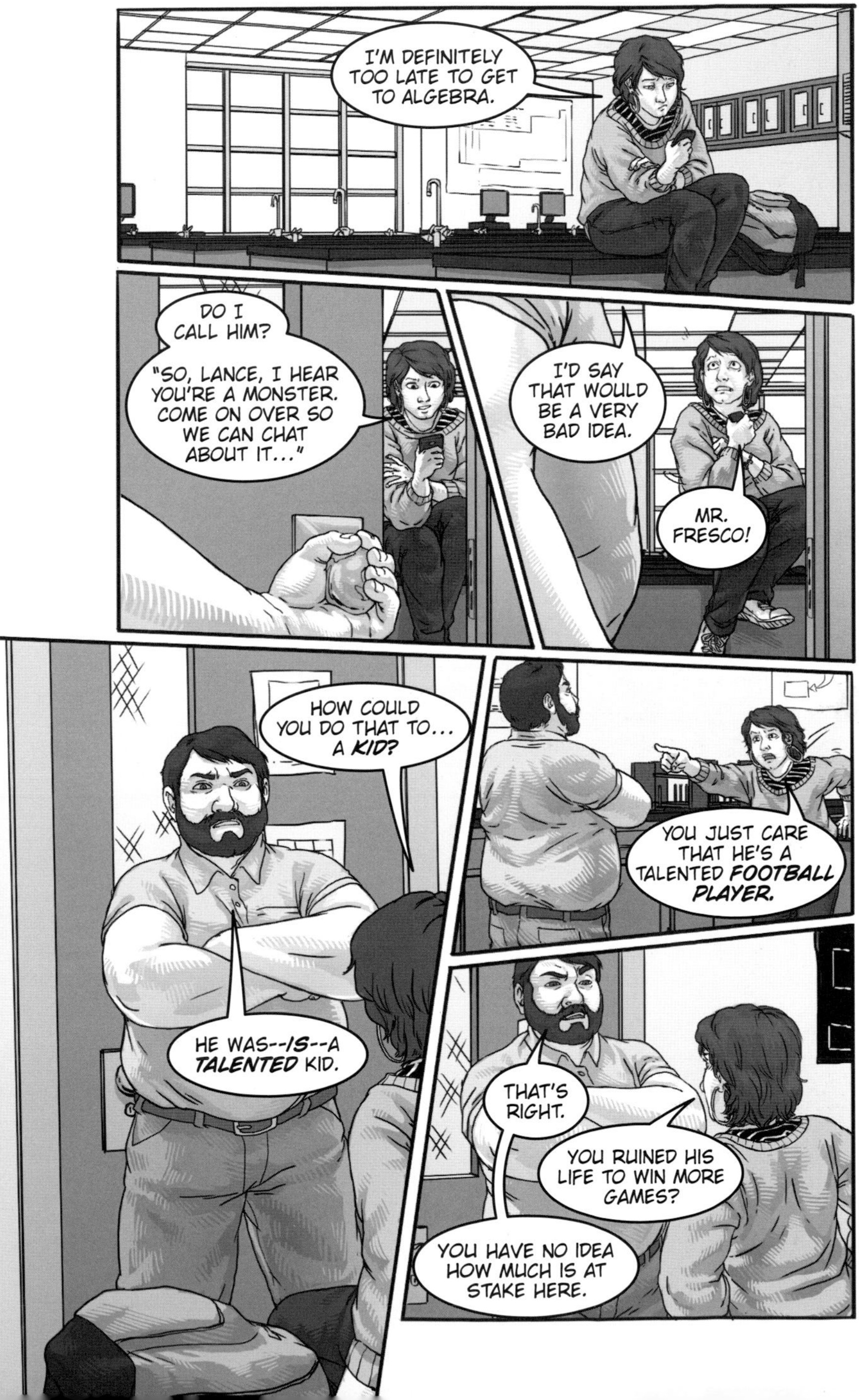
I'M DEFINITELY TOO LATE TO GET TO ALGEBRA.
DO I CALL HIM?
"SO, LANCE, I HEAR YOU'RE A MONSTER. COME ON OVER SO WE CAN CHAT ABOUT IT..."
I'D SAY THAT WOULD BE A VERY BAD IDEA.
MR. FRESCO!
HOW COULD YOU DO THAT TO... A *KID?*
HE WAS--*IS*--A *TALENTED* KID.
YOU JUST CARE THAT HE'S A TALENTED ***FOOTBALL PLAYER.***
THAT'S RIGHT.
YOU RUINED HIS LIFE TO WIN MORE GAMES?
YOU HAVE NO IDEA HOW MUCH IS AT STAKE HERE.

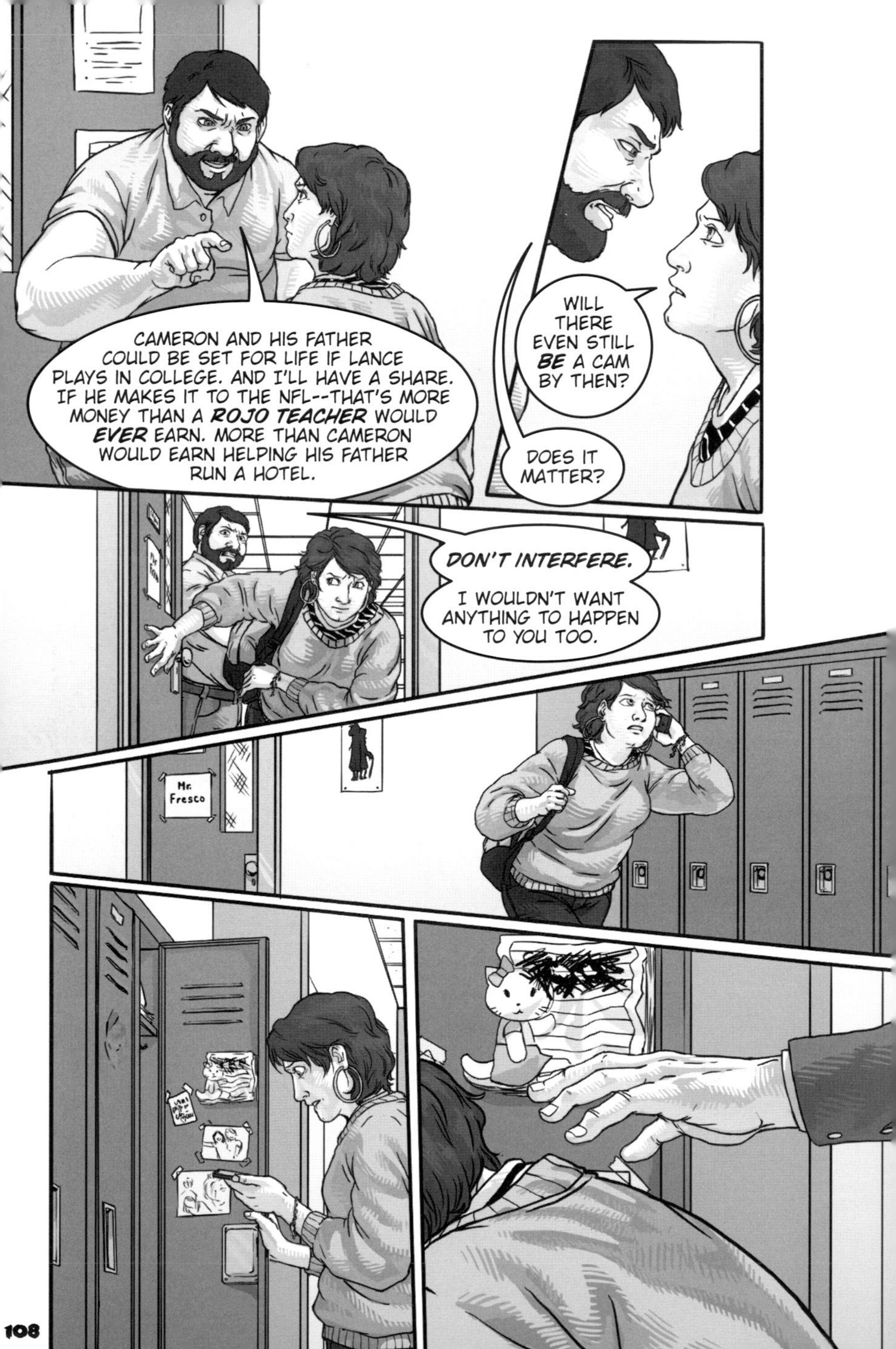
CAMERON AND HIS FATHER COULD BE SET FOR LIFE IF LANCE PLAYS IN COLLEGE. AND I'LL HAVE A SHARE. IF HE MAKES IT TO THE NFL--THAT'S MORE MONEY THAN A ROJO TEACHER WOULD EVER EARN. MORE THAN CAMERON WOULD EARN HELPING HIS FATHER RUN A HOTEL.
WILL THERE EVEN STILL BE A CAM BY THEN?
DOES IT MATTER?
DON'T INTERFERE.
I WOULDN'T WANT ANYTHING TO HAPPEN TO YOU TOO.
Mr. Fresco

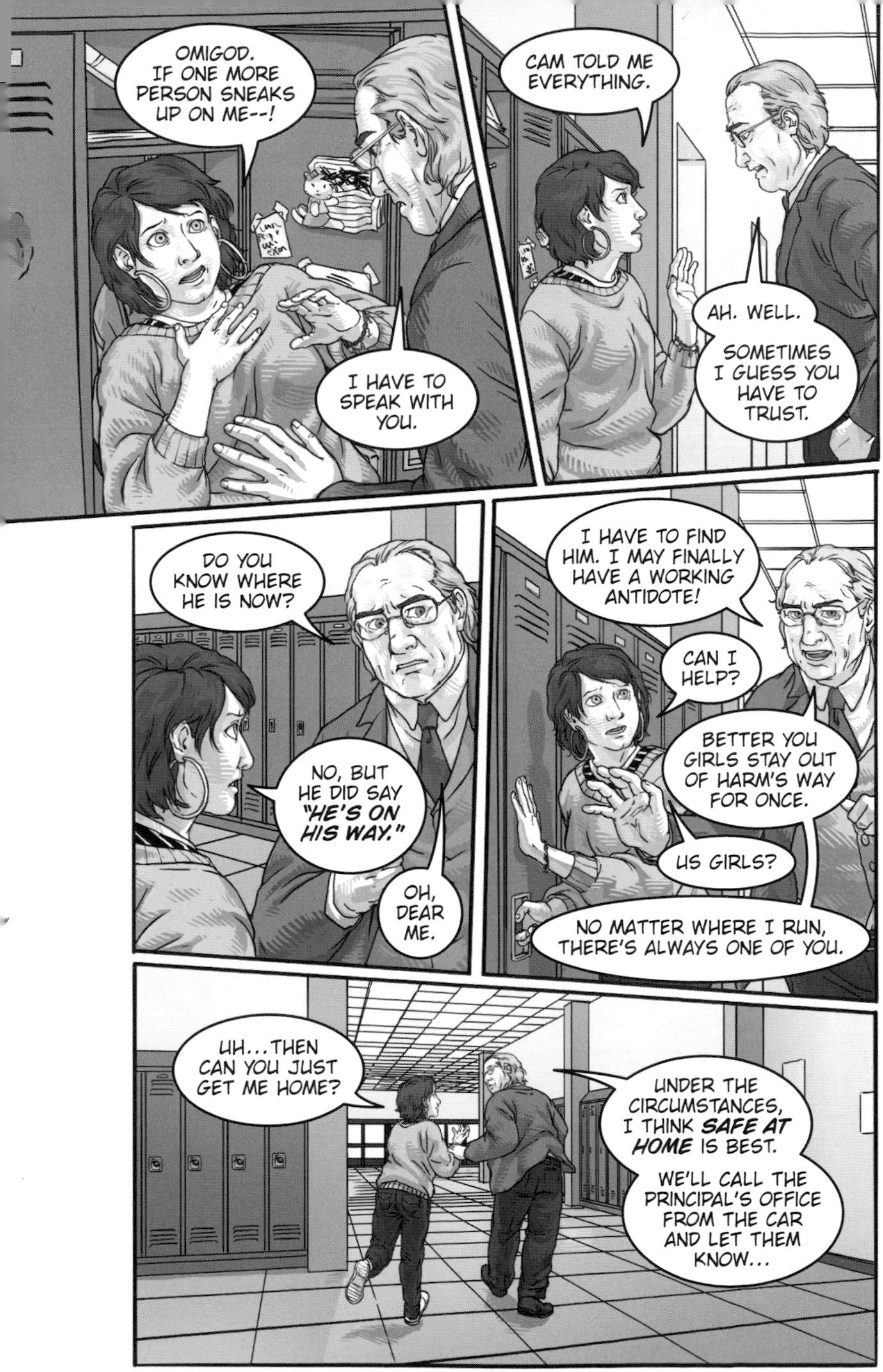
OMIGOD. IF ONE MORE PERSON SNEAKS UP ON ME--!
I HAVE TO SPEAK WITH YOU.
CAM TOLD ME EVERYTHING.
AH. WELL.
SOMETIMES I GUESS YOU HAVE TO TRUST.
DO YOU KNOW WHERE HE IS NOW?
NO, BUT HE DID SAY *"HE'S ON HIS WAY."*
OH, DEAR ME.
I HAVE TO FIND HIM. I MAY FINALLY HAVE A WORKING ANTIDOTE!
CAN I HELP?
BETTER YOU GIRLS STAY OUT OF HARM'S WAY FOR ONCE.
US GIRLS?
NO MATTER WHERE I RUN, THERE'S ALWAYS ONE OF YOU.
UH...THEN CAN YOU JUST GET ME HOME?
UNDER THE CIRCUMSTANCES, I THINK *SAFE AT HOME* IS BEST.
WE'LL CALL THE PRINCIPAL'S OFFICE FROM THE CAR AND LET THEM KNOW...

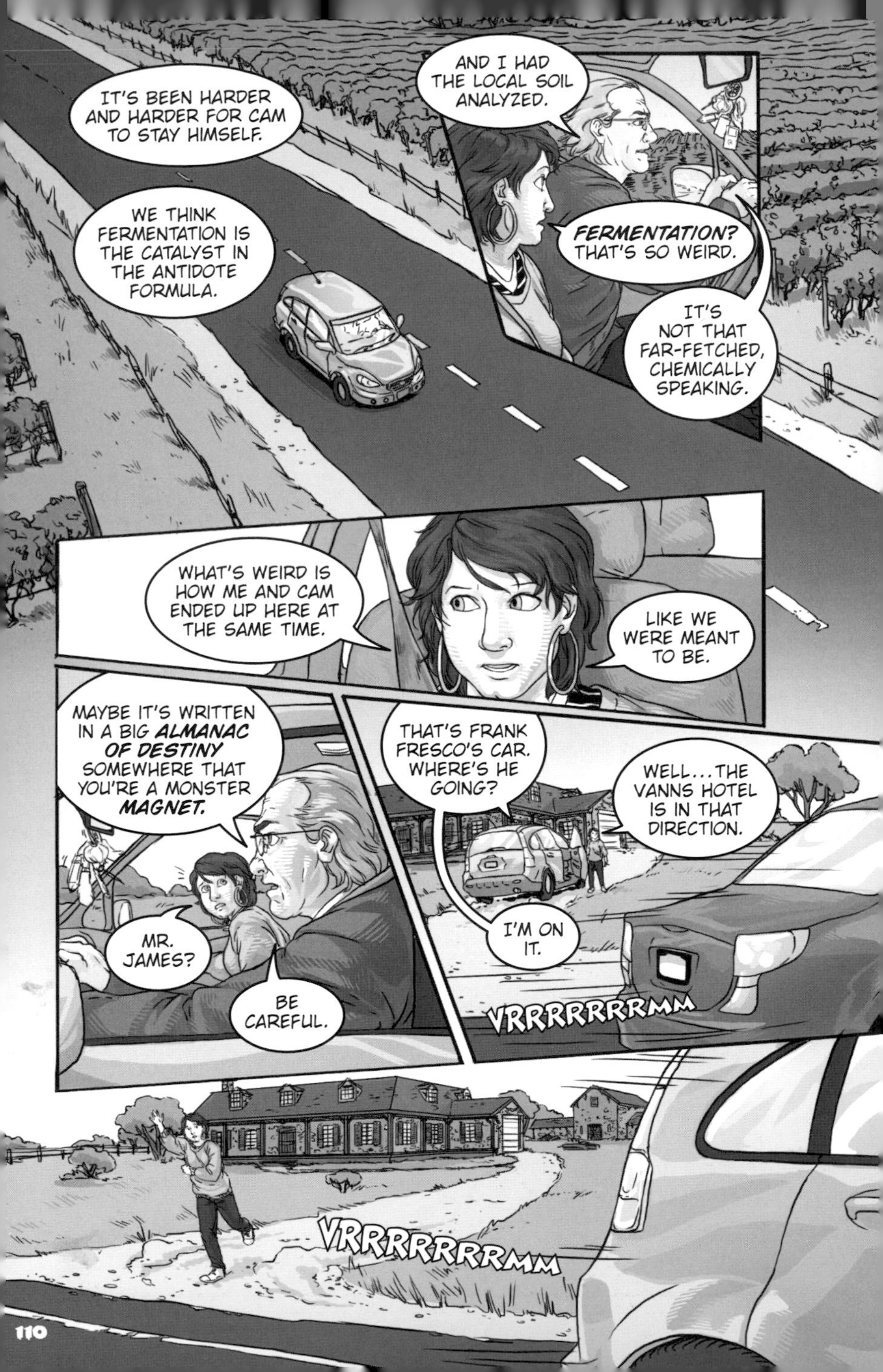
IT'S BEEN HARDER AND HARDER FOR CAM TO STAY HIMSELF.
AND I HAD THE LOCAL SOIL ANALYZED.
WE THINK FERMENTATION IS THE CATALYST IN THE ANTIDOTE FORMULA.
FERMENTATION? THAT'S SO WEIRD.
IT'S NOT THAT FAR-FETCHED, CHEMICALLY SPEAKING.
WHAT'S WEIRD IS HOW ME AND CAM ENDED UP HERE AT THE SAME TIME.
LIKE WE WERE MEANT TO BE.
MAYBE IT'S WRITTEN IN A BIG ALMANAC OF DESTINY SOMEWHERE THAT YOU'RE A MONSTER MAGNET.
MR. JAMES?
BE CAREFUL.
THAT'S FRANK FRESCO'S CAR. WHERE'S HE GOING?
WELL...THE VANNS HOTEL IS IN THAT DIRECTION.
I'M ON IT.
VRRRRRRRRMM
VRRRRRRRRMM

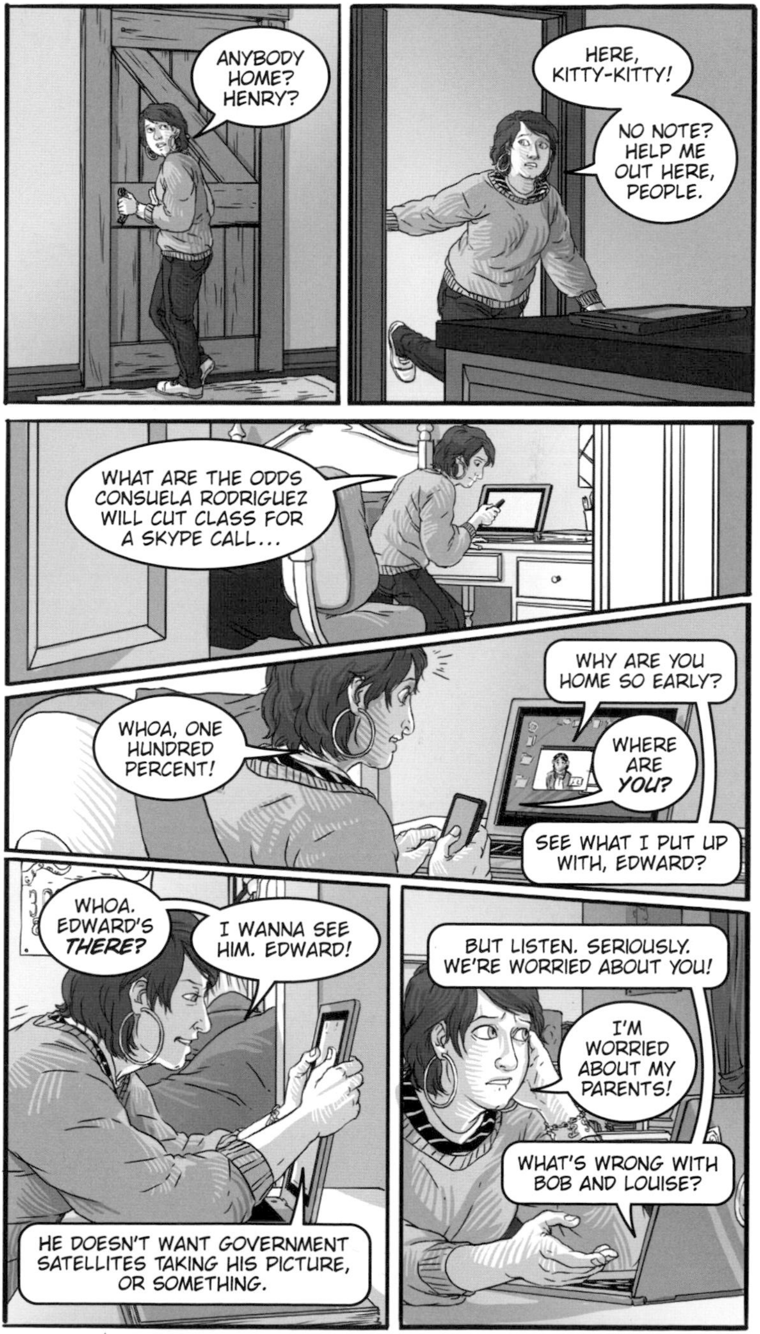
ANYBODY HOME? HENRY?
HERE, KITTY-KITTY!
NO NOTE? HELP ME OUT HERE, PEOPLE.
WHAT ARE THE ODDS CONSUELA RODRIGUEZ WILL CUT CLASS FOR A SKYPE CALL...
WHY ARE YOU HOME SO EARLY?
WHOA, ONE HUNDRED PERCENT!
WHERE ARE *YOU?*
SEE WHAT I PUT UP WITH, EDWARD?
WHOA. EDWARD'S *THERE?*
I WANNA SEE HIM. EDWARD!
HE DOESN'T WANT GOVERNMENT SATELLITES TAKING HIS PICTURE, OR SOMETHING.
BUT LISTEN. SERIOUSLY. WE'RE WORRIED ABOUT YOU!
I'M WORRIED ABOUT MY PARENTS!
WHAT'S WRONG WITH BOB AND LOUISE?

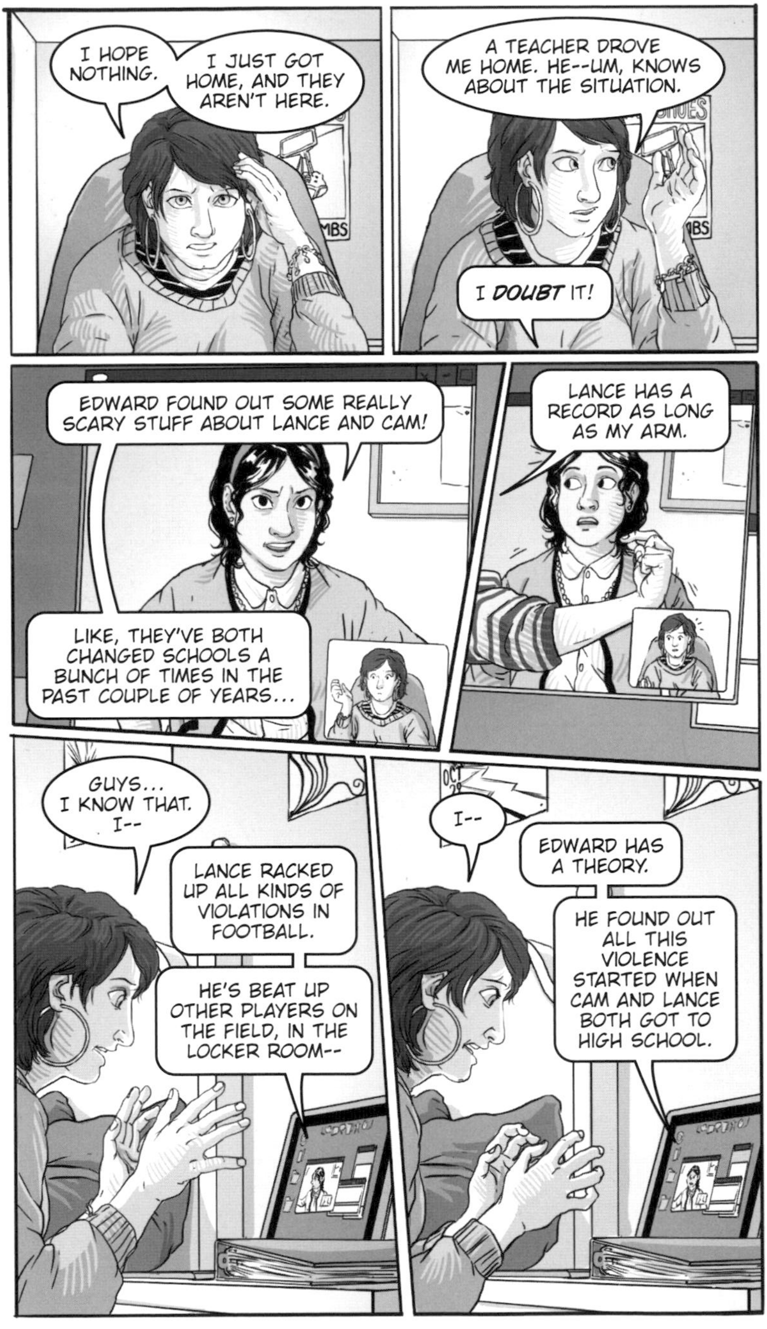
I HOPE NOTHING.
I JUST GOT HOME, AND THEY AREN'T HERE.
A TEACHER DROVE ME HOME. HE--UM, KNOWS ABOUT THE SITUATION.
I *DOUBT* IT!
EDWARD FOUND OUT SOME REALLY SCARY STUFF ABOUT LANCE AND CAM!
LIKE, THEY'VE BOTH CHANGED SCHOOLS A BUNCH OF TIMES IN THE PAST COUPLE OF YEARS...
LANCE HAS A RECORD AS LONG AS MY ARM.
GUYS... I KNOW THAT. I--
LANCE RACKED UP ALL KINDS OF VIOLATIONS IN FOOTBALL.
HE'S BEAT UP OTHER PLAYERS ON THE FIELD, IN THE LOCKER ROOM--
I--
EDWARD HAS A THEORY.
HE FOUND OUT ALL THIS VIOLENCE STARTED WHEN CAM AND LANCE BOTH GOT TO HIGH SCHOOL.

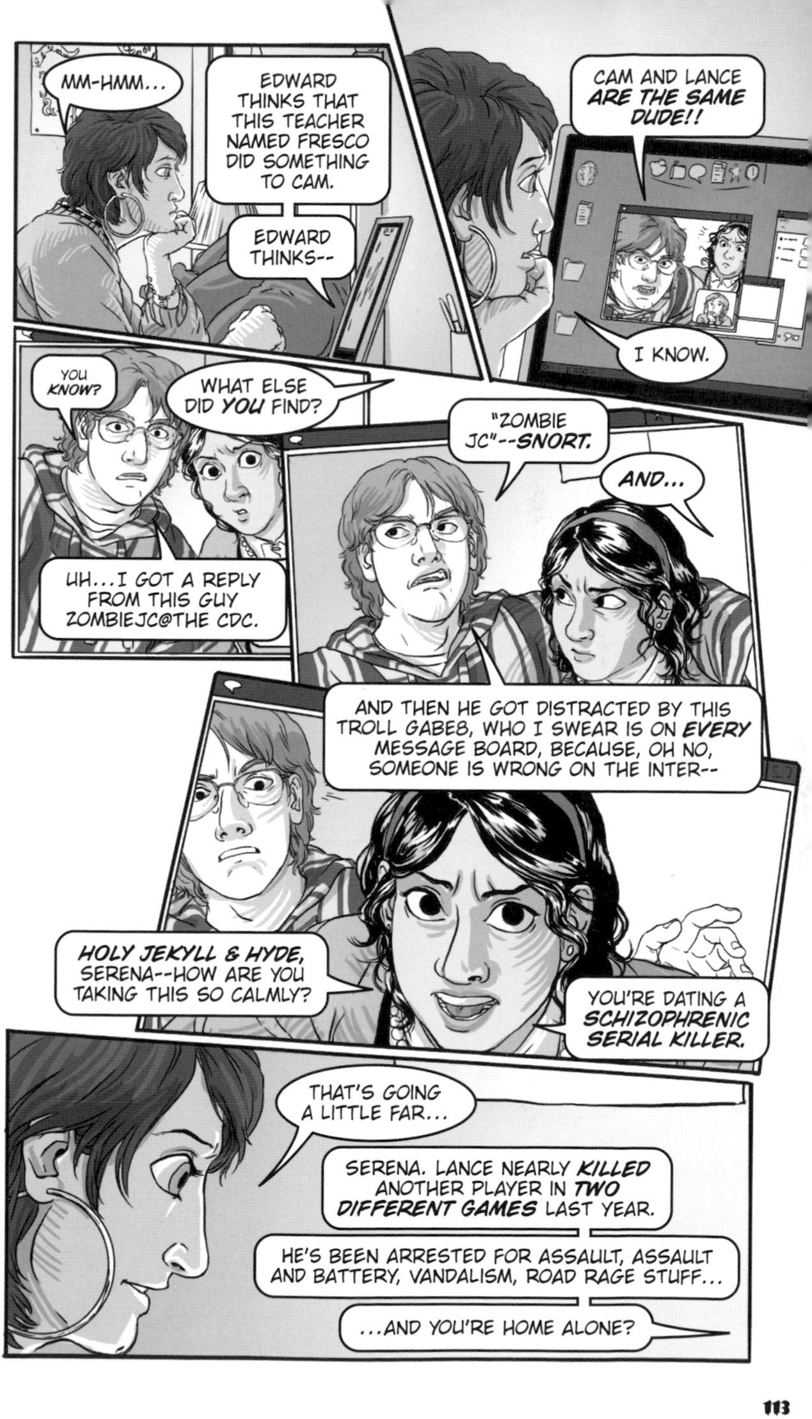

MM-HMM...
EDWARD THINKS THAT THIS TEACHER NAMED FRESCO DID SOMETHING TO CAM.
EDWARD THINKS--
CAM AND LANCE ARE THE SAME DUDE!!
I KNOW.
YOU KNOW?
WHAT ELSE DID YOU FIND?
UH...I GOT A REPLY FROM THIS GUY ZOMBIEJC@THE CDC.
"ZOMBIE JC"--SNORT.
AND...
AND THEN HE GOT DISTRACTED BY THIS TROLL GABE8, WHO I SWEAR IS ON EVERY MESSAGE BOARD, BECAUSE, OH NO, SOMEONE IS WRONG ON THE INTER--
HOLY JEKYLL & HYDE, SERENA--HOW ARE YOU TAKING THIS SO CALMLY?
YOU'RE DATING A SCHIZOPHRENIC SERIAL KILLER.
THAT'S GOING A LITTLE FAR...
SERENA. LANCE NEARLY KILLED ANOTHER PLAYER IN TWO DIFFERENT GAMES LAST YEAR.
HE'S BEEN ARRESTED FOR ASSAULT, ASSAULT AND BATTERY, VANDALISM, ROAD RAGE STUFF...
...AND YOU'RE HOME ALONE?

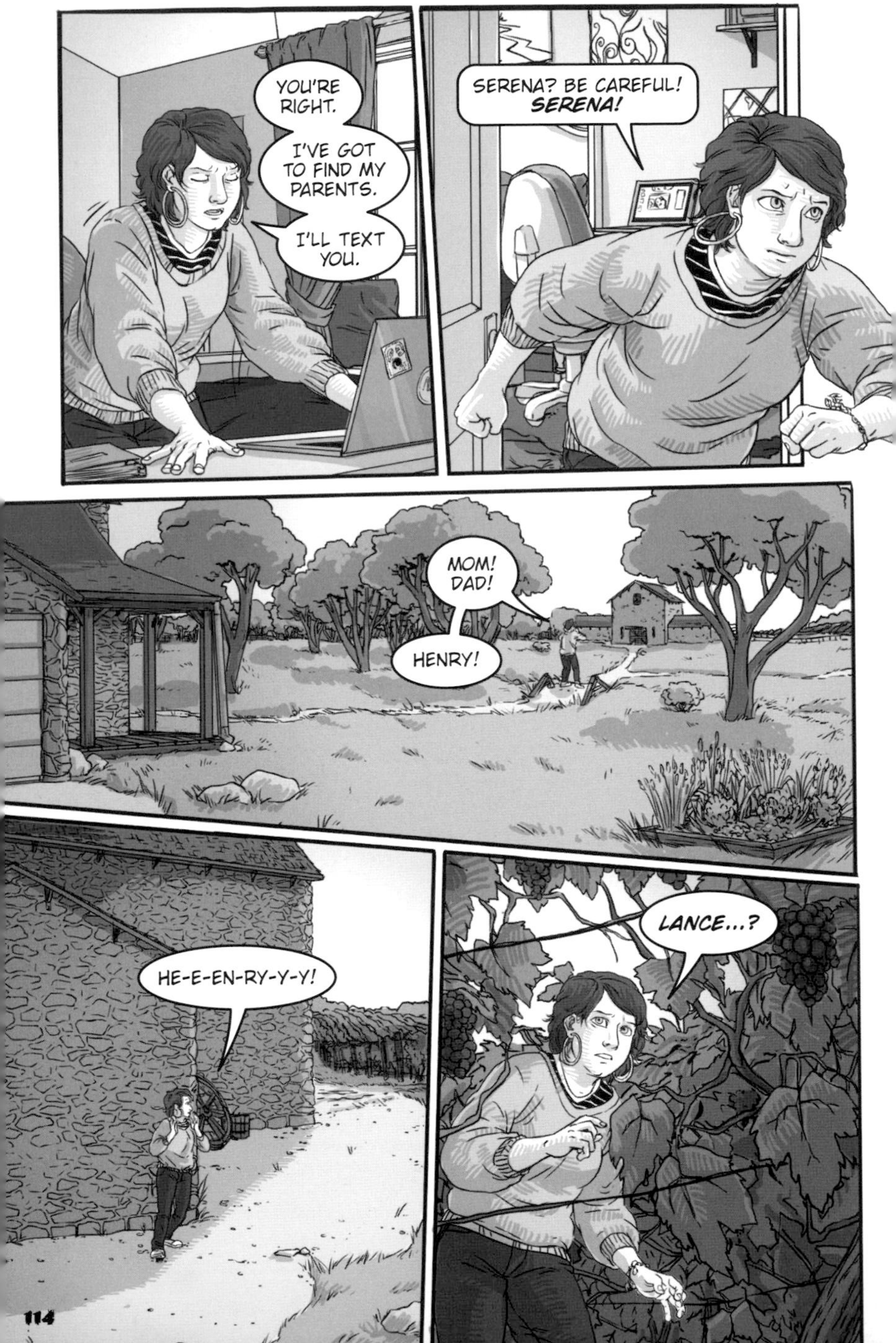
YOU'RE RIGHT.
I'VE GOT TO FIND MY PARENTS.
I'LL TEXT YOU.
SERENA? BE CAREFUL! SERENA!
MOM! DAD!
HENRY!
HE-E-EN-RY-Y-Y!
LANCE...?

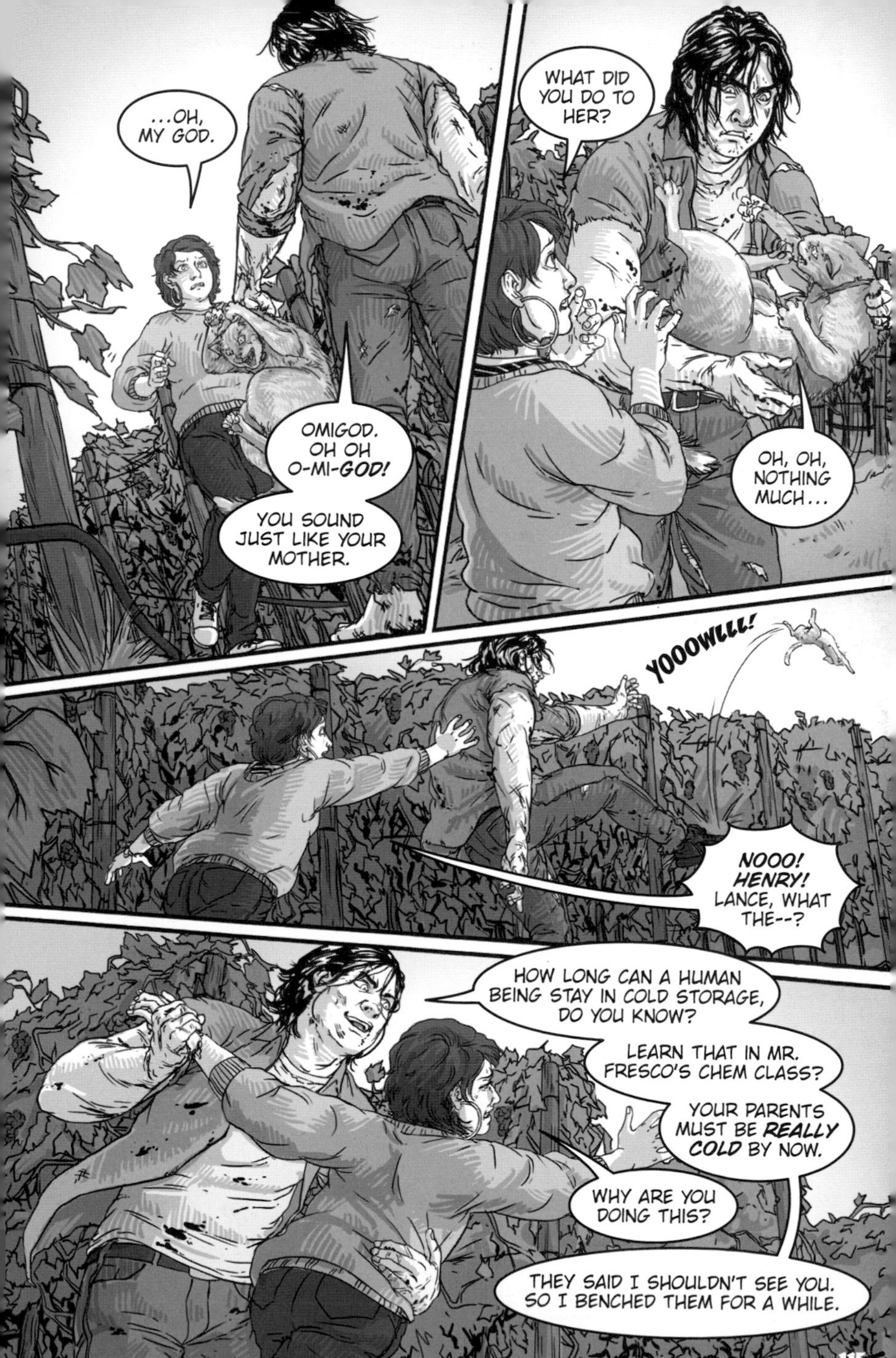

...OH, MY GOD.
OMIGOD. OH OH O-MI-GOD!
YOU SOUND JUST LIKE YOUR MOTHER.
WHAT DID YOU DO TO HER?
OH, OH, NOTHING MUCH...
YOOOWLLL!
NOOO! HENRY! LANCE, WHAT THE--?
HOW LONG CAN A HUMAN BEING STAY IN COLD STORAGE, DO YOU KNOW?
LEARN THAT IN MR. FRESCO'S CHEM CLASS?
YOUR PARENTS MUST BE REALLY COLD BY NOW.
WHY ARE YOU DOING THIS?
THEY SAID I SHOULDN'T SEE YOU. SO I BENCHED THEM FOR A WHILE.

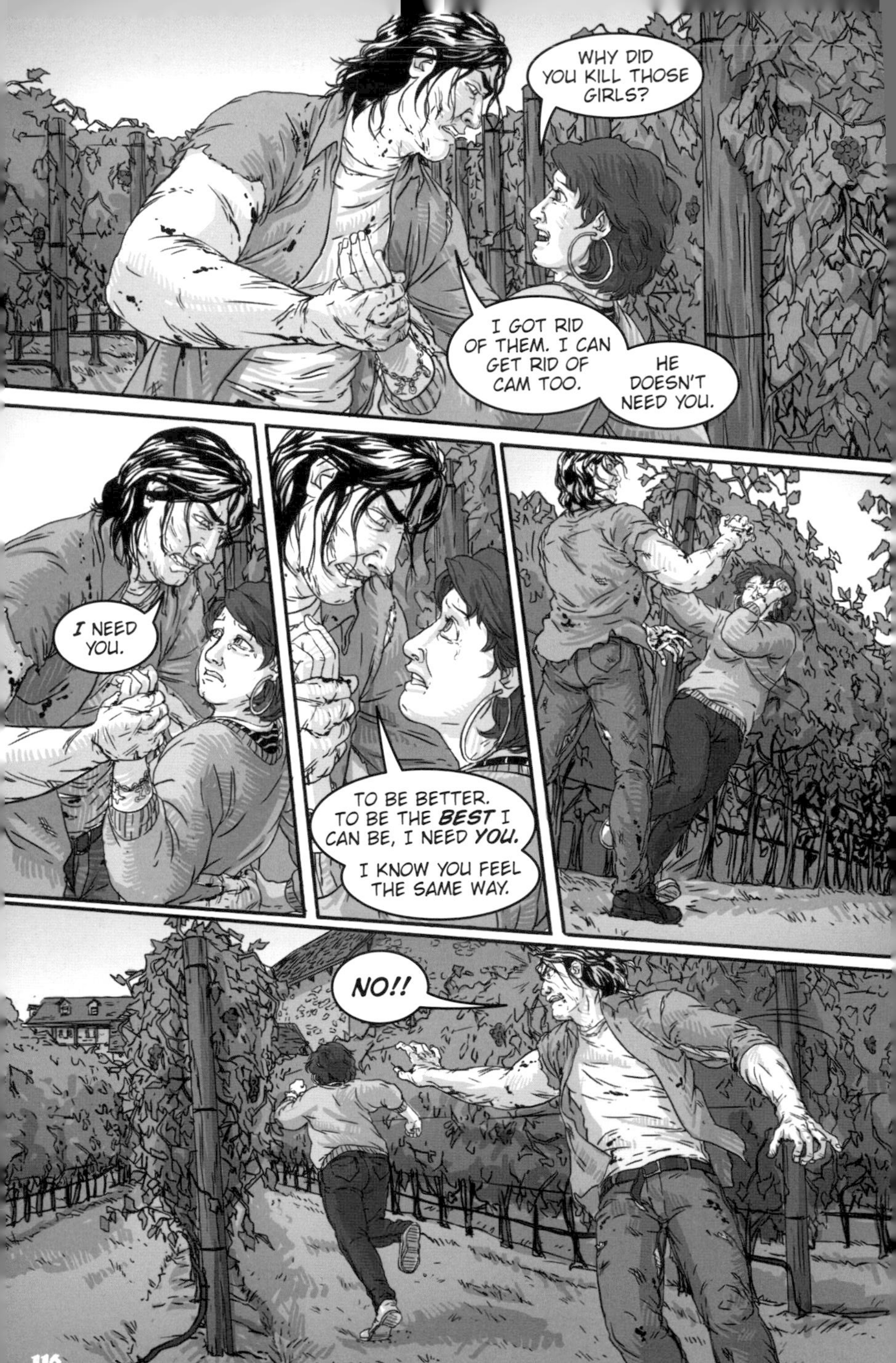
WHY DID YOU KILL THOSE GIRLS?
I GOT RID OF THEM. I CAN GET RID OF CAM TOO.
HE DOESN'T NEED YOU.
I NEED YOU.
TO BE BETTER. TO BE THE BEST I CAN BE, I NEED YOU.
I KNOW YOU FEEL THE SAME WAY.
NO!!

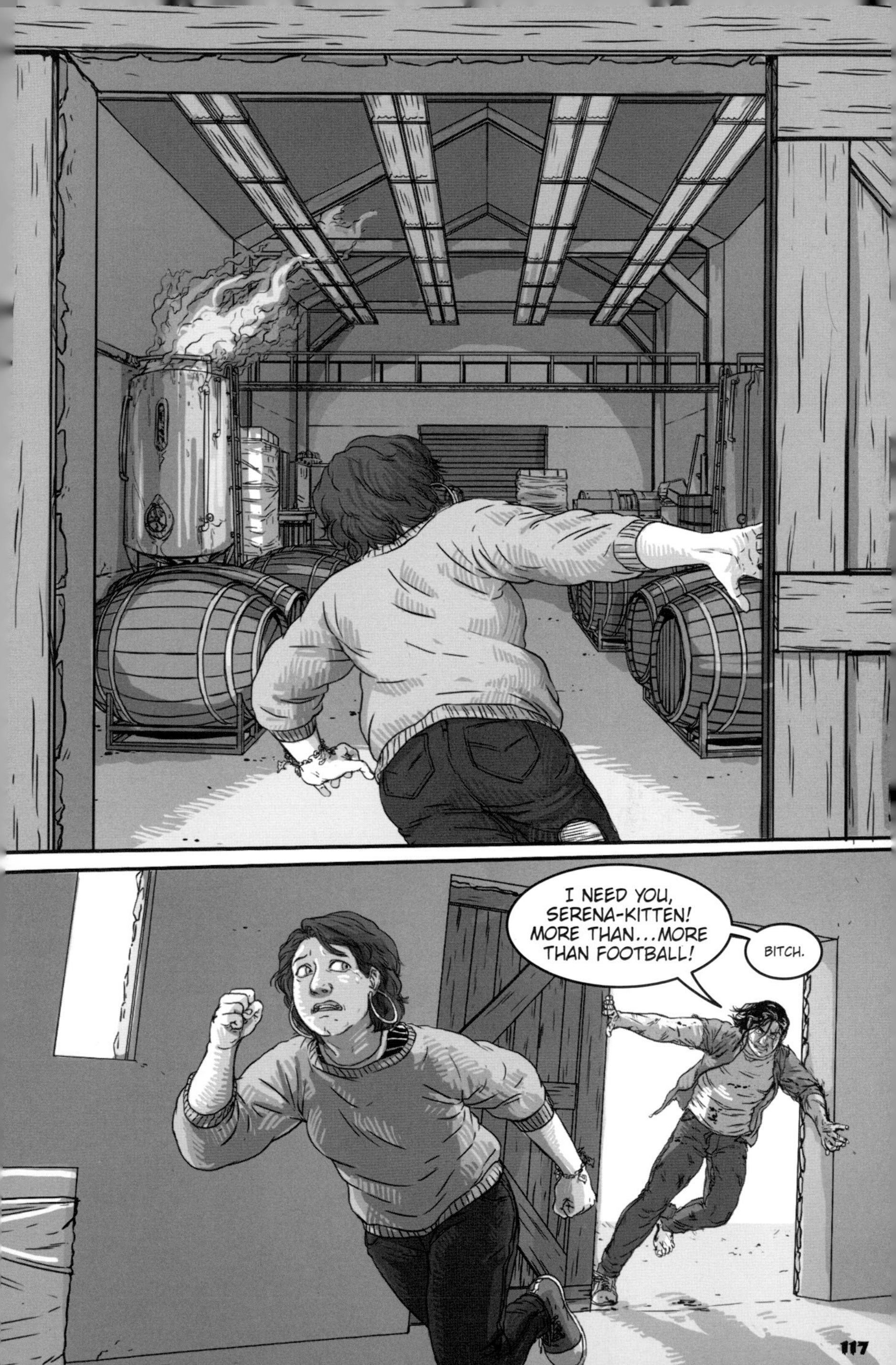
I NEED YOU, SERENA-KITTEN! MORE THAN...MORE THAN FOOTBALL!
BITCH.

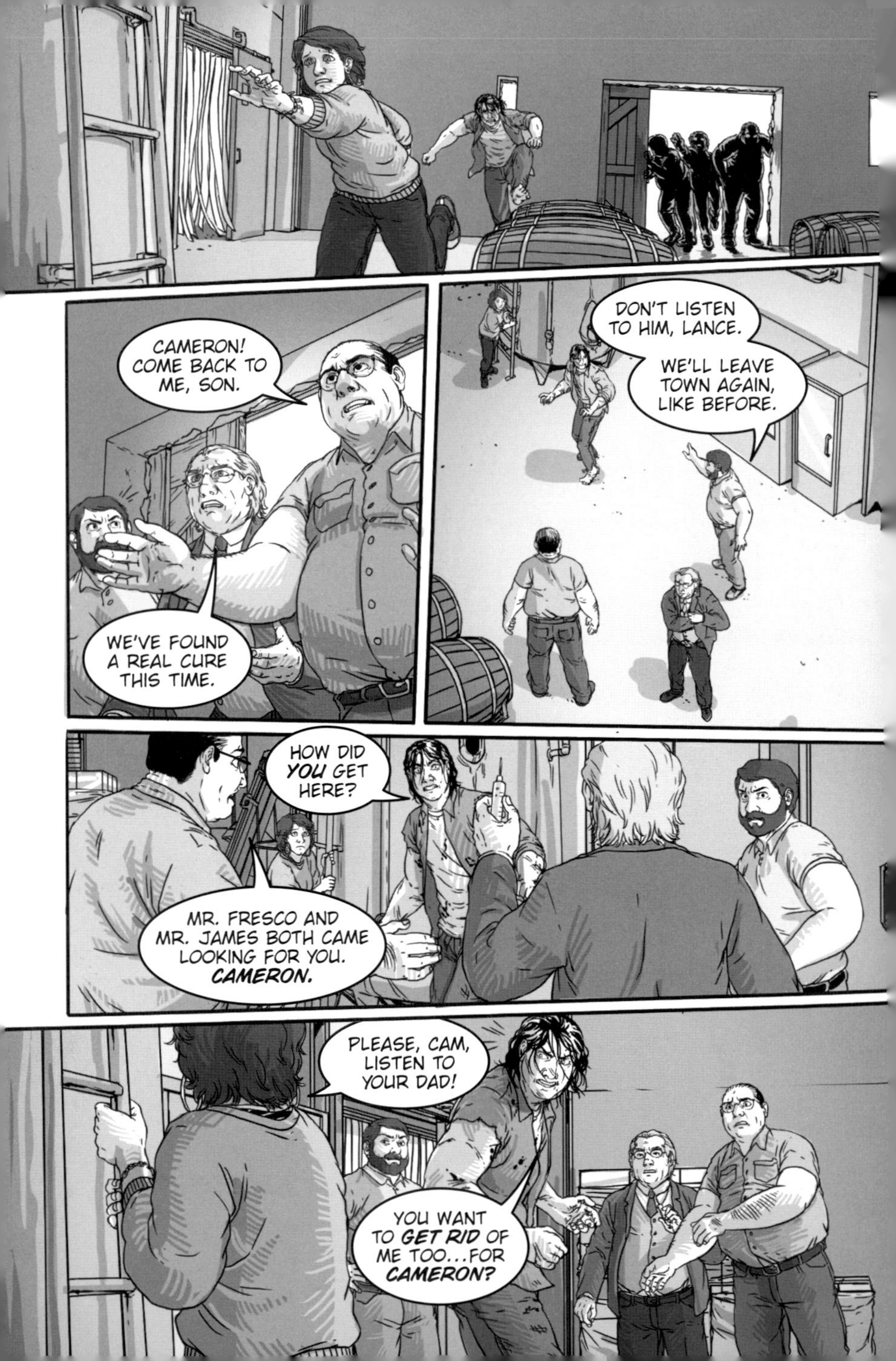
CAMERON! COME BACK TO ME, SON.
WE'VE FOUND A REAL CURE THIS TIME.
DON'T LISTEN TO HIM, LANCE.
WE'LL LEAVE TOWN AGAIN, LIKE BEFORE.
HOW DID *YOU* GET HERE?
MR. FRESCO AND MR. JAMES BOTH CAME LOOKING FOR YOU. *CAMERON.*
PLEASE, CAM, LISTEN TO YOUR DAD!
YOU WANT TO *GET RID* OF ME TOO...FOR *CAMERON?*

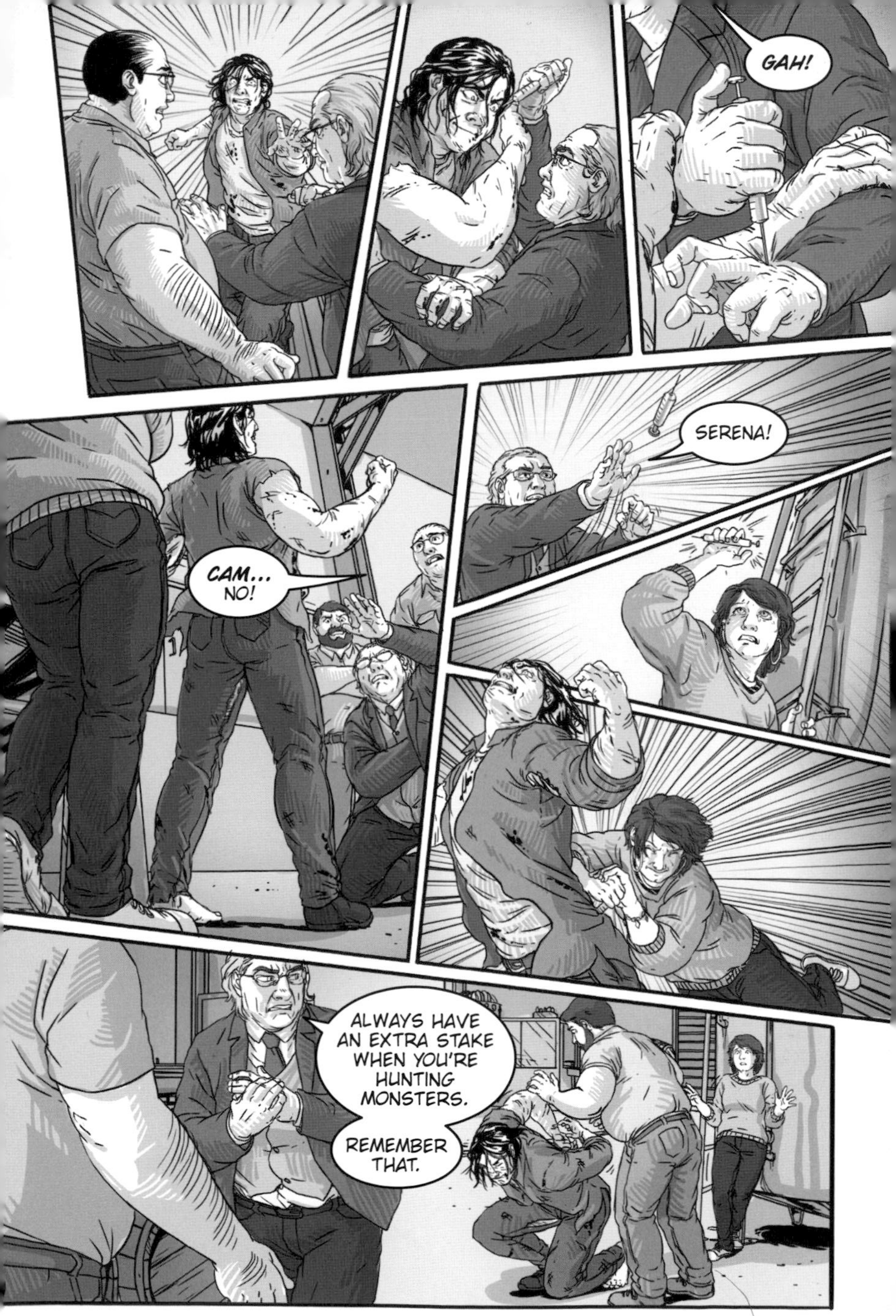
GAH!
CAM... NO!
SERENA!
ALWAYS HAVE AN EXTRA STAKE WHEN YOU'RE HUNTING MONSTERS.
REMEMBER THAT.

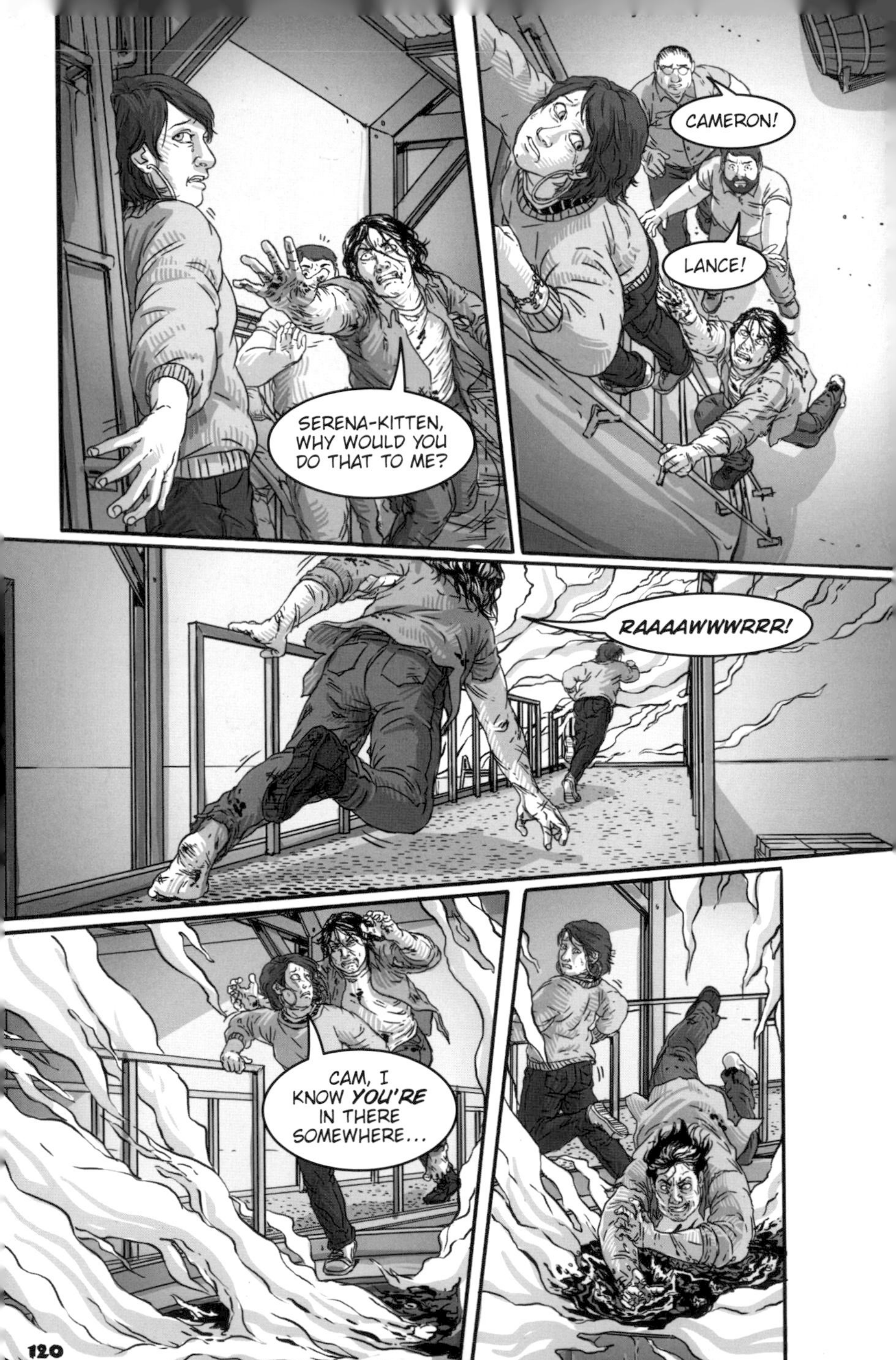

SERENA-KITTEN, WHY WOULD YOU DO THAT TO ME?
CAMERON!
LANCE!
RAAAAWWWRRR!
CAM, I KNOW *YOU'RE* IN THERE SOMEWHERE...

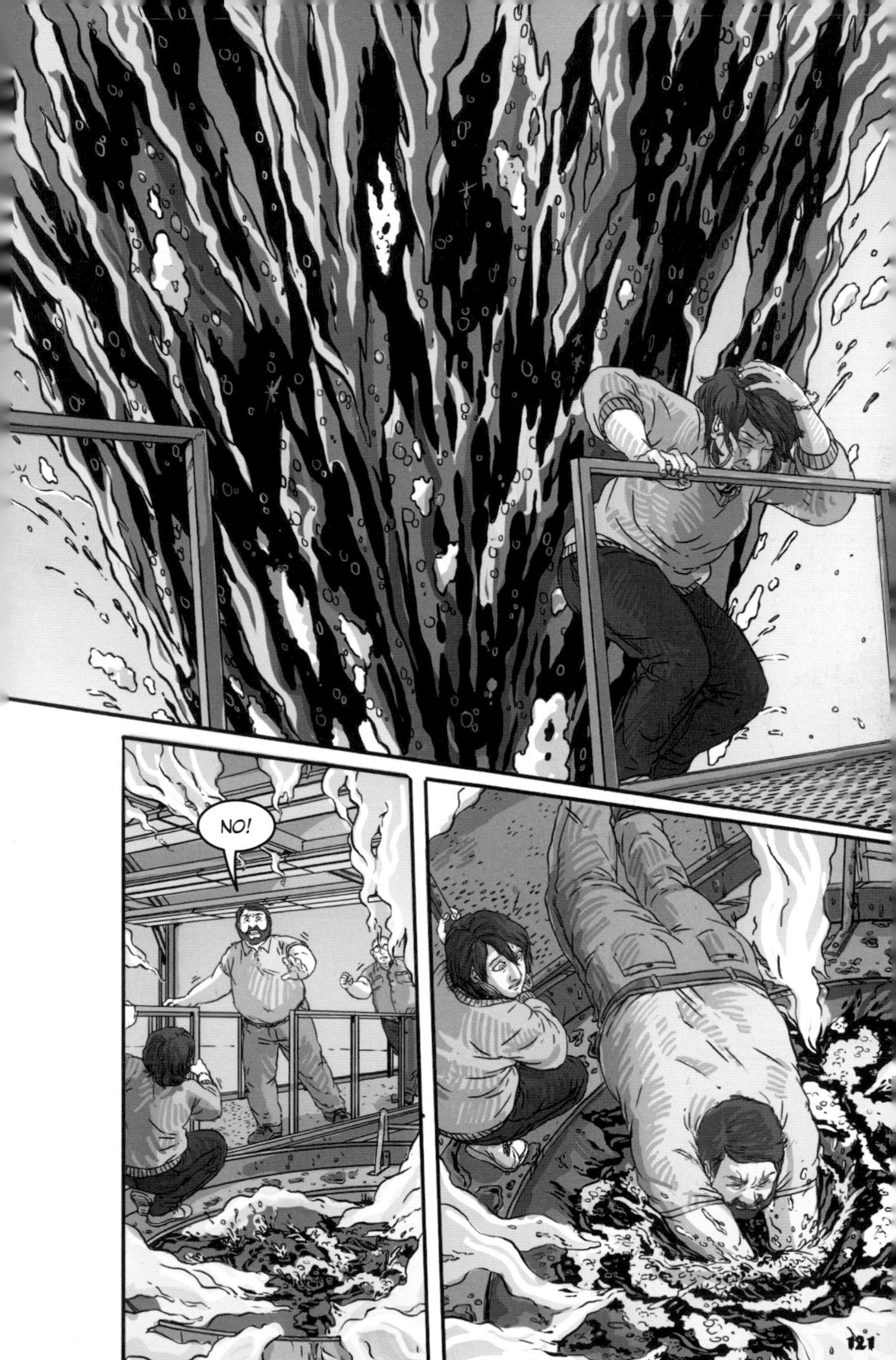
NO!

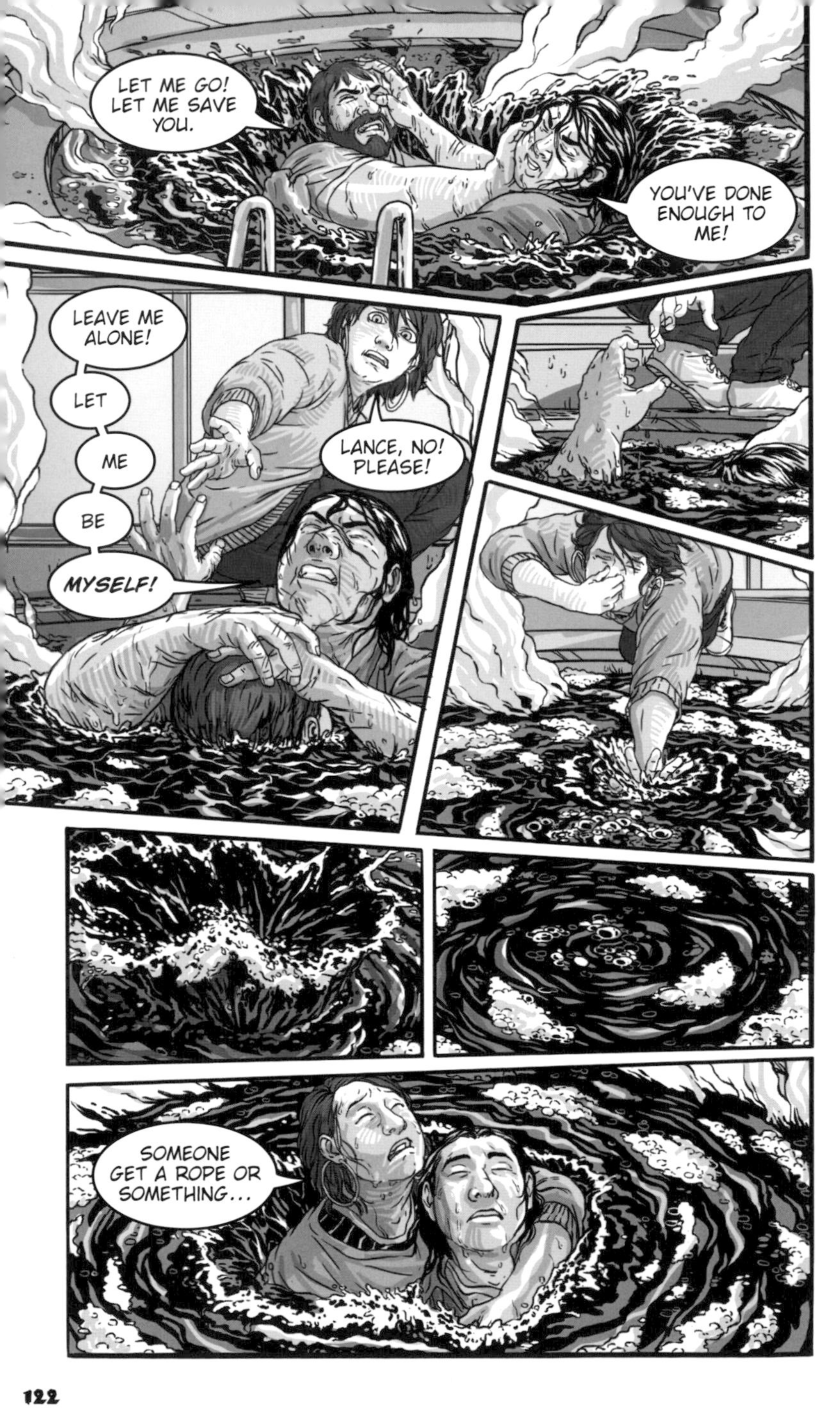
LET ME GO! LET ME SAVE YOU.
YOU'VE DONE ENOUGH TO ME!
LEAVE ME ALONE!
LET
ME
BE
MYSELF!
LANCE, NO! PLEASE!
SOMEONE GET A ROPE OR SOMETHING...

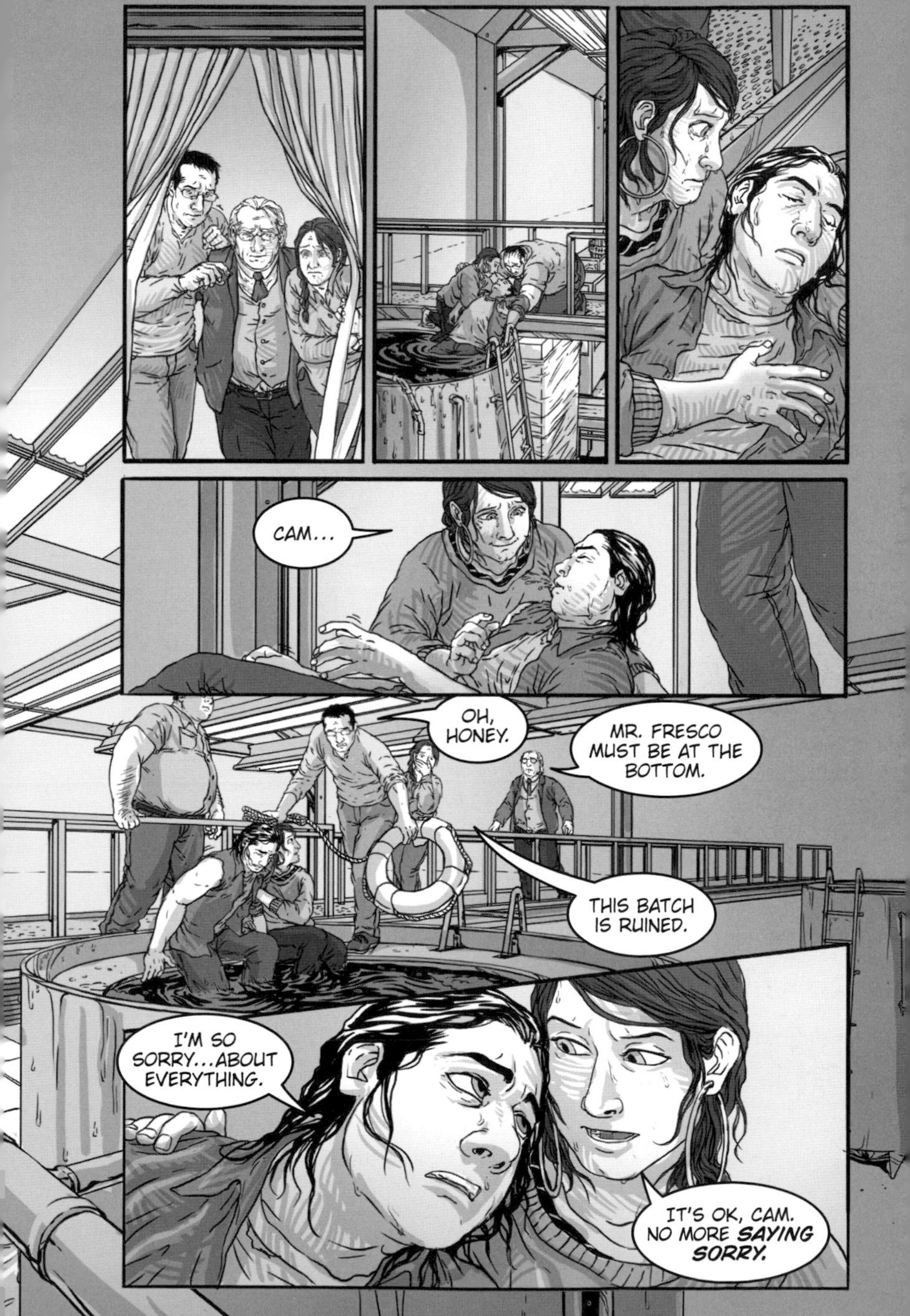
CAM...
OH, HONEY.
MR. FRESCO MUST BE AT THE BOTTOM.
THIS BATCH IS RUINED.
I'M SO SORRY...ABOUT EVERYTHING.
IT'S OK, CAM. NO MORE SAYING SORRY.

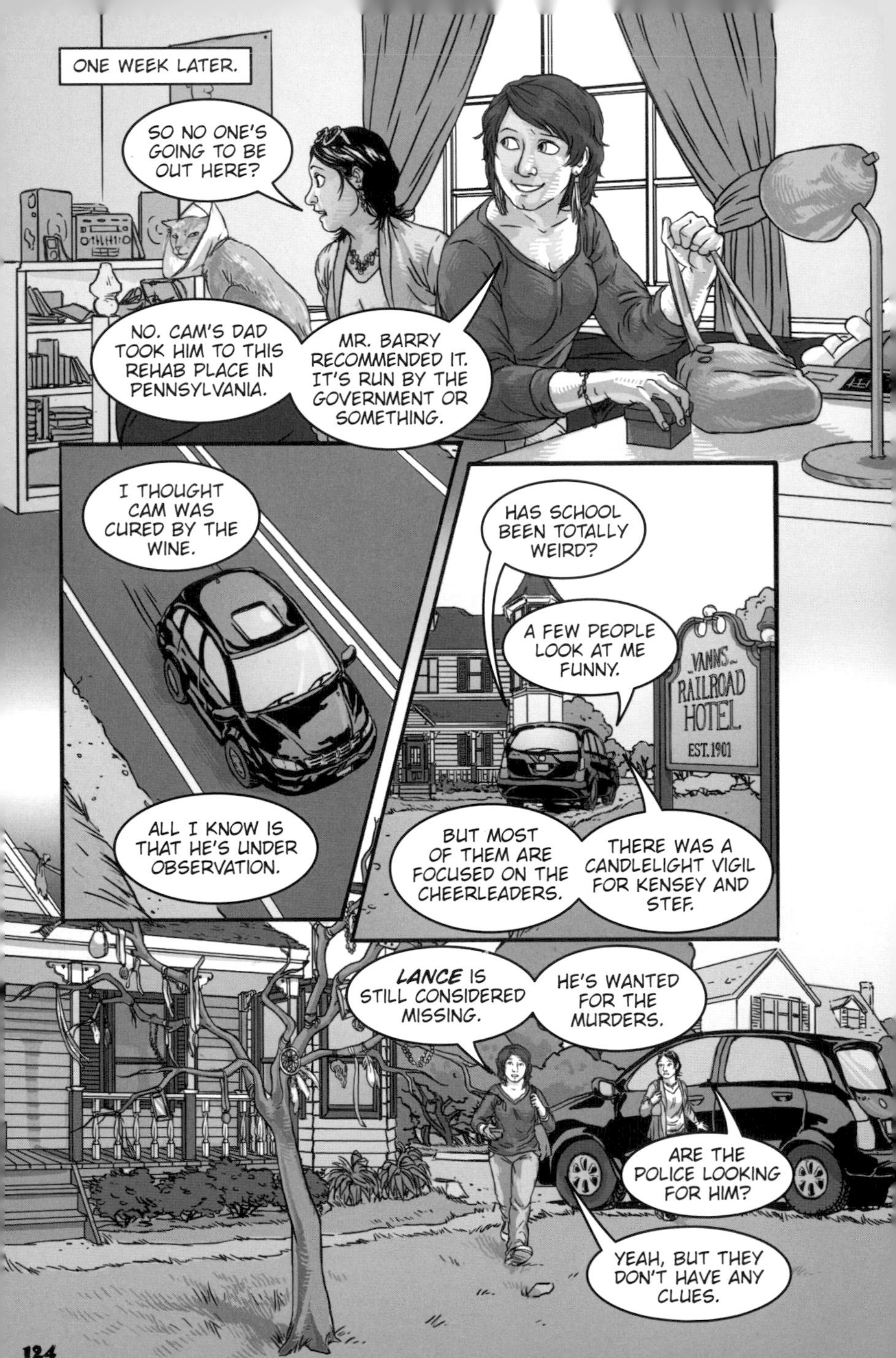
ONE WEEK LATER.
SO NO ONE'S GOING TO BE OUT HERE?
NO. CAM'S DAD TOOK HIM TO THIS REHAB PLACE IN PENNSYLVANIA.
MR. BARRY RECOMMENDED IT. IT'S RUN BY THE GOVERNMENT OR SOMETHING.
I THOUGHT CAM WAS CURED BY THE WINE.
ALL I KNOW IS THAT HE'S UNDER OBSERVATION.
HAS SCHOOL BEEN TOTALLY WEIRD?
A FEW PEOPLE LOOK AT ME FUNNY.
VANNS RAILROAD HOTEL EST. 1901
BUT MOST OF THEM ARE FOCUSED ON THE CHEERLEADERS.
THERE WAS A CANDLELIGHT VIGIL FOR KENSEY AND STEF.
LANCE IS STILL CONSIDERED MISSING.
HE'S WANTED FOR THE MURDERS.
ARE THE POLICE LOOKING FOR HIM?
YEAH, BUT THEY DON'T HAVE ANY CLUES.

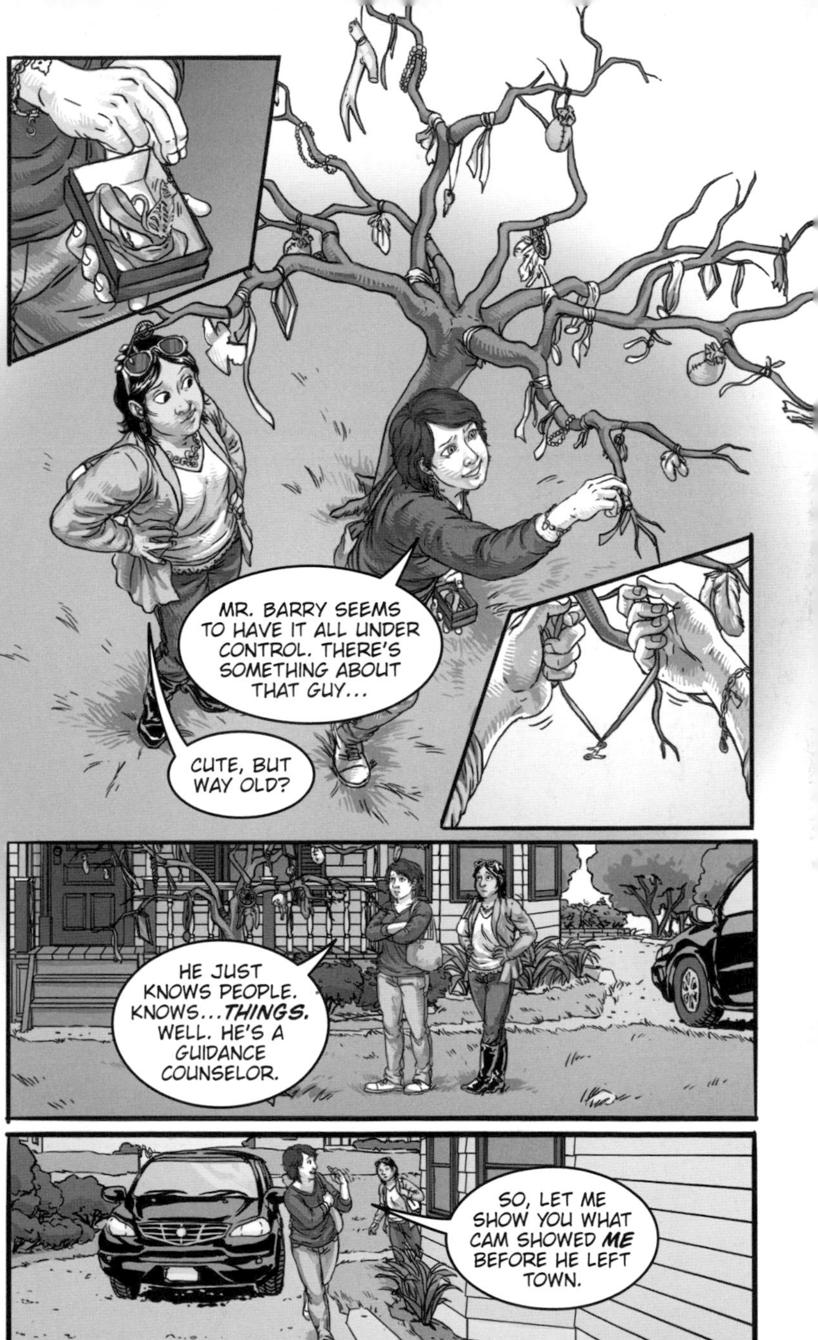
MR. BARRY SEEMS TO HAVE IT ALL UNDER CONTROL. THERE'S SOMETHING ABOUT THAT GUY...
CUTE, BUT WAY OLD?
HE JUST KNOWS PEOPLE. KNOWS...*THINGS.* WELL. HE'S A GUIDANCE COUNSELOR.
SO, LET ME SHOW YOU WHAT CAM SHOWED *ME* BEFORE HE LEFT TOWN.

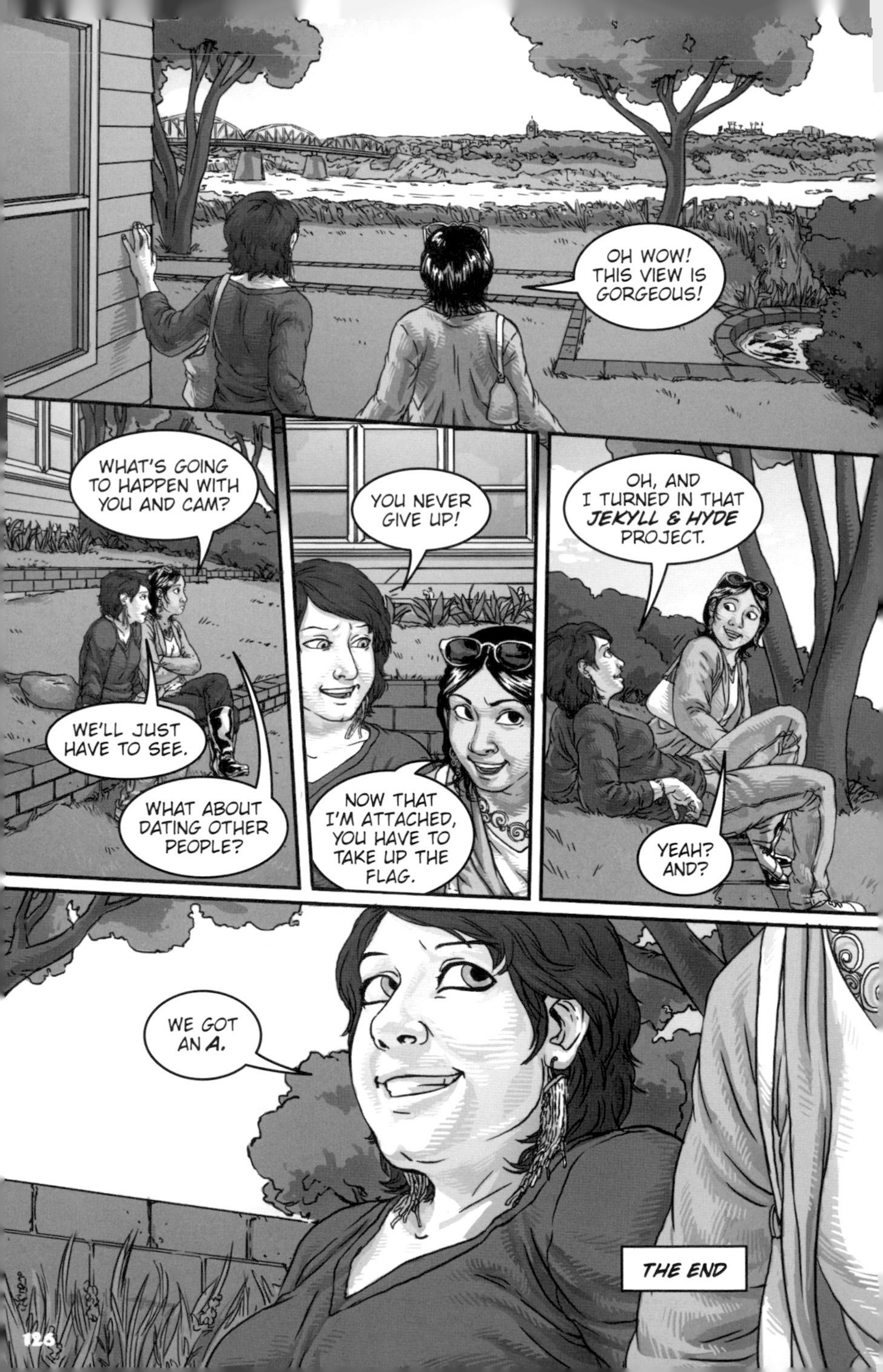
OH WOW! THIS VIEW IS GORGEOUS!
WHAT'S GOING TO HAPPEN WITH YOU AND CAM?
WE'LL JUST HAVE TO SEE.
WHAT ABOUT DATING OTHER PEOPLE?
YOU NEVER GIVE UP!
NOW THAT I'M ATTACHED, YOU HAVE TO TAKE UP THE FLAG.
OH, AND I TURNED IN THAT JEKYLL & HYDE PROJECT.
YEAH? AND?
WE GOT AN A.
THE END

s We —
Hate

Delete!

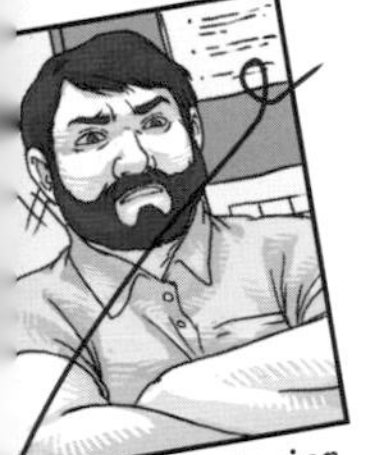

Francisco Javier "Frank" Fresco

Mr. Fresco is already one of our fave teachers. He's known to wear jeans sometimes, he grades easy, and he brings homemade guacamole to class.

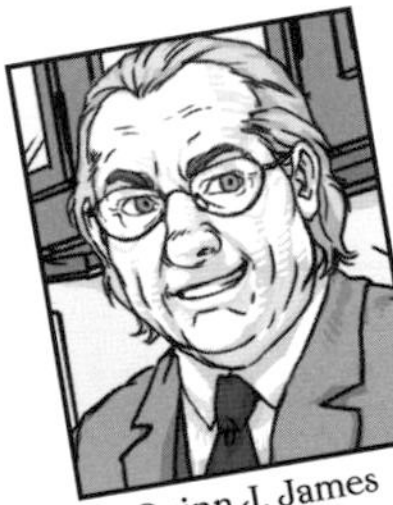

Quinn J. James

Not everyone can get away with wearing wing tip shoes, but Mr. James pulls it off. Our top hats are off to you, Mr. James.

t to
ical
e he
the
dent.
ake
eve!"

Class Favorites

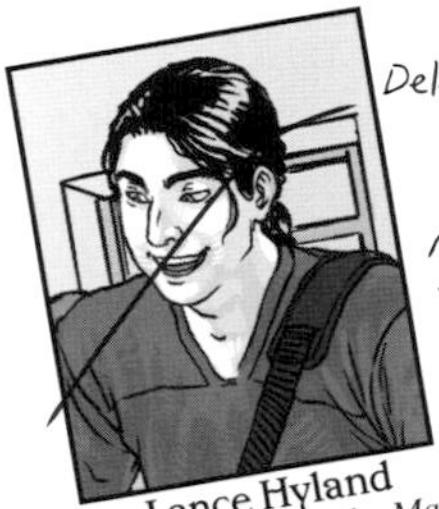

Delete!

Move this to tribute page?

Lance Hyland

Most Likely to Succeed—Male
Rojo's star quarterback is our class favorite by a landslide. With that hair, those eyes, and that arm, he could go all! the! way! to the NFL.
Favorites: The Dallas Cowboys, old-school country music, paranormal movies, driving to Austin for a Chuychanga after the game.

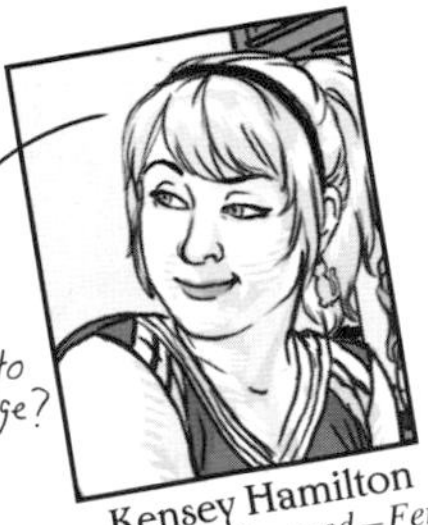

Kensey Hamilton

Most Likely to Succeed—Female
She's a cheerleader, she's pretty—and she's super nice. Clearly, she's going places.
Favorites: North Star Mall, musicals, cheerleading, and her Pomeranian, Peeta. (We don't judge.)

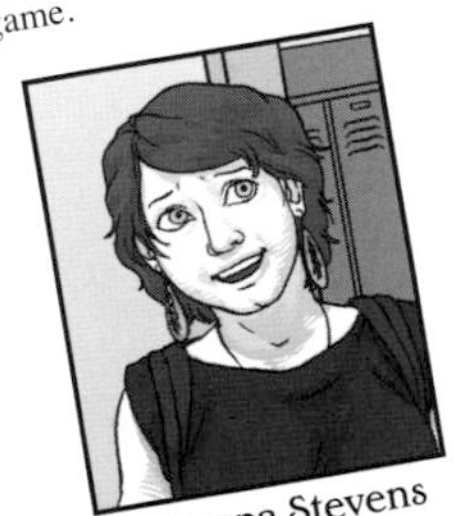

Serena Stevens

Most Likely to Date Your Boyfriend She may be new here, but she's already dating our starting quarterback, and rumor puts her with Cameron Jacobs as well. Girls, lock up your guys!
Favorites: Cats, turquoise jewelry, cats, English literature...and did we mention cats?

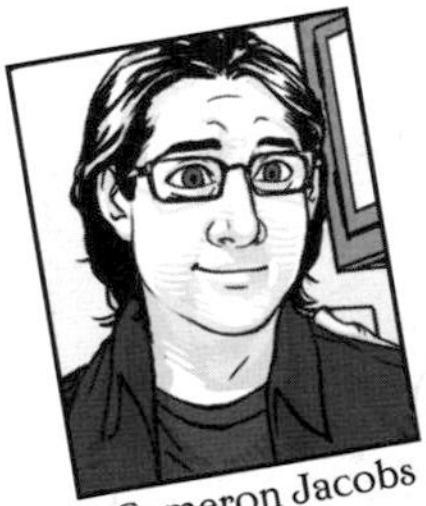

Cameron Jacobs

Most Mysterious
Does Cameron actually go to school here? Or does he just show up in the chem lab ever often to set girls' hearts on fi Your guess is as good as our we're guessing he's going to a Nobel Prize one day.
Favorites: We have no idea Serena Stevens...oh yeah, went there!

yearbook_proof.pdf

yearbook_proof.pdf

The Rojo High Reflections

ABOUT THE AUTHOR
AND THE ARTISTS

ROBIN MAYHALL has been writing since she could hold a pen. She is a corporate communications writer by day and a published speculative fiction poet and fantasy author. An honors graduate of the University of Texas at Austin with a bachelor's degree in journalism, she lives in Louisiana with three cats who only occasionally attempt to sit on her keyboard. Her previous title for Graphic Universe is Twisted Journeys #16, *The Quest for Dragon Mountain.*

KRISTEN CELLA hasn't gotten out much—out of Illinois, that is. She was born in Chicagoland, grew up in the suburbs, graduated from Northern Illinois University in 2009, and has no plans of quitting the state anytime soon. While she has a multitude of interests that have come and gone and come again, including playing soccer and the violin, her love for art and stories has always stayed constant. She indulges both of these through her webcomic *Antagonist,* which can be found at antagonist.swimtrunkstudio.com.

DIRK I. TIEDE, creator of the manga series *Paradigm Shift,* has been posting comics online since 1999. His artwork was featured in Season 3 of NBC's *Heroes.* His website is dirktiede.com.

JANE IRWIN is the creator of *Vögelein,* an independent comic book, and the *Clockwork Game* weekly webcomic about the world's first chess-playing automaton. Her website is vogelein.com.

JENN MANLEY LEE was a founding member of the Stumptown Comics Foundation and works as a graphic designer. She keeps the home she shares with spouse Kip Manley and daughter Taran full of books, geeks, art, cats, and music.